Ellery Queen's Mystery Bag

Ellery Queen's
Mystery
Bag

25 stories from Ellery Queen's
Mystery Magazine

Edited by ELLERY QUEEN

WORLD PUBLISHING
TIMES MIRROR
NEW YORK

724891

ACKNOWLEDGMENTS

The editor hereby makes grateful acknowledgment to the following authors and authors' representatives for giving permission to reprint the material in this volume:

Ellen Arthur for *Cal Always Said,* © 1971 by Ellen Arthur

Jon L. Breen for *The Fortune Cookie,* © 1971 by Jon L. Breen

Curtis Brown, Ltd., for *The Payoff* by Stanley Ellin, © 1971 by Stanley Ellin; and *This One's a Beauty* by Patricia McGerr, © 1971 by Patricia McGerr

Collins-Knowlton-Wing, Inc., for *Comedy of Discomfiture* by Michael Innes, © 1970 by Michael Innes

John Cushman Associates, Inc., for *Accessories After the Fact* by Michael Gilbert, © 1970 by Michael Gilbert; and *Experiment in Personality* by Julian Symons, © 1971 by Julian Symons

Ann Elmo Agency, Inc., for *The Perfect Servant* by Helen Nielsen, © 1971 by Helen Nielsen

Anthony Gilbert for *When Suns Collide,* © 1971 by Anthony Gilbert

Kathryn Gottlieb for *The Gun,* © 1970 by Kathryn Gottlieb

Edward D. Hoch for *The Leopold Locked Room,* © 1971 by Edward D. Hoch

International Famous Agency, Inc., for *A Single Minute of Fear* by Richard A. Selzer, © 1970 by Richard A. Selzer

Virginia Kidd for *Summon the Watch!* by Avram Davidson, © 1971 by Avram Davidson

Dana Lyon for *The Bitter Years,* © 1971 by Dana Lyon

Florence V. Mayberry for *The Beauty in That House,* © 1971 by Florence V. Mayberry

Scott Meredith Literary Agency, Inc., for *Falling Object* by William Brittain, © 1970 by William Brittain; *Someone at the Door* by Evan Hunter, © 1971 by Evan Hunter; *The Real Shape of the Coast* by John Lutz, © 1971 by John Lutz

Dennis O'Neil for *Report on a Broken Bridge,* © 1971 by Dennis O'Neil

James Powell for *The Gobineau Necklace,* © 1971 by James Powell

Carole Rosenthal for *A Specialist in Still Lifes,* © 1970 by Carole Rosenthal

Larry Sternig Literary Agency for *After the Lights Are Out* by Mary Louise Downer, © 1971 by Mary Louise Downer

R. L. Stevens for *The Physician and the Opium Fiend,* © 1971 by R. L. Stevens

Jeff Sweet for *Nightmare in New York,* © 1971 by Jeffrey Sweet.

Published by The World Publishing Company
Published simultaneously in Canada
by Nelson, Foster & Scott Ltd.
First printing—1972
Copyright © 1970, 1971, 1972 by Davis Publications, Inc.
All rights reserved
ISBN 0-529-04562-1
Library of Congress catalog card number: 75-183098
Printed in the United States of America

WORLD PUBLISHING
TIMES MIRROR

CONTENTS

INTRODUCTION

Dear Reader:

We live in an age when many of us, perhaps most of us, are trying to escape anxiety by looking backward.

Today is my sixty-sixth birthday; so I have even more reason to pause, catch my breath, and look back . . . back to the crucial event of my boyhood that did so much to shape the rest of my life.

I first wrote about the event in the introduction to an anthology published in 1944. This anthology was suppressed shortly after publication because of an unintentional violation of copyright; all unsold copies were destroyed, contracts for foreign editions canceled; as a result, the anthology has been out of print for twenty-seven years and copies are exceedingly hard to find.

A slightly expanded version of the nostalgic anecdote (am I, at sixty-six, in my anecdotage?) was included in a volume of essays and causeries published in 1957; this book had a small sale and was reprinted three years ago, again in a limited edition. Other versions and adaptations have appeared in various publications, all intended to appeal only to highly selective audiences, thus widening the readership but slightly.

So it is more than likely that you have not come across this personal reminiscence in your previous reading. Let me tell you then of my initiation into mysteryhood, of my first meeting with Sherlock Holmes.

When I was twelve years old, my family moved from Elmira, in upstate New York, to New York City, and for a time we lived with my maternal grandfather in Brooklyn. It was in my grandfather's house, in the winter of 1917, that I first met Sherlock Holmes.

I was ill in bed when the great moment occurred. In those far-off days I was afflicted with an abscess of the left ear. It came year after year, with almost astronomical regularity—always, I remember, during the week of school exams. My grandfather had an old turnip of a watch that he used to place flat against my left ear, and it always astounded him that I couldn't hear the tick of his Big Ben even after the ordeal of having had my ear lanced.

I was lying in bed, in a cubbyhole of a room, on just such a day as Dr. Watson has so often described—a "bleak and windy" day with the fingers of winter scratching at the windowpane. One of my aunts walked in and handed me a book she had borrowed at the nearby library.

It was the *Adventures of Sherlock Holmes.*

I opened the book with no realization that I stood— rather, I sat—on the brink of my fate. I had no inkling, no premonition, that in another minute my life's work would be born. My first glance was disheartening. I saw the frontispiece of the Harper edition: a picture of a rather innocuous man in dress coat and striped trousers holding the arm of a young woman in bridal gown. "A love story," I said to myself, for surely this unattractive couple were in a church about to be married. The quotation under the illustration—"The gentleman in the pew handed it up to her"—was not encouraging. In fact, there was nothing in that ill-chosen frontispiece by Sidney Paget to make a twelve-year-old boy sit up and take notice, especially with his left ear in agony.

Only an unknown and unknowable sixth sense prompted me to turn to the contents page, and then the world brightened. The first story—*A Scandal in Bohemia* —seemed to hold little red-blooded promise, but the next story was, and always will be, a milestone.

A strange rushing thrill challenged the pain in my ear. *The Red-Headed League!* What a combination of

simple words to skewer themselves into the brain of a
hungry boy! I glanced down quickly—*The Man with the
Twisted Lip—The Adventure of the Speckled Band*—and
I was lost! Ecstatically, everlastingly lost!

I started on the first page of *A Scandal in Bohemia*
and truly the game was afoot. The unbearable pain in
my ear . . . vanished! The abyss of melancholy into
which only a twelve-year-old boy can sink . . . forgotten!

I finished the *Adventures* that night. I wasn't sad—
I was glad. It wasn't the end—it was the beginning. I had
knocked fearlessly on the door to a new world and had
been admitted. There was a long road ahead, even longer
than I realized. That night, as I closed the book, I knew
I had read one of the greatest books ever written. And
today I marvel how true and tempered was my twelve-
year-old critical sense. For in the mature smugness of my
present literary judgment I still feel—unalterably—that the
Adventures of Sherlock Holmes is one of the world's mas-
terworks.

I could not have slept much that night. If I did, I
merely passed from one dreamworld to another, with the
wide-awake dream infinitely more wondrous. I remember,
when morning came, how symbolically the sun shone
through the window. I leaped from bed, dressed, and with
that great wad of yellow-stained cotton still in my ear,
stole out of the house and made my shaky way to the
public library. Of course it was too early for the library
to be open, but I sat on the steps and waited. And though
I waited hours, it seemed only minutes until a prim old
lady came and unlocked the front door.

But, alas, I had no card. Yes, I might fill out the form,
and take it home, and have my parents sign it, and then
after three days—three days? three eternities!—I could call
and pick up my card.

I begged, I pleaded, and there must have been something irresistible in my voice and in my eyes. Thank you now, Miss Librarian-of-Those-Days! These thanks are long overdue. For that gentle-hearted old lady broke all the rules of librarydom and gave me a card—and told me with a twinkle in her eyes where I could find books by a man named Doyle.

I rushed to the stacks. My first reaction was one of horrible and devastating disappointment. Yes, there were books by a Doyle on the shelves, but so few of them! I had expected a whole libraryful, rows and rows of Sherlock, all waiting patiently for my "coming of age."

I found three precious volumes. I bundled them under my arm, had them stamped, and fled home. Back in bed I started to read—*A Study in Scarlet,* the *Memoirs* (with a frontispiece that almost frightened me to death), *The Hound of the Baskervilles.* They were food and drink and medicine—and all the Queen's horses and all the Queen's men couldn't put Ellery together again.

But my doom had been signed, sealed, and delivered in the *Adventures.* The books that followed merely broadened the picture, filled in the indelible details. For who can ever forget that tall, excessively lean man with his razorlike face and hawk's bill of a nose . . . or his mouse-colored dressing gown and amber-stemmed pipe . . . or the way he paced up and down that legendary room at 221B Baker Street, quickly, eagerly, his head sunk upon his chest . . . or the way he examined the scene of a crime, sometimes on all fours, his nose to the ground. . . .

Who could ever forget that gaunt, dynamic figure and his incisive speech . . . or the mysterious Victorian household appliance called a gasogene . . . or the Persian slipper in which the master kept his tobacco and the coal scuttle in which he kept his cigars . . . or the patriotic bullet pocks on the wall and the scraping violin that produced such weird melodies . . . or the hypodermic syringe (what a shock that was to my fledgling sensibilities!) . . . or the ghostly hansom cab that loomed out of the London mist—with a twelve-year-old boy clinging by some miracle of literary gymnastics to its back as it rattled off to perilous adventure. . . .

Two days in the faraway past, two unforgettable days that happened more than half a century ago.

Now, fifty-four years later, the reading of mystery stories is still my bag, and I'll be hooked till the day my eyes and ears and fingertips give out.

In the meantime let me share my reading pleasure. Here are twenty-five stories from the 1971 issues of *Ellery Queen's Mystery Magazine*: stories of detection—all kinds, intuitive, deductive, procedural; stories of crime—all kinds, from theft, kidnapping, and con games to impersonation, blackmail, and murder; stories of bizarre concealments, terrifying experiments, desperate encounters, baffling locked rooms; stories that will bring you minutes of high excitement, hours of suspense and suspension of disbelief, days of escape and entertainment. You will even find detection in an insane asylum, with the detective not the doctor in charge but one of the inmates!

So, once again, this isn't the end, it's the beginning. You have knocked on the door to a new world and have been admitted. Come in, dear reader, come in and join the club. You have many wondrous and amazing meetings ahead of you—twenty-five in this book alone.

Sincerely,
Ellery Queen

Larchmont, New York
October 20, 1971

Ellery Queen's Mystery Bag

*Here is another of James Powell's charming stories of San
Sebastiano . . . and sharpen your wits—clever, crafty,
cunning, this Louis Tabarin, diamond merchant extra-
ordinaire; when Tabarin wanted a diamond necklace for
his antique-jewelry collection—even if it was the last of a
family's heirlooms and with a potent legend to protect
it—he left no stone (no pun intended) unturned.*

JAMES POWELL

The Gobineau necklace

In the Riviera principality of San Sebastiano the name
Tabarin et Cie means diamonds of the first water and
pearls of great price. Louis Tabarin's jewelry shop on the
rue Mazeppa had brought him not only wealth but entry
into the best society where he was admired for his impec-
cable sense of style and envied for his air of bored imper-
turbability. And yet here he was, stopped dead in his
tracks and his mouth ajar, on the Opéra's broad marble
and onyx staircase as the intermission crowd pushed by
him on both sides. Below, just inside the refreshment
salon, was the most exquisite diamond necklace the re-
nowned jeweler had ever seen.

Tabarin moved closer. The salon was crowded and
he was able to stand almost next to the diamonds and the
weak-chinned little woman who wore them. The stones
were all six-sided, an old-fashioned cut which the ancients

believed brought good luck. The setting was superb: sixteenth century, definitely from Rotterdam and probably by Van Gelder.

As Tabarin watched, the woman was presented with a glass of punch by a short man with sad bulging eyes and a thin black mustache. Together they were a study in gentility gone to seed: His cigarette holder was gold-inlaid ivory, but his brand, Grand Moguls, was the cheapest; her dress—a dusty mauve with mutton-chop sleeves—belonged to quite another age. And yet the necklace was worth at least three quarters of a million francs—even more to Tabarin, who was a passionate collector of antique jewelry.

Tabarin admired the necklace until the sound of a buzzer announced the final act. Reluctantly he returned to his box, resolved to have the necklace for his collection. Of course, as he knew from past experience, acquiring it might prove to be a delicate matter. More often than not, the direct approach, the blunt offer to buy, proved disastrous. Once Tabarin had coveted a twelfth-century episcopal ring, the last valuable possession of a certain Lady Milgrain who lived in a damp bed-sitting room in a squalid house run by an immense ox of a woman with bad teeth. Several visits to Lady Milgrain had failed. "As the last of my line I intend to take the ring with me to the grave," she told him over weak tea and broken cookies. "Perhaps a tradesman would find that hard to understand," she had added with a little smile.

But that particular story had a satisfactory ending. A few months later Lady Milgrain passed away in her sleep. It was the landlady who found her body. So when the ring was not among the dead woman's effects, Tabarin knew where to go. With a wink and a poke in the ribs the landlady had sold him the ring for a fraction of its value.

Outside the Opéra, Tabarin located the couple again

just as they were getting into a cab, she wearing a woolen shawl over her shoulders, he a plastic raincoat. Tabarin followed them across the Pont des Coeurs and into the once fashionable Faubourg St. Médor. Their destination was the Hotel Sébastopol, a narrow, decaying structure wedged in between a shuttered drugstore and a pastry shop.

As Tabarin entered the lobby, the couple's feet were just disappearing up the wrought-iron cage of the elevator shaft. The concierge came out of a room behind the hotel desk. "May I help the gentleman?" he asked.

"I thought I recognized the man and woman who just arrived," said Tabarin.

"You mean the Count and Countess de Gobineau," said the concierge, throwing his shoulders back proudly as if to say, "Imagine them staying in a hotel like this," and then shrugging as if to add, "It is a pity they've fallen so low."

Tabarin started to go. But then he turned back and dropped a business card on the desk. "The countess placed a necklace in the hotel safe, did she not?" he asked.

"I was sure I knew you from somewhere, Mr. Tabarin," said the concierge, pulling a racing form from under the counter. "The Beaulieu racetrack. I too am a follower of the sport of kings. I—"

"I would like to examine that necklace," said Tabarin, laying a bank note on the counter.

The concierge drew back. "Ah, no," he said firmly. "Maybe we aren't the Hotel Prince Adalbert, but still, our guests have rights!"

"I admire your discretion," said Tabarin. "It should be rewarded." He tapped the bank note. "This plus a sure thing at Beaulieu tomorrow."

The concierge bit his lip and looked nervously to the left and right. Then he motioned Tabarin behind the counter and into the back room. He watched from the doorway while Tabarin examined the necklace diamond by diamond with a pocket glass. The diamonds were magnificent—each stone without flaw, and all drawn together in a setting at once bold and delicate.

"Trottoir in the third," said Tabarin, returning the necklace to its green leather box and the box to the concierge. "And you needn't mention this to the count and countess."

Among the inhabitants of the fringe of San Sebastiano high society was Madame Olga Knapp, a cynical, aggressive widow who supported herself on commissions earned for bringing customers to the more expensive shops. Tabarin's question surprised her. Yes, as a matter of fact, she had met the Count and Countess de Gobineau at a lavish dinner party thrown by the Bile King—her contemptuous nickname for an American patent-medicine tycoon with a childlike reverence for titled nobility. But Madame Knapp dismissed the couple with a wave of her hand.

"The countess didn't say 'boo' all evening," she said. "And the count added nothing to the occasion but a hearty appetite. A pathetic couple. I find pathetic people a bore, don't you?"

Tabarin left the question unanswered. "I'm having a few friends over for drinks this evening. Perhaps you would care to join us, Madame Knapp," he said.

An invitation to Tabarin's house was a rare and coveted honor. Madame Knapp was quick to accept. "Excellent," said Tabarin coldly. "And perhaps your friends the Count and Countess de Gobineau would care to join us as well." This, his tone made clear, was the price of her invitation.

The evening began tediously. Nothing Tabarin said could put the timid little countess at her ease in the presence of the rich, the famous, and the witty. As for the count, what few opinions Tabarin could get him to utter were painfully mundane.

Finally Tabarin decided to make his move. General Klostermann, retired chief of staff of the army of San Sebastiano, had just launched off on his favorite topic: the nature of war following the nuclear holocaust when, Klostermann believed, the saber charge would come into its own again. He liked to illustrate this point down on his hands and knees using lead uhlans and spahis, which he carried with him everywhere in a large cardboard box.

Tabarin chose this moment to show de Gobineau his study, including his shelf of rare first editions ("I'm not much of a reader," said the count), his collection of erotic engravings ("What'll they think of next," said the count), and his admirable still life of oranges, apples, and cheese by Marbeuf ("Cheese gives me heartburn," said the count).

"But antique jewelry is my great weakness," said Tabarin, revealing the wall safe behind the Marbeuf. "Usually I keep my collection at the shop. My insurance company prefers it that way." Tabarin drew out a box containing a pendant, brooch, and signet ring. "But now and then, much to their dismay, I bring a few pieces home to enjoy them at my leisure."

Tabarin waited. What could be more natural than for the count to mention his antique diamond necklace? When he did not, the jeweler had to snap his fingers. "Ah," he exclaimed, "I knew I had seen you some place before. Last night at the Opéra. As I recall, your wife was wearing a rather unusual antique necklace."

"The necklace is beautiful, isn't it?" De Gobineau said a bit sadly. "The last of our family heirlooms."

"I suppose you've had it appraised?" asked Tabarin in an offhand way.

The count sighed. "Pointless," he said. "Regretfully I can never sell it."

"Because it's encumbered in some way?" asked Tabarin, straining to keep the apprehension out of his voice.

The count shook his head. "Because of the family legend," he said. "The Gobineau necklace was lost at sea during the Eighth Crusade, stolen by marauding Yorkshiremen during the Hundred Years War, sold to pay off creditors under the Sun King, and so on and so on. But always it came back to us. Always. For example, the family fled to Russia during the French Revolution, but not before a local Jacobin leader had confiscated the necklace in the name of the Republic. This Jacobin later fled the Girondists across the Rhine and into the Duchy of Altdorf, where he was promptly executed as a spy, and the necklace was added to the duke's treasury. It was later returned to France as part of German reparations following the Battle of Jena. Seven years later in Odessa my great-great-grandfather won the necklace at cards from a Cossack officer who claimed to have found it in baggage abandoned by Napoleon in his retreat from Moscow. So you see, knowing that the necklace must come back to me, how could I in good conscience sell it?"

"Not even for a million francs?" said Tabarin flatly.

The count smiled. "I'm sorry," he said.

Tabarin didn't press the point. Nor did he give up. He was reminded of the Baron Haegg, who had an ancient emerald clasp he refused to sell. After all, it had been in his family for generations. And the baron's income was adequate for a sensible, temperate man. Which was what Haegg had been, until Tabarin introduced him to the voluptuous Magda Schmettering, sometime model, sometime movie starlet. Well, the bounteous Magda would be wasted on the count. But there were other ways.

Later when the other guests were taking their leave, Tabarin drew the count aside. Protesting that the evening was still young, he invited the count and his wife to the Casino.

The count raised an eyebrow. "We never never gamble," he said.

"I'd hardly expect my guests to risk their own money," laughed Tabarin. "I, of course, will provide the stakes. You might find it interesting."

The count weighed the invitation thoughtfully. "Perhaps I would," he agreed.

Three days later Tabarin was offering the count a chair in his office. "And how is your charming wife?" he asked.

The count leaned forward with a conspiratorial smile. "I'm afraid she half suspects the reason for my visit," he said. "She's waiting for me in your showroom."

"Then this isn't a social call?" said Tabarin smoothly.

The count was carrying his plastic raincoat over one arm. He drew a green leather box from the pocket and set it on Tabarin's desk. The jeweler examined the necklace carefully with his loupe, pretending to see it for the first time, impressed once more by its dazzling beauty. "I assume you've reconsidered selling," he said.

"No," said the count. "I've already explained why that is impossible." He cleared his throat. "First, Mr. Tabarin, let me thank you for introducing me to the first great passion of my life. Some men are lucky at roulette; others are not. I've discovered that I am one of the lucky ones."

"Then you've been winning at the Casino?" asked Tabarin uneasily.

The count smiled broadly and nodded. "That is, until yesterday, when I encountered a losing streak. Quite temporary, of course. But I've exhausted all my available funds."

"I see," said Tabarin, relieved.

"I knew you'd understand," said the count. "So I would like to borrow one hundred thousand francs from you, using the necklace as security. And with the stipulation that I will forfeit the necklace if I cannot repay the money by the end of the month."

Tabarin couldn't believe his ears.

The count nodded emphatically. "Yes," he said, "why shouldn't I force my luck a bit? Since I can't really lose the necklace—I explained our family legend, didn't I?—then by gambling with money borrowed on it I'm bound to win." He smiled at his own clever logic and tapped his temple.

For a brief moment Tabarin pitied the count. But a fool had no right to such a magnificent necklace. He quickly drew up their agreement in the form of a receipt for the diamonds and was just about to write out the check when his secretary came to the door. She said the countess wanted to speak to her husband. In fact, the countess was right behind her, craning to look into the office.

Tabarin quickly snapped the green leather lid over the necklace. In the next moment the count was on his feet and had dropped his raincoat over the box. "What is it, Florence?" he said sharply.

"Alfred," said the countess, "the salespeople have shown me so many expensive things. I'm sure they expect me to buy something."

"In a moment, my dear," said the count.

Tabarin's secretary closed the door, but not before she reminded him he was late for an appointment. He made out the check and handed it to the count, who had picked up his raincoat. "If you hurry you can still make the bank before it closes," the jeweler said. "In fact, it's on my way. Let me drop you there."

With a final admiring glance at the necklace Tabarin left it with his secretary, instructing her to place it in the vault.

That evening there was the opening of a new art gallery on the rue de Bégat. Afterward Tabarin dined with a group of friends at a Tripolitanian restaurant of which San Sebastiano had several, all throwbacks to its nineteenth-century fling at empire in North Africa. It was someone else at the table who suggested a visit to the Casino.

So they arrived, a handsome, laughing group. To Tabarin's surprise the count was not there. Surely he hadn't lost the money that quickly. Gautier, the steward, shrugged. He hadn't seen the count all day. Tabarin frowned. Had the count abandoned his crazy scheme?

There was no way out of it, Tabarin had to call the Hotel Sébastopol. The concierge informed him that the count and countess had checked out late that afternoon, leaving no forwarding address.

"Have you taken ill, sir?" asked Gautier, as Tabarin put down the receiver.

Each time the night watchman limped by the office doorway on his rounds he shook his head at the sight of Tabarin, jaw clenched, staring down at a necklace on his desk. The necklace was a fake. The count had pulled a switch, probably when his wife had come to the door. The money wasn't important. The fact that the little con man had taken him wasn't important. But Tabarin was desperate to have the real necklace back. And by the first light of day a plan had taken shape in his mind.

Not far from the Marché St. Nicholas, or Thieves Market, was the Café Dureville, the dismal habitat of sleepy night people squinting against the early morning sun. Sitting in the corner was Babar the Elegant, a third-rate burglar and safecracker with a weakness for shot-silk suits, flowered shirts, and silver ties. Babar had a head cold. He hunched his broad shoulders over a glass of hot grog, inhaled the fumes deeply, and said, "In deals to defraud the insurance boys the customary split is fifty-fifty."

"My reasons for wanting this done do not involve

insurance," said Tabarin. "I'll give you five hundred francs now. There'll be another two thousand for you inside the wall safe."

Babar dipped a sugar cube in the grog and sucked on it thoughtfully. "One thousand now," he said.

"Agreed," said Tabarin. Then he hurried off to the photographer's studio where he met Magda Schmettering, who was still grumpy from being wakened before noon. She had brought the bikinis he had requested. Tabarin made his choice carefully. Then, while she was changing, he explained to the photographer exactly what he wanted. Magda posed for the picture with all the radiance of a woman who believes the necklace she is wearing is worth a million francs.

And that was that. Now all Tabarin had to do was tell his secretary that he was taking the Gobineau necklace home with him that night.

By afternoon of the next day the theft of the diamond necklace from the Tabarin residence was front-page news all over Europe. What editor could resist running that picture of the necklace worn by a bikinied Magda which Tabarin had supplied to the wire services? Even the police inspector, after clucking over the pierced wall safe, had commandeered a second copy of the photo for his personal file. And Ortalon, the investigator for Gibraltar Insurance, when he was finished scolding Tabarin for keeping a necklace worth a million francs in a "glorified breadbox," had requested an extra copy of the photo and Magda's phone number. "In these cases," he told Tabarin, "we always question the last person to wear the stolen item."

Tabarin sat back and waited. If the count fell for his little trick, if he believed that the fake necklace had been stolen before Tabarin discovered the switch, then he would be hurrying back to San Sebastiano. "I've come to repay that little loan and redeem my necklace, Mr. Tabarin," he would say with an innocent smile. "A theft? Why, no, I hadn't heard of any theft. I am overcome. Even though I know you will make good the loss, how can a mere million francs replace a family heirloom?"

Then Tabarin would produce the fake necklace and offer the count a simple choice: Either he would go to jail for fraud—and how many more of his victims would step forward when the story hit the papers?—or he would sell the real necklace to Tabarin at the jeweler's price. A carefully calculated price, not so low that the count would prefer a few years in jail or so high that it wouldn't hurt. Tabarin wanted the swindler to know he was being swindled.

Tabarin was anticipating the pleasure of that encounter as he reached his door that evening. Suddenly there was a loud sneeze and Babar the Elegant emerged from the shadows. Babar had read the newspapers. "You trying to muzzle the ox that grinds the grain, Mr. Tabarin?" he demanded. "I told you if it was a caper to take the insurance boys that I get half."

"Patience, Babar," said Tabarin. "In a day or two you'll see it wasn't that at all."

But the count didn't appear the next day or the day after that. Obviously he suspected a trick of some kind. Yet sooner or later he would have to come. Tabarin imagined him like a wild animal slowly approaching a trap, wary and nervous but drawn by the overpowering lure of the bait.

By the morning of the third day Tabarin was tense and expectant. To his annoyance his first visitor was Ortalon. The insurance investigator announced grandly that Gibraltar, famous on two continents for promptly satisfying customers, was once more to justify that reputation. Tabarin cursed to himself. He wanted the necklace, not Gibraltar's million francs, which he obviously couldn't accept. So now he would have to admit to a fool like Ortalon that he, Louis Tabarin, had been taken in, outwitted, by a con man.

Tabarin started to speak. But Ortalon raised a hand for silence and lay a garland of light on Tabarin's desk. The Gobineau necklace! Trembling, Tabarin examined it stone by stone under his loupe. The diamonds were real. This was the original necklace. "But how?" asked Tabarin.

"Last night we were contacted by the thief who offered to sell the necklace back to us for half a million francs," said Ortalon. "And now, if you'll just sign this receipt—"

Tabarin signed the paper quickly. In his bewilderment only one thing was clear: The genuine Gobineau necklace was in his hands again. Suddenly his office had filled up with shouting reporters and pushing photographers. "I took the liberty of breaking the story to the press. Good publicity for you—and for Gibraltar," said Ortalon.

When the insurance investigator and the last of the reporters had left, Tabarin tried to shake off the blind spots from the flashbulbs and struggled to order his thoughts. But events were moving too fast. The phone rang. Babar the Elegant had heard the news over the radio. Was Tabarin trying to cheat him out of his share of the half million? If so, Babar threatened to make a deal with the police and put Tabarin behind bars for a long time. The jeweler was quick to promise Babar his quarter million. After all, the necklace was cheap at the price.

Tabarin had just put down the phone when his secretary announced the Count de Gobineau. The count took a seat and then he looked at the surprised jeweler and smiled. In one swift moment Tabarin knew what the little man was going to say. Nevertheless he waited for the words. That gave him a few more moments to hold the necklace in his hands.

The count lit a Turkish cigarette and nodded at the diamonds. "I see you've been expecting me, Mr. Tabarin," he said. "Yes, I've come to redeem my necklace. You see, last night I came into a considerable sum of money."

A most unusual background for detection—the State Institution for the Criminal Incurably Insane; and a most unusual dramatis personae—*mainly, the six patients in Cottage D. But it is not, as you might expect, the doctor in charge who is the detective; and it is not an attendant or any sane person. The detective is one of the patients. An incurably insane criminal the detective? Surely a "first"—perhaps the most unusual "first" in the 131 years since Poe's preternaturally sane Dupin.*

JOHN LUTZ

The real shape of the coast

Where the slender peninsula crooks like a beckoning finger in the warm water, where the ocean waves crash in umbrellas of foam over the low-lying rocks to roll and ebb on the narrow white-sand beaches, there squats in a series of low rectangular buildings and patterns of high

fences the State Institution for the Criminal Incurably Insane. There are twenty of the sharp-angled buildings, each
rising bricked and hard out of sandy soil like an undeni-
able fact. Around each building is a ten-foot redwood
fence topped by barbed wire, and these fences run to the
sea's edge to continue as gossamer networks of barbed
wire that stretch out to the rocks.

In each of the rectangular buildings live six men, and
on days when the ocean is suitable for swimming it is part
of their daily habit—indeed, part of their therapy—to go
down to the beach and let the waves roll over them, or
simply to lie in the purging sun and grow beautifully tan.
Sometimes, just out of the grasping reach of the waves,
the men might build things in the damp sand, but by evening those things would be gone. However, some very
interesting things had been built in the sand.

The men in the rectangular buildings were not just
marking time until their real death. In fact, the "Incurably Insane" in the institution's name was something of
a misnomer; it was just that there was an absolute minimum of hope for these men. They lived in clusters of six
not only for security's sake, but so that they might form
a more or less permanent sensitivity group—day-in, day-
out group therapy, with occasional informal gatherings
supervised by young Dr. Montaign. Here under the subtle
and skillful probings of Dr. Montaign the men bared
their lost souls—at least, some of them did.

Cottage D was soon to be the subject of Dr. Montaign's
acute interest. In fact, he was to study the occurrences
there for the next year and write a series of articles to be
published in influential scientific journals.

The first sign that there was something wrong at Cottage D was when one of the patients, a Mr. Rolt, was
found dead on the beach one evening. He was lying on
his back near the water's edge, wearing only a pair of
khaki trousers. At first glance it would seem that he'd

had a drowning accident, only his mouth and much of his throat turned out to be stuffed with sand and with a myriad of tiny colorful shells.

Roger Logan, who had lived in Cottage D since being found guilty of murdering his wife three years before, sat quietly watching Dr. Montaign pace the room.

"This simply won't do," the doctor was saying. "One of you has done away with Mr. Rolt, and that is exactly the sort of thing we are in here to stop."

"But it won't be investigated too thoroughly, will it?" Logan said softly. "Like when a convicted murderer is killed in a prison."

"May I remind you," a patient named Kneehoff said in his clipped voice, "that Mr. Rolt was not a murderer." Kneehoff had been a successful businessman before his confinement, and now he made excellent leather wallets and sold them by mail order. He sat now at a small table with some old letters spread before him, as if he were a chairman of the board presiding over a meeting. "I might add," he said haughtily, "that it's difficult to conduct business in an atmosphere such as this."

"I didn't say Rolt was a murderer," Logan said, "but he is—was—supposed to be in here for the rest of his life. That fact is bound to impede justice."

Kneehoff shrugged and shuffled through his letters. "He was a man of little consequence—that is, compared to the heads of giant corporations."

It was true that Mr. Rolt had been a butcher rather than a captain of industry, a butcher who had put things in the meat—some of them unmentionable. But then Kneehoff had merely run a chain of three dry-cleaning establishments.

"Perhaps you thought him inconsequential enough to murder," William Sloan, who was in for pushing his young daughter out of a fortieth-story window, said to Kneehoff. "You never did like Mr. Rolt."

Kneehoff began to splutter. "You're the killer here, Sloan! You and Logan!"

"I killed no one," Logan said quickly.

Kneehoff grinned. "You were proved guilty in a court of law—of killing your wife."

"They didn't prove it to me. I should know whether or not I'm guilty!"

"I know your case," Kneehoff said, gazing dispassionately at his old letters. "You hit your wife over the head with a bottle of French Chablis wine, killing her immediately."

"I warn you," Logan said heatedly, "implying that I struck my wife with a wine bottle—and French Chablis at that—is inviting a libel suit!"

Noticeably shaken, Kneehoff became quiet and seemed to lose himself in studying the papers before him. Logan had learned long ago how to deal with him; he knew that Kneehoff's "company" could not stand a lawsuit.

"Justice must be done," Logan went on. "Mr. Rolt's murderer, a real murderer, must be caught and executed."

"Isn't that a job for the police?" Dr. Montaign asked gently.

"The police!" Logan laughed. "Look how they botched my case! No, this is a job for *us*. Living the rest of our lives with a murderer would be intolerable."

"But what about Mr. Sloan?" Dr. Montaign asked. "You're living with him."

"His is a different case," Logan snapped. "Because they found him guilty doesn't mean he is guilty. He says he doesn't remember anything about it, doesn't he?"

"What's your angle?" Brandon, the unsuccessful mystery bomber, asked. "You people have always got an angle, something in mind for yourselves. The only people you can really trust are the poor people."

"My angle is justice," Logan said firmly. "We must have justice!"

"Justice for all the people!" Brandon suddenly shouted, rising to his feet. He glanced about angrily and then sat down again.

"Justice," said old Mr. Heimer, who had been to other worlds and could listen to and hear metal, "will take care of itself. It always does, no matter where."

"They've been waiting a long time," Brandon said, his jaw jutting out beneath his dark mustache. "The poor people, I mean."

"Have the police any clues?" Logan asked Dr. Montaign.

"They know what you know," the doctor said calmly. "Mr. Rolt was killed on the beach between nine-fifteen and ten—when he shouldn't have been out of Cottage D."

Mr. Heimer raised a thin speckled hand to his lips and chuckled feebly. "Now, maybe that's justice."

"You know the penalty for leaving the building during unauthorized hours," Kneehoff said sternly to Mr. Heimer. "Not death, but confinement to your room for two days. We must have the punishment fit the crime and we must obey the rules. Any operation must have rules in order to be successful."

"That's exactly what I'm saying," Logan said. "The man who killed poor Mr. Rolt must be caught and put to death."

"The authorities are investigating," Dr. Montaign said soothingly.

"Like they investigated my case?" Logan said in a raised and angry voice. "They won't bring the criminal to justice! And I tell you we must not have a murderer here in Compound D!"

"Cottage D," Dr. Montaign corrected him.

"Perhaps Mr. Rolt was killed by something from the sea," William Sloan said thoughtfully.

"No," Brandon said, "I heard the police say there was only a single set of footprints near the body and it led from and to the cottage. It's obviously the work of an inside subversive."

"But what size footprints?" Logan asked.

"They weren't clear enough to determine the size," Dr. Montaign said. "They led to and from near the wooden stairs that come up to the rear yard, then the ground was too hard for footprints."

"Perhaps they were Mr. Rolt's own footprints," Sloan said.

Kneehoff grunted. "Stupid! Mr. Rolt went to the beach, but he did not come back."

"Well—" Dr. Montaign rose slowly and walked to the door. "I must be going to some of the other cottages now." He smiled at Logan. "It's interesting that you're so concerned with justice," he said. A gull screamed as the doctor went out.

The five remaining patients of Cottage D sat quietly after Dr. Montaign's exit. Logan watched Kneehoff gather up his letters and give their edges a neat sharp tap on the tabletop before slipping them into his shirt pocket. Brandon and Mr. Heimer seemed to be in deep thought, while Sloan was peering over Kneehoff's shoulder through the open window out to the rolling sea.

"It could be that none of us is safe," Logan said suddenly. "We must get to the bottom of this ourselves."

"But we are at the bottom," Mr. Heimer said pleasantly, "all of us."

Kneehoff snorted. "Speak for yourself, old man."

"It's the crime against the poor people that should be investigated," Brandon said. "If my bomb in the Statue of Liberty had gone off— And I used my whole week's vacation that year going to New York."

"We'll conduct our own investigation," Logan insisted, "and we might as well start now. Everyone tell me what he knows about Mr. Rolt's murder."

"Who put you in charge?" Kneehoff asked. "And why should we investigate Rolt's murder?"

"Mr. Rolt was our friend," Sloan said.

"Anyway," Logan said, "we must have an orderly investigation. Somebody has to be in charge."

"I suppose you're right," Kneehoff said. "Yes, an orderly investigation."

Information was exchanged, and it was determined that Mr. Rolt had said he was going to bed at 9:15, saying good night to Ollie, the attendant, in the TV lounge. Sloan and Brandon, the two other men in the lounge, remembered the time because the halfway commercial for "Monsters of Main Street" was on, the one where the box of detergent soars through the air and snatches everyone's shirt. Then at ten o'clock, just when the news was coming on, Ollie had gone to check the beach and discovered Mr. Rolt's body.

"So," Logan said, "the approximate time of death has been established. And I was in my room with the door open. I doubt if Mr. Rolt could have passed in the hall to go outdoors without my noticing him, so we must hypothesize that he did go to his room at nine-fifteen, and sometime between nine-fifteen and ten he left through his window."

"He knew the rules," Kneehoff said. "He wouldn't have just walked outside for everyone to see him."

"True," Logan conceded, "but it's best not to take anything for granted."

"True, true." Mr. Heimer chuckled. "Take nothing for granted."

"And where were *you* between nine and ten?" Logan asked.

"I was in Dr. Montaign's office," Mr. Heimer said with a grin, "talking to the doctor about something I'd heard in the steel utility pole. I almost made him understand that all things metal are receivers, tuned to different frequencies, different worlds and vibrations."

Kneehoff, who had once held two of his accountants prisoner for five days without food, laughed.

"And where were *you*?" Logan asked.

"In my office, going over my leather-goods vouchers," Kneehoff said. Kneehoff's "office" was his room, toward the opposite end of the hall from Logan's room.

"Now," Logan said, "we get to the matter of motive. Which of us had reason to kill Mr. Rolt?"

"I don't know," Sloan said distantly. "Who'd do such a thing—fill Mr. Rolt's mouth with sand?"

"You were his closest acquaintance," Brandon said to Logan. "You always played chess with him. Who knows what you and he were plotting?"

"What about you?" Kneehoff said to Brandon. "You tried to choke Mr. Rolt just last week."

Brandon stood up angrily, his mustache bristling. "That was the week *before* last!" He turned to Logan. "And Rolt always beat Logan at chess—that's why Logan hated him."

"He didn't *always* beat me at chess," Logan said. "And I didn't hate him. The only reason he beat me at chess sometimes was because he'd upset the board if he was losing."

"You don't like to get beat at anything," Brandon said, sitting down again. "That's why you killed your wife, because she beat you at things. How middle-class, to kill someone because of that."

"I didn't kill my wife," Logan said patiently. "And she didn't beat me at things. Though she was a pretty good business woman," he added slowly, "and a good tennis player."

"What about Kneehoff?" Sloan asked. "He was always threatening to kill Mr. Rolt."

"Because he laughed at me!" Kneehoff spat out. "Rolt

was a braggart and a fool, always laughing at me because I have ambition and he didn't. He thought he was better at everything than anybody else—and you, Sloan—Rolt used to ridicule you and Heimer. There isn't one of us who didn't have motive to eliminate a piece of scum like Rolt."

Logan was on his feet, almost screaming. "I won't have you talk about the dead like that!"

"All I was saying," Kneehoff said, smiling his superior smile at having upset Logan, "was that it won't be easy for you to discover Rolt's murderer. He was a clever man, that murderer, cleverer than you."

Logan refused to be baited. "We'll see about that when I check the alibis," he muttered, and he left the room to walk barefoot in the surf.

On the beach the next day Sloan asked the question they had all been wondering.

"What are we going to do with the murderer if we do catch him?" he asked, his eyes fixed on a distant ship that was just an irregularity on the horizon.

"We'll extract justice," Logan said. "We'll convict and execute him—eliminate him from our society!"

"Do you think we should?" Sloan asked.

"Of course we should!" Logan snapped. "The authorities don't care who killed Mr. Rolt. The authorities are probably glad he's dead."

"I don't agree that it's a sound move," Kneehoff said, "to execute the man. I move that we don't do that."

"I don't hear anyone seconding you," Logan said. "It has to be the way I say if we are to maintain order here."

Kneehoff thought a moment, then smiled. "I agree we must maintain order at all costs," he said. "I withdraw my motion."

"Motion, hell!" Brandon said. He spat into the sand. "We ought to just find out who the killer is and liquidate him. No time for a motion—time for action!"

"Mr. Rolt would approve of that," Sloan said, letting a handful of sand run through his fingers.

Ollie the attendant came down to the beach and stood there smiling, the sea breeze rippling his white uniform. The group on the beach broke up slowly and casually, each man idling away in a different direction.

Kicking the sun-warmed sand with his bare toes, Logan approached Ollie.

"Game of chess, Mr. Logan?" Ollie asked.

"Thanks, no," Logan said. "You found Mr. Rolt's body, didn't you, Ollie?"

"Right, Mr. Logan."

"Mr. Rolt was probably killed while you and Sloan and Brandon were watching TV."

"Probably," Ollie agreed, his big face impassive.

"How come you left at ten o'clock to go down to the beach?"

Ollie turned to stare blankly at Logan with his flat eyes. "You know I always check the beach at night, Mr. Logan. Sometimes the patients lose things."

"Mr. Rolt sure lost something," Logan said. "Did the police ask you if Brandon and Sloan were in the TV room with you the whole time before the murder?"

"They did and I told them yes." Ollie lit a cigarette with one of those transparent lighters that had a fishing fly in the fluid. "You studying to be a detective, Mr. Logan?"

"No, no." Logan laughed. "I'm just interested in how the police work, after the way they messed up my case. Once they thought I was guilty I didn't have a chance."

But Ollie was no longer listening. He had turned to look out at the ocean. "Don't go out too far, Mr. Kneehoff!" he called, but Kneehoff pretended not to hear and began moving in the water parallel with the beach.

Logan walked away to join Mr. Heimer, who was standing in the surf with his pants rolled above his knees.

"Find out anything from Ollie?" Mr. Heimer asked, his body balancing slightly as the retreating sea pulled the sand and shells from beneath him.

"Some things," Logan said, crossing his arms and enjoying the play of the cool surf about his legs. The two men—rather than the ocean—seemed to be moving as the tide swept in and out and shifted the sand beneath the sensitive soles of their bare feet. "It's like the ocean," Logan said, "finding out who killed Mr. Rolt. The ocean works and works on the shore, washing in and out until only the sand and rock remain—the real shape of the coast. Wash the soil away and you have bare rock; wash the lies away and you have bare truth."

"Not many can endure the truth," Mr. Heimer said, stooping to let his hand drag in an incoming wave, "even in other worlds."

Logan raised his shoulders. "Not many ever learn the truth," he said, turning and walking through the wet sand toward the beach. Amid the onwash of the wide shallow wave he seemed to be moving backward, out to sea. . . .

Two days later Logan talked to Dr. Montaign, catching him alone in the TV lounge when the doctor dropped by for one of his midday visits. The room was very quiet; even the ticking of the clock seemed slow, lazy, and out of rhythm.

"I was wondering, Doctor," Logan said, "about the night of Mr. Rolt's murder. Did Mr. Heimer stay very late in your office?"

"The police asked me that," Dr. Montaign said with a smile. "Mr. Heimer was in my office until ten o'clock, then I saw him come into this room and join Brandon and Sloan to watch the news."

"Was Kneehoff with them?"

"Yes, Kneehoff was in his room."

"I was in my room," Logan said, "with my door open to the hall, and I didn't see Mr. Rolt pass to go outdoors.

So he must have gone out through his window. Maybe the police would like to know that."

"I'll tell them for you," Dr. Montaign said, "but they know Mr. Rolt went out through his window because his only door was locked from the inside." The doctor cocked his head at Logan, as was his habit. "I wouldn't try to be a detective," he said gently. He placed a smoothly manicured hand on Logan's shoulder. "My advice is to forget about Mr. Rolt."

"Like the police?" Logan said.

The hand patted Logan's shoulder soothingly.

After the doctor had left, Logan sat on the cool vinyl sofa and thought. Brandon, Sloan, and Heimer were accounted for, and Kneehoff couldn't have left the building without Logan seeing him pass in the hall. The two men, murderer and victim, might have left together through Mr. Rolt's window—only that wouldn't explain the single set of fresh footprints to and from the body. And the police had found Mr. Rolt's footprints where he'd gone down to the beach farther from the cottage and then apparently walked up the beach through the surf to where his path and the path of the murderer crossed.

And then Logan saw the only remaining possibility— the only possible answer.

Ollie, the man who had discovered the body—Ollie alone had had the opportunity to kill! And after doing away with Mr. Rolt he must have noticed his footprints leading to and from the body; so at the wooden stairs he simply turned and walked back to the sea in another direction, then walked up the beach to make his "discovery" and alert the doctor.

Motive? Logan smiled. Anyone could have had motive enough to kill the bragging and offensive Mr. Rolt. He had been an easy man to hate.

Logan left the TV room to join the other patients on the beach, careful not to glance at the distant white-uniformed figure of Ollie painting some deck chairs at the other end of the building.

"Tonight," Logan told them dramatically, "we'll meet in the conference room after Dr. Montaign leaves and I promise to tell you who the murderer is. Then we'll decide how best to remove him from our midst."

"Only if he's guilty," Kneehoff said. "You must present convincing, positive evidence."

"I have proof," Logan said.

"Power to the people!" Brandon cried, leaping to his feet.

Laughing and shouting, they all ran like schoolboys into the waves.

The patients sat through their evening session with Dr. Montaign, answering questions mechanically and chattering irrelevantly, and Dr. Montaign sensed a certain tenseness and expectancy in them. Why were they anxious? Was it fear? Had Logan been harping to them about the murder? Why was Kneehoff not looking at his letters and Sloan not gazing out the window?

"I told the police," Dr. Montaign mentioned, "that I didn't expect to walk up on any more bodies on the beach."

"You?" Logan stiffened in his chair. "I thought it was Ollie who found Mr. Rolt."

"He did, really," Dr. Montaign said, cocking his head. "After Mr. Heimer left me I accompanied Ollie to check the beach so I could talk to him about some things. He was the one who saw the body first and ran ahead to find out what it was."

"And it was Mr. Rolt, his mouth stuffed with sand," Sloan murmured.

Logan's head seemed to be whirling. He had been so sure! Process of elimination. It had to be Ollie! Or were the two men, Ollie and Dr. Montaign, in it together?

They had to be! But that was impossible! There had been only one set of footprints.

Kneehoff! It must have been Kneehoff all along! He must have made a secret appointment with Rolt on the beach and killed him. But Rolt had been walking alone until he met the killer, who was also alone! And *someone* had left the fresh footprints, the single set of footprints, to and from the body.

Kneehoff must have seen Rolt, slipped out through his window, intercepted him, and killed him. But Kneehoff's room didn't have a window! Only the two end rooms had windows, Rolt's room and Logan's room!

A single set of footprints—they could only be his own! *His own!*

Through a haze Logan saw Dr. Montaign glance at his watch, smile, say his good-byes, and leave. The night breeze wafted through the wide open windows of the conference room with the hushing of the surf, the surf wearing away the land to bare rock.

"Now," Kneehoff said to Logan, and the moon seemed to light his eyes, "who exactly is our man? Who killed Mr. Rolt? And what is your evidence?"

Ollie found Logan's body the next morning, face down on the beach, the gentle lapping surf trying to claim him. Logan's head was turned and half buried and his broken limbs were twisted at strange angles, and around him the damp sand was beaten with, in addition to his own, four different sets of footprints.

In so many ways a "second story" is even more important than a "first story." It means that the new author hasn't rested on his or her laurels; it means the new author is continuing to write—persisting, persevering, producing.

Kathryn Gottlieb's first story, "An extremely Civiliz-ed Murder," appeared in the March 1966 issue of Ellery Queen's Mystery Magazine. *Now, we give you her second story, and we have a strong hunch we won't have to wait so long for her third. "The Gun" is a sensitive and percep-tive love story—yes, we said "love story"; and yet, as you will see, it belongs in a mystery-suspense anthology. It is "extremely civilized"—a compulsive story that makes compulsive reading.*

KATHRYN GOTTLIEB

The gun

I was sweating. The month was July, the city was New York, the air-conditioner in the office of the Consulate of the African Republic of Matanzia was noisy and blew hot air at me, and the news was bad. "They've held back the cash," said Joseph Arundu. "You'll have to forget the job." He shook his head. "I regret it exceedingly."

"You regret it!"

He looked at me gravely from the far side of the ma-hogany desk. "We do, you know. We need you."

"Oh, look, what the hell—I mean, I'm sorry, forgive me, but what am I supposed to do? On the basis of our contract I terminated my job, I gave up my lease." I was trying to keep the anger out of my voice, which left the whine in. "I gave up my women," I said, lightening it. I wanted the job badly. I am a civil engineer, the job was water resources development, I liked Arundu and the others of his countrymen I had talked to some months before, and I wanted to go to Africa. I had been looking forward to it the way one looks forward to a new life. "What do you want me to do?"

Arundu was a big man, handsome and somber. He was wearing a white robe of some kind and a small Nehru-type hat with bits of mirror glass set in around the edge. Outside of that he was just like you and me, only more interesting.

"Wait for us," he said. "In three months we'll have the funds to get started. I'm sure of it. The bank has promised." He shook his head and looked at me with a small smile. "It is only at the last minute that the bank advised us of the delay. Red tape. Red tape! You have this also in your country? Look." He leaned forward confidentially. "Do you want me to settle your contract?" He looked me sturdily in the eye. "We're broke. I can offer you a lifetime supply of coconuts."

Go fight City Hall. "I'll wait," I said. "I'll wait."

And that was the beginning. If the International Bank for Development had come through with the cash on schedule, I wouldn't be writing now from this place of confinement.

I'd said I'd wait, but meanwhile I had to live. I called my old friend Tom Stanley, who is president of a small upstate outfit called Paleotronics. Tom said he could fit me into a temporary slot in engineering and so I shortly found myself up in Elsinore, a small town forty miles west of Albany, New York, and a long way from Africa—but now, in July, just as hot.

Elsinore is the kind of town where if you want to stay overnight you have to buy a house; so Tom and his wife, Jane, made room for me in their own split-level for

a week and then Jane found me a place of my own, primitive quarters in the gatehouse of a boarded-up estate just
outside of town, northwest of the plant. There I lived
happily on delicatessen, reading Joseph Conrad, stayed
away from the Stanleys. I saw no one else, formed no ties,
worked some evenings on stuff I brought back from the
office—they were busy there at Paleotronics, expanding
into bankruptcy—and wandered in the summer nights
through the rankly overgrown and scented garden and
thought of Africa.

So far so good.

One night—I had worked late, it was after seven—
I stopped at Pete's Delicatessen, bought a half pound of
ham, two rolls, and a six-pack, put the package on the
car seat, then sat there with the car keys in my hand,
watching the late July sunlight blasting down Main Street,
which runs west and uphill at that point, and watching,
listening to and inhaling the traffic, which is heavy—there's
a lot of trucking along this route. I was tired. Hot, tired,
bored, edgy, worried, and critical.

I watched the poor skinny high-school girls and their
poor skinny little mothers walking down the street, with
their lifelike faces, and then I scowled at a car that pulled
into the space ahead of me. I disapprove of sloppy driving,
and this car stopped well short of the curb, its tail sticking
out into traffic just enough to annoy. The driver, a woman,
got out slowly, no hurry, and walked over to the parking
meter, a straight-backed, idle walk with a lot of don't-care
in it.

My first sight of Kay Bannerman. I watched her with
idle dislike. She was tall, looked about twenty-seven, and
cared little for the opinion of humanity; being washed but
not, I think, combed—her hair, a kind of dull brownish
gold, was yanked back from her face and held by a barrette at the nape of her neck. She was wearing a limp gar-

ment made in two pieces that failed to meet in the middle, washed out and worn out; she needed starch, or embroidery, or a collar and tie.

I stared at her as she fumbled in her purse for a coin to put in the meter. She had a firm profile, high cheekbones, and a human-looking mouth. She wasn't wearing any makeup. She caught my glance and looked at me with hatred. She was beautiful. She gave up on the coin hunt and sauntered away from the meter. Violation, it said.

I watched until the screen door of the delicatessen, slamming behind her, made her invisible. The sun was hot, the fumes were shortening my life, and the noise offended my ears. I drove home. The ham was sweating and the beer was warm. I kept thinking of her. I did not know at the time either her name or what it was she had against the world.

I soon enough found out both.

The Stanleys gave a cocktail party. There must have been forty people jammed into the little recreation room that I had slept in that first week. I was in a friendly mood, glad to see people for a change. I hadn't really seen anyone to talk to outside the Paleotronics office and I hadn't heard a word from the Africans. I was beginning to worry and I was glad of the distraction. I got there pretty much on time and found the place already jammed with the prompt.

I had a couple of drinks and talked to various people and then through a momentary clearing in the crowd I saw a tall girl standing at the end of the room. She was alone. Her back was to the rest of us and she was staring at a picture on the wall. I had a vision of sweated ham and blinding sun that came and went like an aberration before I recognized the back in the black dress. Under that dress was the thin white waist I know so well that dwelled between the top and bottom of that unspeakable two-piece.

I elbowed my way across the room saying sorry, sorry, and when I got near her I saw that the hair was piled on top of her head this time and held in a sort of French knot by, I think, the same barrette. The hair was the dark gold I remembered and strands had come unfastened or had never been fastened and were straggling down the back of a really beautiful neck. I came up even with her and she never looked around at me until I said hello.

Then her eyes looked right at mine. They were a dark shade of blue and set in deep, nicely spaced sockets. She had a somber expression that reminded me of Joseph Arundu's. A lot of people are finding the world heavy going these days.

She spoke. "You," she said.

I acknowledged it. Would she like a drink?

She would.

I plowed my way to the bar and back again and we drank our drinks together. People left a little space around us.

"Tell me," she said. She looked amused. "Where you come from, are there women?"

"Cleveland. Yes."

"Delicatessens?"

"The world's best. Why?"

"Then how is it you never saw a woman walk into a delicatessen before?"

"I stared at you," I said. I felt the color come up in my face. "If you don't want to be looked at, then don't go out like that."

The faint smile faded. "Like what?"

"That thing you were wearing," I said. "That garment. Like the things you see flapping on lines in people's yards on country roads when you're driving by at high speed. It forces people to look at you. It"—I was groping for words, or for a thought—"it forces intimacy. And don't go around with hair straggling down your neck."

Her hand went up to smooth back her hair and my stomach gave a lurch. She was wearing a wedding band. I'm not a poacher. But now it was too late.

She saw the movement of my eyes. "Dead," she said. "He's dead. Lying in the cold cold ground."

"That's not nice," I said. "To talk like that."

"You wanted to know." And then—"I'm going. I have to go home." She looked around, stooped, and put her glass down on the floor next to the wall out of the way because there was no other place, and then she was forcing her way out through the people who were looking at her oddly and I stood there saying to myself: "Let it end, let it end now"; and then I found myself walking down the room after her and it took time because the people had come together in her wake, and when I got to the end of the room, she was walking out the door.

"Don't go," I called after her. I didn't even know her name. Behind me someone tittered. A knot of people came between us and when I got to the door she was gone. I stood outside on the flat stone step. The night was warm and the air was moving softly. Out on the street a motor was spinning and not catching. The battery had run down. I didn't want a woman. I didn't want to want a woman. I didn't want to care about anyone. This was not the time in my life for it, for ties and bondage, for the Tom-and-Jane life, for the nine-to-five. *After* Africa.

Silence in the street. Then she came walking back over the lawn. When she came up to me I caught her wrist. She said, "I think I must have left the radio on."

"I'll take you home."

She looked dismayed. "You mustn't leave the party. You mustn't leave here with me."

"The party's all right. I'll come back and say good night. Come on."

'But my car—"

"I'll call a garage. Don't worry. All right?"

She told me her name was Kay Bannerman, and where she lived.

Her house was out in the same direction as mine, but not so far. It was an old-fashioned-looking place, almost a mile beyond the last split-level and with fallow fields on either side of it; waiting for the developers, growing weeds and money. I turned off the engine and we listened to the summer evening. The tree frogs were making a lot of sound. I leaned back against the window at my left and looked at her. She stared straight ahead. Her profile was beautiful and strong, her expression vulnerable and sad.

After a long time I got out of the car and went around and opened the door on her side. She got out and stood facing me. The street light was shining on her face. She was very beautiful, like Ingrid Bergman on the late-late TV movies. I wanted to touch her face in the lamplight, but I folded my arms. "Look," I said, "I'm going to Africa."

"Don't be angry," she said. She was smiling faintly. "I'm not going to stop you." She turned away from me and went up the path to her front door. I stood where I was and watched until she opened her door and I saw a light go on behind it as it closed.

I went back to the Stanleys' and said good night and thank you. I picked up a lot of sideways looks there, including one from my host. I went back to the gatehouse and spent a sleepless night, my haven destroyed. At three in the morning I turned on the light and picked up Mr. Conrad's book, since that gentleman spoke to my condition.

The next morning at Paleotronics, George Russell, who had been at the Stanleys' party, stopped at my desk, smiled unpleasantly, and passed on without comment.

Russell is a man with transparent red hair and a badly assembled face—he has thin lips that don't appear to meet at the corners, and yet they must.

I left promptly at five and drove directly to her house. As I drew near, looking across the open fields I saw her working in the garden beyond. Even at that distance I had no doubt it was Kay; she was dressed in coveralls and her hair was tucked up under a railroad cap, but her bearing was distinctive. She was picking something and putting it in a basket. I drove up the weed-grown driveway, stopped behind the house, and got out. She turned and came up to me, not hurrying. The vegetable patch was a good distance behind the house, maybe three hundred feet. She was carrying a small basket of tomatoes under one arm and holding onto a bunch of rooted cuttings of some kind. Chrysanthemums. A sharp end-of-summer smell wafted off them.

"Come onto the porch," she said. She sounded as though she had expected to see me there.

We sat on the wooden steps leading up from the garden to the kitchen porch. The paint was peeling from the steps. "Isn't it lonely here for you," I wanted to say, but I kept silent. I was afraid she would think I wanted to take advantage of her loneliness and I didn't want her to think a wrong thing of me. What I felt for her had to do with her self and not with her being alone.

She took off the railroad cap and loosened her hair. Her fingers left tracks of topsoil on her forehead. I felt that I knew her very well—as parker, shopper, drinker, digger—yet didn't understand her at all. "It's hard to know you," I said.

She made a face. "I'm simple," she said. "Either silent or shouting. Look, I've got to get these in the ground." She showed me the chrysanthemum sections. "Maybe later, when the sun's gone down. I'm late with them. I should have divided them a month ago. Wait here." She got down from the steps, then disappeared around the corner of the house for a few moments, and came back empty-handed. "I've put them in the shade."

The back of the house faced west. The hot late sunlight was pouring across the garden and into our faces. A rough-barked oak grew just beyond the steps, high-limbed and choked with dead wood. The shade fell on the driveway, and beyond. I squinted up into the tree. "You want to get those dead limbs out of there," I told her. "It's bad for the tree. Don't you know anything about trees? You could get some of that lumber on your head someday."

She didn't answer. A squirrel was posed out on the end of one of the dead limbs. Very pretty. "Oh, for God's sake," I said.

"What?"

"Nothing. Those are nice-looking tomatoes you've got there."

She looked pleased. "They're good. It's a new variety from the Ag Station up here. It's just got a number, no name yet. They're meaty and the plants don't wilt. We used to grow Rutgers but they weren't always good. A friend of mine with the college gave me the plants." I felt jealous of the friend with the college and the we who used to grow Rutgers. Both.

"It must be lonely for you here," I said.

She got to her feet. "I really must get those sections in the ground."

"That's stupid, to put them in now. You don't want the sun on them. Can't we talk for a little while longer?"

"All right," she said. But she didn't sit down again.

"Have you lived here long?"

"In this house? Five years. Six. We started those chrysanthemums from seed. Hardly anyone bothers to do that anymore. But you really ought to see them. A lot of singles, but all colors. All the colors you can imagine. And every plant is different."

We were standing very close. I was astonished to see tears come into her eyes. "And I intend to see them in bloom again. I'm staying. They all thought I'd be out of here a long time ago. But I'm not going to leave until I'm ready. Not a minute before. I'm going to plant them, pinch them, water them, weed them, and pick them. By the middle of October they'll be finished. Hard frost. Then I'll leave."

"Where will you go?" I asked her. I was dismayed that she was going and that made no sense, because by the fall I would have gone a lot farther myself. Remember Africa.

"I don't know where I'll go. But," she said again, "I'm not going to leave until I'm ready."

Pariah. I remembered her standing alone at Tom's party.

I gestured at the garden. "He died, you said."

She nodded. "Oh, yes," she said. "He died."

Well, how? I wondered. It was no long respectable illness. All that vigorous gardening. And he must have been, probably was, young. Drink? An accident? Maybe she was driving. Maybe that was it. "How did he die?"

Her voice was matter-of-fact. She was back on familiar ground. "I shot him."

Then she turned and walked up the kitchen steps, quickly but not running. The door slammed behind her. The basket of tomatoes was lying on the step in the sun. I left it there and drove home.

I kept away the next day and the next day and the one after that. Then I went back. I drove into the driveway. The weeds seemed taller to me, like a threat. She was sitting on the back steps staring out across the garden. She got to her feet as I walked to her. I took her hand. We didn't say anything. After a while she said, "Come into the house. I'll fix you something to drink."

After that time I went to her every evening directly

from the office. Sometimes I took her out to dinner at a place I found up the road near Tompkinsville where we didn't run into anyone she knew. More and more often she cooked something or threw a salad together, or I picked up cold cuts or a couple of steaks. The tomatoes from the Ag Station seeds were very good—tasty and solid. In the evenings we weeded the garden or sat on the back porch steps and talked, or were quiet. Sometimes we went in the house. I was in love with her.

I liked the quiet times best. I liked to watch her work in the kitchen or in her garden. She had a quiet, put-together way of moving. I liked to look at the back of her neck and the slope of her shoulders and the arms and the back, and the narrow long waist and round hips. I remembered my first sight of her, walking into the little store and the screen door closing behind her.

"I can't believe there was a time I didn't know you," I said. It was a wrong kind of thing to say, under the circumstances. Cruel, even. The time when I wasn't going to know her was going to start again very soon. And I said other things like that.

She never answered directly but she'd look as though I'd given her some secret drink of intoxicating power. Something in her eyes and in the set of her mouth would change. I didn't say it to make the effect. I'd hear myself saying the injudicious things, as if the truth were compelled out of me. And all the time the end of summer was coming and I lived one day at a time.

She talked to me freely about killing her husband. Matter-of-fact, sitting across from me at the kitchen table, telling me about it in a steady voice, getting it out of the way. It had been, she said, an accident. He had liked to hunt. She had not, but she had gone with him, on occasion, anyway. "I'm companionable," she explained to me, smiling a little, smoothing back her hair with her strong, long-fingered hand—a gesture I got to be familiar with. She was silent a lot, she told me. But companionable. It was not a mean silence, just her nature.

The shotgun that killed him had been returned to her by the police. If I cared to see it I could look up to the bend in the stairway, just crane around from where I sat. I didn't have to. I had seen the gunrack on the landing when I came in; it was a funny old house, full of nooks and angles and useless space. The stair landing was visible from the kitchen.

"Look at it and know it," she insisted. "It's the middle one. Otherwise you'll be wondering and sneaking looks." I looked. I didn't expect to feel anything about it and oddly it gave me a jolt. The middle one; she had taken it in her hands and killed a man with it, a man who had slept with her. I turned back to her, meeting her eyes with conscious effort.

"There," she said to me, "that's over with." She told me the rest of it. He had died here, in the kitchen. "Where you are sitting," she said. He had asked her to bring him the gun. She had gotten it from the rack and it had fired as she gave it to him. She sounded like a child reciting something learned by rote. "I sound like a parrot," she said at the end. "I have told it over and over. But that is what happened."

There had, of course, been an inquiry, of a fairly extensive nature. Their friends had stood by her; they had been well liked as a couple. "People liked Dick better than they liked me," she said. "I seem cold, or standoffish. I'm not really. But I seem so. Dick was the hearty type. We knew a lot of people. You met some of them at Tom and Jane's. Those two are still kind to me. They are the only ones. But everyone stood by me when Dick died. It was important that they did. There were no witnesses, after all, to the shooting. The police relied on what they could find out about me, my character, about my relationship with Dick. The gun was in my hands when he was shot. I told them so. I was bringing it to him and I tripped over a torn edge of the linoleum."

I looked, involuntarily, downward.

"I keep meaning to have it fixed. But I tripped, so that I fell against the table, and the gun went off, and Dick fell over, very slowly. It was like slow motion, the whole thing, or something happening in a dream. It seemed to me at any moment of its happening that I could have stopped it or made something else happen, but it kept happening. There was nothing I could do, I was off balance, and I suppose it all took just a few seconds, really."

"But I don't understand about everyone," I said. "The people in town, I mean. Your friends. What's gone wrong?" I was remembering George Russell, the leers, the suggestive glances, the silences, the odd looks on the night of Tom's party. And I seemed to have been ringed with a peculiar atmosphere ever since that night. It was a small town and I was sure that everyone who knew me, and a lot of people who didn't, knew where I spent my time.

"They testified, you see, that Dick and I were very happy. That they knew us very well, and that I could not conceivably, in their view, have wished to kill Dick, or even to hurt him. Then when it was all over, the inquiry closed and the gun back in this house, they turned their backs on me."

"Why?"

She shrugged. "Because they all lied. Out of kindness to me, or maybe they were squeamish. Maybe they didn't want the trial and the publicity and all that. I don't know people's motives. Maybe they didn't want me to die or spend a lot of years in prison because of something they said or guessed. Maybe it was bad enough that Dick had died here in the kitchen. We quarreled, you see, the two of us. Like cat and dog. Everybody knew it. It was an ugly habit we had gotten into. And it had been going on for, I don't know, three years.

"We had our first public quarrel, and after that we never seemed able to get back on common ground. Sometimes I think Dick hated me. I'm not an easy person and we were too different. We never should have married each other. We'd have had good marriages, I think, with other people. Dick's temper got worse and worse. Twice, two different times, he hit me. In front of people. I don't know how much longer we could have gone on together. I don't believe in divorce, really."

She paused and sighed. Those eyes, in their beautiful deep sockets, were downcast. She was staring at the table. "So you see, they lied for me. And they all believe that I killed him. Which I did. But they think I wanted him to die. Or killed him in a fit of temper. They think I murdered him. If they had just turned their backs on me," she said with a sort of sad intensity, "it wouldn't be so painful. But they—"

"What? What has everyone done to you?"

She raised her eyebrows, then smiled. "Just that. Turned their backs. That's all. It's enough, really. It has been very difficult for me here. I feel like the leper with his little bell."

"Lonely."

"No. I'm not lonely. I'm alone. I don't want to be with them. Come on." She jumped to her feet. "I'm hungry. Would you like something cold? Or steak? Steak and salad?"

"But all that gardening," I said. I was bewildered. "I thought you must have been very happy. People that gardened together."

She laughed. "It was the only time we didn't quarrel. Gardening together. We were tired and our hands were full and we worked side by side. It was the only good thing. Wait until you see Dick's chrysanthemums. He was a wonderful gardener."

"I'll be gone by then," I said. I hated Dick.

She stood very still, upright, by the sink. "Don't say that," she said. "I don't want to know that."

A couple of nights later I said to her, "But why do they hate you? You're not hateful. Do they really think you meant to kill him?"

"Do they? I don't know. Do they think so? Do you think so? After the hearing, when everything was quiet again, a couple of the men thought I must be lonely. You know? And I wasn't, not for them. So they all turned against me. First one, then another, then everybody."

That conversation took place on a Monday night. The next day George Russell caught up with me at the water cooler and said something filthy about Kay. I punched him in the mouth. I didn't know I'd done it until I saw the blood well up from his lip. I looked at my knuckles. They were white and turning red. He smiled at me with his mouth wet and red as though he'd scored a point.

"You're a pair," he said. "You're a pair."

Before the day ended, Tom Stanley called me into his office. I apologized for the business at the water cooler. "Why don't you stay away from her?" he asked me. "It's none of my business what you do, but she's bad news, believe me."

"I don't believe you," I said.

But all the same, I was full of unease, and anger, and distrust. It seemed to build inside me as time went on.

We were, it should be plain, in the midst of a love affair. There seemed to be no way I could put a stop to it. I lived for the time of day when I could be with her. I was drawn to her. She asked nothing of me, and never said, even, will I see you again. She was steady and loving and I couldn't believe she had killed in anger. Yet, under

the steadiness I began to sense that she knew they all had
got to me. She grew sad as time went on. Withdrawn. Not
passing moods; something barely felt, but always there.

August was ending, and I would soon be hearing
from the Africans. We never spoke of it directly. But she
spoke about the future, once or twice; not ours, not mine,
just her own. When the garden was finished in the late
fall she would shut up the house and go away.

"What will you do?" I asked her.

"I don't know. I used to do editorial work. But I feel
as though that were in another age. I don't want to do
editorial work. I wish I could just be someone's gardener.
I just don't know. My mind hurts."

But often she shook off the mood and was gay and
lively and amusing. I loved to watch her being domestic,
fixing things at the kitchen sink. I couldn't imagine being
with any other woman. She was quick-tempered, I found,
as I have always been, and we began to quarrel over little
things, things that don't matter, always ending in laughter
and lovemaking.

The summer wore on. The earliest of the chrysanthemums began to bloom. The house became like my own
house, familiar in all ways: its chipped paint, a loose ban-
ister I had nailed into place. I was always conscious of the
gunrack and its contents. It seemed remarkable to me that
the police had brought back that shotgun. And yet, why
not? It belonged to the Bannermans and it had been involved in an accident. Just that. When I stood beside the
refrigerator and turned a certain way I could see it there
on the landing and my eyes were drawn to it.

One evening—it was the start of the Labor Day weekend—she noticed me staring at it.

"I've used it since, you know," she said.

"Used it?"

"There were rabbits in the garden. I tried everything
to make them stay away. They were destroying the last
of Dick's garden. There was a little redbud tree, a variety

that he had rooted. They ate it to the ground. It seemed too bad. I felt that enough of him had been destroyed," she said passionately. "I couldn't stand it about his flowers and things. I know what you think of me. Don't think I don't know what goes on in your mind. But I couldn't stand it about the rabbits. I went out there and I shot at them, not to kill them but to frighten them away. Not just once"—she had turned to face me directly, her eyes intent, holding mine—"not just once. On three separate successive evenings. Then they stayed away."

That night we made love like strangers.

Then, just a week later, I had to say the thing we had both been waiting for. Usually she was outside, working in the garden or sitting on the steps, just waiting for me, when I drove in. This time she was in the kitchen and I walked in and sat down at the table where her husband used to sit. I remember looking down at my hands clasped on my knees, my arms, bare in the heat, tanned, the hair bleached with the sun. I felt the news was printed on my forehead. She had been standing at the sink, cutting a stalk of celery into bits. She turned around, the knife in her hand, and looked at me without saying a word.

"They called me today," I said. "They want me out there by the first of October."

She kept staring at me like a blind woman, but a blind woman who saw everything. Then she dropped the knife, not on the counter but on the floor, and came to where I sat and dropped to her knees and put her arms around my legs. She crouched there for minutes, her face buried in the cuff of my trousers. Then she looked up at my face. Her eyes were dry. I felt the tears start in my own.

"No," she said.

"I have to go."

"Please." Her voice broke. She caught her bottom lip between her teeth.

But she didn't cry.

I stood up and pulled her gently to her feet. I put my arms around her, and she stayed quite still in my embrace. After a while she put my arms away from her and moved back to the sink. Her face was pale and almost without expression. She stooped and picked up the knife and straightened again, put back the hair from her forehead, every line of her body, every gesture and movement so known to me.

"I can't let you go," she said. As I came to her she shook her head. "No," she said. "Don't touch me. I've got to think. You know, I know what we'll do. We'll eat. Then I'll think. I'll think later." She sounded as simple as a child, a child in pain and determined not to show it. She turned back to the sink and started to cut the celery again. Now she was crying.

"Do you think I want to leave you? Do you? Do you?" I was hoarse.

She turned to face me again. "I don't know."

"Kay, I have to go. Try to understand. It's something I *have to do*. I promised this to myself. I gave up a good job for this and I got rid of everything that mattered to me and every *one* that mattered to me. I have to explore the world a little and explore myself. This is the time of my life when that's the thing I *have* to do. Now. *This* time. The time isn't going to come again. Kay, *I have to do it.*"

I was terrified I wouldn't be able to leave her; not that she could make me stay but that *I* wouldn't go. "I have to do it," I said again. "Do you think I want to go now? Do you think I want to leave you?"

"I don't know," she repeated, shaking her head. "I just don't know. I only know if it were myself, I could never leave you. How can we leave each other?" She made a small gesture of asking, or of despair. She was still holding the knife. "Do you love me?" She sounded shy.

"Yes, I love you."

"Then how can I let you go? How can I?"

Suddenly I couldn't stand it anymore. "Will you stop that! Will you? Will you?" I was shouting. "And will you put down that damn knife!"

Her head came up and her mouth opened. She looked as if I'd struck her. She fumbled behind her for the counter and put the knife on it without even turning around.

I hated what I was doing. I hated myself for it. I hated her for standing in my way. I hated her because I loved her. I was standing with my back to the refrigerator. I wrenched my eyes away from her and my glance fell on the gunrack. "Get that damned thing out of the house!" I shouted. I raced up the stairs after it. The case was unlocked. I grabbed the middle gun out of the rack and tramped back into the kitchen with it.

"You must be crazy to keep this in the house," I shouted at her. "You have no feelings. None at all. If you had any feelings you couldn't have this gun in the house."

I flung open the screen door and walked heavily out onto the back porch. The sun was still in the sky, warm and golden, much farther to the south than when we had first stood here together. How many times had we not stood or sat together on these steps, time after time, before love and after love, in the beneficence of the summer evenings. I looked at the gun in my hand as though a stranger had put it there. I was bitterly ashamed. I heard her open the kitchen door behind me and I turned. She was calm, not crying.

"I must have been out of my mind," I said.

"No," she said. "It's difficult, that's all. My situation. And you going away. The whole thing is difficult. I shouldn't have tried to keep you. I swore to myself that I wouldn't stand in your way when the time came. I'm sorry. I really am."

"But I love you."

She smiled a soft and gentle smile—the calm after the storm. "You'd better put down the gun," she said. "I think it's loaded."

I set it down hastily, propped in the angle of the porch railing and the top step. I smiled back at her. Some kind of madness seemed to have passed. The gun was simply an instrument for frightening rabbits. I trusted her absolutely. And I never loved her more than in that moment.

"I'll get on with dinner," she said and turned back to the kitchen. At the screen door she hesitated. "Pick us some tomatoes?" she asked me. "Pick two. No, three. And make sure they're ripe. You brought me some green ones last time."

Tomatoes. At the far end of the garden. Three hundred feet in a straight line—and the loaded gun between us.

I didn't trust her after all.

But I loved her and I had hurt her enough. And I am, though this would not have occurred to anyone, a gentleman. "All right," I said, my lips tight across my teeth.

I walked down the steps, leaving the gun where it stood. To have moved it would have been to destroy her. When I had gone a dozen paces into the garden I turned and looked behind me, because she hadn't gone into the kitchen. I should have heard the door. She was still standing there, her back against the door, looking after me, still faintly smiling.

I turned and walked on, stiff-legged as though I were forcing my way through water. I didn't want to move but I had to keep going. The tomatoes were still fifty yards away and maybe farther than that, maybe on the other side of eternity.

I plowed on, fighting the undertow. I passed a small clump of chrysanthemums starting to show color, and I thought of the man whose flowers they were. Helpless to stop myself, I turned once again and looked back at her.

She still stood there, looking after me. In the oak beside the porch two squirrels spiraled up and down the trunk, hell-bent for happiness. She saw me look at them, and I think she laughed. Then she turned and opened the screen door and walked into the kitchen. The door slammed behind her and the shotgun toppled over and I flung myself to the ground.

There was a great bloody gully across my thigh, nothing to inconvenience me, and a scattering of lesser wounds from the ankles on up. The pattern, Kay said admiringly in the hospital, reminded her of the way one is supposed to scatter crocus bulbs.

I have now been confined in this place for two weeks. My bags are packed for Africa—Kay packed them—and her bags are packed for Africa; all the summer clothing she could buy in the local stores. Tomorrow morning I will get out of this place and on Friday morning we will get married, the Stanleys in attendance. Then we will drive down to the city and that night we will fly to Matanzia together. Being, both of us, incapable of looking after our own selves, we are going to look after each other. Put another way, the battle between us has only begun and will now be carried on at infinite length and in a hotter climate.

It is evidence of growth and versatility when an author writes a nonseries story that is as interesting as, or even more interesting than, his series stories. In "Falling Object" William Brittain outdoes himself in a tale about a brilliant physicist who is forced by circumstances to take "pointless, dead-end, menial jobs" but who remains a man with a life purpose—a deadly life purpose.

WILLIAM BRITTAIN

Falling object

Edmund Plummer stood on the roof of the Talmadge Building and peered over the parapet. He could see the flat stainless-steel-and-glass side of the building seeming to become smaller as his gaze traveled downward to the street twenty stories below. There were no setbacks, no architectural gewgaws to break the edifice's severe rectangular lines; it was a triumph of modern efficiency, providing the maximum of office space with the minimum of materials.

But Plummer thought he had discovered something unusual about the building. If true it might make necessary a revision of his original set of equations. He raised his bifocal glasses and bent forward to peer once again through the telescope of the surveyor's transit he had set up on the roof. Then he checked the measurement gauges on the instrument and jotted some figures into a notebook in neat precise columns.

There could be no question about it. Instead of rising at a precise right angle from the pavement below, the sides of the Talmadge Building leaned to the south almost three inches—two and seven-eighths inches, to be exact.

Edmund Plummer wished to be exact.

He looked at his watch, startled that his time on the roof had passed so quickly. Down below, on the fourteenth floor, men and women would be leaving their offices to go home. Then it would be Plummer's job to sweep and mop and carry away the mountainous pile of wastepaper and other debris created each day in order to keep a few of the wheels in that remarkable machine called American Business running properly.

Plummer neither liked nor disliked his job as a cleaning man. He had felt the same way about his previous job as a dishwasher and the one before that when he went from door to door handing out advertising leaflets for a chain of department stores. They were ways to keep alive, that was all. And even in these menial occupations, sooner or later he would have to quit and move on. Eventually, no matter where he was or what he did, someone would recognize him as the man whom the law had freed but whom everyone knew to be a—

Plummer tried to keep the word out of his mind. But it was impossible. Besides, it was all down in the official government records, which were now probably yellowing and gathering dust in a warehouse somewhere.

He managed to smile to himself, wondering what the secretaries on the fourteenth floor, who were so pleasant and so condescending to him, would think if they ever found out that the odd little man who emptied their ashtrays and dusted their desks and smiled vacantly at them had received his Ph.D. in physics at the age of twenty-three. Would they still giggle and call him "Plumsy" if they became aware that during the fall of 1942 and the spring of '43, at the height of World War II, he had been considered potentially more valuable to the Allies than a squadron of bombers?

And what would their reaction be if they discovered that their genial janitor had once stood in the dock of justice accused of being a traitor?

There was nothing thrilling or sensational about what had happened to Plummer; the whole grubby business had been a tragedy of errors from beginning to end. During October of 1942—at about the time that British bombers were stepping up their incessant pounding of the German industrial cities—Plummer was hard at work on a device of his own invention. It was an improved bombsight.

As any bomber pilot of that time could testify, the most dangerous part of a mission was the "bombing run" —the approach to the target. At that point the plane had to be kept straight and level for a period of approximately thirty seconds, allowing the bombardier to adjust his sight, make the correct allowances for speed, direction, and altitude, then release his bombs. During that thirty-second period the plane was a sitting duck at the not-so-tender mercies of both the cruelly accurate antiaircraft batteries on the ground and the best fliers the German Luftwaffe could put into the air. Men who have been through it are willing to swear that the thirty seconds over the target really lasted thirty years.

Plummer's new bombsight was designed to reduce that period of time by a full seven seconds. Seven seconds —the entire R.A.F. would have been willing to sell its collective soul to obtain seven seconds of grace on their flights through the shrapnel-filled hell.

But the device was never to reach the men who so desperately needed it.

Near the end of October 1942 certain "bugs" started cropping up in the new bombsight. On several occasions, problems that had seemed near solution proved to be more complicated than was first supposed, forcing not only Plummer but his entire staff to spend valuable time readjusting their theories to fit cold, hard, unyielding facts.

At about the same time Plummer received a visitor at his small apartment near the Baltimore research center.

The visitor gave his name as Norman Gant. He had heard of Plummer's work on the bombsight, and he wondered if he might discuss—no, of course not. The government would be keeping close watch on the progress of such an important device. Still, Gant explained, there were those who were interested in seeing that such an invention did not come into use *too* soon. Perhaps certain problems that Plummer was having might delay final production for a year, maybe longer. Those whom Gant represented would be willing to pay a huge sum for such delay.

Plummer had thrown the man out of the apartment.

But unfortunately he had neglected to report the offer of a bribe. And even more unfortunately the progress on the bombsight came almost to a halt. First, the optical system had to be scrapped; then the unit refused to function reliably at any altitude above 100 feet; and the focusing gauge tended to jam in wet weather. Everything that could possibly go wrong seemed to do so.

And in April of the following year, during a raid on an apartment suspected of harboring German nationals, the man who called himself Gant was picked up by the F.B.I. He was quickly identified as Josef Schissel, a former guard at one of the Vernichtungslager—the Nazi extermination camps. Having spent several years in the United States as a youth, Schissel spoke English without an accent, and in addition he was familiar with American slang. The Abwehr, the German Intelligence Bureau, had received word of the device on which Plummer was working, and Schissel had been smuggled into the United States by way of Mexico for the sole purpose of rendering the new bombsight project ineffectual. This Schissel proceeded to do—simply by swearing that the young scientist had indeed accepted money from him to slow down work on the bombsight. Schissel's confession, coupled with the almost total lack of progress on the device itself, was enough to make the authorities gravely suspicious that Plummer had sold out his country.

At the ensuing trial Plummer was pitifully unable to refute the circumstantial evidence against him. Why, it was asked, hadn't he reported his meeting with Schissel immediately? His answer—that he considered the man just another antiwar crackpot—was the object of derisive laughter by the prosecuting attorney. Plummer pointed out that his standard of living hadn't changed a bit since the supposed payoff. The prosecution, however, took the position that a man as intelligent as Plummer would be far too clever to begin spending the money immediately. Secret Swiss bank accounts were hinted at. And yet the government could produce no real evidence of anything more serious than poor judgment. Plummer might even have convinced everyone of his innocence—except for Schissel's testimony.

When the small clean-shaven German was placed on the witness stand he requested and was granted the privilege of making a statement to the court. Everyone present expected him to scream curses at the government which was holding him captive. The judge held his gavel ready to hammer down any such attempt.

Instead, Schissel began by thanking the court as well as his captors for the extreme courtesy they had shown to him, an enemy agent. He commended the judge for his fairness. Under the circumstances, Schissel went on, he was sorry to have placed the judge in such a difficult position. He realized that the judge would find it necessary to declare Plummer innocent because of the value of his brain to the Allies.

"You must find him innocent because the government forces you to do so," Schissel concluded in a low voice. "It is a pity that the law must yield to expediency." Stretching out his hand, Schissel pointed dramatically at Plummer. "Nevertheless, that man is a traitor to his country."

It may have been that Judge Randall Barth felt compelled to prove that in his courtroom the law still reigned supreme; perhaps Schissel's humble manner and his obvious willingness to take the entire punishment on his own shoulders evoked some sympathetic vibration in the judicial conscience. Whatever the reason, the fact remains that the enemy agent's words had an astounding effect. "That agent really got under Judge Barth's skin," one reporter was overheard to tell another. "The old man's liable to set Schissel free and hang Plummer instead."

In his final summation Judge Barth left no doubt that he considered Plummer to be the lowest form of human scum. He stated that he would personally see to it that the complete testimony of the trial was made available to any prospective employer foolish enough even to consider giving employment to such a person. Nevertheless, on the basis of the evidence alone—

Forcing each word through teeth clenched in anger the judge pronounced the accused not guilty. The reporters rushed from the building to file their stories.

In the court of law Plummer was innocent. But public opinion does not operate by rules of evidence. In a world of defense contracts and top-secret information Plummer found himself an outcast. His fiancée returned his ring; there was no note attached. He learned that while a rising young physicist attracts friends as honey attracts bees, a suspected traitor attracts only curses and looks of scorn and disgust. The two years in which he went without work wiped out his small savings. And then began the series of pointless, dead-end, menial jobs. He didn't live; he merely existed from day to day.

Then one morning in 1956 he found a cast-off newspaper on a park bench. He was about to pass it by when his eye was attracted by a small headline containing a familiar name. After thirteen years of imprisonment, the article stated, Josef Schissel, a spy for the Nazis during World War II, was to be released.

Schissel would be free. And Plummer resolved to kill him.

There followed for Plummer several years of keeping painstaking records on Schissel's whereabouts. He was returned to Germany. There he was influential in the exposure of three major Nazi war criminals. A general, grateful for Schissel's assistance in rounding up the wanted men, pulled some political strings to obtain a visa to enable the former spy to revisit the United States. The visa was twice renewed. Finally, in 1965, Schissel was granted permission to live permanently in the United States. Three years later he bought a small delicatessen only a couple of blocks from the Talmadge Building. Within a few months word of his delicious coffee and generously large slices of rich pastries had been passed to several of the secretaries in the building, and Schissel was commissioned to make daily deliveries for the morning coffee breaks.

It was then that Plummer applied for a job in the Talmadge Building as a janitor. He was hired.

At that time Plummer had no idea which method he would use to kill Schissel. It was enough to have finally located the man who had ruined his life.

During his first day on the job Plummer found out that the coffee-break items were delivered by Schissel himself; the Talmadge Building provided the major part of his income, and he did not trust any of his helpers to make the deliveries properly. But try as he might, for the first week on the job, Plummer could not catch sight of his intended victim. He began to wonder what changes twenty-five years had made in Schissel's appearance.

During the second week Plummer was sent to the roof of the building to clean away a pile of debris left by some workmen. It was hard work, and when he finally finished, he leaned against the parapet, enjoying the cooling breeze which never reached the sidewalk far below. He saw a panel truck pull up to the curb in the alley next to the building. A man wearing a white apron got out. From where Plummer was standing, the figure was curiously foreshortened. The man, who from that distance resembled a tiny white insect, opened the rear of the truck, took out a small wheeled cart, and began to fill it with coffee urns and trays wrapped in white paper. Then the man wheeled the cart around the corner to the building's front entrance. There the doorman greeted him cordially and even opened the door for him. It was several seconds after the man had entered that Plummer realized who he must be.

Schissel! There below him in the street, the man whose lies had made Plummer's existence a living hell was calmly making his daily delivery. Heart pounding furiously, Plummer raced down the stairs from the roof. He ran to the door of the service elevator and was about to punch the button when he stopped. As he withdrew his hand he smiled grimly.

He knew now how Schissel would die.

A few days later, from his meager savings, Plummer purchased a small but heavy steel strongbox. By going without lunches for several weeks he saved enough money to buy a secondhand surveyor's transit, complete with tripod, from the pawnshop around the corner from the shabby room in which he lived. The following Sunday he carried the transit to several points within two blocks of the Talmadge Building. From each of these spots the entire height of the structure was visible, and at each he took readings with his transit.

Then Plummer began his calculations. They were comparatively simple for a man who had once designed a bombsight. The Talmadge Building was 242 feet high. Five feet, eight inches—he guessed that to be Schissel's height—would have to be subtracted from that, making the distance 236½ feet. Weight, of course, was not important. It was the mass that counted, barring the neg-

ligible effect of the air itself. Wind needed to be taken
into consideration, so he would choose a calm day. A rate
of acceleration of 32.2 feet per second (approximately)
meant a distance of 16 feet the first second (approximately) and—no! Approximations were not good enough.
The figures had to be exact. But Plummer was trained to
be exact.

And he knew that a heavy strongbox, dropped from
the roof of the Talmadge Building at precisely the correct
instant, would smash into the head of Josef Schissel on the
sidewalk below with the velocity of a cannonball. Even if
it were to hit only Schissel's shoulder or back it would
most certainly kill him.

There was one further aspect of the problem that
Plummer found intriguing. Schissel certainly wasn't going
to just stand there and wait for the box to hit him. No,
Schissel would be moving too. But this did not disturb
Plummer. With the exception of the fact that the target
as well as the "bomb" was in motion, these were the same
calculations that bombardiers had performed over enemy
factories. It was merely necessary to see that the target
and the bomb collided at the same place at the same time.

From one of the secretaries on the fourteenth floor
Plummer borrowed a stop watch. Each day, just before
the coffee break, he went to the roof and observed Schissel
unloading his trays and urns, wheeling them around the
corner of the building, and entering through the front
door. The time it took Schissel to push the cart from his
truck to the front entrance varied only because he was not
always able to park his truck in the same place. Plummer
began measuring the time from the moment Schissel passed
a fire hydrant and he noted that the man could be de-
pended on not to change his pace. His movements were as
regular as clockwork.

The strongbox would be released to hit Schissel's
head just as the man reached the corner of the building,

since at that spot he cut the corner sharply, coming within two feet of the side of the building.

As a final step in his preparations Plummer managed "accidentally" to spill a blob of white paint on the sidewalk several yards down the alley from the corner. The spot had been chosen after several days of observation and calculations. When Schissel reached the blob of paint, the box would be dropped; Schissel would continue to walk ahead, and at the precise moment he arrived at the corner, the plummeting heavy metal box would have reached a point five feet, six inches, above the pavement. Finis.

And now Plummer had discovered that the Talmadge Building leaned two and seven-eighths inches to the south.

For a moment he wondered if it would be necessary to revise his entire plan. Then he shook his head. No, there was really no need for it. He would merely hold the box a bit farther out from the parapet before dropping it. A larger object than the box would, of course, be desirable in reducing the margin for error, but something heavy and yet small enough to be smuggled up to the roof was essential. The strongbox would do admirably. Besides, Plummer had another use for it.

Before dropping it on Schissel's head Plummer planned to fill the box with all the newspaper clippings he had saved concerning the German so the world might fully understand the reasons why he had to die.

The following day was rainy. The day after that a high wind sprang up early in the morning, and the same evening a gray mass of fog settled in, remaining for forty-eight hours. Plummer wondered if he would ever be able to put his murder plan into operation.

Friday morning arrived, sunny and cool and without a breath of wind. Looking through the window of his dingy room, Plummer smiled and hummed a happy tune to himself. It was a perfect day for walking with a girl in the park, for lying on the grass and watching the sky, for taking a trip to the country—and for murder.

Now that the time had come to carry out his plan, Plummer found himself curiously at ease. He whistled gaily at his image in the shaving mirror. He decided to skip breakfast, using the time instead to thumb through his thick packet of newspaper clippings for a last time. The earliest ones, dated April 1943, he handled gingerly. They were brittle with age but still quite readable. SUSPECT GOVERNMENT SCIENTIST OF SELL-OUT read the one on the top of the pile.

Replacing the clippings in their envelope, he crammed it into a jacket pocket and left the room. As he reached the sidewalk he remembered that he had forgotten to lock the door. He considered going back and then decided against it. There was nothing he possessed that was worth stealing.

He was six minutes late getting to work. In the basement of the Talmadge Building he went to his locker and changed into his blue coveralls, his mind on the steel strongbox waiting on a shelf of the broom closet on the fourteenth floor.

At 9:40 Plummer was on a stepladder, busily polishing the globes of the lights in a hallway on the fourteenth floor. Only twenty more minutes, he thought to himself. At ten o'clock. Then I'll put away the ladder in the closet, take the box, and go to the roof. Schissel will drive his truck up to the curb at 10:15, just as he always does. But he'll never make it to the front door. All these years I've spent waiting for this chance, and now there's just a few more minutes to—

"Plummer?"

It was Ed Malenski, who worked on the floor above. He must have come down the stairs; Plummer hadn't seen anyone get out of the service elevator. "Yeah, Ed," he answered.

"Dandridge wants to see you in his office right away.

He couldn't reach you on the phone, so he called me and told me to let you know."

Jerome Dandridge was the head of the maintenance department of the Talmadge Building. Plummer supposed he was going to be reprimanded for being late. He didn't mind. Just as long as it didn't take too long. He rode the service elevator to the basement, got out, and knocked softly on the door of Dandridge's office.

"Come in." Plummer opened the door. Dandridge was sitting at his desk, and another man, conservatively dressed, stood beside him. The second man was a stranger to Plummer, and Dandridge made no attempt to introduce him.

"Mr. Dandridge, I'm sorry about being late, but—"

"That's not why I wanted to see you," Dandridge rumbled. "How long you been with us, Plummer?"

"About four months."

"And before that? What did you do before that?"

"Dishwasher—other things," Plummer replied. "It's all in my application. Why?"

Without answering, Dandridge turned to the other man and picked up a paper from his desk. "Says here he never completed high school," he muttered. "What d'ya think, Mr. Ross?"

"Hard to tell," was the answer. "A long time has gone by since then. People change."

The man called Ross turned to Plummer. He reached into a pocket and pulled out a leather folder. "Mr. Plummer," he began, "I'm Joseph Ross. I'm with the F.B.I., and—"

Plummer was only half listening. Something had fallen from Ross's pocket when the agent had produced his identification. It was a small yellowed piece of paper with print on it. Automatically Plummer bent down to pick it up. His eyes widened. The black print screamed at him from the newspaper clipping.

SUSPECT GOVERNMENT SCIENTIST OF SELL-OUT.

They knew who he was! It wasn't fair. Not today. Not after all these weeks of planning.

"No! Not now!" he shouted. Running to the office door he dashed through it, slamming it behind him. Across the hall was the service elevator, its doors open. He scurried inside and punched the button for the top floor. As the doors slid shut he had just time to see Ross and Dandridge burst out of the office in a vain attempt to halt the elevator.

The car rose swiftly to the twentieth floor. Plummer stepped into the corridor and looked around. It was empty. They were probably waiting in the basement for the indicator to show which floor he had stopped at. He had only a few seconds before—

Behind him the elevator doors closed and he could hear the car starting downward.

He ran to the stairway leading to the roof and pounded up the steps. Opening the thick door with his passkey, he moved out into the sunlight. Inserting the key into the outer lock, he turned it hard in the wrong direction. The key snapped off. Perhaps that would be enough to jam the lock. To make doubly sure he inserted some small pieces of wood at the edges of the door, forcing them into place with the heel of his hand.

How much time? He glanced at his watch. Three minutes, ten seconds, before Schissel was scheduled to arrive. Please, please let the door to the roof hold for a few minutes. Just until he had enough time to drop—

The steel box! He had forgotten to take the box. It was still on the fourteenth floor, in the broom closet.

There had to be something else. A brick. That was it, a brick. He scanned the entire roof.

There was nothing but tiny scraps of wood which the slightest movement of air would blow off course. Even if they were to fall perfectly straight, Schissel would hardly feel them when they struck. He had to find something heavy.

There was nothing.

Plummer heard a pounding on the door to the roof. The lock rattled, but the thick iron door remained closed. "Plummer! Open up!" called a muffled voice.

Far below he could see the sunlight glinting off the top of a panel truck as it moved up the alley at the side of the building. A tiny antlike figure got out and opened the rear doors. The cart was piled high with trays. The coffee urns were put into place.

And in that instant Plummer found the weapon that would kill Schissel. It was one he should have thought of long ago—so much better than the strongbox. He removed the packet of clippings from his pocket and grasped them tightly in his hand.

Behind Plummer, Ross and Dandridge had managed to open the door a scant two inches before a wooden wedge at its base again jammed it. "Plummer, listen!" shouted Ross through the opening. "The army just located a report that Schissel sent to his superiors back in '43. That's why I'm here. It only landed on my desk two days ago and—"

But Plummer, deep in concentration, did not hear. Down below, Josef Schissel closed the doors of his truck and gripped the handle of his cart. He took a step forward —two—three—

"Open up, Plummer. The government's willing to do anything in its power to make amends. You're cleared! You're inno—"

The front wheels of Schissel's cart glided over a white paint stain on the sidewalk. The rear wheels followed. And then Schissel's right foot came down on the white spot.

With the soles of his heavy work shoes poised on the parapet 236½ feet above Schissel's head, Edmund Plummer folded his arms tightly across his chest, smiled through the tears streaming down his cheeks, and stepped off the parapet and out into space.

Sam and Sophie had been married twenty-three years. A happy marriage—not exciting, but normal. Then they both got the bug—painting. Sophie developed into a "modern," but Sam stuck to his delicate little flower studies and his realistic little still lifes. Indeed, entirely in his own way, Sam became a specialist.

CAROLE ROSENTHAL

A specialist in still lifes

The crowd from the art gallery next door pressed and swirled around me in the front of the restaurant. I stood, peering into faces, trying to locate my wife. We had arranged to meet here as soon as she was finished looking at the exhibition. But naturally, she was late again.

"Darling, he knows his *craft* so well, but I certainly wouldn't call him an artist," someone near me was saying.

"Did you see Sari Pendleton's sculpture? The *idea* of using *real* livestock to make her point!"

"So McLuhanesque!" a voice wailed into my left ear. "Whatever happened to tradition?"

"Don't be an idiot," came the reply on my right.

Their voices, as they stood near the bar, rose like little birds of prey, circling the room and soaring above the clatter of knives, forks, and dishes. A passing elbow knocked into my ribs, and simultaneously I felt a sharp pain in my foot.

"Excuse me," I said to the man next to me, pulling my foot from under his shoe. But he looked past me to a hard-edged woman with a high, brittle black hairdo who stroked her head absorbedly as she chattered.

I found myself gradually propelled to the back of the restaurant, where there were fewer people, and stopped near a table for two, where a small man with wispy eyebrows sat alone, hunched over a roast beef dinner.

"Do you mind if I sit here for a few minutes?" I asked. "I'm supposed to meet my wife here, and there are so many people."

He dabbed at the corner of his mouth with the napkin. "Sit down," he said. "I know how wives are."

He was a mild-looking man with a large nose that jutted out in inverse proportion to his diminished chin, and with narrow sloping shoulders. He seemed misplaced among the conscientiously chic crowd from the exhibition, with their avant-garde costumes and boisterous color combinations.

"Been to the show?" he asked.

"The art show?" I shook my head.

"What else? Isn't that what *they're* all talking about?" He gestured toward the crowd, his bland gray eyes narrowing unexpectedly. "Real art lovers!"

"I wouldn't know," I said apologetically. "I'm not too big on modern art myself. Leslie, my wife, just took up painting recently, and I drove her into town to see the show."

He folded his hands comfortably on the table, regarding me with a very serious expression. "I see," he said. "My wife is also an artist." He cleared his throat.

"But I'm an artist, too," he added. "A specialist in still lifes, you might say. Yes, very still." He smiled as if he'd made a joke, and I waited for the punch line.

He stared at the table for several seconds. "Been married long?"

"Three years," I said.

"Twenty-three for me. No children, though, which I suppose in a way is a blessing." Suddenly he pointed back into the crowd.

"See that woman over there?" he said. "No, no, the skinny one leaning against the bar stool, with the expression like a hawk." He indicated the woman I had noticed earlier, with the hard-looking black hair. "Know her?"

I shook my head.

"I do. Bettina Clarke-Resnikoff." He thrust out the syllables derisively. "A friend of my wife's. Writes the art column for the *Weekly Herald*. Don't have anything to do with her!"

The intensity of his voice startled me. "What do you mean?"

He grunted. It was a deep painful sound. And I suddenly noticed that the man's apparent smallness was an affectation—a mannerism of gesture and posture—as if he had trained himself for insignificance. As he leaned back in the chair he seemed to be growing.

"If you really want an answer to that question I can tell you, but it's a long story." He retreated into a diffident shrug, and added, "In fact, I'd like to tell somebody and a stranger might understand even better than a friend."

I glanced at the wall clock behind his shoulder and nodded.

"Go ahead," I said. If he became too long-winded, Leslie would eventually rescue me.

"A lot of this story has to do with my marriage," he said, "and it's rather personal. But just bear with me and you'll get the total effect."

Leaning back, I pulled out a cigarette and lit it. At first he spoke so softly I had to strain to hear his voice.

"You see," he began, "we had a really happy marriage. Not exciting, but normal. Sophie, my wife, was a little on the domineering side, but frankly I don't mind that. In fact, her get-up-and-go lent a spark to our relationship. We had the usual hobbies and routines—bridge with the Schwartzes on Wednesdays, and movies and TV on weekends. My wife had canasta on Tuesdays and Weight Watchers on Thursdays, and I went bowling with the boys on those nights. Then Sophie took up an interest in art."

He scratched his large nose and smiled. "Sophie started going to painting classes on Saturdays, and pretty soon she was so involved with it that she urged me to start painting, too. 'So good for your self-expression, Sam,' she told me.

"Well, she was one hundred percent right! I took to it like a duck to water and within six months we were spending most of our spare time painting. Together. It was a nice feeling, let me tell you, to look across my easel at Sophie, her face all wrinkled up with concentration, a smudge of yellow ocher on her chin, painting the same still life I was painting. Almost like newlyweds, you might say. Then—"

"You know," I interrupted the little man, leaning across the table, "that's funny. My wife has been trying to get me to paint, too."

"Don't do it!" he said sharply. "Listen!" His eyes strained the net of his lined face for a moment, before the film of mildness restored itself to his expression. "Let me go on with my story.

"Anyway, gradually Sophie started talking about entering art shows. 'What can we lose, Sam?' she asked me. And actually, she began to win. Prizes. I remember it was right after she got third prize in the Maple Hill Shopping Center Show that she told me, 'Sam, you're holding back. The reason I'm winning prizes and you're not is because you're too realistic. People like a little flair these days, you know? Something a little different.'

"But I enjoyed doing realistic paintings, and I don't understand this modern stuff, anyway. So I kept on with the still lifes. Only Sophie was really outpacing me. The next thing, a couple of the exclusive ladies' art clubs asked her to join. And Sophie made all new friends. But since the meetings were for members only, I never met the people she was running around with, and pretty soon we weren't even speaking the same language. She'd look at my paintings and say things like, 'Lacks lyrical qualities,' and 'No creative tension between the colors.' Now, how can you answer charges like that?

"Our whole routine began to collapse. She even wanted to give up our weekly bridge with the Schwartzes.

"Then she met Bettina Clarke-Resnikoff."

The little man's face became suffused with color, and his hands on the table knotted. For several seconds his eyes hardened and fixed on the back of the black-haired woman still chattering shrilly at the bar.

"That was what really changed everything. I could put up with a lot, but this—well, I put up with it, too—but it was too much!

"Bettina Clarke-Resnikoff is a woman who can best be described as a vampire. An articulate vampire, that woman haunting the fringes of arty events, sucking from the artists, and dissecting them out loud or in print as soon as she has a chance. The major thing she's big on is accusing people of being unoriginal. As soon as she understands something she denounces it. And because she talks louder and more often than anyone else, people take her as an expert.

"Well, she began to cultivate Sophie. Maybe she thought Sophie was really talented, or maybe she just wanted to make trouble. Who knows? But they spent hours on the phone with each other every day. And naturally, the next thing I start hearing about is originality. As soon as I come down to breakfast—by this time it's cold cereal instead of hot pancakes, since Sophie's so busy—I hear pronouncements on who's original and who's not original. In no time at all *nothing* is original enough for my wife!

" 'Sam, we're not living *originally* enough. We have to change the furniture.' And out goes my comfortable green armchair and in comes some clear, blow-up plastic model that deflates every time I sit on it.

" 'Sam, don't you think bowling is a waste of time? Bettina says all the really *original* people are taking up improvisational dance.'

"And my painting—well, whoever heard of realism in the mid-twentieth century? 'You might as well take a snapshot, Sam,' Sophie tells me.

"Meanwhile, she converts my den into a studio for herself, since she's started doing these twelve-foot collages out of beer pretzels. Crumbs all over the house! But I don't mind. I work small anyway, so I use a corner of the garage for painting. But what *did* bother me was that *everything* seemed to be changing. Even *Sophie* looked different to me from week to week. And on the day I came home from work and she presented me with an architect's plans for an ovum-shaped house I knew that things were coming to a head. It was only a matter of time before Sophie would realize that *I* was too unoriginal for her.

"Exactly two weeks and three days later, Sophie came into the garage where I was painting a delicate little flower study. She planted her hands on her day-glo hip-huggers and just stood looking at me for a few minutes.

" 'Sam,' she said, making her voice very hard and flat, 'I've thought it over carefully. I've also discussed it at length with Bettina. We just don't have anything in common anymore. I'm becoming so original—as a personality, I mean—and you're so ordinary. I want a divorce.'

"I just stood there. Although I'd been half expecting it, still it took me by surprise. I couldn't get a word out, even though I could feel my lips moving and something like static was crackling in the back of my head. Hadn't I gone along with all her schemes?

" 'It's no use talking about it, Sam,' she said. 'My mind is made up.'

" 'But, Sophie—' I stammered.

"She came over and put her hand on my arm. 'I'm sorry, Sammy,' she said. 'We've had twenty-three good years together, but I didn't really know who I was during that time, and now I'm beginning to find myself. Besides, you know you haven't been happy during the past few months. You don't want to change! You like to stand still. You're so predictable!'

"And suddenly she broke off and started to chuckle. She pointed to my little painting and shook her head.

" 'You see what I mean, Sam, don't you? It's not as if you *couldn't* be original—I mean *anybody* could be—but look at what you're doing right now. Look at this painting! That's just what Bettina meant all along, but I always used to defend you. No originality! Completely predictable! Sam, I want a divorce immediately. I know now you'll never do anything new!'

"I felt very confused. By the time answering words came pouring out—I still don't remember what I said—I found that my fingers had fastened tight around her throat and my thumbs had pressed against her windpipe.

" 'Predictable, am I? You think I'm completely predictable?' and I can still see her laughing at her astonishment—at *my* astonishment—as her hands flapped feebly against my shoulder. She stared wide-eyed at me and her tongue protruded. It was quite funny.

"Small parched sounds came from her mouth. When

I finally unknotted my fingers from her throat she sagged against me. Then she fell to the concrete floor and her head hit with a dull thwacking noise.

"She didn't move. And as I looked down at her I was struck by her helplessness. Gently I slipped a pile of old art magazines under her head. She had such a bulge-eyed expression of surprise on her face! And even though I knew something was wrong I must admit that I *liked* the way she looked.

"And then I got *my* idea! I wanted to paint her. A memento and a tribute! Just as she was, where she was. Why not? All my life I had been balking at unusual ideas, but why not break out of that rut? Besides, my paints were already out.

"So I began. And although my first idea had been to capture her expression of surprise, as I thought about it the urge for something more abstract, more expressionistic, came over me. Hadn't Sophie encouraged me to be original?

"So I painted her eyes a rich purple, and in light strokes of the brush I made her nose yellow. The cheeks were a deep cobalt blue. Then I painted her mouth an acid green—very vivid—but it didn't work very well because paint kept dribbling from the corners of her lips. I guess it's because I had only worked on canvas. And being unused to experimental surfaces I couldn't get the right consistency for the skin—"

"Wait a minute!" My knee struck the table as I jerked upright in the chair. This was incredible! "You don't mean you were painting directly *on* her skin?"

"Didn't I say I was painting her?" he said. He passed his fingers over his forehead, looking vaguely puzzled and alarmed. "I thought I mentioned it.

"Well, by the time I was finished, Sophie looked pretty interesting. Actually it was the most unique thing I had done in my whole life, and I admired her for quite a while before it occurred to me to check her pulse. But of course, just as I'd thought, she was dead.

"At that point, though, the full implication of what I'd done hit me. I panicked. I didn't know what to do. There was my wife of twenty-three years stretched out and painted from head to toe, as colorful as a Byzantine mosaic. Painting her had seemed like a good idea, but when I thought about calling the doctor, or the police, I knew it would look very bizarre.

"Then I remembered something. So I went into the house and checked the calendar. Sure enough, Sophie had written down that this art show was today, and she had already reserved a space in it. So I strapped her to a frame, crated her up very carefully, drove down here, and entered her in the show. Maybe you saw her—she's hanging in the center gallery against the righthand wall as you walk in. The light's not very good, but a lot of people were crowded around when I walked by a while ago."

"But you're mad!" I exclaimed.

"Do you think so?" he asked, raising an eyebrow. "I would have said so, too. But do you know what Bettina Clarke-Resnikoff commented when she saw my entry in the show?"

"What?" I whispered.

" 'Highly original. Is it your own idea?' "

He smiled ironically and raised his napkin to his lips.

I stared at him. Preposterous! He must be mad! How could I gracefully excuse myself and alert the police? The important thing, of course, was not to panic.

"*Darling,* I'm so sorry to keep you waiting!" Leslie, my wife, had squeezed through the crowded restaurant without my seeing her, and she stood at our table now, pulling off her gloves. "It was the most unusual show."

She paused, looking at the little man, then back to me. Evidently she was waiting for an introduction, though it took me a moment to remember to behave normally.

"My wife, Leslie," I said. "This is Mr.—?"

"Roseman," he said, half rising behind the table. "Sam Roseman."

Leslie beamed. "Not *the* Sam Roseman?"

He shrugged, embarrassed.

"Well, congratulations!" Leslie pumped his hand up and down. "You know, your entry just won first prize!"

For a moment the little man looked startled. He puckered his forehead and scratched the tip of his nose. A wide smile spread across his face.

"My wife shares in this triumph," he said, sliding his eyes sideways at me. Abruptly I rose and pulled Leslie toward the front door.

"Really, darling," Leslie protested as I pushed our way through the crowded restaurant, "I wish you were more interested in culture. You didn't have to act so rude to the man just because you don't understand art. After all—"

Suddenly she broke off and began waving enthusiastically to the brittle, black-haired woman at the bar.

I dropped her arm. Had the whole world gone mad? "Do you know *her?*"

"That's Sam Roseman's wife," Leslie said, tucking her hand in mine. "Really a nice woman. And I understand her husband is a very original, extremely witty person. Were you talking to him long?"

I turned slowly around toward the table. The little man, catching my eye, was lowering one eyelid in a careful, deadpan wink.

―――――――――――

Another solid, substantial, satisfying crime-detective story by Anthony Gilbert, with the author's usual fine sense of "the spirit of the place," and her equally fine delineation

*of characters who, even if you've never met people exactly
like them, will give you the shock of recognition that
comes with the conviction it all could have happened
just as Anthony Gilbert has related it.*

ANTHONY GILBERT

When suns collide

There may be some people at Summerley Green who don't
remember when Mary Totten came to us, but there can
be few who have forgotten the day she left. Mary wasn't
native to the Green; she came at the time the local authorities challenged public opinion by acquiring the old
Manor Farm just beyond the village and turning it into a
home for autistic children. At that time quite a number of
people didn't know what an autistic child was, and when
they found out, there was a good deal of indignation, almost as much as if the proposal concerned an open prison
or a Borstal.

My editor wanted me to get the story—I was working for the *County Argus* then, and this kind of institution
wasn't as commonplace or as easily acceptable as it has
since become. I've moved around the world a lot since
that time—I suppose you could say I've gone up in it—but
I don't recall summers nowadays so brilliant, or winters so
keen, or springs so full of promise as they were then.

I was twenty-four and Mary was two years younger.
On my way to the home I ran into Jed Wilson. We'd

been to the local school together, and when our contem-
poraries started to fan out and make for the big cities or
countries overseas we'd stayed on, he in his uncle's building firm, and I as a cub reporter, though I at all events
didn't mean to stay in Summerley Green all my life.

We walked up the hill to the Manor Farm compan-
ionably. I didn't guess then that he was going to become
my brother-in-law. When we reached the old Manor Farm
we both stopped automatically, though for different reasons. He was interested in the structural changes that had
been made; the council had shown a lot of imagination,
and Jed's uncle had had a hand in the work.

"Not bad," he said, looking to me for approval. But
I had eyes only for Mary Totten.

Perhaps no one could be quite so beautiful as she
seemed to me at first sight. She was dark and slender and
her features would have enchanted an artist, but there
was more to it than that. There's an expression that gardeners use: They say a man has a green thumb, which
means that whatever he plants prospers—flowers bloom
and shrubs burgeon. Mary had a green thumb for life; just
by existing she seemed to create fresh beauty in the
world. A lot of water has flowed under the bridges since
that day, but I've never changed—not at least until our
last meeting and then, you might say, events were dead
set against us. . . .

Those children were lumped together in the minds of
the majority with the mentally handicapped and the sub-
normal. But Mary would have none of it.

"They are children who live in a world of their own,"
she insisted, "and who are we, who can't enter their world,
to say it's inferior to ours? All we can do is try to provide
a bridge so that they can move back and forth." But she
made it clear that there must be no compulsion, that the
children were free beings.

"You saw her with those kids?" I remarked to Jed

later when we were having a pint at The Black Lion. "What would she be like with children of her own?"

"Don't try and upset the applecart," Jed warned me, quite sharply for him. "Any girl worth her salt can beget children, but this girl is different. She belongs to *their* world, she's their means of communication. If you destroy a bridge over a river," he amplified, as if he thought me too dumb to grasp his meaning, "what happens to the people isolated on the far bank? Either they plunge for themselves and drown, or they sicken and die—most likely of starvation."

That was like Jed. A normal enough chap in the ordinary way, he had these moods of perception—though that wasn't what I called them in those days—that he voiced without the least self-consciousness. It was an odd thing: My guardian when I was a boy talked apparently the same language, but it never sounded the same. I suppose the difference was that Jed was always sincere. Neverthe less, I couldn't see Mary Totten staying long at the Manor Farm. I didn't believe the local lads would let her.

I was wrong, though. It wasn't that she didn't have her chances—half of us had our hearts at her feet; but none of us was the lucky man. There was speculation as to whether there was a secret someone in the place she'd come from, but I know now that wasn't the case. The gossips, not without a touch of malice, began to prophesy that if she wasn't careful she'd join the ranks of those who wouldn't take the walkers and whom the riders had passed by.

She was barely twenty-five by that time, but in Summerley Green we marry young. Only Jed didn't seem surprised. At all events, he wasn't among her worshipers, though he liked her well enough.

"I've always been sorry for prince consorts," he told me. "A man should rule in his own kingdom, and the average chap's going to have his work cut out trying to live up to all that brilliance."

That was just before he married my healthy plain sister, Nora. And they had two children and a third on the way before Charles Holland arrived to startle the Green as Mary had some years before. I was in The Black Lion the first time I saw him. He came into the bar, not showing off or anything—it was clearly his normal manner; but he gave the impression of being ten feet high. I was reminded instantly of the morning I'd first set eyes on Mary Totten.

Holland was a fair giant of a man; I got the impression that if the place had been plunged into darkness he'd have glowed like a torch. A blind man would have realized something had happened. And if he wasn't as handsome as he seemed at first sight, he was still striking enough to be the center of attraction, wherever he went. My first coherent thought was: Here's someone at last who might match up to Mary Totten.

I turned impulsively to Jed, but he was in another of his prophetic moods. "What an old matchmaker you are, Bill," he said. "But you can forget about it. It would never work."

"You think you know it all, don't you?" I snapped.

"Use your loaf," Jed advised me. "What happens when two suns collide? You don't get double illumination. On the contrary, the results are ruin and destruction, explosions that desolate and leave barren two worlds."

Charles Holland had come to manage the big wood-pulp factory that had just been erected in the new township of Summerbridge a few miles away. If there'd been an outcry in the Green about the Manor Farm establishment, it was nothing compared with what the old residents had said when they saw the factory going up and the new town being built all around it. A lot of the land the factory used was agricultural, but farming wasn't doing so well then and the value of the land for building purposes was, by comparison, astronomical. The inhabitants of Summerbridge didn't mind; it meant jobs for their young men and women who'd otherwise go far afield. Only the diehards like Freeman of Loseby Farm fulminated against the newcomers, seeing in the development the beginning of the end of what he considered civilization.

"Those clever scoundrels!" he declared. "One of these days they'll find a way to put a factory up on the Downs—by computers, I wouldn't wonder—and we'll all be run by machines." And he was by no means consoled when one of the younger generation retorted insolently, "Why worry, Dad? It won't be in your lifetime."

What followed seemed to me as natural as the night following the day. I wasn't actually in Summerley Green, not even in England, when Mary Totten married Charles Holland. My paper had given me an overseas assignment that kept me out of the country for three months, and when I came back, the tongue-wagging, such as it had been, was over. Not that there had been nearly as much of this as the neighborhood had anticipated. The wedding had taken place in London and the couple had gone abroad for the honeymoon. Summerbridge thought this normal, the Green considered it something of a slur.

In a way you could say that Mary became a stranger within a year of her marriage. I don't believe she meant to separate herself from local interests, but Charles Holland entertained a lot in the ostentatious and, to my mind, hideous house that had once been a pleasant small-scale manor, and the most we saw of Mary was through the glass of the biggest car in the county, wearing the kind of clothes no one else would have dreamed of buying, not only because of the cost but because they wouldn't have any opportunity for wearing them. They traveled quite a bit, Charles' interests being legion. As for the children who were going to startle everyone, they didn't materialize. It seemed the unkindest quirk of fate that two such splendid potential parents should remain childless more than three years after the wedding.

Nora and Jed had produced another child, the sort you'd have expected Mary's to be. I thought: Heredity's an odd thing—hawk-faced Jed and plain good-natured Nora producing such a beauty.

"Poor Mary!" Nora said to me when I went down to inspect the newborn. "I used to think it would be marvelous to be married to a rich man. I didn't realize then that gold can build prison gates as well as castles."

"I can't see Mary allowing herself to be imprisoned by wealth," I assured my sister warmly.

Nora gave me an affectionate sisterly punch. "You never did see any further than the end of your own nose," she told me.

I suppose it was a few months later that I saw for myself how matters stood between the Hollands. I had met Mary once or twice, and though to me her beauty was still untarnished, there was a change in her that shocked me. The widely spaced eyes, the lovely lines of brow and chin—these nothing could change; but the spirit behind that loveliness seemed to be burning low.

But after I saw Charles Holland in London at a function I attended in an official capacity, I began to understand why. Though he spent so much of his time between walls, he had a broad open-air streak. Jed said once it was a pity we had no pack of hounds in the neighborhood—Holland would have looked well in a pink coat. He was clearly enjoying himself the night I saw him, and giving equal pleasure to his companion—only she wasn't Mary. This girl was dark-haired, but that was about all the two had in common. This one was as alluring as a tigress and

about as trustworthy. She was younger, of course. Mary
was now in her thirties, and this girl couldn't be more
than twenty-two or twenty-three. I was sure, the instant I
set eyes on her, this was the reason for Mary's changed
appearance. Later Jed was to say to me, "One of the reasons would be more accurate. You must be about the only
member of the old gang who didn't know."

The trouble was that at that stage Mary recognized
her husband for what he was—and still loved him. At all
events, that was the way I read it.

On this particular evening a man named Percy Bedford whom I'd met on more than one assignment moved
over to say, "Doesn't the great Charles Holland come from
your part of the world?"

"He catapulted into it a few years ago," I said.

"Prides himself as a gambler," Percy continued. "At
least, that's what we hear. All I can say is, he's going to
need all his luck to handle a girl like Pamela. She's Pamela
Cross, you know. And that type always holds out for a
wedding ring."

"Then she's wasting her time," I snapped. "Charles
Holland's got a wife of his own."

Percy gave me a grin and a nudge. "Wake up, Rip
Van Winkle. Did you never hear of divorce?"

"Divorce Mary to marry that little tramp?" I exclaimed.

Percy's eyebrows rose. "That little tramp, as you call
her, is likely to inherit if not the earth at all events a siz-
able portion of it when Grandpappy hands in his dinner
pail." His eyebrows twitched again. "Why the heat, Bill?
Not declaring an interest either way, are you?"

I was surprised to realize the force of my feeling for
Mary after so long. And the folly of it, the sheer waste.
Like keeping some huge bonfire burning with no one
there to see it. It didn't make sense, of course, but so little
that has to do with love ever does. What, I ask you, was

the sense of Mary wasting herself on a man who was not only unfaithful to her but apparently didn't care who knew it?

It was Nora who remarked, when next we met, "It won't surprise me if one of these days the great Charles Holland bites off more than even he can chew."

"Why shouldn't Mary divorce *him*?" I demanded.

"Why should she?" Nora said. "He's like those war-mongers in the Old Testament, whose vocation was to slay and to lay waste wherever they went. He's spoiled Mary's life, so why should she set him free to ruin some-one else's?"

I only saw Mary once more, and that was some months later when a line I was following up for my paper took me in a homeward direction. I still thought of the Green as home, since I had no other.

After Mary, all women seemed dull and insipid. In my mind's eye I always remembered her as she had looked on that first day—so radiant, so unquenchable.

Later that afternoon my car broke down with the suddenness and thoroughness that all car owners know. I left it at Martin's Garage and was told to return in a couple of hours to find out what could be done. I'd known Martin's father when I was a boy, and young Martin as-sured me they'd treat my jalopy as a special job.

A damp, unpromising morning had turned into a fine and spirited afternoon. I phoned through my story and on impulse decided to see if Mary was at home. All about me, pasted onto fences, nailed to tree trunks, were notices of a fair to be opened by a celebrity that afternoon, which presumably accounted for the general emptiness of the Green. Most probably Mary would be at the fair with all the rest, but I'd nothing else to do, so I went to look for her.

Charles Holland had contrived to disfigure what had

been a charming small Manor House with various additions and embellishments that might have come straight from a Hollywood set. The gardens weren't allowed to ramble; everything was cut back and planned as carefully as a jigsaw puzzle. I decided they'd been laid out by landscape gardeners in the same way that illiterates sometimes buy books—at so much a yard to impress their neighbors with their scholarly propensities.

I went through the elaborate iron gates, half expecting to be accosted by a liveried figure demanding my business; but, except for a faint breeze, nothing stirred. Nobody came when I knocked and rang. I supposed all the domestic staff had gone off. Even men like Charles Holland, for all his wealth, can't persuade the independent Summerbridge women to live in. And I daresay Mary didn't really want them.

Anyhow, as I say, no one came, so on my second impulse of the afternoon I wandered away from the front door and peeped through the windows of the long room that ran from the front to the back of the house. To my mind it was more suited to a showplace than to a home, with a good deal of overdecorative furniture and gaudily painted china in corner cupboards. There was a heavy brocaded couch and chairs, and French windows opening onto a sort of loggia.

I could see clearly through the glass, and that's how I saw Mary. She was leaning back in an artificial-looking white-painted chair of Italian design, and she was dreaming or asleep, since she hadn't heard my bell. I went round the side of the house. A second white chair had been pushed back from the table, as though someone had risen hurriedly. On the table itself were two coffeecups, used but empty. Mary lay back, unmoving; she didn't even turn her head when I called her name.

It was then that I saw the small red-capped vial that had rolled to the ground at her feet.

Unthinking, I picked it up. It was empty now and bore the usual anonymous label—Tablets—and a warning that an overdose could be fatal. I didn't know how many tablets it had contained originally, but it didn't matter anymore. I stood there numbly, not quite believing at first that this could be the end of the rare, the beautiful, the brilliant Mary Totten.

I found I was rolling the little vial up and down my sleeve and unthinkingly I dropped it into my pocket.

You know the expression: Time stood still. It stood still for me, then, though probably for not more than a minute or two; but it seemed endless. Then my mind began to function again. Surely I should call someone—but who? The doctor? The police? I didn't even think of Charles.

I pushed at the door leading into the house from the garden and it opened easily enough. There was a rack of coats at this far end of the passage that widened beyond the staircase into the handsome hall. I recognized an old green coat that Mary sometimes wore for gardening. I wondered whether she ever wore it now or had merely kept it for auld lang syne. Next to it was the checked sports jacket that Charles Holland used to wear when he walked round what he'd called his estate. At first glance it was like anyone else's, but if you looked again, you'd detect the fine cloth, the perfection of cut and dash; and even the buttons were unusual. It was faintly damp, so I supposed he'd been wearing it that morning. I supposed he'd gone to the fair—it would be expected of him—and I wondered what excuse he made for Mary's absence. Or hadn't he bothered?

There was no telephone in the hall, and I didn't fancy opening any of the closed doors to look for one. After all, I could use the public booth on the Green. I stood there for quite a while, pondering. When I put my hand in my pocket to find a handkerchief, because I was now sweating, I was struck by the extraordinary quality of the silence all around me. It was the kind of stillness you only find in a deserted house. And it occurred to me that's what this house was—deserted.

In the end I didn't telephone anyone. Mary, I reminded myself, was dead. Nothing I could do would help her now. I walked slowly back and stared down at that dead uncomprehending face. A police officer I once met told me that no matter how a man died, the after-expression was always the same—a kind of anonymous peace. Unless someone's been at work on him with a knife or a gun, he added. I looked for peace in Mary's face, but all I could see was a shell whose occupant had departed. I didn't even say good-bye. There was nothing there to say good-bye to.

I left the premises through the rear garden by a wooden gate in the wall, opening onto tough countryside. In the far distance a car went by, but nothing else moved. I didn't see so much as a squirrel. It was too early to go back for my car, and even if I'd felt like a drink, The Black Lion wouldn't be open; so I climbed the north down lying beyond the commonland. Local legend declares that during the Ice Age there was a tremendous split in the earth's surface, resulting in an abyss that made a man giddy to gaze into. Yet human resource had made a road there, had even built a few solitary homesteads far down in the valley, remote from the world. They looked like toys from where I was standing.

Fifty years ago, they say, you could walk the downs from dawn to dusk and see no one but an occasional shepherd tending his flock. But I saw no shepherds that afternoon—not the human kind, that is. As a race, they're like hedgers and ditchers—modern life has rendered them obsolete. I saw the silhouettes of some cattle on the horizon and a church with a square tower among the distant trees. I thought how farsighted it was of the old builders to erect a tower, rather than a spire that might be snapped off by the pitiless winds that race across the downs in winter.

On the farther side of the valley a great flock of sheep had turned their noses homeward. They trotted in the stumbling flurried fashion of their kind, as if driven by an invisible shepherd. Then I saw the shepherds themselves, a pair of them, half-bred collies, rounding up their charges with a skill and patience that no human could have exceeded. I stood watching for the sheer joy of it. They went about their job with the precision of regimental sergeant-majors. I waited, seeing one of the dogs turn, retrace his steps, to hunt out a stray lamb that had gotten separated from the main body. Back he came, driving his bleating charge in front of him. I waited till they, too, were like toys against the sky. At last I came back by the lower road to claim my car.

"I've been watching the sheep on the north down," I told Martin. "That's a fine pair of dogs."

"They'd be Mr. Freeman's two," Martin said. "Took them to the sheepdog trials in London, he did, and they beat the rest of 'em hands down." He'd had some good offers for them, Martin continued, but Freeman said he'd as soon sell his wife as his dogs. "Wouldn't let 'em be shown on the telly neither," young Martin added, taking my notes and making change. "I reckon Bess Freeman nigh clawed his eyes out when she heard, but mine are working dogs, Tom Freeman told her, and a working dog's like a workingman, he's got no time for that sort of foolishness."

By the time I'd left Martin's, The Black Lion had a few chaps standing about outside waiting for the door to open. I listened, but Mary Holland's name wasn't mentioned. I'd told Jed I'd be down this way this afternoon, so it was no great surprise when he pushed the door open, though as a married man he wasn't the customer he used to be. He'd changed less with the years than any man I knew. He didn't envy any of the go-getters who'd done so well for themselves; he was satisfied with life the way it was. He might look like an easygoing sort of fellow, but the man who thought that would soon discover his mistake.

We got chatting, and still there was no mention of Mary. It seemed uncanny to me. When you know a thing yourself, you can't quite credit that no one else knows it. We were still swapping yarns and Jed was saying that Nora was expecting me up at the house that evening when Charles Holland came bursting in. He was a bit heavier, a bit older, but he hadn't lost that air of vitality that would have made him stand out in any crowd. He looked as though he didn't have a care in the world. I said as much to Jed in a wry voice, knowing Holland was going to be worried enough pretty soon.

Jed was as cool as the proverbial cucumber. "Peter Pan was never my favorite character," he remarked. "Chaps of that age should be worried, feel the weight of their responsibilities. Could be that's his trouble—that he's never accepted them."

Before I could ask him—because I was curious—just what he meant, the door was pushed open again and Sergeant Larkin came in. He made straight for Charles Holland, who grinned at him, but the sergeant didn't grin back.

"Going to give me a parking ticket?" Charles inquired.

But it would be a grim tombstone that could equal the expression on Larkin's face. He said something to Charles that none of us could hear, and Charles stopped smiling, as though someone had rubbed a hand over his mouth. He put down his tankard and got off his stool.

"Accident?" I heard him say, as the pair of them went past without a glance in our direction. "What sort of an accident?"

But nobody could hear what the sergeant said.

Jed and I had another pint, and when we came out of The Black Lion the brilliant light had dimmed. The last stragglers were coming back from the fair. Peace seemed to surround us like a lake.

But it was all illusory. There wasn't going to be much peace hereabouts for quite a while to come. No one knows how the village grapevine works; presumably the neighbor who had found Mary and called the sergeant had spread the news. At all events, within the hour the rumor had spread from lip to lip. Mary Holland was dead; more than that, it was said she'd taken her own life.

"I don't believe it," said Jed bluntly, when he heard. "Mary was not the suicide type. I'd easier believe that Charles Holland killed her."

And that, believe it or not, was the official verdict.

When it got round that Charles Holland had been arrested for the murder of his wife by poison, the whole place gasped, and no one, I am sure, gasped louder than Charles.

"You're out of your senses," he told the inspector who came over and made the formal arrest. "I left my wife drinking coffee, and as well then as I was myself. I'd been urging her to come to the fair, but she said she had a headache. Then there was this phone call and I went in to take it"—that, I supposed, explained the pushed-back chair —"and after changing my coat I went straight to meet this fellow straight up to the fairgrounds."

It all sounded very neat, but the police mistrust neatness. And there was more than one witness to testify that Charles had been asking for a divorce and Mary had refused him. It came out, too, that Charles had made the coffee, so that the village woman who came to "oblige" could get off in time to put on her finery for the fair. She drew a rather attractive picture of him pouring the coffee directly into the cups.

Well, Nora said, anyone could have known he made

it. A woman would have put the cups on a tray. And it turned out that he'd added a drop of whiskey to each cup —what's called Irish coffee. Nor did it pass unremarked that the smell of whiskey may disguise another smell that preferably should be undetected.

It was a good story that Charles put up and he might have got away with it but for one thing. When the police started to look for the vial that had held the tablets, they found it in about the last place you might have expected —in the pocket of Charles' green sports jacket. And there was proof that he'd been wearing the jacket that very morning.

The prosecution's case was that he dropped the vial into his coat pocket when he poisoned Mary's coffeecup, meaning, of course, to dispose of the vial later, or possibly to hang around till the poison started taking effect, and then drop the vial where, in fact, I had actually found it. But apparently he'd been caught off guard by the phone call, which, it turned out, wasn't from a chap at all, but from the latest of his women, threatening trouble; so he'd dashed away, they said, and only remembered too late about leaving the vial in the sports jacket.

Anyway, his plan to be the one to find Mary on his return misfired, because a neighbor came in to bring her something from the fair, found her, and, unlike me, rushed to notify the authorities. Another thing that told against him was that the vial was rubbed clean of fingerprints. I remembered rolling it up and down my sleeve before dropping it into the pocket of Charles' sports jacket. . . .

I was in court when the jury brought in a verdict of guilty. Even then Charles didn't accept it. Some miracle would save him at the eleventh hour; this kind of thing couldn't happen to the great Charles Holland. Of course, we don't hang men for murder anymore, and a life sentence doesn't have to be more than ten years; but those who have endured it will tell you the sentence doesn't come to an end when the prison gates open. And the world to which Charles Holland will return one day will prove as strange and inimical as the prison where he now lives.

And isn't that right? Isn't that the way it should be? Wasn't it a life sentence the judge gave him?

Sometimes, when I walk over the great North Down and feel the wind in my face and hear the curlews calling, I remember a man who used to like walking there, too. You can't get much exercise in a prison yard.

"Is this British justice?" he'd shouted as they led him away from the court.

Perhaps not. But it's rough justice as I see it, and it was the best I could do on the spur of the moment.

O. Henry's real name was William Sydney Porter. He was born in 1862 in Greensboro, North Carolina, left school at the age of fifteen, and worked for five years in his uncle's drugstore in Greensboro. In 1882 he went to Texas for his health, and between 1884 and 1894, in Austin, he earned his living as a clerk, bookkeeper, draftsman, and bank teller. In 1894 he bought Brann's Iconoclast, *which he retitled* The Rolling Stone. *It was in this short-lived humorous weekly that some of O. Henry's early stories and poems appeared.*

Among his contributions to The Rolling Stone *was a series of stories about "The Great French Detective." In these flagrant, fragrant parodies of Vidocq, O. Henry hit on an inspired name for his detective—Tictocq. So far as we have been able to check, only two Tictocq stories have been included in O. Henry's seventeen books—"Tictocq" and "Tracked to Doom," both in* Rolling Stones *(1912), the latter a case in which Tictocq is not only the eyewitness of a murder but also the earwitness of the murderer's confession, and yet "the murderer of Marie Cusheau was never discovered." (Tie that for detective perspicacity if you can!)*

We now offer you a tale of Tictocq that was first published in the June 23, 1894, issue of The Rolling Stone *and has never appeared in print since (except in EQMM last year). It is typical of the Tictocq series—a "condensed novel" of outrageous 'tec tomfoolery; it is also an enjoyable discovery, a hitherto "unknown" O. Henry story that was lost to devotees of detection for seventy-seven years.*

O. HENRY

Tictocq, the great French detective; or, The murder in Rue St. Bonjour

CHAPTER I

"Make way, messieurs; make way for the great Tictocq."

It is midnight in Paris.

In the salon of the concierge in the Rue St. Bonjour

a gaping crowd of grisettes, gens d'arme, and bourgeoise stand around the body of a murdered man.

Tictocq, the great French detective, pushes his way through the crowd and kneels by the corpse.

"Ventre St. Gris," says Flaubert, the rag picker.

"Mille tonnerre, mon ami, je suis petit bon toadstools en fin de frogs' legs," answers old Marie Bonfallong, the daughter of Grisi Tonjours, the street sprinkler.

"Tiens! Will you be quiet, canaille?" says Tictocq.

"Be quiet, vraiment!" hisses Gaspard de Toot, the gendarme. "Tictocq has found a clue."

The great detective closely examines the body of the murdered man and enters the following memoranda in his pocketbook.

"Stranger; age about forty years; about five feet ten in height; hair dark; left eyebrow missing; linen marked E.J.; cause of death, violent concussion over left temple; residence, politics, religion and favorite poet unknown."

On the table in the salon is a plate of butter.

Tictocq carefully examines the plate and draws forth a long, glittering, golden hair.

"Mon Dieu," he says, holding it up. "In three days I will deliver the murderer to Monsieur le Prefect of the Police. Clear the room!"

The bourgeoise, the canaille, and the sans-culottes are driven from the salon.

The captain of the gens d'arme and Tictocq the detective follow, carefully locking the door behind them.

When they have gone, the murdered man rises to his feet, places a long black hair in the butter, laughs a low, sardonic laugh, and goes out the back door.

CHAPTER II

It is the next night.

The banqueting hall of the Prince Bonbonette is magnificently lit with lights.

In the antechamber the Chevalier du Nord and Father Roguin, the famous bon-vivant priest from the cathedral of Honi soit qui mal y pense, have just taken off the limit.

The guests are at supper.

The gold and silver plate on the table must have cost over $76.

About the center of the long table, just beginning to cut open a can of sardines with a silver jeu d'esprit, sits the most beautiful woman in France.

It is the Countess Villiers.

She has all the wild seductive grace, the abandon, the bonhomie, the university-girl-at-a-football-game empressement that one seldom sees outside of the Champs Elysées, or the Sixth Ward, Austin, Texas.

Her hair of a beautiful lustrous golden hue hangs down her back in long, undulating, shimmering waves.

The company is the most famous that Paris can produce.

Among the guests are Madame Tully, Madame Duke, Napoleon IV, Madame Ruppert, and Lydia Pinkham.

Every few minutes the prince touches a silver gong, and servants enter bearing freshly cut watermelons and patty for grass.

The conversation is the most brilliant to be found in any Parisian salon. Wit, satire, bon mots, repartee, and epigrams fly upon the air as a new keg comes in from the Faubourg St. Germain brewery.

"Voilà! Madame Tully," says the prince, shaking his jeweled hand back at one of the most beautiful ladies of the court, "you have only eaten three watermelons. What is it Rousseau says: 'Bong le bong, bong, bunghole gehaben?'"

"Diable, mon prince," replies the madame, "you flatter me! I am not rien de plus cubebs. I believe what Montesqueioux says is true—'Scratchez vous mon back, and I'll scratchez votre. Nicht wahr?' "

"Ah, madame," laughs the prince. "I know you of old. There is no putting the kibosh on you."

The Abbé Meatmarquette is relating some delicious morceau to the Duchess Camusot. She is listening with the utmost enjoyment, her eyes sparkling, with a piece of watermelon in her hand and one foot on his chair.

"Monsieur l'Abbé, you are too funny for anything," laughs the duchess. "But come! Where do you get all this knowledge of the gay and fashionable undercurrent of our most exclusive Parisian circles? You are better informed than the *Revue de Deux Mondes,* or the *Figaro* itself, and you à soi distant and entre nous father in the church. Where do you get all this fund of information?"

"Parbleu, madame, where else but in the New York *Sunday World?*"

"Mes enfants," says the prince, rising, "the dancing hall awaits us, and Terpsichore will probably jolt some of this watermelon down for us. Allons à la dans."

The prince is approaching the Countess Villiers with the intention of asking her hand for the cakewalk, when the doors are suddenly burst in and 127 gens d'arme enter the salon with Tictocq, the famous French detective, at their head.

"Ti donc, messieurs. What means this intrusion?" says the prince, reaching back for his hip pocket.

"En le nom de l'empereur," says Tictocq. He draws from his pocketbook a long golden hair and compares it with that of the Countess Villiers.

"Madame la Comtesse, you are my prisoner," says Tictocq.

"On what charge?" asks the countess, coolly picking her teeth with a corkscrew.

"The murder of a stranger in the Rue St. Bonjour yesterday."

"Your proofs?"

"This hair was found in the butter on the table by the murdered man."

The countess laughs.

"Regardez vous, Monsieur Tictocq," she says, removing her hair and handing it to the detective. "I bought this hair in the Rue St. Montmartre at four o'clock this afternoon."

"Foiled again!" hisses Tictocq, taking a watermelon under his arm and leaving the salon.

CHAPTER III

The office of the Prefecture of Police.

Several gens d'arme stand about the room.

The stage manager, call boy, and all the supes are arranged R. and L. as audience.

Suddenly the door opens and the great Tictocq enters with a prisoner.

"Qui est votre ami?" says the prefect.

"The murderer of the stranger in the Rue St. Bonjour."

A murmur of admiration runs around the room.

The gens d'arme hope for the day when they will become world-renowned detectives like the great Tictocq.

"Can you prove an alibi?" asks the prefect of the prisoner.

"No, monsieur."

"Were you drunk?"

"No, monsieur."

"Had your victim provoked you in any way?"

"No, monsieur."

"Mon Dieu! What cold-blooded savagery. Away with him to the Bastille."

"Hold!" says the captain of the gens d'arme. "There is one thing in the prisoner's favor that should be considered."

"What is that?" asks Tictocq with a dark frown.

"He is the murdered man himself."

"Is this true?" asks the prefect.

"It is," says the prisoner.

Tictocq draws himself up proudly.

"Monsieur le Prefect," he says, "have I ever failed in bringing a criminal to justice?"

"Not this week, anyhow," says the prefect.

"Then," says Tictocq, "is not my word better than that of a man who murders himself and then escapes?"

"Ma foi, certainement," says the prefect. "Away with the prisoner to the Bastille."

"Parbleu!" say the gens d'arme one to another. "Is there another in the world like the great Tictocq?"

———————————

There are certain writers who often reveal a curious point of view, an unusual vision, an odd or offbeat sense of humor about what's happening around us in this fruitcake world we inhabit—such contributors to Ellery Queen's Mystery Magazine *as Avram Davidson, James Powell, and Robert McNear—and we must never forget the late Gerald Kersh, Lord Dunsany, and Ben Hecht.* Sui generis, *every one of them, bless them all.*

Florence V. Mayberry also has a different kind of vision of people and how they think and what they do. You will find this beguiling point of view in her story

*"The Beauty in That House"—a strange story, but then
every story that Florence V. Mayberry has written for
EQMM has been a strange one.*

FLORENCE V. MAYBERRY

The beauty in that house

So.

Willie. And me.

At least, I hope it will turn out that way. Just Willie
and me.

William doesn't suit him as a name. But then neither
does Willie. But he enjoys the nickname. It sounds affectionate.

Willie has this big beautiful house. Filled with trink-
ets—at least, that's what he calls them. Like a Chinese lion
maybe 5,000 years old. Russian ikons from the czar's
court. A shaving mug once used by Franz Josef of Aus-
tria. Paintings, carvings, illuminated manuscripts. Satin-
hung walls. Not wallpaper made to look like satin—real
brocaded satin. The candelabrum on Willie's piano doesn't
have crystal drops; the drops are jewels. All this is just a
start. Those are just the few things I noticed the first night
I went to Willie's house for dinner.

Willie gave me the creeps. Oh, he looked good. Too
good. His hair had that new fluffy cut, the one achieved
when the hair is blown, snipped, then blown and sprayed.
It covers any bald spot. Not that Willie was anywhere

near bald. Willie had lots of hair, the sandy-blond kind that happens when gray gets mixed in. His eyes were almost as pale. His mouth was well shaped, but when he wasn't talking he held it as if he had just bit in half an hors d'oeuvre about the size of a dime. But when he talked, his mouth opened full and looked fine. His words came out big and round like an elocution teacher's.

His chest was deep. But it didn't look strong and virile. Pouter-pigeon. He was tall, with plenty of flesh on him. But it didn't make him look strong. More like a hothouse plant that has been overforced. Like I said, Willie gave me the creeps.

But his house and all the beautiful things in it didn't. Willie knew all about them. Their history. Why they were valuable. How they were made and who made them. I finished high school at night classes—in my twenties, while working in the daytime to support a sick husband. They didn't have anything in those night classes about jewels and paintings and the history of art. So all I knew was that when I looked at Willie's treasures chills went up my spine. And I got a funny crying sensation in the pit of my stomach from the way the soft light of a lamp—alabaster, Willie called it—fell across the painting of a woman whose throat seemed to throb in the glow. I would have sworn, almost, she had a pulse. And the old polished chest with the inlaid design—I felt I had to rub it. When I did, Willie smiled, showing two pointed rat teeth, and he said, yes, rub it, that shows true appreciation, get the feel of the artist in your fingers.

What he said was right. A feeling came into me, as though I had made the chest myself. Then Willie handed me a small jade walnut. A thousand years old, he said. Hold it, he said, rub it; thirty generations more or less of Chinese aristocrats have rubbed that walnut and soothed away their tensions. And now so did he. Well, that did it.

The jade had a lovely smooth cool touch. But Willie was all over it. When he turned his back to show me something else I put it down.

So how would it be to touch Willie?

Can you believe it? Willie's personal bathroom had walls of mother-of-pearl. At least, they looked like that. There was a deep white rug all over the floor, and a painting baked in the porcelain of his washbasin. And me with cheap prints in cheap frames on my living-room walls.

Willie's bedroom looked like the pictures in *House Beautiful*—only better because I was actually in the room, my feet sinking into the Chinese rug. The big bed had a black lacquered headboard. On one side was a large lacquered chest, on the other was an inlaid writing cabinet. French, made at the time the wealthy French went all out for Chinese objets d'art. On top of the desk was a figurine of a Chinese lady I could have kissed, she was so elegant and pure and lovely. "Pick her up. Touch her," Willie urged.

A man with all that money should have had those rat teeth filed off and capped. "Do you," I asked, "touch her?"

"Indeed I do," Willie said. "She is my darling, my lovely. She's a court lady of China, you know. Oh, what fun I'll have teaching you about my beauties! You'll make an apt student, my dear."

He reached for me. But I slid away as though the sudden sight of a framed Chinese scroll was just too much for me, as though I had to get to it fast and lose myself in it. Just for a minute I wished I could dive into Willie's swimming pool, which was just outside his bedroom, beyond sliding glass doors. Only that wouldn't have been possible. Two beautiful boys, maybe twenty or twenty-one, were swimming in it. They were good swimmers, tall, strong, gleaming boys, tanned to a sun-gold. They would have rescued me. Because Willie would tell them to. Not because they wanted to.

Willie came behind me and put his hands on my shoulders. It felt as if little worms were crawling up and down my arms. "You're as lovely as my figurine, Courtney. And how that name suits you, my darling. It's so regal, so aristocratic."

"I'm not an aristocrat," I said. "My people came from the hill country of Kentucky. It's an old family name. I always hated it because it's a boy's name, and I'm a girl."

"Who wants a silly girl's name?" he said. "You're not a silly girl. You're an exquisite mature woman. You will look so right as hostess of this house. A lovely jewel." He didn't add "in an exquisite setting," but that's what he meant. And he'd make me into that jewel. With his money.

I turned and faced him. "Willie, I have to be honest. To be comfortable with myself. I don't love you. But I love this beauty. I've never had it. Only cheap imitations."

"How wonderful that you can have it now," Willie said. "Now I'll show you the room that will be yours. If you want it redecorated, we'll do it. But it is done in exquisite taste. It was my sister's."

Willie's sister had died, oh, maybe a month before he began asking me out. He'd known me for a year or so before that, but I was only the clerk who usually waited on him at the bookstore.

That same week, after he had shown me my room, Willie and I were married. Willie wanted to make a big thing of it, invite everybody who was anybody for miles around. But I said no. I didn't want to be shown off. So we had a civil ceremony in another state. Nobody we knew—not even the two golden boys, Ferdie and Maurice —was present.

I wonder if anyone who hasn't had yearnings like mine and squelched them all her life could understand the way I felt when I went to live in Willie's house. Even the way the light shone through the thin, thin Irish Belleek china cups at teatime made me shiver. Before I married Willie I had one cup and saucer nearly that thin. I used it when I wanted to cheer myself up. Finally the cup cracked and then it looked like any other piece of the thrift-store china I was always picking up. Willie's house had two whole sets of Belleek.

I suppose a woman of forty-three ought to have had by that age more of the things she has always wanted. But I was a widow with no training for a job, other than selling things. And not anything special at that. Just a low-keyed salesclerk, which is why I fitted well in book-stores. So I satisfied my yearnings by reading books about beauty and looking at beautiful things in stores and museums. I could sew and had a knack for style. Willie noticed that when he came in the store to buy books, usually accompanied by Ferdie or Maurice. But after his sister died, Willie began to come in alone. Next thing I knew I was having dinner at Willie's house, with two Filipino servants waiting on us. Willie was shopping for a woman in his household.

I hated myself for being Willie's front. Not Willie, I didn't hate him—in part I was grateful to him. I just hated me. Ferdie and Maurice helped out with that. They hated me, too—especially Ferdie.

One day when I thought they were all away I decided to take a swim. The swim was more than a luxury, it was therapeutic. But I never used the pool if the boys were around. Their eyes had taken on a veiled laughing look the one time I came out in my bathing suit in front of them. But who could blame them? One leg thin and twisted from the polio I'd had as a teen-ager. The fact that the rest of me was round and slender and well put together didn't hide that leg.

While I was swimming, Ferdie suddenly came into the pool area. Well, my bad leg couldn't be seen in the water. So I waved at Ferdie and kept on swimming. I figured he would leave. He couldn't stand me. Instead he came to the pool's edge. "Could I speak with you, Mrs. McKinley?"

I stopped swimming, stood up in the water. "Yes?"

"Please. Come over here, the servants might be listening," he said, beckoning to me. I swam to him. He reached down his beautiful muscled arm. And suddenly I was yanked up on the side of the pool. "It will be easier to talk up here," he said, smiling, but his eyes like flames on dark coals.

I was miserable and awkward, knowing how my leg looked. I turned quickly to reach for my robe. Ferdie told Willie later that I slipped. But if I had slipped, bent as I was to pick up the robe, the bump would have been on the front of my head, not on the back.

Ferdie said that as I fell I struck my head on the pool's edge, then sank in the water.

"Ferdie knocked me into the pool. He banged me on the head with something first," I told Willie when I was up to talking. "If you hadn't come home when you did, Ferdie would have left me in the pool to drown." Both Willie's bedroom and mine had two sets of sliding glass doors, one set opening into the pool area, the other set into the patio. Willie came into his bedroom just after I fell, saw Ferdie staring down—shocked, Ferdie explained —rushed out and ordered Ferdie in after me. "He would have told you I fell in while no one was around. Or that he didn't know anything about it."

Willie's eyes clicked. Like a computer putting things into place. Don't ever think Willie wasn't intelligent. He had a supermind. I don't know what he said to Ferdie. But Ferdie went away for a while. When he came back he moved out of the main house into the garden guesthouse. There was a kitchenette in it and he even ate his meals there.

After that Maurice put himself out to be darling to me. Maurice was always a weaker character than Ferdie. Ferdie was sinuous, pantherlike. Maurice was blond, as muscled as Ferdie, but the muscles seemed unused. He was, oddly, like a gorgeous wax replica of a gorgeous male model. Actually handsomer than Ferdie—so handsome that if one didn't spend too much time at it, it was a stark and startling pleasure simply to look at him. But only to look. The boy was cold all the way through.

Willie was fonder of Ferdie than of Maurice. Ferdie was mean, but he wasn't cold. Maurice was a thing of beauty to be displayed like one of the antiques, paintings, or carvings. But there was raw emotion, a kind of flame, in Ferdie. He was dark gold, with large and lambent eyes. He carried a jungle in him.

Perhaps that was why it seemed so natural when Ferdie bought the lion cub. One morning Willie looked out the window of the breakfast room, into the patio. He took a deep breath. Then he smiled. "Come here, darling," he said to me. "Look what that Ferdie has done."

Ye gods, what? I thought. Set fire to my bedroom? Dug a pit for me to fall into? I went to the window and saw the cub sniffing at the plants. It was an adorable creature. Big, slappy feet, its head round and furry and innocent-eyed. I love animals. Perhaps better than people. Even if they are vicious there's an honesty about them. Especially I love cats, so graceful, so self-sufficient. But working all the time as I did before I married Willie, I had gotten out of the habit of wishing I had one.

Impulsively I slid back the glass doors, went into the patio, and touched the cub's head. It was purring, so loud the purr sounded like a growl. It rubbed against my negligee that was trimmed with eider. The cub caught a mouthful of eider and made funny faces as the feathers tickled his nose. I laughed, kneeled, and put my arms around its neck. Ah, the lovely pure thing! It was the loveliest thing in all that house of beauty.

Willie stood over me, his eyebrows peaked, his expression admiring. "Well," he said. "You *are* a constant surprise. Ferdie, aren't you pleased that my wife loves your new pet?"

Ferdie was standing beside the doorway to the garden guesthouse, a leash in his hand. Glowering. He forced a smile and slanted his eyes so their expression couldn't be read. "They make a charming picture," he said tightly. "But I had hoped to have the lion solely attached to me. The animal trainers advised that it should be taught to recognize only one person as its master."

I stood up, staggering a bit as I always do because of my weak leg. Without a word I went in the house, back to my breakfast. It was difficult to swallow the coffee. For I knew exactly what Ferdie had in mind. Train that cub. Then when it grew up, one day, the end of me. How he'd bring it off I didn't know. Perhaps toss a steak on me. Or grapple me when Willie was away and then toss me to the lion.

Willie joined me. "Darling," he said, "how good Ferdie really is at heart. He has given the cub to you because you were so beautiful together. He said that now he would never be happy owning it just for himself—it was so apparent the cub instinctively loved you."

"I don't want Ferdie's cub."

"It isn't Ferdie's cub," Willie said sleekly. "Ferdie doesn't want it anymore. If you don't accept it I'll have to send it back to the animal people."

As I mentioned, Willie is very intelligent. He wanted me in his household. Alive. Impulsively I went to Willie and kissed his cheek. Then I hurried back to the patio and my cub. When we were through playing my robe was stripped of feathers and the cub had a pink eider mustache.

I had dreamed many times of the gorgeous cats I might own someday—Persians, Siamese, Burmese. But never of a lion. That was for Hailie Selassie, an emperor.

Or for a lion tamer. Now I owned one, and with my surroundings I felt royal. The cub, even so young, had strength and a dignified confidence. The way it padded around me, rubbing against me, with a soft show of muscles beneath its loose baby skin, was thrilling. Along with the bold and lovely way it looked into my eyes. All that spring we played, the cub and I. Willie hired an animal trainer to give me pointers, for the cub was growing and becoming rougher in play.

Willie began to spend a great deal of time in the patio with us. Not Ferdie, who sulked in the guesthouse. And certainly not Maurice, who had let out a terrified squeak like an oversized mouse at his first sight of the cub and then had fled to the roof above the pool area for his interminable sunbaths. Even in that safe place he shuddered and chittered to himself as he watched us play below.

Willie's reason for staying in the patio was not because he was worried about the cub attacking me. If that had been all, he would have hired a guard. He stayed because he was fascinated. By the pair of us. Sometimes he looked at me as though he had never seen me before. And sometimes, to tell the truth, I looked at myself in the mirror as though I had never seen me before. The reflection was of a woman who should have a lion for a pet. Tawny-haired as the cub. Sinuous in line when standing still, when not walking and showing the limp. A woman that the beauty in that house had rubbed off on.

Willie took up sketching that summer. He had a gift for it. An amateur's gift, yet with true feeling coupled with delicacy of line. He liked to catch the cub and me in motion. He grew better and better at it and his trips to New York, or wherever he went, became quite rare. He had always kissed me on the forehead when we said good night and I went to my room. Now he began kissing my lips. One night when a tear trickled down my cheek he kissed it away. Willie no longer gave me the creeps.

One cloudy morning in early fall, as I stepped out of my bedroom onto the shallow brick step leading to the patio, I tripped and fell over something. My knees struck the bricks and for a minute I closed my eyes and rocked back and forth, easing the pain. Then I looked to see what had tripped me. It was the cub's bloody head.

Yes. Hacked off. My beautiful cat. My darling, soft, purring, playing love. My pure strong lion.

I just sat there. I never wanted to get up. It was too late to help the cub. And who wanted to get up and move and live where hate crouched on the edge of peace and beauty?

Willie found me like that. He helped me into the house and made me take something—some pill, I didn't even know or care what it was. It wasn't long until I began to fade away into sleep. And as I did I thought I heard, far away, someone crying.

When I woke, the cub was gone. Ferdie, too. Maurice, of course, wouldn't have come near enough to the cub to kill it. Willie and I never discussed it. But he began to pay even more attention to me than he had before.

Even though no blame fell on Maurice, Willie ignored him. Maurice often looked like a lost soul—no Ferdie to talk to or fight with—and he kept wandering from his room into the pool, then up to the roof for his sunbaths. And always smiling and fawning at the dinner table, like a nasty child that people can't bear to pick up and cuddle.

Willie was taking me a great many places. Not like before, which had been only to big events where everyone would see us. But suddenly now to dinner in some special little restaurant where we knew no one. Or on his New York trips where he made me do a lot of shopping. He insisted one time in New York on buying me a leopard coat. "You don't know yourself, Courtney," he said. "I do. I'm a connoisseur. You need leopard."

Whoever would have thought that Courtney Aikins,

born in southern Indiana, once crippled with polio, who had spent most of her life as a mediocre salesclerk, could look as if the leopard coat had grown out of her. But it did. My gray eyes seemed to turn green and slant catlike as I looked in the long mirror. And my skin from being in the sun so much was tawny gold to match my hair. How the saleswoman oohed and aahed, while Willie looked sleek and proud, not unlike a cat himself.

Willie finally relented about Ferdie. One morning there Ferdie was, calling from the door of the garden guesthouse to Maurice, who was lying face down on the roof taking his sunbath. Maurice raised up and answered with something sharp—I couldn't make out the words. Ferdie shouted back and Maurice flipped over and dangled his golden legs over the side of the roof as though he would jump into the patio. Willie went out and they both became silent.

After that, every time Ferdie and Maurice spent more than five minutes in each other's company, they had a spat. And from the tense expression on Maurice's face, and the jerky nervous way in which he talked and laughed, it was clear that he was as uptight as I was about Ferdie's return.

One day as Willie and I started out the driveway, headed for lunch at the beach club, I discovered I had forgotten my purse and gloves. While Willie waited, I went back to my room for them.

Ferdie and Maurice were at it again, out in the pool, just beyond my partially opened door. Their voices were high and shrill. It was the servants' day off, and as far as the boys knew, the house was empty. Ferdie accused Maurice of killing the cub. In a rage Maurice admitted it, saying he had poisoned the beast first, then got the idea about cutting off its head. "Something they would be sure only you would think of!" he shrieked. "You—jealous because she took away your lion! And if you couldn't kill her, like you tried, you'd kill her pet! And that's what

they did think. Go ahead and tell on me! They'll never believe you. They'll believe you're making more trouble
and you'll get run off again!"

I slipped out.

I could have—maybe I should have—gone right out
and told Willie. But that would have left me with Ferdie.
Probably for keeps. No doubt Willie would be terribly
remorseful and do everything he could to make it up to
Ferdie. So I didn't say anything.

That morning, the day of the murder, Maurice and
Ferdie chanced to come into the pool area at the same
time and saw me swimming. Ferdie turned on his heel
and left. Then I heard the bang of the guesthouse door.
Maurice smiled, feathered a kiss toward me, and walked
up the stairs to the roof. He knew I didn't like anyone
else in the pool when I used it.

I never told anyone, not even Willie, that I saw Ferdie go up to the roof. And come back down again. Because
I didn't see him. Of course, anyone would know that it
would be easy not to see. For I went into the steamroom
after swimming. It was a habit of mine. The steam helped
my leg. I was still there when I heard screams from the
patio. I grabbed my robe and hurried out. There was
Maurice, his head smashed against the bricks, the golden
face trickled with blood.

The screams were coming from Ferdie, standing over
Maurice.

"Have you done it again?" I asked. "Like you killed
my cub. Like you tried to kill me!"

He sprang at me, grabbed my throat, shook me,
screaming, "You lie, you lie! I never killed the cub! Maurice killed the cub! You did it, you pushed him off the
roof! You'd like both of us dead!"

Which is what he wished, for Maurice and me.

I was half unconscious by the time the gardener
came, the cook jabbering behind him. I could scarcely
move my neck for a week.

Willie was in New York at the time. So it had to be me, when I could talk, who called the police. Then I walked over to the sobbing Ferdie and slapped his face. Hard. "You listen to me," I said. "You're the only one with the strength to pitch Maurice over the edge. I couldn't shove him an inch. The servants had no reason to do it. And you know how I am about stairs, how I avoid stairs. And you hated Maurice. Almost as much as you hate me."

"I didn't, I didn't! I was in my room, listening to my stereo."

"Perhaps," I said. "Between times. I have other ideas. But in this case we have to think of Willie. Accusations and counter-accusations such as we might make in this household will give a poor picture of Willie to the world. I'll phone Willie and have him hurry home. Until then I advise you to say simply that you found Maurice in the patio. And I will say just what happened, that your screams brought me out of the steamroom. It's your problem to think up some explanation for why you choked me."

Willie flew right home. Terribly shaken. Shocked by Maurice's death, and perhaps even more shocked at the thought of any scandal.

Ferdie and I, of course, had to make statements to the police before Willie arrived. So did the gardener and the cook, and the gardener told about having to pull Ferdie off my throat. Ferdie cried and said how sorry he was, that the sight of his friend's dead body had so shaken him that he must have been temporarily out of his senses.

"He's a very highstrung boy," I said. "And he had just come for a visit with Maurice after not seeing him for a long time. It was a shock. Poor Maurice, perhaps he fell asleep, then turned in his sleep because the sun was getting strong, and simply rolled off. The roof should have a railing."

That was certainly the way it looked. Although, as I said, I had my own ideas.

The reporters attempted to make something out of Maurice's relationship to our family. "He was like a son," I said. "Mr. McKinley is a wealthy man and has endowed several schools. In addition he has educated quite a few young people on an individual basis."

After that the newspapers referred to Mr. McKinley's lovely, dignified wife whose "face was pale and set with grief" over the tragic accident.

Willie gave Ferdie a peaked-brow, probing look when he arrived from New York. And they had a private discussion. Ferdie apparently didn't tell him that Maurice had killed the cub, possibly for fear Willie would begin to tie in revenge with Maurice's death. I thought of telling, but then Willie might want to know why I didn't exonerate Ferdie earlier. It might solidify Ferdie's position.

For after all I couldn't prove that Ferdie returned to the pool that morning while I was in the steamroom, then slipped up the stairs and pushed Maurice over the edge.

It was chilling to have Ferdie back in the house. Yes, once more in his old room. Eating dinner with us every night. Now when Willie was away and the servants not nearby, I moved around like a cat who has suddenly been brought into a house full of dogs.

"Why don't you ever wear your leopard coat? You look so beautiful in it," Willie said one night when we were about to take another trip to New York. It was winter and snowing up north.

"The cleaners did a bad job on it. It looks queer, some of the hair doesn't come up, it's matted and uneven. And it's shedding."

"I'll complain to the furrier," Willie said. "After all, they're the best in New York, they should make good. It cost enough."

"It was probably the cleaner's fault."

"Then the cleaner should make good. People like that oughtn't to be in business."

"All right, Willie," I said. "I'll talk to them. In the meantime I have the tweed and it's fur-lined."

"You're not the tweed type," he said fussily. "We must get you another coat."

But we were so busy doing other things that we didn't get around to it that trip. Later he asked about the leopard coat, but casually because by then we were planning a trip to Tahiti and fur coats seemed silly.

Some woman in some thrift store certainly found a bargain. Oh, sure, the fur would be matted down here and there. But a little more cleaning in the right spots would put it right. It was just that the coat had stayed too long in the steamroom. I forgot to take it out until after I had gone to my room and dressed. Then when I did get it, I tucked it inside my robe and put it far back in my closet, still wet and steamy. Anyway, I never wanted to see it again. So it dried queer in spots.

The morning Maurice died, Ferdie was in the guest-house. I heard his stereo playing, and it was in his bedroom on the side away from the patio. The music was loud. Ferdie always played the music so loud when Willie was away that it kept me from concentrating on any music I might want to hear.

I went to my room and got the leopard coat. Then I draped it over one of those silly inflated seahorses we had in the pool, the kind one floats around on. It was difficult for me not to stumble, going up the stairs with that clumsy thing in my arms. My bad leg was trembling, because this was the second time I had gone up those stairs. Just a few minutes before, I had dried off my feet and climbed to the roof. I had seen Maurice lying on his stomach, cheek on his hands, elbows thrust out. He was facing away from the stairs, breathing slowly and deeply. His foot gave an involuntary twitch, as happens when one is asleep.

So then I went down for the leopard coat and the seahorse. And came back, quietly, quietly. I knelt down so I couldn't be seen from the patio and thrust the leopard-covered seahorse against Maurice, hard and quick. He woke up, whirled his head to see what it was. His eyes sprung wide, terrified. He must have thought it was another cub, a leopard cub. He let out a choked yip and rolled to get away from it.

"Why, it's only a joke, Maurice," I said. "I was only playing."

I said it as he pitched over the edge. If he had survived that fall I would have said again, "It was only a joke, I was only playing."

Willie has invited Ferdie to go with us to Tahiti. Ferdie hates me. I hate Ferdie. I wonder which one of us will be the first to do something about it? I wonder. . . .

An occasion for cheers—the first "Charlie Chan" short story, a pastiche respectfully written by Jon L. Breen. . . .

Earl Derr Biggers, the creator of Charlie Chan, wrote only six stories about his "patient, aphoristic Chinese-Hawaiian-American" sleuth. All six were full-length novels and all six appeared first as serials in The Saturday Evening Post *(in those "good old days"). And from these six stories, by the miracle of Hollywood, have come more than forty feature-length motion pictures, the Lord-knows-how-many radio shows, numerous commercial tie-ins, and, we are reliably informed, an imminent TV series. And not long ago Pyramid Publications issued all six novels in paperback—*Charlie Chan Carries On, The Black Camel, Behind That Curtain, The Chinese Parrot, Keeper of the

Keys, *and* The House Without a Key *(the last named was actually the first Charlie Chan novel, originally published in 1925, nearly fifty years ago).*

Among current pastichists (pastichers? pasticciosos?), Jon L. Breen is the logical writer to bring us the first Charlie Chan short story. You will remember that Breen has already given us pastiches of Frank Merriswell, Ed McBain's 87th Precinct, S. S. Van Dine's Philo Vance, and parodies of Ellery Queen's L. Larry Cune, John D. MacDonald's Trygve McKee (Travis McGee), and, soon to appear in Ellery Queen's Mystery Magazine, *John Dickson Carr–Carter Dickson's Sir Gideon Merrimac. And now he presents an adventure of the one and only Charlie Chan—to help publishers and producers, readers and reviewers, perpetuate the alliterate (and literate) Charlie Chan as a household name.*

JON L. BREEN

The fortune cookie

Bill Artemas watched the lights of San Francisco twinkle and recede in the distance. It was a clear night, and standing on the first-class deck of the SS *Waikiki* he could feel the brisk sea air on his face. Memories of his last night in the gleaming bay city now mingled with imagined delights of Honolulu, making his frame of mind happy when it could easily have been apprehensive.

Bill was young—twenty-three on his last birthday—and, being young, he felt no qualms at all about the fact that he was virtually broke. He had spent the last of his inheritance booking passage on the *Waikiki*, and he knew no one and had no job waiting for him in Honolulu. But such things do not trouble the young, especially if they have Bill Artemas' range of accomplishments: a splendid tennis game, particularly strong on the forehand; a good background in English literature gained during four subsidized years at Stanford University; three months of valuable experience as a cub reporter on the San Francisco *Call;* and manners polished to a fine gloss by his acceptance in San Francisco high society, of which only Boston's is any higher.

Taking a deep breath of the clean night air, Bill wondered why he was alone on deck on such a lovely night, only a few minutes out of port. True, it was a bit chilly and less hardy souls might find it intolerably so, but being young—Bill suddenly realized he was no longer alone on the deck.

When Bill looked away from the fading lights of the bay city to see who had joined him, his first thought was that he need never look at lights or shimmering water again, only at this lovely face, heart-shaped and framed in dark brown hair. But he wasn't to look on her startling beauty for long. She grasped his hand, put something in it, and hurried away as quickly as she had come.

It gradually dawned on Bill that she had had terror in her eyes and that he now had a Chinese fortune cookie in his hand.

"And when I cracked it open, Mr. Chan, it was empty!"

It was early afternoon of the *Waikiki*'s first day at sea, and Bill Artemas sat in the grandly appointed lounge opposite one of the ship's most illustrious passengers, a plump and middle-aged Chinese of self-effacing and friendly manner. Charlie Chan, of the Honolulu police, was on his way home from a law-enforcement conference in San Francisco. During his stay he had been the object of much gratifying yet faintly embarrassing personal publicity, so he was not surprised to find himself consulted by a fellow passenger for an off-duty investigation of a shipboard mystery.

"Mr. Chan," Bill went on excitedly, "I don't know who that girl is, but I'm sure she's in danger. Maybe she's being held prisoner or something. I—"

Bill broke off sharply as a steward approached.

"May I get you gentlemen something to drink?" asked the steward. "Some coffee or tea—or something stronger?"

Bill Artemas was cheered by the suggestion. "Scotch and soda. It's good to be able to order a drink again without feeling like some sort of criminal!"

Charlie Chan's black eyes twinkled. Before Prohibition started, Bill Artemas was undoubtedly too young to order anything but milk.

"Those temperance people went too far, gentlemen," the steward remarked. "And to go too far is just as wrong as to fall short. In trying to reform drinkers they merely created more. What's your pleasure, Mr. Chan?"

"Juice of orange, thank you so much."

"Coming right up."

When the steward was out of earshot, Bill leaned over the table and regarded Charlie Chan imploringly. "What can we do, Mr. Chan? Who is she? What does that empty Chinese cookie mean? Is it a message of some kind?"

Charlie regarded the other man searchingly. "Girl you saw was Chinese?"

"Oh, no," Bill Artemas said quickly, "she was beautiful!" After a moment's pause he added, "I hope you don't misunderstand me, Mr. Chan. I mean, Chinese girls are beautiful, too."

The detective chuckled. "No apologies necessary. Poets of all nations have told us where beauty truly lies: in eyes of men. To this poor person, apogee of all that is beautiful resides in home on top of Punchbowl Hill. To others merely large uninteresting family of Chinese."

Despite the other's unoffended air, Bill was becoming more embarrassed. "No, really, Mr. Chan, I really do think Chinese girls are beautiful. In a strange and special way. Even more beautiful than white girls on the whole."

"But beautiful in a way that is unattainable. Society decrees that Chinese girl as unavailable to you as another man's wife. Thus an exotic beauty to be admired but not to seek for company. Not to make you lovesick as you are over girl on deck. Is it not so?"

"I think you're right, Mr. Chan. One glimpse of that girl has changed my life. If only we knew who she is."

"One hurdle already cleared. I know young lady's identity."

"You do?" Bill exclaimed.

The Chinese detective nodded slightly and pulled a newspaper clipping from his jacket pocket. He offered it to Bill for inspection.

PROFESSOR SOUGHT IN
UNIVERSITY MURDER

Dr. Albert Kane, University of California Professor of Chinese Classics, is being sought by Berkeley police in connection with the murder of a student, Wilbur Clayton of Santa Rosa.

Young Clayton was found shot to death last Sunday in Strawberry Canyon on a secluded part of the Berkeley campus. Close friends report that Clayton, a Chinese Classics student, had threatened to take action for plagiarism against Kane, claiming substantial parts of a recent book by Kane were actually Clayton's work.

Detectives found evidence that Professor Kane has fled

his Berkeley apartment. Also apparently missing is Karen Drummond, a secretary in the Chinese Classics Department.

Photographs of Kane, a nondescript fair-haired man of early middle age, and of Karen Drummond, a young and strikingly attractive brunette, were included in the newspaper report. Bill stared fixedly at the girl's picture.

"Missing girl and girl on deck are the same young lady perhaps?"

"No perhaps about it. That's her! But how did you know?"

"Young lady's thoughts simple enough for simple man to follow. Young lady wishes to tell us she is being held against her will, finds chance to give message to fellow passenger without detection by person accompanying her. She has saved fortune cookie served with Chinese dinner in San Francisco, has saved same in one piece, maybe a souvenir. Has removed fortune slip, for even rare lady who can leave cookie uncracked cannot leave fortune unread. Many fortune cookies allow removal of fortune slip without cracking.

"Lady chooses fortune cookie to represent silent call for help. Her action doubly clever: Bright young man, confronted with mystery and with supposedly Chinese confection, naturally seeks out only Chinese detective on board. Due to undeserved attention gathered by this humble person, search fairly easy to consummate.

"There is clue for you. Clue for me: Young and desperate lady attaches great importance to supposed Chinese symbol. Secretary of Chinese Classics professor who may be murderer is missing. Connection not too difficult to see."

"But, Mr. Chan, this Kane fellow may have found out she's trying to make contact with people. She could be in great danger. He could throw her overboard."

"More calm, please. Calm much more helpful than

panic, is it not so? Why did girl accompany fleeing murder suspect?"

"Well, maybe she saw something, saw the crime committed. And he forced her to come with him."

"Then why would murderer not kill her at once?"

"Well—I don't know—"

"And if fleeing, why would murderer bring girl? Flight strong indication of probable guilt. If guilt admitted through flight, why carry off witness?"

Bill looked blank.

"Kane loves young lady," Charlie explained. "Freedom alone not enough for suspect's happiness. Must have girl as well. Murder suspects and even murderers are men as you and I, Mr. Artemas."

This unquestionable truth dawned on Bill Artemas. "He wants to make her love him. Like Lon Chaney in *The Phantom of the Opera*."

"Maybe girl love him, too. Maybe not know about murder until vessel leave, then saw newspaper and realized traveling companion is murderer."

"I don't think she could love him," Bill said fiercely. "That story sounds very fishy to me."

"Sound much like gilled creature to humble self as well," said Charlie, smiling. "Abduction more likely theory than love reciprocated by young lady. But girl could feign love. Is plenty smart."

"We'd better try and find the professor quick, though. She may not be able to fool him much longer, if that's what she's doing. How can we find him?"

"Maybe not so difficult, Mr. Artemas."

Bill looked thoughtful. "I'll bet he's disguised."

Charlie bowed. "Most helpful, thank you so much. Kane's face hard to recognize—look like many men. Still must cover face somehow—maybe beard, dark glasses. Or maybe more subtle way of concealing features."

Bill cast a surreptitious glance around the room and

saw that likely candidates abounded. An elderly man in a wheelchair seemed a likely possibility to the aspiring sleuth. With a nod Bill pointed out the man to Charlie.

The Chinese detective chuckled. "Thank you so much, but hanging skin of neck, liver spots of hands, dead look in eye bespeak talent for makeup worthy of aforementioned Mr. Chaney. Maybe carry comparison too far?"

"I guess so." But Bill Artemas was not discouraged. He had learned at Stanford never to give up, especially if the adversary was from Berkeley.

He lowered his voice. "The gent with the bald head and monocle. He looks like a stage Englishman to me."

"Shares said quality with many real Englishmen. Distinguished gentleman is Lord Barnstock, former Home Secretary. So sorry."

The steward returned with their drinks.

"There we are, gents—Scotch and soda and orange juice."

Bill Artemas paid for both drinks automatically, his good breeding pushing him even closer to pennilessness.

"Thank you so much," said Charlie Chan.

"Your first trip to Hawaii, Mr. Artemas?" the steward inquired politely.

"Yes, it is," Bill replied. "I hear it's beautiful."

"Oh, yes, indeed. You will—"

A growling voice from another table interrupted the steward who seemed about to embark on a travel lecture. "Steward, blast you! I want some service!" The growler was a fat balding businessman in a flowered shirt. He was accompanied by a pleasant-looking lady who seemed somewhat ashamed of his behavior.

"You'll excuse me," said the steward. "When the wind blows, the grass must bend, as they say."

He scurried away.

"That man's a boorish sort," said Bill, glancing at the angry tourist.

"Very drunk early in day. When sober, maybe different."

"Could he be the professor? That would be quite a disguise—but the fat looks real, and who could the lady with him be? Besides, he probably wouldn't call that much attention to himself."

"Maybe," said Charlie, looking thoughtful. "And maybe exact opposite. By observing man's fault, you may know his virtues."

"Huh? Who said that? Confucius?"

"Yes, a man often quoted. A very wise man, but not always quoted for his wisdom."

Bill Artemas looked puzzled. "I don't understand."

"Soon will."

Charlie lifted a finger and summoned the steward, who rushed over, having placated his rude customer.

"Yes, Mr. Chan? Can I get you something else? Or is something wrong with the drinks?"

"Should there be something wrong with them?"

"I doubt it. I made them very carefully. The cautious seldom err."

"But the foolish do, Dr. Kane! Sit down, please."

The steward swallowed. "I'm not allowed to. But why did you call me that name? I'm not—"

"You make no attempt to disguise features, Dr. Kane. Why not? You think maybe steward go unnoticed like 'Invisible Man' in story by Mr. Chesterton? You are maybe too confident. Much too confident when foolish vanity makes you quote Confucius three times to Charlie Chan and not think he will associate you with missing professor of Chinese Classics. 'To go too far is just as wrong as to fall short.' 'When the wind blows, the grass must bend.' 'The cautious seldom err.' Not the best translations, but meanings clear."

The steward smiled slightly. "I'll be damned. I took you too lightly."

Bill Artemas absorbed this with an open mouth.

Finally he remembered his heroic role and asked the impostor-steward, in a low voice between clenched teeth, "What have you done with Miss Drummond? Where is she?"

"She's safe," he said. "She didn't want to come, but I forced her to. I should have known it was no good. I killed Will Clayton. I'll confess it—it's good to have it off my chest."

Dr. Albert Kane walked slowly down the passageway to the crew's quarters and pushed open the door of his cabin. The three men accompanying him—Bill Artemas, Charlie Chan, and Captain Vernon, the SS *Waikiki*'s veteran skipper—couldn't all enter the cubbyhole, but they could see the girl sitting on the edge of the bunk.

Bill saw the same terror-stricken eyes he'd seen the night before on the deck. She stared from face to face, as if unsure of their intentions.

Bill smiled encouragingly. "You're safe now, Karen." But the fear did not leave her eyes.

Captain Vernon looked from the frightened girl to Albert Kane. "So we signed on an escaping murderer, eh? It was easy for him—he worked for us years ago, but under another name. George Allison, he called himself."

"Summers when I was in college," explained Kane. "I used an assumed name because I didn't want my family to find out I was working as a ship's steward. I'm glad this is over with. I made a terrible mistake in shooting Clayton and then kidnapping Karen and now I'm ready to pay for it."

Charlie Chan spoke for the first time in several minutes. "Contradiction, please. Case not closed that easily." He turned to Bill Artemas. "Humbly regret deceiving you, Mr. Artemas, by not telling all I know of Clayton murder case. I have worked with honorable Berkeley police in this case and have facts you do not. But I think facts you see lead to same conclusion reached by humble self."

Charlie paused, but none of his listeners spoke. They watched him intently, wondering what his next words would be.

He turned to the girl sitting on the bunk. "You are murderer of Wilbur Clayton, Miss Karen Drummond."

The stricken look in the girl's eye told everyone present why terror had not left her when it seemed her rescue had been effected.

"Berkeley police get in touch with me shortly before we leave San Francisco: They find plenty evidence pointing to Karen Drummond as murderer of Wilbur Clayton. Motive is jealousy. Clayton leave her for other girl. Karen, plenty angry, pay attention to advances of Professor Kane, who love her all of two years she has worked in his office. But she want to stop plagiarism suit by Clayton, who got secret evidence of same from Karen Drummond.

"So she kills Clayton when meeting him alone in Strawberry Canyon. Convinces Kane he number-one suspect, must flee. He takes old job on ship under old alias, helps her to stow away. Everybody thinks she fleeing with him, but he fleeing with her."

Bill Artemas looked angry. He had three reasons which he threw at Charlie one after the other.

"You didn't solve this case! The Berkeley police did! And how'd they know Kane would take this ship?"

Charlie bowed. "Very true that police work always cooperative venture. But Berkeley detectives not know Kane and Miss Drummond taking SS *Waikiki*. They gave findings to humble self because of earlier consultation on case. This poor person's small contribution only to find professor among possible disguises on ship—and he has only disguise of servitude and anonymity."

"You lied to me, Mr. Chan. You said Kane was the murderer."

"Correction, please. Never say Kane is murderer. Only tell you what girl wants us to think."

"All right, all right, but how the heck could I have figured all this out?"

"Should be quite clear to you, Mr. Artemas, if not blinded by youthful infatuation. Girl on deck more likely murderer than Kane. She gives you fortune cookie to suggest desire to escape. But why does she not speak? Why not run to captain for safety? How can Kane hold her? Terror clearly feigned, desire to frame Kane for murder, then disappear and cover own tracks. For her love for Professor Kane not real as his for her. She gladly throw him to police, knowing he will take blame, not implicate her in crime.

"Final and conclusive link: Kane brings us here and shows us girl sitting in unlocked cabin and not tied at all. How could he keep her thus against her will? If you not know real murderer when we find untied girl in unlocked cabin, still terrified after rescue, symptoms of lovesickness clear indeed."

"It's true, all true," admitted the girl on the bunk. "I shot Will and I'd do it again—and if I had to, I'd kill you all."

Bill looked at her face, beautiful even in treachery, and felt remorse at this vicious statement. But then he looked at the distraught professor and Bill knew he'd escaped comparatively easily in the painful game of love.

With both fugitives in the captain's custody, Bill walked down the passageway seeking the deck's bracing sea air. Charlie was by his side.

"Plenty beautiful girls in Hawaii, Mr. Artemas," the Chinese detective said. "I take you home to Punchbowl Hill for plenty good dinner. You will come?"

"Yes, I will, thank you. Chinese girls really are beautiful, you know. Do you have daughters, Mr. Chan?"

---

*Julian Symons' "Experiment in Personality," as the title
implies, reveals his probing, inquisitive, restless mind.
Let us quote from the story, and if you can resist beginning to read at once, you are less susceptible to temptation
than your editor.*

*". . . To be 'not yourself,' what did that mean? Did
it mean that you were somebody else?"*

*". . . For some reason they were talking about the
nature of experience."*

*" 'You mean that we sometimes become somebody
else?' "*

*Join a disturbing daymare game called Anonymous
People—disturbing in its overtones and undertones, a daymare in its implications and insinuations. But we must
warn you: Play the game vicariously, only by reading
about it. Don't ever play it in dead earnest.*

JULIAN SYMONS

Experiment in personality

As the years passed it seemed to Melly that the party at
the Estersons had been the turning point of her life. In a
literal sense this was true, because she met her husband,
Frederick, for the first time on the night of the party; but
there was more to it than that. The Estersons' party was
crucial because of what happened there, the thing about

which she never afterward said anything to anybody, not even to Frederick. And then again, as time went by, she had flickerings of doubt about whether anything had happened at all. Everything, in any case, seemed to depend on the party.

It was a time when she was young and silly, or perhaps when she was recovering from the effects of being young and silly. Her mother had died when she was three years old, and she had been brought up in Singapore by her father. It was true that he sent her to school in England but she made few friends, and the months of each year spent in England seemed to her tedious spaces between the events of her real life.

This life began again with each holiday when she flew back to Singapore and met her father at the airport, a tall, distinctive, immediately recognizable figure, with his Panama hat and ebony walking stick. She knew that he was proud of her from the way in which he introduced her with imperturbable sweet gravity to strangers at parties.

"This is my daughter, Melisande," he would say. "She was named after my favorite opera." When she was small he would sometimes read to her a poem about Melisande, a poem that began:

> Pale little princess, passionate and shy,
> With delicate small hands and heavy hair,
> A simple childlike creature, wild and fair,
> Yet shadowed by a haunting mystery.

The poem seemed to her very beautiful, and she always called herself by her full name, refusing to speak to the girls at school who abbreviated it. Really, as she afterward realized, she saw her father very little, for even when she was at home he was at his office all day, often came home late at night, and sometimes did not return that day at all.

So she was alone a great deal, and although she was not conscious of being lonely it was, as he said, no life for a young girl. When she was nineteen she went off (I was *sent* off, she thought later) to a secretarial job in England. He consoled her when she wept, reciting two more lines from that sad poem, lines about her Pelleas entering at the door.

"You don't want to spend your time with an old fellow," he said. "In England your Pelleas will be waiting for you."

He gave her the boyish smile that made the words about being an old fellow quite ridiculous. It was only later, again, remembering the servants giggling together and recalling things hinted by acquaintances, that she realized he had carried on frequent affairs and that the presence of a young daughter must have been an embarrassment. Only later too she understood the meaning of a scene she had witnessed when she was ten years old.

She had come early from the local school because she felt unwell, to hear a murmur of voices and laughter. One of the voices sounded like her father's, although there was an unusual note in it. The voices came from the living room and, delighted to find him at home, she opened the door. Her first impression was that he was playing a game with a child on the floor. Then she saw that the child was a Chinese girl and that she wore no clothes.

The Chinese girl stared straight at Melisande with no expression at all. Melly could not see her father's face and retained an impression only of a crouching powerful animal with huge hands that moved up the little Chinese girl's arms to grip her shoulders and, as it seemed, to shake her. Then Melly closed the door and ran to her room.

That was one of the nights on which her father stayed away. The next day he picked her up at school and took her out for a picnic. He never referred to the incident and she did not see the Chinese girl again. A few months later Melly was sent to boarding school in England.

She got the secretarial job through a letter written by her father to a director in a publishing firm, whom he had known long ago when they were undergraduates. Very soon she met a young man who might, she thought, be Pelleas. His name was Archie and he was a commercial artist, but he was suitably ethereal and elegant. He took her out to dinner and to concerts, and kissed her in taxis. She did not greatly enjoy the kissing, and although she permitted him to seduce her in his flat one night because he seemed to expect it, she found that also not particularly enjoyable. He did not say, "I love you," and what happened seemed very unromantic and unlike the ideal relationship between Pelleas and Melisande.

The affair with Archie, if it could be called an affair, ended abruptly a few days later when she received a cable saying that her father had died suddenly of a heart attack. She flew back to Singapore for the funeral and there learned that he had died in bed with his latest mistress and that he had left nothing but debts. Behind the sympathy of friends she detected a kind of malicious satisfaction. She returned to England as soon as possible. For some reason she had a horror of seeing Archie again and refused to speak to him when he telephoned.

In the weeks that followed she took a great many pills of various kinds, some on the instructions of her doctor, pills to tranquilize and to enliven, and she mixed these pills with drink so that she was in what seemed a state of continual light-headedness. She worked for Mr. Radcliffe, the editorial director who had known her father, and he was very gentle; but he was also ponderously dignified and somehow she was put off by the rimless glasses he wore and the sniffs that punctuated his remarks. When he asked her out to dinner one night, the sniff was distressingly in evidence as he pondered what to order. Then she was irritated when he consulted her about the wine. Her father would never have consulted any lady about the wine.

"The truth is I feel a little responsible for you, my dear. After all, I did know Charles. A remarkable man. He was the leader among our little group at the university, you know. I always thought—"

Mr. Radcliffe did not complete the sentence and she did not ask him to do so because it seemed to imply that her father had promised more than he had performed in life, and if that was his opinion she did not want to hear it. "But in the last few weeks you've been obviously—well, not yourself." He sniffed.

She sipped the wine. "Does that mean you want to get rid of me?"

"Not at all. It's just that—well, you've suffered a great tragedy. I think it has affected you."

"It's true I'm not myself," she admitted. There was consolation in uttering the words aloud. To be "not yourself," what did that mean? Did it mean that you were somebody else?

"I should like you to feel that you could come to me with any problems." Sniff. "If it would help you to have a few days off, that could easily be arranged."

"I'm perfectly all right. But thank you, Mr. Radcliffe."

I do believe, she thought, that he's making approaches to me, a man old enough to be— She did not complete the sentence even in her mind. But perhaps she was wrong, for although Mr. Radcliffe drove her back to the apartment she shared with another girl he did not even put his hand on her knee, and he refused her invitation to come up for a nightcap. On the following day he was his usual ponderous self and it seemed impossible that he had ever suggested she should call him Donald.

Mr. Radcliffe was a bore, there was no denying it,

and to her surprise most of the authors she met in the office were boring, too. Although some of them wrote about young people they were almost all of them well over forty, and in spite of the fact that, as she gathered with astonishment, few of them made a living from their books, they were tremendously puffed up with their own importance. Some of them tried to flirt with her—it was the only word she could use—and one of them took her out to lunch and talked about his own books all the time.

Gabriel Esterson was interesting because he was so unlike the other authors. He was tall and fair, with bright blue eyes, a lick of hair that came down over his forehead, and an enthusiastic manner. He wore turtleneck shirts or close-fitting suits with high rolled lapels. He wrote what she supposed were science-fiction stories—about subjects like the last man left alive after an atomic war and the way in which he repopulated the world by constructing a machine able to bear children, a procedure worked out in much technical detail. During the course of the story the machines learned how to reproduce with each other and at the end they killed the last man.

One day Esterson stopped in her small office after having seen Mr. Radcliffe and asked if she liked the book.

"It was interesting."

"You didn't like it? Why not say so?"

He sat on the edge of her desk. This was one of his turtleneck days.

"All right, I didn't like it."

"No need to be uptight about it. What's your name?" She told him and he turned down the corners of his wide mouth. "Ever have fantastic fun?"

"I don't know what you mean."

"I don't either, baby." The door of Mr. Radcliffe's room opened. He stood there frowning behind the rimless glasses. Gabriel got off the desk and raised a hand. "See you."

"That young man is *not* a very desirable character," Mr. Radcliffe said later.

"How do you mean?"

"To my mind there is something unwholesome about his books. Although of course he is a clever writer, which is why we publish him. I may be old-fashioned." A sniff. She offered no contradiction. "He has a strange wife. Her name is Innes. I shouldn't be surprised if she takes drugs, she is like a skeleton."

"Oh."

"And then they give very odd parties."

"You've been to them?"

"To one only. We wore masks painted to represent politicians and animals."

She echoed stupidly, "Politicians and animals."

"They fought together. Or pretended to fight. It was all something to do with the release of energy, according to Esterson. I found it distasteful."

Distasteful, or fantastic fun? A week later Esterson telephoned and asked her to a party on the following Saturday. "Bring a boyfriend if you want to, but I'd like to know now. The number of guests is important."

"I'll be alone." She had had no boyfriend since Archie.

"Fantastic."

"Is there something special—"

"Baby, about my parties there's always something special. Not before nine o'clock, not after ten. After ten the gates are locked, we shut the prisoners in. And wear old clothes. Don't dress up, dress down."

His laugh was infectiously gay. She looked forward to the party. He was not exactly her image of Pelleas and in any case he was married, but there was something exciting about the whole prospect. And maybe she would meet Pelleas at the party.

On Thursday she got the flu. She stayed in bed and Olivia, the girl with whom she shared the apartment, telephoned Mr. Radcliffe. During the day she took a variety of pills and felt better, but in the evening she was running a temperature.

On Friday morning she was a little better again, and then in the evening felt really ill. Olivia was going away to her parents for the weekend. She wanted to call a doctor. Melisande told her not to be ridiculous.

"But, Melly—"

"My name is Melisande."

"You're just being stupid."

"I'm going to this party tomorrow night, remember."

"You must be crazy."

Melisande had difficulty getting Olivia into focus. Sometimes she wavered about as though under water and at other times she was quite distinct, but there were two of her. Olivia took off her clothes preparatory to changing her dress and stood, naked but for brassiere and briefs, in the middle of the room. Melisande looked away for some reason. Olivia was a rather flat-faced girl with dark eyes, and for a moment Melisande had the impression she was looking at the Chinese girl in Singapore.

"You—" She sat up in bed.

"Yes?"

"Nothing. You are Olivia?"

"Look here, I think you're delirious."

"No, I was just being stupid. You said so, remember? I'm perfectly all right."

She watched to see if Olivia changed again while she dressed, but nothing happened. When she rushed off finally to catch her train after dithering about making fresh lemon juice, Melisande felt nothing but relief. She took four of her pills and fell asleep almost immediately.

When she woke, light was filtering through the thin curtains. Her vision was clear, her mind vacant, and she stared for what seemed to be minutes at the pattern of wild flowers on the wallpaper, and then she put out her fingers to touch them. The wall was tangibly there but that created a problem, for it meant that she was at home, really at home again in Singapore.

Turning over and closing her eyes she saw again and more vividly the wild flowers on the wallpaper, a pattern which her father had ordered because he said she looked like a wild flower herself. Columbine, eglantine, larkspur, what were the names? The larkspur was a brilliant blue. In a moment she would hear the padding feet of the servants or her father singing an old song as he always did before taking his bath:

Don't go walking down Lovers' Lane
With somebody else . . .

He always said "somebody else" instead of the correct words, "anybody else." Who was somebody else? She opened her eyes and looked at the clock, which said ten minutes past four. How could it say that when daylight was showing through the curtains? She turned over again and looked at the wall, which was now a neutral biscuit color, devoid of any kind of flower. She was in her rather dingy bedroom in the apartment.

"Afternoon," she said. "I've slept for twenty-four hours."

It was not twenty-four but she could not be bothered to work out the exact number. She got out of bed, went to the lavatory, drank a glass of water, and tried without success to find her pulse. She stuck a thermometer into her mouth and took it out when she felt her eyes closing. The reading seemed to be 102. Utterly weary, she crawled back into bed again and closed her eyes.

She opened them a moment later and looked at the clock, which now said eight-fifteen. She remembered the party, got out of bed, and decided that she felt much better. The thermometer lay on the bathroom shelf but she did not use it. Instead she ran a very hot bath, put in double the amount of bath oil she generally used, and immersed herself for twenty minutes. Later she rubbed the steam from the mirror and considered her face and body.

Pale little princess, passionate and shy—but in fact she was a biggish girl, with bones that distinctly stuck out, long twine-colored hair, a face with neat ears and bright eyes but rather too long a nose, breasts of no particular importance, a good flat stomach, and reasonably attractive legs. It was unremarkable physical equipment for a princess, but would Pelleas think so?

An hour later, after eating with difficulty a tuna fish sandwich and taking two pep pills, she was on her way to the party. She was lucky enough to find a taxi just at the door.

There is an area lying between St. John's Wood and Maida Vale where the streets are wide, the houses large and Victorianly solid, and the pervading air is one of decayed gentility which has not yet changed to smartness. The Estersons lived in one of these houses.

Gabriel came to the door, took both her hands in his, then decided to kiss her.

"Baby, you're here. Fantastic. This is Innes. My wife. Melisande."

"Melisande." Her name was repeated faintly, with a dying fall. Innes Esterson was tall and extremely thin, with a long white face and drooping shoulders. She wore a bright green shirt and tight-fitting trousers. She peered through short-sighted eyes and murmured again, "Melisande." Then she added, "Your clothes."

Melly had not quite known how to take Gabriel's instructions and was wearing a blue dress which although not fashionable hardly came in the category of old clothes.

"Perfectly all right," Gabriel said. "Super. Come and meet people."

Twenty of them were standing in a large high-ceilinged living room. Most of the men and some of the women wore pullovers and narrow trousers, but she was glad to see some other dresses. She found a drink in her hand, sipped it, discovered that it had a pleasant bittersweetness like some dimly remembered medicine, and drank it down. The glass was refilled almost at once.

She sat on a sofa with a young man who wore long sideburns and talked about underground films. Names slipped off his tongue—Grabowski, Smith, Flugheimer. She caught hold of one and repeated it faintly. "Masters?"

"Bud Masters. That's me."

"You're an—underground film maker." She had a vision of him living underground. He made films there, working in large windowless rooms like boxes. Men and women moved around in them, oscillating slowly and never speaking. At his word of command, "Action," they speeded up and began to jerk, never straying from their set positions while he moved among them with his handheld camera going snap, snap. Later in the dark room, in the darkest of the windowless boxes, he developed the films which showed—what did they show?

"Does underground film making take place underground?" This reasonable question was answered with a laugh. Then Bud Masters vanished and a woman with short-cut hair and a thin nose, wearing a monocle, sat next to her.

"Darling, you're a wit."

"Who are you?"

"I'm Lenya. What do you do?"

At that moment she could not remember, and so repeated the question. Lenya laughed and her monocle dropped. She replaced it.

"I'm on the box."

On the box? "The underground box?" Melly ventured. "No windows?"

Lenya laughed again. This time the monocle stayed in. "The idiot box, darling, the hot cod's eye, on your nelly, the telly. 'Down Our Street'—it's been my bread and butter for six months. But they're killing me next week."

"I'm sorry."

Lenya leaned toward her and their shoulders touched. "What's the idea tonight, what's Gabriel up to?" Melly shook her head and sipped her drink. "I mean, he's always up to something. He's a fun man, isn't he? Were you at the Lies and Truth party?"

"No."

"We all wore masks and had to tell lies about our past lives. Of course they were almost all about sex. Then there was a psychologist here who analyzed the stories. To Gabriel it was a kind of game—everything's a game to him."

"And Innes?"

"Innes, of course, is—well, I mean, she's Innes. But Gabriel, he's never grown up."

Melisande withdrew her shoulder from the warmth of contact. Gabriel was standing over them, with two men beside him.

"Get up, Lenya, this is round one, and clinches are not allowed until round five." He took Lenya by the hand and raised her to her feet.

"You know what you are, Gabriel, you're just a damn creep," she said without heat.

"Better men than you have said worse. You can't monopolize the loveliest girl in the room. Upsadaisy." His hand, which felt very cool, took Melisande's and she was standing up. Her body felt weightless. He introduced her to the two men, but she did not hear their names. One was an artist and the other a public-relations man connected with an American film company.

She listened to them, but although she heard what they said it did not quite seem to make sense. Even the words they used were unfamiliar. Psychedelic she had heard often, although she was never quite sure what it meant; but what was "a hard-edge painting?" And what was "kinetic art?" She began to drift, or float, away from them but was hauled back by a question.

"Is this your thing?" It was the artist, plump and red-cheeked. "I mean, Gabriel's kind of thing, does it put you on?"

"I don't know," she said truthfully. "What kind of thing is it?"

"That's the question." The artist looked at the public-relations man. "Isn't that the question, Bruno?"

"You're right there, Whit. With Gabriel that's always the question." Bruno had a bristly mustache and bulging eyes. "Shall I tell you something? I fancy you."

If I had some vanishing cream, she thought, I could smear it on that nasty little mustache and it would disappear. And if I had *enough* vanishing cream I could smear it all over him and then *he* would disappear. The idea made her giggle.

"What's so funny?" asked Bruno Mustache, but without answering this she did drift or float away to find herself talking to Innes, who spoke in a faint expiring voice, in gasps like a swimmer pushing a head up out of water and then dropping back. For some reason they were talking about the nature of experience.

"You don't think then—that there's anything in—mysticism? In getting—beyond the self?"

Melly considered this. "I don't know. I've never had an experience like that."

"Gabriel believes that what Western man feels—is limited by his—environment." Innes' eyes were little colorless pills set in deep sockets alongside her long nose. "He thinks we should try to—reach out—to something beyond—ourselves."

The words seemed to sound an echo in her mind. "Yes."

"That's what his work is—all about." Innes raised an

arm almost as thin as a clothesline and let it drop again. In a hopeless voice she said, "Experiment is—necessary, don't you think?"

"You mean that we sometimes become somebody else?"

A squat toadlike figure appeared at Innes' side. "Why, *Adrian*," Innes said in that expiring voice. She offered a papery cheek which he touched ceremoniously. Innes made a feeble gesture in Melisande's direction. "This is —" Her voice died away altogether. Adrian ignored Melisande. She moved away and met Frederick.

He was leaning against a wall with a glass in his hand, a tall man with a brown face, and he gave her at once an impression of reliability. It was connected somehow with his old tweed jacket and his polished shoes, but there was something reassuring even in the way he nodded to her, said hello, and asked if she knew everybody. She replied that she knew nobody at all.

"I'll tell you a secret, neither do I." His face showed deep creases, like crinkles in well-worn leather, when he smiled. "And I'll tell you something else. I'm older than anybody else here, and I'm feeling my age. What's your name?"

When she told him he said, "Beautiful. But rather a mouthful for a practical man like me. I shall call you Melly."

Somehow she did not feel any resentment when he used the abbreviation, and when he said that his name was Frederick Thomas she thought a moment and then said it suited him.

"I feel that's a criticism," he said.

For a moment she had trouble in keeping him properly focused. But she blinked and it was all right again.

"If you're a practical man and you don't know anybody—" She lost track of what she wanted to say, then came out with it triumphantly, "—why are you here?"

"I'm a computer engineer and I've been helping Gabriel with his last book."

"The one about—about the machines who had children?"

"That's it. He wanted to make the mechanical details plausible, and they are. A remarkable character, our Gabriel."

"I work for his publisher."

He nodded. "Melly, are you feeling all right?"

"Perfectly." But the considerate tone in which he spoke almost brought tears to her eyes. "Only I don't think I like this drink very much." She gave it to him and he put it on a shelf.

"There's some food over there. Would you like anything?"

She shook her head. "My name really is Melisande, there's a poem about me. 'Pale little princess, passionate and shy,' it begins. Do you know it?"

"I don't read much poetry. I'm afraid I'm an uncultured character. But I'll tell you something, it suits you."

"I like your jacket." She touched the rough cloth of it at just the moment when Gabriel clapped his hands.

He stood looking down on them, and her momentary impression was that some act of levitation had been performed. Then she saw that he was standing on a table. His blue eyes glittered, his fair hair hung down over his forehead. She had been aware even in the staid office surroundings of some magnetic quality about him and now this magnetism was intensified so that he looked like a woodland demon.

"We are going to conduct an experiment in personality." There was a faint murmur from the group which might have been laughter or excitement. "I'm not talking about pot or LSD—you know what I think about them, they're simply means of heightening sensation artificially. In the long run they have no meaning, they don't say anything about what you *are*. They turn you on or they don't, all right. But supposing we dispensed with artificiality's aid, could we still turn ourselves on? What sort of people *are* we?"

"Respectable," somebody said. There was a small ripple of laughter. Gabriel threw back his head and joined it. Melisande looked at his neck, white and smooth. Something about the shape made her uncomfortable. She turned her head and saw Innes. Her eyes were closed, her lips moved as if in prayer.

"All right. Each of us has his own identity, and most of those identities are respectable. But suppose we were anonymous, suppose A were the same as B, supposing all differences of sex were suddenly wiped out—"

"Shame," somebody said, but there was no laughter.

"—Are you convinced you would be the same person? Might you not become somebody else?" Gabriel's voice had quickened.

"How are you going to make us anonymous?" That was the underground film man, Bud—what was his last name?

"That's the game. I call it Anonymous People. It's a scientific experiment, but there's one rule. When you're playing, don't speak." Gabriel paused. "If people speak, sex differences will be noticed—that's the point. Otherwise, just have fun. One more thing."

He looked around and they stared up at him expectantly. "Open your minds to the possible. Don't hold back. Anyone who doesn't want to play, say so."

Nobody moved. Gabriel paused as though considering whether to say more, then jumped down. Was Innes still praying? She seemed to have disappeared.

"But, Gabriel darling, what do we *do*?" Lenya asked.

Gabriel said mockingly, "Since you ask, Lenya darling, you can be first. Through there." He opened a door, which was not the one through which they had come in, gave her a gentle push, closed it again, and stood beside it. "One at a time."

Frederick spoke from beside her. "You said there was only one rule."

"Not once you're on the other side of the door. Except that you don't come back here. There'll be a little wait. I suggest you all pour yourselves another drink."

Half a dozen people did so, but there was an uneasy silence. After a minute there was a buzz, rather like that heard in a doctor's waiting room. Gabriel jerked a thumb at Bud Masters, who went through the door.

The process was repeated at about the same intervals of time. Once there was a longer waiting period, perhaps of two minutes, and Gabriel opened the door, then quickly closed it again. Beside her Frederick said something.

"What's that?" she asked.

"I don't much like this. He's playing with things he doesn't understand."

"It's a scientific experiment." Her words came out slowly.

"It's Gabriel getting his kicks."

"Frederick," Gabriel called. Frederick smiled at her, went across to the door, and passed through it.

Now that he had gone she felt very tired. She sat down in an armchair and closed her eyes. Behind them some recollection seemed to burn. She was in a plane which swooped in circles lower and lower toward the ground, the ground becoming bigger, the details of it frighteningly large. Bump, bump, they had landed, but where was her father? He appeared at the door of the plane and swept off his Panama hat with a smile that was not reassuring but mocking. She got up to greet him but something, a pressure on one shoulder, held her back in the seat.

With an effort she opened her eyes. Gabriel's hand was on her shoulder. He said, "Your turn, baby." There were only two other people left in the room. He opened the door for her and with a feeling of physical dread she passed through it.

She found herself in Gabriel's study. There was a work chart on one wall, a neat desk beside it. It was all perfectly ordinary, but then what had she expected? And what was she meant to do? A single lamp burned over the desk but some other light disturbed her. Slowly, and again with effort, she swiveled her eyes and saw over a door an extemporized sign with a light behind it, which said in capitals: TAKE OFF SHOES, MEN TAKE OFF JACKETS, PUT ON CLOTHES AND GLOVES, LEAVE BY THIS DOOR.

Now she saw a row of shoes on the floor, looking as though they had been left outside a hotel bedroom; men's jackets were flung on a sofa, a bundle of clothes was beneath the sign. She picked up the clothes. There were three pieces of clothing in each bundle and they were made of rubber. Three-piece suit in rubber, she thought, and checked her laughter. Rubber gloves lay beside the clothes.

The trousers had an elastic waist and slipped on easily after she had taken off her shoes, and the upper part was quite simple too, a sort of rubber windbreaker, again elastic at the waist, which clung in some places and was loose in others. The helmet-style headpiece had holes in the mouth and nostrils through which to breathe, but otherwise it fitted closely.

"I must look like something from Mars," she thought and looked around the room to find with a shock that she could hardly see it. The eyepieces of the rubber helmet must have been made of some partly opaque material that made everything look dim. She had to grope rather than walk.

"Come on," a voice snapped. Gabriel had opened the door from the living room and was looking in. She raised a rubber hand and opened the door below the lighted sign. As she passed through and closed it she heard the buzzer sound.

It was like entering another world. No, no, she thought. I mustn't use a cliché like that; rather it was like being a partially sighted person, aware of everything yet unable to see properly. She was in a hall, and this must be the entrance hall of the house, but it looked entirely different through these blurry eyepieces.

She opened a door but it seemed to be only that of a closet under the stairs, so she closed it again. The staircase was by her side, a passage loomed ahead, and the element of choice involved in the question "Which way shall I go?" suddenly seemed important. As slowly as an invalid she made her way along the passage to find at the end of it another flight of stairs leading downward.

She descended, holding onto the stair rail, and again the loss of tactile sensation because of the rubber suit was disconcerting, although she told herself that it was only like wearing rubber gloves for washing up. At the bottom of the stairs there were three doors. Which one to choose, and where was everybody?

She opened the middle door and made a small sound of surprise when she saw a reflection of herself inside. Then the figure raised a rubber arm and saw another rubber figure holding a knife and she realized that everybody was dressed alike. What was it Gabriel had said—"supposing A were the same as B"—that was it precisely. The knife descended, carved a slice off some kind of meat that looked like ham, pinned it with the knife, and offered it to her. She was in the kitchen.

She shook her head and the figure began to push the ham through the small breathing slit in the headpiece made for the mouth. She watched with revulsion as the meat disappeared bit by bit rather as though it were being consumed by a snake. Half of the piece of meat dropped off and fell to the floor. With a slight bow the figure offered her the knife and she took it automatically while watching the other man—or woman?—who had opened a refrigerator and was peering inside.

A bottle of milk was ceremoniously taken out, held up, the top removed. For drinking? Unbelievingly she saw the milk—she knew that it was milk although in this dim light the color was indiscernible—poured onto the floor. Ham-nibbler wagged a reproving finger. Milk-pourer put the empty bottle back into the refrigerator and spread out arms like a conjurer who has performed a successful trick. Melly turned and walked out of the kitchen.

Anonymous People, she thought as she opened a second door which proved to be that of a dining room in which another rubber figure was arranging knives and forks on the table in an elaborate star pattern; I don't like anonymous people. She stumbled a little as she hurried up the stairs thinking, I want to get out of this, I am not an anonymous person.

She went to the door of Gabriel's study and shrank back as another anonymous person came out and passed apparently without seeing her. With one rubber paw on the door handle she remembered that Gabriel had said, "Don't come back here," and thought how conspicuous she would make herself by going back. I can play the game for a little while longer, she thought; after all, I don't have to join in and *do* anything. She could find some place in a room upstairs and just sit there quietly.

On the second floor she was again confronted by a choice of doors. Like Alice in Wonderland, she thought vaguely, although was it really like Alice? She played a game of her own in front of the doors, saying eeny-meenie-minie-mo to decide which one to open. It turned out that she had picked the bathroom, and she shut this door quickly when she saw a rubber figure standing under the shower with water pouring all over it, him, her. The figure capered about at sight of her and she remembered her father saying when she was a small child, "Come on in, the water's lovely."

The sense of outrage she felt about the man—it must have been a man, no woman would have done such a thing—came from the feeling that he was doing the wrong thing; she could not have put it more precisely than that. When she opened the adjoining door, she entered what turned out to be a bedroom and sat down on a bed; at first she thought there was nobody else in the room and that she had escaped from the world of wrong behavior.

Then she saw the rubber man—she was prepared, it turned out, to identify all of them as men—sitting at a small writing desk. It took her a moment or two to see what he was doing, and another few seconds before she believed it. He had a screwdriver or chisel in his hand and he was using it to force open the top of the desk. The effect, as the top opened, was rather that of an old silent film, for she saw the splintered wood where the lock had been forced and yet because of the rubber suiting she could hear nothing. But now the sense of outrage was strong enough for her to try to stop him.

She got off the bed and advanced toward the man. He was not aware of her presence until she was almost on him. Then he jumped up, backed away, turned, and ran out of the door. She did not understand why he had seemed so frightened until she looked down and saw that the knife given to her in the kitchen was still clasped in her rubbery right hand. He had thought an attack was being made on him, and perhaps he was right. Perhaps she would have attacked him with the knife. She might have done the wrong thing, too.

The thought was upsetting. She went over to the desk and closed it, resisting the very real temptation to look at the letters she could see inside. I must stop it, she said to herself, and knew that to get away from temptation she must hide. She knew the place for hiding. She hurried out of the bedroom, passed two figures as she ran down the stairs—one of them tried to stop her—reached the ground floor, opened the door of the closet under the stairs, and got inside.

She sat down because there was no room to stand up, pulled the door almost completely shut, and had instantly the most wonderful feeling of safety. She was at once perfectly relaxed and very tired. She put the knife on her knees, leaned back, and closed her eyes. . . .

She could not remember afterward how long she had slept, or indeed whether she had slept at all. The inside of the closet was dark, and it made little difference to what she saw or didn't see whether her eyes were open or closed, as she found when she flapped them up and down like tiny shutters. And it was as she did this flapping—if my eyes were wings, she thought, I could use them to fly —that she became aware of another presence. She did not *hear*—that was not possible—but she knew there was somebody else with her.

Strangely enough, perhaps because of her utter re-laxation, she was not frightened. She was prepared for something to happen, yet when it did happen she had at first a failure of apprehension so that she shifted her body slightly away from the thing that was touching her. The thing moved with her, rippled down her backbone, and she realized its nature. A hand was moving up and down her back.

The activities of this disembodied hand gave her pleasure. It began at the small of her back, moved gently in circles that radiated out from the backbone and rose to the nape of the neck, which reassuringly did not feel like the real nape of a real neck because the whole thing was made of rubber. The effect was soothing; it made her feel at peace, yet one of the agreeable things about it was the undercurrent of excitement, the sense that this was a preliminary activity.

She knew that the body behind her would move closer, and it did. The hand moved around to the front of her body, and just when she was wondering whether this was a one-handed man, the other hand made itself known. The two rubber hands linked together across her middle—how clearly she saw them in her mind's eye! —and then moved upward, upward.

The sensation she experienced then was of a piercing sweetness previously unknown to her. Certainly the affair with clumsy Archie had offered nothing comparable to it. The other body pressed against her urgently now, and the hands now gripped hard where they had previously stroked. She wanted to turn her head but it seemed to be fixed, and what would she see but a mask made of rubber?

The knowledge that no fulfillment was possible heightened her pleasure and even when the hands moved up to her neck, the pleasure remained undiminished. Then the hands tightened and she was struck with panic, trying to turn her head to ease the pressure on her windpipe, twisting to convey that he was pressing too hard, pulling at the hands with her feeble paws, groping for the knife on her knees, and using it to jab upward awkwardly once, twice.

And yet, before she lost consciousness, she wanted to express regret for this action and to make it known somehow her predominant feeling had been one of pleasure, almost of ecstasy. . . .

"Rather a success," Gabriel said. "Perhaps it should have been more carefully organized, but still distinctly a success. Several plates and dishes smashed, one desk forced open, one bathroom semiflooded, three chairs and a small table thrown out of a window. Some odds and ends broken, probably by accident. Would any of you have done such things if you hadn't been anonymous? Of course not. Two regrettable incidents. One couple found removing their suits for extracurricular purposes. I won't name them. And one faint—from heat, I expect. Sorry about that."

She heard all this very vaguely, but felt the need to protest. "I didn't faint. Somebody tried to—" She stopped at that. She was lying on a sofa in the sitting room and now she looked up at the faces around her, some anxious and some amused. Gabriel's face was amused. The room wavered. She closed her eyes.

There was a hand on her forehead. A voice said, "Burning hot. She ought to be in bed."

She opened her eyes again. "How did you find me?"

Gabriel answered. "You were flat out on the floor in the hall, darling. I brought you in here and gave you some brandy."

"In the hall? Not in the closet under the stairs?"

"The glory hole? No, baby. Were you there?"

"I thought so. Did you find a—a knife?"

He raised his eyebrows, shook his head, and she wondered if he had been the man with her. Articulating with conscious clearness she said, "I was in what you call the glory hole. You were in there with me, weren't you?"

There was a murmur, one distinctly of amusement. Gabriel said gently, indulgently, "If you say so. And what happened in the glory hole, baby?"

But what had happened—the burning pleasure she had felt and her intense desire to repeat it—was something she could not say out loud. She shook her head and stared at him. His blue eyes looked back at her searchingly, and his words seemed to have a peculiar emphasis. "What you've got to remember is that nothing happened, nothing at all. You fainted and I found you on the floor in the hall. Anything else was your imagination."

She nodded, to show that she was prepared not to accuse him again. Her hand went to her neck, which did not ache or feel sore. Was it true then? Had she imagined it all? She looked wonderingly around at the faces—Bud Masters with his sideburns, monocled Lenya, Bruno Mustache, drooping Innes, and the others. They stared back at her with concern. There was a silence, broken by Bruno.

"Can't imagine what you think you've proved, Gabriel. Just got a lot of stuff smashed up, that's all."

Now Gabriel's gaze shifted from her, and his manner eased. "I don't set out to prove things. Except to myself. And to Innes perhaps."

Lenya, hovering beside Melisande, said, "You look pretty wild, you know. As if you're not really here. Come with me and I'll put you to bed."

"Not necessary." That was Gabriel. "We can easily put you up here, can't we, Innes?"

"No." The thought of staying in that house terrified her. She saw Frederick's leathery face and spoke to it. "Please take me home."

She barely said good-bye to Gabriel and Innes and did not speak to the rest of them. On the way back in the taxi Frederick said it had been a damned stupid party and that Gabriel was a silly man. She felt too tired to contradict him.

Back in her apartment he said, "Now, if you can get yourself to bed I'll make some hot milk. Any aspirin about?"

"Yes, but I've got pills—"

"No pills. Just aspirin."

He sat beside the bed while she drank the milk and aspirin. She waited for him to kiss her, but he only looked at her with dog-brown eyes like her father's. Or had her father's eyes been blue like Gabriel's? It worried her that she could not remember.

"Feeling better?" She felt just the same but said she was better. He spoke earnestly. "You weren't feeling well enough to go out, and it was terribly hot inside that rubber gear. You fainted and Gabriel found you. Nothing else happened."

"Nothing else happened," she echoed like a child, closed her eyes, and was asleep. She felt his lips brush her forehead in a good-night kiss like her father's—or was that a dream, too?

On the following morning he phoned to see how she was and asked her out to lunch as soon as she felt up to it, any day, any day at all. She did not really feel up to it, but she had lunch with him that day and dinner the day after. A month later they were married.

Frederick had sufficient money to buy a little house almost in the country, but not too far away from his work. She left the publishing firm because she did not want to see Gabriel again and got a few other secretarial jobs; but Frederick did not want his wife to work and she settled down to becoming a housewife.

He called her Melly because Melisande, he said, was rather ridiculous in this day and age, and she accepted this. Their lovemaking was infrequent, inhibited, and produced no children. Frederick became in time an administrator, in charge of a large department. Melly took up social work connected with juvenile delinquents, which she found interesting. They were good solid citizens, and as their friends used to say, real assets to the community.

Frederick never again mentioned the Anonymous People party to her, and as time went by she felt increasing doubt that anything had happened. Had she imagined it all, or were there other possibilities in her personality that remained unfulfilled? And not only in her personality.

How could she ask if the long deep scratches on Frederick's arm—the scratches she had noticed when he brought her the milk in bed that night—if they had been made by her knife when it tore through the rubber windbreaker? She was willing—or was she?—to bury the events of that evening, so that she never knew whether for one single hour of his life, he—like Melisande—had become somebody else.

A little gem of a tale . . .

R. L. STEVENS

The physician and the opium fiend

The lamplights along Cavendish Square were just being lit, casting a soft pale glow across the damp London night, as Blair slipped from the court behind Dr. Lanyon's house. It had been another failure, another robbery of a physician's office that yielded him but a few shillings. He cursed silently and started across the square, then drew back quickly as a hansom cab hurried past, the horse's hoofs clattering on the cobblestones.

At times he wished it could end this easily, with his body crushed beneath a two-wheeler. Perhaps then he might be free of the terrible craving that growled within him, forcing him to a life of housebreaking and theft.

William Blair was an opium fiend. He still remembered the first time he had eaten opium, popping the little pill of brown gum into his mouth and washing it down with coffee as De Quincey had sometimes done. He remembered the gradual creeping thrill that soon took possession of every part of his body. And he remembered too the deadly sickness of his stomach, the furred tongue and dreadful headache that followed his first experience as an opium eater.

He should have stopped the diabolical practice then, but he hadn't. In three days' time he had recourse to the drug once more, and after that his body seemed to crave it with increasing frequency. It was his frantic search for opium which now led him nightly to the offices of famous physicians, to the citadels of medicine that lined Cavendish Square. He had broken into ten of them in the past fortnight, but only two had yielded a quantity of opium sufficient to ease his terrible burden.

And so it was in a state bordering desperation that Blair entered the quiet bystreet that ran north from the square. He had gone some distance past the shops and homes when he chanced to note a high, two-story building that thrust forward its windowless gable on the street. He was familiar enough with doctors' laboratories in this section of London to suspect that here might be one, hidden away behind this neglected, discolored brick wall. But only a blistered and distained wooden door gave entry into the building from this street, and the door was equipped with neither bell nor knocker.

Hurriedly he retraced his steps to the corner, avoiding a helmeted bobby who was crossing the street in the opposite direction. He waited until the police officer had disappeared from view, his hand ready on the dagger in his pocket. As he moved on, a few drops of water struck his forehead. It was beginning to rain.

Round the corner he came upon a square of ancient, handsome houses. Though many were beginning to show the unmistakable signs of age, the second house from the corner still wore a great air of wealth and comfort. It was all in darkness except for the fanlight, but the glow from this was sufficient for him to decipher the lettering on the brass nameplate. He had guessed correctly. It was indeed a doctor's residence. He set to work at once as the rain increased.

It took him only a few moments of skillful probing with the dagger to pry open one of the shuttered windows. Then he was through it and into a flagged hall lined with costly oaken cabinets. The doctor was obviously wealthy, and Blair hoped this meant a well-stocked laboratory. He moved cautiously along the hall, fearful of any noise which might give the alarm. The house could have been empty, but it was possible the good doctor had retired early and was asleep upstairs.

Blair made his way to the rear of the first floor, heading in the direction of the windowless gable he had observed from the street. He passed into the connecting building and through a large darkened area that, by the light of his Brymay safety matches, appeared to be an old dissecting room, strewn with crates and littered with packing straw, and dusty with disuse. Blair moved through it to a stairway at the rear. This would lead to the second floor of the windowless gable, his last hope of finding a supply of opium.

The door at the top of the stair was a heavy barrier covered with red baize, and it took him ten minutes ere he finally forced it inward with a loud screech. The disclosed room proved to be the small office-laboratory he sought—his work had not been in vain! The remains of a dying fire still glowed on the hearth, casting a pale orange glow about the room. The laboratory had been in use that very night, and in such a home the storage shelves would be well stocked.

It took him but a brief search to discover, amid the chemical apparatus, a large bottle labeled LAUDANUM. This was a tincture of opium, he knew, and no less an authority than De Quincey had reckoned twenty-five drops of laudanum to be the equivalent of one grain of pure opium. Yes, this would satisfy his need.

His hand was just closing over the bottle when a voice from the doorway rasped, "Who is there? Who are you?"

Blair whirled to face the man, the dagger ready in his hand. "Get back," he warned. "I am armed."

The figure in the doorway reached up to light the gas flame, and Blair saw that he was a large, well-made, smooth-faced man of perhaps fifty, with a countenance that was undeniably handsome. "What do you want here, man? This is my laboratory. There is no money here!"

"I need—" began Blair, feeling the perspiration collecting on his forehead. "I need opium."

There was a sharp intake of breath from the handsome doctor. "My God! Have conditions in London come to this? Do opium fiends now prowl the streets and break into physicians' homes in search of this devilish drug?"

"Get out of my way," returned Blair, "or I will kill you!"

"Wait! Let me—let me try to help you in some way. Let me summon the police. This craving that obsesses you will destroy you in time. You need help, medical treatment."

As he spoke, the doctor moved forward slowly, forcing Blair back toward the far wall of the room. "I don't want help," sobbed the cornered man. "It's too late to help me now."

The doctor took a step closer. "It is never too late! Don't you realize what this drug is doing to you, man? Don't you see how it releases everything that is cruel and sick and evil in you? Under the influence of opium, or any drug, you become a different person. You are no longer in command of your own will."

Blair had backed to the wall now, and he could feel its chill firmness through his coat. He raised the dagger menacingly. "Come any closer, Sawbones, and I swear I will kill you!"

The doctor hesitated a moment. He glanced at the darkened skylight above their heads, where the rain was now beating a steady tattoo upon the glass. Then he said, "The mind of man is his greatest gift. To corrupt it, to poison it with drugs, is something hateful and immoral. I hope that I am never in a position where I lose control of my free will because I have surrendered to the dark side of my nature. You, poor soul, are helpless in the grip of this opium, like the wretched folk who smoke it in the illegal dens, curled upon their bunks and oblivious of the outer world."

"I—I—" began Blair, but the words were lost in his throat. The physician was right, he knew, but he was beyond caring now, beyond distinguishing between right and wrong. He only knew that the doctor had forced him further from the bottle of laudanum.

"Let me call the police," urged the doctor, softly.

"No!"

The physician's hand moved, all in a flash, seizing one of the bottles from the shelf beside him and hurling it upwards through the skylight. There was a shattering of glass and a shower of silvery white pellets from the bottle. Then a sudden violet flame seemed to engulf the entire skylight, burning with a hissing sound that ended almost at once with a burst of explosive violence.

Terrified, Blair tried to lunge past the doctor, but the large hands were instantly upon him, fastening on his coat and wrist, forcing the dagger away.

They were still locked in a life-and-death, silent struggle when, moments later, a helmeted bobby burst into the laboratory. "What's happening here, sir? I saw the flame and heard the explosion—"

"Help me with this man," shouted the physician. "He's trying to steal opium!"

Within seconds Blair was helpless, his arms pinioned to his sides by the burly police officer. "Take me," he mumbled. "Take me and lock me up. Help me."

Another bobby arrived on the scene, attracted by the noise and flame. "What was it?" he asked the doctor.

"I had to signal you somehow," he told them. "There were potassium pellets in the bottle and I took a risk that enough rainwater had collected on the skylight to set off a chemical reaction. Potassium reacts even more violently with water than does sodium."

"You were successful," returned the second policeman. "I heard that boom two streets away."

The doctor was busy moving some of his equipment out of the rain which was still falling through the shattered skylight. "I think with treatment this man can be saved," said he. "It is his addiction that has led him into a life of crime."

"I would not worry too much about him, sir. He could have killed you with this dagger."

"But I do worry about him, as I would about any human being. As for myself, I was much more fearful that he would wreck my laboratory. I have been engaged in some important experiments here, relating to transcendental medicine, and I feel I am on the verge of discovery."

The first police officer pulled Blair toward the door. "Then we will leave you alone to clean up, sir. And good luck with your experiments." He was halfway out the door when he paused and said, "Oh, by the by, sir, I will need your name for my report. I did not have time to catch it on the brass outside."

"Certainly," replied the physician, with a smile. "The name is Jekyll. Doctor Henry Jekyll."

This was the 349th "first story" to be published in Ellery Queen's Mystery Magazine, *now in its thirty-second year of publication—an exceptional first story, filled with suspense and a growing sense of terror.*

The author, Dr. Richard A. Selzer, told us little about himself. At the time he submitted "A Single Minute of Fear" he was a forty-one-year-old surgeon practicing in New Haven, Connecticut. He has a wife and three children for (as he expressed it) "comfort, comedy, and comeliness" (assign the nouns as it may strike your fancy). He confessed to "a lifelong envy of the purveyor of the printed word" (note the professionalism indicated), and in his next life he "would like to be a tenor and say everything in high B flat" (cryptic and provocative).

RICHARD A. SELZER

A single minute of fear

She had sat wrenlike on the edge of an old ladder-back chair—small, thin, white-haired, with blue eyes and a startlingly youthful voice. It had struck him that if he had heard that voice without seeing her he would have expected a young girl. The voice was clear, light, with a bit of boldness in it. For an instant he had a vision of a beautiful young girl imprisoned in an old woman's body.

"Yes, it is a big house, I suppose, but it's home," she

was saying. "I was born here and never lived anywhere else. From up here on the hill you can see the lights on the water in the harbor. Come, I'll show you."

They walked up the curving staircase to the library. From the window the lights far below darted and zipped, like phosphorescent bugs. It was so quiet. That was what he liked best—he could study here, undisturbed. Warren was older than the other students and needed to regain the discipline of studying. Five years of solitude in the Forestry Service had depleted his drive. Passive and shy at his return to the world, he needed the isolation he saw here.

When they returned to the living room, she had said, her blue eyes pale and unswerving, "Of course, no girls in the house. And no liquor."

"May I smoke?"

"In your room."

They arranged for him to work out his rent in chores, giving her eight hours of work each week. She always took in forestry students, she said. "They understand hedges and grass. You really can't get much out of a classicist." She had made that mistake once and that year had ended up hiring a gardener.

His room was on the third floor, really more than he had hoped for. The walls were dark walnut, rather somber, but less distracting than wallpaper. There was a bathroom with ancient porcelain fixtures and a naked bulb at the end of a string. One window was darkened by the middle branches of a pine tree. The other window looked down over the steep curving drive of the private road.

He had meant to keep his distance, do his chores, and stay in his room. For a while it worked out that way, and days would go by when he wouldn't see her. Once or twice, while mowing or raking on the grounds, he had the feeling he was being watched, but when he turned to look up at the house all the windows were blank.

Then one night she met him at the door.

"Won't you have dinner with me tonight?"

"Yes, thank you, Mrs. Pierson. I can't stay long, I have so much to do, but I'd like it very much." He was downstairs at six and went to the kitchen.

"Sit down in the dining room and I'll serve in a minute."

At dinner they had talked of many things. She was an aggressive conversationalist, initiating each subject and asking questions. She seemed far more interested in his history than in recounting her own. "Not quite in character," he thought. He was pleased, nevertheless, and enjoyed telling her of his experiences in the Forestry Service.

At the end she said, "I'm glad you're here, Warren. I feel safe. These days it's not good for an old woman to live alone in a big house. There are too many burglars."

After that first dinner he found himself spending more and more time in her parlor. It became a matter of course that they would eat dinner together. Warren reluctantly admitted to himself that he enjoyed her company. Actually she knew many things and could talk intelligently on a number of subjects, from jury duty to conservation. Unlike other women he had known, she had an earnestness, an open strength of mind, that appealed to him. After the years of solitude he relished her company and, no less, the semblance of family life that she offered.

After his classes he did not adjourn to the coffee shop with the other students but went home, more and more eagerly, and always with a sense of impending comfort. There was the night she talked of her father.

"He was a hunter—not great, but certainly avid." She smiled in nostalgia. As for herself, she admitted a reluctance to shoot animals for sport. "In fact, after he died, I removed stuffed birds and beasts from every mantel and cabinet in the house, and put them in the attic. Why, there was even a great horned owl on the piano, if you please. No wonder I hated to practice, with those re-proachful eyes on me. Would you like to see his gun col-lection?"

"I would indeed, Mrs. Pierson. I know a bit about guns myself."

"I'm sure you do. Well, after dinner I'll show them to you."

Later she unlocked a large breakfront in the library and he took one gun after another from its rack, feeling the polished barrels, the rich wood. They still had a faint odor of oil about them. She stood aside and watched him expertly cock a rifle. She seemed immensely pleased at his excitement.

"There are boxes and boxes of shells of all sizes in the drawers. See?"

She opened a drawer and he noted the carefully labeled, neatly stacked boxes.

"Have you ever shot a gun?" he asked her.

"Heavens, no! I'm not strong enough for that."

"It doesn't take much strength if you know how. Someday I'll show you."

"I'd love to watch you shoot. There's plenty of room on the back lawn."

"Good. I'll set up a target and we'll have some fun."

What had started as a game quickly assumed a more and more central focus in the time they spent together. They would meet in the library and after a brief consulta-tion at the gun cabinet would walk together down the great staircase to the back of the house.

One day she said, "May I try?" There was timidity in her voice.

He had stood behind her. It was all so gentle. Out-side, on the far end of the lawn, in front of a cluster of copper beeches, the targets he had set up stared up at them like bloodshot eyes. His left hand helped her sup-port the weight of the rifle, his right guided her eye to the sight, her finger to the trigger.

"Now," he had whispered in her ear. The tiny body jerked once beneath his steadying grasp, but remained straight, defiant, before the recoil. She learned quickly. He felt all the pride of the trainer, the tamer of beasts, the drawer forth, the realizer of potential. She was elated at her progress, ran to examine the target, and kept her score with a scrupulousness that was almost fanatical.

At dinner they talked of guns and bullets.

"I must learn to protect myself," she said. "An old woman like me all alone. There are burglars throughout the neighborhood. They know we're helpless. Now we can fight back, can't we, Warren? Thanks to you, we can give a good account of ourselves."

She seemed then to imagine the very confrontation itself, and discovery of the intruder, the gun raised, the breathless moment of aiming, the report, the impact, the stung body's crumple and fall.

"Well, I doubt you'll ever need to use it," laughed Warren. "I suppose it doesn't hurt a bit to let them know you've been target-practicing. But it's fun."

"Yes, it is," she said, with a voice that seemed not to have finished the sentence. . . .

Warren had lived in Mrs. Pierson's house for eight months. It was November and the big house seemed darker than ever. After five o'clock in the evening there was virtually no light from the outside.

For the past few weeks he had been increasingly restless, bored. His rehabilitation at school was complete. He was tired of the old lady's company now, tired of her constant talking of guns and shooting. She was obsessed with it. He began to get home later and later in the afternoon. Often it was too late and too dark for any practice, and on those days she seemed quieter, not glum but disappointed, and he ate quickly and went upstairs to study.

There was a girl who worked as a secretary in the Forestry School, and he had begun to watch her. One day she sensed his gaze, looked up, and smiled. For Warren that smile was a kind of liberation. They had talked, eaten lunch together, and he had taken her to the movies. Later he had kissed her, feeling the warm sweet-smelling body through her thin blouse. From then on he was with Paula every day.

"I won't be home for dinner tonight, Mrs. Pierson."

"Why? Is anything wrong?"

"No, I—I have some work to do in the library." Somehow he couldn't tell her about the girl. She had looked at him for one moment extra.

"We'll have coffee when you come home, then."

"I think I'll be too late tonight. Thanks, anyway."

That was the first time. In the beginning he would tell her each morning that he wouldn't be home for dinner, but when it happened every day he stopped telling her. The more he saw of Paula—and that "more" had developed into a love affair, his first—the less he saw of Mrs. Pierson.

For the past week he had merely lived there in the big dark house. They had not had occasion to speak and he tried to avoid her when possible, waiting until he heard her in the kitchen before he came quickly downstairs and ran out the front door. He felt a certain guilt in the abrupt way he had terminated their relationship, but it only bothered him when he saw her standing, tiny and silent, at the library window upstairs. The rest of the time he did not think about it.

And now tonight. He had left Paula at six o'clock. They had arranged to meet at ten for a beer. As he walked up the long steep driveway he thought he saw Mrs. Pierson at the library window. He looked again, but saw nothing.

He was stopped in his tracks by the sound of the shot and the spray of pebbles that kicked up not five feet in front of him. He was nailed to the spot. Raising his hand to shield his eyes he peered up at the dark house. Another shot rang out, and the paved driveway bore a gouge several feet to his left.

Galvanized, he ran half crouching to the safety of the garage. Now she could not see him. He knew it was she, beyond any doubt. He unlocked the door of the garage that led to the basement and went inside. "I've got to get to her," he thought, "before she hurts herself. Crazy old bitch. I'll sneak up behind her and grab the gun. Then out I go, out of here permanently."

He noted that the house was in complete darkness, and thought, "Better not turn on any lights." He crept up the back stairs to the kitchen, flattening along the wall, then into the great hall and up the curving staircase. It was completely dark and utterly quiet. At the door to the library he stopped. The shots had come from there.

Should he run in, flick on the light, and rush her? Or creep in on the floor? He slipped off one shoe and, stepping well out of range, threw it into the library. There was a resounding crack and zing which echoed for a few moments. His skin crawled with tension.

The gun cabinet! He had to reach it and get a rifle. He had to meet her on more equal terms, so that if she were truly insane or wouldn't talk to him, if worse came to worst he could shoot, not to kill but to disarm.

The gun cabinet was at the far end of the room, near the back entrance to the library. A frontal assault was out of the question. Retreating, he slipped off the other shoe and threw it into the library. There was another shot, followed by the tinkle of shattered glass. At the same time he raced lightly and silently through a side hall to the other entrance of the library. The cabinet was now no more than three feet away.

He dropped to his haunches and inched his stockinged feet toward the cabinet. For what seemed an hour he crouched there, staring out into the blackness, then reached up to try the glass cabinet door. It was open! He had thought to quickly smash it and snatch a weapon through the broken glass. He knew which ones were already loaded. She must have forgotten, in her nervousness, to close and lock the door.

"Take one," came the youthful voice.

He froze.

"Take one. I won't shoot while you're there."

He waited. His eyes were accommodating to the darkness and he saw her as a small mound of blackness between the large windows in the far wall. He reached for a rifle and quickly slid it from the cabinet. An open box of shells stood on the lower shelf, and he took a handful and dropped to the floor. Crablike, he scuttled backward to the doorway and out of the room. No sooner had he left the library than two shots in quick succession flew across the room. He heard the glass of the gun cabinet shatter.

"Please, Mrs. Pierson, this is crazy. Can't we stop and talk about it? Someone can get hurt."

He tried to keep it light, give her a chance to quit, laugh, agree that it was only a game, and that it was now time to stop and have dinner. She answered with a shot that cracked at the other end of the dark room, spending itself in metallic echoes. Warren knelt at the turn of the hall leading out of the library.

"You need help, Mrs. Pierson. You're sick. Come on, put down the gun. Come out where I can see you. I won't shoot and I won't hurt you. I'll get you a doctor, and when you get well we'll forget the whole thing."

His voice was too loud, he knew, but it was hard to control. He was frightened.

"Mrs. Pierson," he called. "Please. Mrs. Pierson, let's stop this. Calm yourself. Why are you doing this? Why do you want to kill me? You're upset, and maybe I—I don't blame you. But surely we could talk about it."

A pause. "Can't we?" There was no answer. "Look,

Mrs. Pierson." He made his tone firm, slightly menacing.
"If it comes to that, you can't outshoot me. I taught you a
lot but not everything." And then more gently, "I don't
want to hurt you. Answer me, damn it!" he shouted. Still
no answer. "O.K., that's it."

He hated her now, hated her for frightening him,
threatening him. Hated her as much as she must hate
him. He could feel her hatred and his own like two dark
clouds filling the house, insinuating poisonous strands into
each other's substance. It amazed him how immediately
hatred arose, full-grown. All it took was a single minute
of fear. Good lord, how he hated her now!

What had she expected? A lasting emotional attach-
ment? Warren could not imagine the basis for her desire
to possess him. All right, they had both been lonely, but
that was certainly not new to her, and he had honestly
enjoyed her company. At what point did reason and propriety snap? When did she announce, in silent authority,
her ownership of him? It was only thwarted possession
that could produce such a murderous jealousy. Even now
the irony of having been the instrument of his possible
destruction did not escape him.

Maybe there was time to get out of the house. He
rose halfway and backed into the side hall. A shot. He
ducked and fled into the library again, coming out the
front entrance. Good! She had gone down the side hall,
thinking he was still there. He crossed the hall and raced
into a bedroom. He knelt there next to the doorway, rifle
ready. At the very first sound he was going to shoot.
Maybe that would scare her and make her surrender.

He stared out into the blackness; then, on the other
side of the stairwell, he saw the dim shape floating toward
him. He raised the gun to his shoulder, took aim at a point
just behind the shape, and fired. She did not so much as
start or change her speed.

"I've got to get out of here or get her." He rose to his

feet, fired two shots in the direction of her shape, then plummeted down the stairs to the first floor. As he reached the bottom he heard the crack of a rifle and simultaneously felt a breathtaking pain in his left hip. There was a moment of terror, when he wanted to slump to the floor and give in to his wound; but steeling himself he plunged on, feeling his trousers grow warm and wet from the blood.

He was sweating heavily. That shot had been too close for comfort. She couldn't be that good, she couldn't. He was forced to admit that she had improved a great deal in the last weeks of their practicing. The thought crossed his mind for the first time: What if she gets me? True, he was a better shot, but she knew this house. It was like an extension of her own body. For over sixty years it had surrounded her like a carapace. Surely that would count in her favor.

"Don't be careless, Warren," he thought.

He had never wanted to kill anything so much as he wanted to kill her. The hate was like a hot branding iron in his head. He twisted and clenched to contain it, but each minute that it went unslaked was torture. He felt his brain draw itself together like an animal, grow dark and concentrated, sitting poised on the floor of his skull, ready to spring. Was he to pay for a lifetime of her spinsterhood?

"The bullet didn't hit the bone, or I couldn't run," he reasoned.

He raced across the open expanse of the living room into the solarium. This was a long narrow room with a French door at each end. It was completely windowed and full of plants. He flattened against a wall and waited for her. He knew now that he would have to shoot—to shoot to kill. And he wanted to kill her.

Then he knew she was there, in the room with him, at the other end. He could not see her but her presence was palpable. He had to kill her with the first shot or she would kill him by learning the origin of his blast. His hip was throbbing unbearably, and his right sock was sticky with blood. He had to kill her soon.

From where he crouched, Warren watched with mounting alarm as slowly, icily, the moon slid across the windows, frosting the dark leaves of the plants with a sinister shine. Here and there on the walls, tapers of its cold glare threatened to dilute the thick darkness to a vulnerable dusk. In another moment he would be revealed.

Then suddenly, absurdly, the telephone rang. His muscles jumped in fright, making his hip throb anew. It rang again and again and then again. In the middle of the fourth ring it stopped and he heard the youthful voice say, "Hello?"

Lurching forward he fired shot after shot in the direction of the telephone. It stood on a small table at the other end of the solarium. When he stopped, another shot screamed into his ear, hard, grating at first, then purifying into a single silver sound that filled his head.

"My God, she's at the other phone."

From the extension in the living room he heard, or thought he heard her say, "Police—hurry. I've just killed a burglar."

This was the 357th "first story" to be published in Ellery Queen's Mystery Magazine. *Can a story be, at one and the same time, charming and creepy? Delightful and terrifying? Try this one for size—and shivers.*

The author, Jeff Sweet, was a senior at New York University when he submitted "Nightmare in New York."

He was studying the art of film and was spending most of his nonschool hours "pursuing a career as a playwright-critic-composer." His "immodest ambitions" also included being an actor and a director, and he has studied critical writing under Clive Barnes, songwriting under Paul Simon, and has attended the Eugene O'Neill Memorial Theater Center's National Critics Institute. He comes by all these interests genetically: His mother was a concert violinist and his father a speech writer. . . . And now, read Mr. Sweet's strange story of Mr. Stanley's shoes.

JEFF SWEET

Nightmare in New York

I found it in my mail—an envelope with the picture of a simple, dignified tie shoe in the upper-left corner under which was a logotype reading: *Stanley Shoes, Mail Order Sales Department.* My first instinct was to toss it into the trash with the other junk mail, but for some reason best explained by behavioral psychologists I opened it and removed the sheet inside.

Mimeographed on stationery also bearing the illustrated logotype was the following:

Dear Friend:
I was very happy to receive your note expressing interest in making extra money selling our high-quality shoes to friends and neighbors. Many people across the country—men, women,

young and old—have found selling Stanley Shoes a steady source of outside income. Why, they practically sell themselves!

Mr. Harry Grench of East Orange, New Jersey, sold seven pairs of our super-cushioned footwear on his very first day! Miss Sally Timble of Winnetka, Illinois, cleared over $300 in commissions in less than a month! In addition, both have won many fine prizes for themselves and their respective families.

Your Stanley Sales Outfit should arrive within a few days. Good luck!

Sincerely yours,
Milton Stanley

Of course I'd never sent Mr. Stanley a note expressing even the slightest interest in selling his high-quality shoes to friends and neighbors. All I could figure was that someone had sent in my name as a gag.

Though there was a time not too long ago when I might have considered peddling sandals. I'd just moved to New York and my career in commercial art was—well, let's say Peter Max wasn't the slightest bit worried. Then I met Susan—attractive, intelligent, rich. We were soon engaged, and we plan to get married when she has finished school. In the meantime she has seen to it that her fiancé hasn't been wasting away.

All of which added up to a thanks-but-no-thanks to Mr. Stanley. And with a superbly executed backhand flip I tossed letter and envelope into the wastebasket.

A few days later, just as Milton Stanley had promised, it arrived—my Stanley Sales Outfit. It consisted of a brightly colored booklet with pictures of all the various styles in which the high-quality shoes came plus a sample of the special super-cushion that made Stanley Shoes so comfortable that "you feel like you're walking on the clouds of Heaven!" And there was another mimeographed letter from Milton Stanley.

Dear Friend:

Here is your complete Stanley Sales Outfit—all you need to sell our high-quality shoes to friends and neighbors. Soon you too will be earning high commissions part-time the Stanley way!

Since my last letter, Mr. Harry Grench of East Orange, New Jersey, has sent in his latest order, this time for 62 pairs of our super-cushioned footwear! And Miss Sally Timble of Winnetka, Illinois, has won a free, all-expenses-paid vacation to India and the Orient!

I look forward to seeing your first orders.

Best wishes,
Milton Stanley

The Stanley Sales Outfit followed the first Stanley letter into the hands, ultimately, of the Department of Public Sanitation.

I thought no more of Mr. Stanley and his shoes for the next two months, though I did derive much comfort out of squeezing the sample of the Stanley super-cushion in moments of distress. Then, almost two months later to the day, I received another letter.

Dear Friend:

I'd like to speak to you man to man.

Two months ago, at your request, I sent you a Stanley Sales Outfit—all you needed to start you on the road to high commissions in your spare time. We are still waiting for your first order. Frankly we've been wondering where we went wrong. Is it something we've done?

I have in front of me Mr. Harry Grench's latest order. (You remember Harry. East Orange, New Jersey, ring a bell?) He hit the $1100.00 mark—a new record for sales! I also have here a letter from Miss Sally Timble. She has left Winnetka, Illinois, for a brand-new home in Park Ridge, and with her commission money has moved her mother into a rest home in Virginia!

Please let us hear from you.

Hopefully,
Milton Stanley

Feeling waggish, I took Mr. Stanley's letter and sat down at the typewriter, a Scotch and water within arm's reach. And I composed the following letter:

Dear Milt,

Glad to receive your last letter. Hope you and the kids are feeling well. Has Aunt Betsy gotten over the flu? And how about business? Business good? Recession hurt you?

Now, about the letter you sent me. Why, of course you may speak to me "man to man" any time you wish. I mean, didn't I always have a sympathetic ear whenever you were having problems with Jill back at old State U.? It is with a smile that I remember you timidly knocking at my door as if afraid I would jump out and brain you or something. (I think you were a freshman and I was a junior.) But we got to be good friends after that. Those midnight beer blasts and all. I can hardly keep from shedding a nostalgic tear. But back to your letter. I'm sorry if your faith in me has been shaken. But after Dorothy left me, I tell you, Milt, I just gave up the will to sell shoes. No, no, don't laugh. It's true. I used to consider selling your super-cushioned shoes a kind of sacred mission. But Dorothy—well, she left me and, well, I haven't told this to anyone, but she ran off with my sample super-cushion and my booklet and defected to Thom McAn! But don't worry about me. I'll be all right. I admit I was in a blue funk for a while, but I met this wonderful girl named Susan in the Rare Books Room at the library, and I think it's going to be O.K. from now on.

Give my best to Harry and Sally.

Kevin Ivers

I folded the letter, put it into an envelope, addressed

it to Mr. Milton Stanley in care of his factory, stamped and mailed it. Good God, did I feel clever! I could just picture Stanley getting the letter and wondering, "Who the hell is Kevin Ivers?" and racking his skull to remember those beer blasts. Yes, I was very satisfied with myself and celebrated by eating dinner out at Nathan's.

A week later, however, I found another envelope with the Stanley Shoes logotype in the upper-left corner waiting for me in my mailbox. I pulled out the contents— another letter on the company stationery. But this one was typed, not mimeographed! It read:

Dear Kev,
Sorry to hear about Dorothy, but that's the way the cookie crumbles. Women are like that, you know. Susan sounds nice. I hope you and she find what you're looking for, though God knows in these troubled times how hard that is!

I'm afraid all is not well with me. My brother Roger—he's in charge of production here at Stanley Shoes—he's started a power play with some of the other board members to try to force me out of the company. He denies it, of course, but I have the evidence! And the strange looks he's giving Jill. I can't quite describe the looks exactly, but they're not the kind you give another man's wife.

Also Aunt Betsy's flu has gotten worse. She was taken to the hospital last week where she is in fair condition. I suppose all I can do is pray.

I may be in New York soon. I'd like to drop by if it's convenient.

Do you still have the sporty sideburns?

Write soon,
Milton

How the hell did he know I had sporty sideburns?
I was beginning to get a little scared. No, not scared, nervous. Actually, sort of scared nervous. How did Milton

Stanley know about my sideburns? The question haunted me. Even squeezing the super-cushion did not bring me any peace. In a fit of anxiety I threw it away.

Other questions crept into my mind. Was it possible I actually knew Milton Stanley in college without knowing it? Had I listened to his problems at State U.? Did we have midnight beer blasts?

And then I'd remember that I hadn't gone to State U. and that as a student I'd loathed the taste of beer.

I shaved off my sideburns.

Soon after another letter arrived. This one was handwritten.

Dear Kev,
I haven't heard from you lately. Has something happened?

I'm afraid things here have gone from bad to worse. Aunt Betsy's flu turned into something else and she passed away last week. Harry and Sally flew in for the funeral. It was nice to see them again. I would have called you about it but I didn't want to upset you. After all, you really didn't know Betsy that well. She was a remarkable woman and the world is poorer for her passing.

Somehow I managed to rally my supporters on the board and blocked Roger and his co-conspirators' move to push me out— for the time being at any rate. I know this isn't the end of it. I can feel him plotting behind my back all the time. What really upsets me is that I'm sure Jill is in on it. You remember those looks I said he was giving her? Now she's giving them to him. I don't like it, Kev.

I heard from Mark Honig the other day. He said he saw you on the street and you'd shaved off the sideburns. He tried to catch up with you, but you and some pretty girl caught a cab before he could talk to you. I guess that must be Susan, right? Anyway, he said it was at Forty-eighth and Fifth.

Oh, what the hell am I writing this for? As if it makes any difference in the grand scheme of things. You remember our conversations about the grand scheme of things when we were in college? I laugh to think how naïve we were then.

Your friend,
Milt

You can imagine what this letter did to me, especially since I remembered grabbing that cab with Sue at Forty-eighth and Fifth! Who was this Honig guy who'd spotted me?

A sudden inspiration. I took out the New York phone book and looked up Mark Honig. I dialed the number with a shaking hand. There came the beginning of a ring on the other end. In the middle of it someone picked up the phone.

"Hello?" someone said.

"Who is this?" I asked.

"Mark Honig," the voice replied. "That you, Kevin?"

I shuddered.

"Kev, are you there?"

"Uh, yeah, yeah," I said.

"What's the matter, Kev? You sound nervous or something." The guy actually seemed to be concerned.

"No, no, I'm O.K.," I insisted.

"Actually, it's a good thing you called. I lost your number and I was supposed to reach you."

"What about?"

"You know—Stinky."

"S-s-stinky?" I stuttered.

"Stinky Stanley. You remember Stinky Stanley, Kev. All those beer blasts in college."

"Right," I mumbled.

"Hey, Kev, what's happening with him? He called me and he sounded all shook up."

"Well, uh, you heard about his Aunt Betsy," I said.

"Yes, too bad. She was a good lady."

"And his brother," I continued. "You know he tried to push Stinky, uh, Milt out of the company."

"I can believe it. Roger's like that."

"Uh, Mark, what was it about Stinky you were going to—?"

"Oh, yes," said Honig. "He's coming into town."

"When?" I asked.

"Tonight. Eight-forty flight from Chicago. Told me he was counting on staying with you a couple days. He tried to reach you himself, but you must've been out. Anyway, that's why I was worried about not having your number. Of course, now you've called, so you got the message and everything's O.K."

"Yeah," I said.

"I've got to run," said Honig. "Dinner date. Give my best to Stinky. The three of us've got to get together at McSorley's or somewhere."

"Right," I said. I wasn't really listening to him. I was thinking of that visitor on his way from Chicago arriving at the airport at 8:40, and if I was scared nervous before, I was plain scared now!

"Give me a call tomorrow," Honig said. "We'll arrange something." After good-byes, he hung up.

I looked at the clock. It was 6:30. I figured mentally that it would take Stanley till nine to actually land and another hour or hour and a half to arrive by cab depending on whether he landed at La Guardia or Kennedy. That meant anywhere from 10:00 on.

My first thought was to pack an overnight bag and get the hell out of here, but then I realized I had nowhere to go. And besides, feeling very fatalistic, I figured that one way or another, some day or another, I'd have to face up to this thing, and it would probably be best to get it over with.

I called Susan and canceled our date for that night.

She was good and mad. She'd picked up a pair of tickets in the orchestra for some new rock musical, but what could I do?

I tried to kill time watching TV, but reruns of "I Love Lucy" and "Gilligan's Island" didn't help much.

At 8:30 my door buzzer rang. I pressed the answer button.

"Hello?"

"It's Jill, Kev. Let me in." Her voice was very firm.

"Who?"

"Jill Stanley, Kev. Open the door—I'm freezing out here."

I obeyed, and a few minutes later Jill Stanley, red-haired and tight-lipped, told me what she had on her mind: "You're going to kill Milton."

"What?"

"Just what I said, Kevin. You're going to kill Milton. I know he's coming over here tonight, and when he does you're going to give him a cup of coffee with a little of this in it." She took a small packet out of her purse. "And at eleven o'clock a mutual friend will drop by and pick him up."

"Mark Honig?"

"Yes, Mark," she said. "He owes me a favor."

"And why am I doing this?" I asked. "Murder *is* against the law, even in New York."

"So is bigamy, Kevin."

I felt the ends of my mouth twitch. "What do you mean?"

"You know what I mean," said Mrs. Stanley. "I mean your wife and kid back in Fort Wayne. What do you suppose your chances of marrying the rich Susan would be if I sent her this family portrait?" She pulled out a photo Christmas card showing Dorothy, Melissa, and me smiling into the camera, little Melissa with her eyes closed from the flash. And in my handwriting—*To Milt and Jill from the Ivers Family.*

"How did you get this card?" I demanded, if it is possible to demand in a shaky voice.

"You sent it to us, two Christmases ago. Don't you remember?"

"But I don't even know you!"

She didn't answer but started glancing at some sample drawings on my desk. "Not bad," she said. "Maybe I'll get Roger to have you design a new trademark for the company after he takes over. The old one is so tacky."

She reached for the card. I held onto it. She smiled.

"Never mind. I have plenty of copies." She moved toward the door.

"Why pick on me?" I asked. "Why don't you do it yourself?"

"Oh, no," she said. "This way is much neater."

"But what if they catch me? They'll trace him to me!"

"How? You don't know him, remember?" She was overdoing that smile as she left.

Milton Stanley arrived a little after ten. . . .

You know something? I don't answer junk mail anymore.

This was the 360th "first story" to be published in Ellery Queen's Mystery Magazine . . . *a sensitive and probing portrait of Emmy, a farmer's wife.*

The author, Ellen Arthur, is in her midthirties, married to a computer analyst, and they have two children. Ellen Arthur has been writing off and on for as long as she can remember. She took short-story courses from Patricia McGerr (also represented in this volume) and Robert Knowlton and "learned more about writing from them than from all the rest" of her formal education.

*The author's hobby is music, and she loves to write
folk tunes. She also loves sports (bowling and golf, in particular), bridge, and "arguing religion and politics." And
oh, yes: Her interest in crime stories originated with her
father, who was a police captain and who "toted me
around quite a bit, and on one notable occasion when
there were no prisoners, even locked me in a cell."*

ELLEN ARTHUR

Cal always said

Emmy hardly noticed the cry the first time she heard it.
The second time, she raised her head to look out the
window, but the cluttered yard looked no different to her
than it should, so she went back to washing up the noon
dishes. Cal told her to clean up good before she came
outside.

Her small red knuckles bobbed rhythmically in and
out of the dishpan except when she paused to shake the
water drops from her hands and lift her skirt to mop off
her face. She did this gingerly, taking care not to touch
the blue-yellow bruise on her temple. It surely was hot,
she thought, for so soon in the spring. Probably on account of the mist rolling in last night. That did always
seem to make it hotter.

In her mind she counted up the things she was supposed to do. There was the stove to clean, the floor to wash

up, and the two rabbits to skin. Ugh, the rabbits! She hated that. One time she tried to tell Cal how much she hated it, but he didn't pay no mind.

She heard the sound again and thought it must be Cal yelling at that horse he'd borrowed off Dilby. It occurred to her that he must be working close by, and for a few minutes afterward she speeded up her work as if perhaps he might be able to glance up and see her through the window of the cabin.

She wanted to get done quick anyways because she was itching to sit out on the porch. Spring and summer were the best times even when it was hot. Lordy, how she used to love being outdoors when she was a kid! Walking in the deep woods was best of all, searching out the small animals with the sharp pointy faces. She liked to puzzle over what they might be thinking. She could lose all track of time doing that. Plenty of times she didn't get on to school at all and got in trouble.

And once, when she was eleven, she got shot in the leg by a man hunting squirrel, and her Pop said she had to keep shut of the woods. That hurt worse than getting shot, and even worse than the doctoring. After a while Pop forgot about it, though. Emmy smiled, remembering how good she felt once she got free again. Her father was sure easier to get around than Cal was. Cal likely never forgot about anything since the day he was born. Some chance she got now to go out walking by herself!

She pushed her rag back and forth over the stove top and wondered why remembering was so easy for Cal and so hard for her. She was always forgetting something and making him mad.

She heard the yell again and she stood still, cocking her head, listening, to see if it would come again. She thought she might've heard her name. Could be Cal wanting her to bring something. It stayed quiet outside—nothing but bird sounds and leaf rustling from a little wind that was coming up. She was glad about the wind. It would be nice out on the porch if some of the heat blew away.

This yelling business was a sticker, though. She folded up the stove rag and sat down at the table so she could figure. Frowning, she ran her thumbnail across the green-painted tabletop. If Cal *was* calling her, could he be doing it just to see if she'd come out when she wasn't supposed to? He'd never done it before, not that she could remember. But with Cal you couldn't be sure. His mind could wind around like a bog trail and be just as dangerous, too.

She went to the window. Nothing she could see out there cleared it up. Shaking her head impatiently, she went to the door and opened it. "Cal!" she called out. "You Cal!" She stood listening for an answer and then shut the door. If he was calling her, then why didn't he answer when she called him back?

She reached down a cup and poured coffee from the pot on the drainboard. It was near cold, but it tasted good. Sipping it, she turned the problem around in her brain. If he was tricking her it was clear she should keep working. Likely he would hit her if she came out when she wasn't supposed to. On the other side of it, if he was needing her to bring something and she didn't—

Again! There was that yelling again! Emmy stiffened and held herself alert. It *was* Cal and he was calling her name! There he was calling her name when just two minutes before he wouldn't even answer her!

Her frail mouth curved up in a smile. It was a game all right. No other reason to call out and then play possum when she answered, and then right away call again. Well, for once she had him outsmarted.

Still smiling she went back to her work, moving quickly now that she knew what to do. She would finish everything he'd told her and then run out to see what he wanted. It was safe as churches. She'd have every right to be outside once the work was done.

When the floor was clean she went straight to the rabbits, handling them as fast as she could. Every now and then she heard Cal call. It seemed like no time at all before she was ready to clean herself up and go out.

Pleased with herself, she trotted across the yard, wondering which way she should go to find him. She wished he'd call out again so she could tell. She decided to try the north side first and right away she saw she'd picked it right. Just over the rise she saw Dilby's horse standing near the ridge, eating grass. Queer he was loose. She couldn't see Cal yet. When she got there, the horse sidled away like he was making room so she could use the ridge for a lookout.

But before she could do it the sound came again, loud, and so close by it made her jump. "Emmy!" It was Cal's voice, hoarse-throated and furious.

She froze. Dilby's horse shuddered and snorted, and Emmy stared at him like maybe he could explain it. Instead, he wheeled and pounded away, leaving her alone on the ridge.

Fearfully she crept to the edge and peered over. Cal was glaring up at her with blazing, hateful eyes. From habit she flinched, though it was plain he was in no shape to hurt her. She stared down in amazement. There was some blood up around his head—not a whole lot, but not what you'd call a little bit either. He looked crooked somehow, like he might've been twisted out of line somehow.

"You're hurt," she said with a nod. It seemed to her his face was a real peculiar color.

"Damn you! Why didn't you come?" He talked in a whispery croak, but there was enough meanness in it to make her careful.

"Didn't know you was hurt."

"You heard me."

"I didn't!"

He struggled, and for a minute she thought he might get up. "I *know* you heard," he said.

"You said I couldn't come out till my work was done!" As soon as she said it she covered her mouth, but it was too late. His face told her plainly she should've stuck to saying she didn't hear him.

"You damn woman, if I could—" His words stopped, but his mouth stayed open like he wanted to suck air. She wondered if he was through being able to talk. After a minute he started up again. "Get yourself over to Dilby's. Say I'm hurt bad and to bring the doc right away. Be sure —be sure you say where I am. Now, tell it back to me like I told you." He made a moaning sound and closed his eyes.

She looked down at him. "Cal? . . . Cal? . . . Are you fainted, Cal?" She tried to think if she should start right off to Dilby's or wait till he got awake so she could say it back like he wanted. She saw him stir and decided to rattle it off quick: "I'm to go over to Dilby's," she said, "and say you're hurt bad and need the doc, and I got to say where you are under this ridge here."

She got up to leave and paused, struck by a novelty in Cal's orders. "Cal, am I supposed to go over Dilby's all by myself?"

"You move!" he shouted. "Run!"

She ran off, muttering angrily. Ten foot! A big man like him getting that bad hurt from falling ten foot! It wasn't fair. Not when she'd done everything so careful, just exactly what he told her. Now she was in bad trouble. Whenever he got able he was going to beat her silly.

She raced down the road toward Dilby's farm. She wondered if running so far would be a bad thing for a baby if she happened to have one in her now. She hoped she didn't. On account of him was why she hoped it. Having that damn Cal for a father wouldn't be much luck for a baby. Her own father was hard enough, but at least you stood a chance if you stayed shy of him when he was drinking. But that Cal!

She slowed down to save her breath. Never get there at all, she thought, if I drop dead running. That Cal! He was itching to get his hands on her. He had a pure killing look on his face down there in the ditch. She saw it plain. He looked just like that time she came on the porch to hear the tractor man talk.

What a silky voice that tractor man had! Just like a man on the radio. Anybody would've wanted to just sit there and hear him. She made sure she sat clear on the other side of the porch and kept her dress pulled down, and she never said a word. She never did a thing but look at him and listen. Cal didn't even act like he minded, but after the man left—

Suddenly Emmy stopped running. The blood washed away from her face. A terrible idea had caught hold of her. What if Maude Dilby wasn't home! Was she supposed to tell Frank Dilby? Cal never ever let her speak to *any* man. She tried to remember Cal's words. Did he say she could tell Frank? Oh, Lordy! Hadn't he half killed her for just *listening* to that other man?

She turned back. The only thing to do was ask Cal. She wished she'd thought of it sooner, before she got so far. But if she went on and Maude really wasn't there, she'd have a longer piece than this to run back.

When she got to Cal he was fainted again. She scrambled down the ridge and tried to wake him. It seemed like a long time before his eyes opened, and when they did they looked clouded over and stupidlike and he couldn't understand what she was asking.

"Cal, Cal! Can I tell it to Frank if Maude's not home? Can I tell it to Frank?"

Finally he heard her. "Oh, God," he whispered, "tell it to Frank."

She started off again, running as fast as she could because Cal certainly seemed bad off. Pretty soon she had to slow down. Her breathing was hurting. She'd run too much. As soon as she could she'd run again.

She walked slowly, trying to get some strength. For the first time she noticed the sounds in the woods around her. It was strange not to have Cal walking with her and keeping his eye on her. Her head felt weak and buzzy. A sparrow flew up out of the dust ahead and she watched it till it was lost in the trees. Her knees were watery. She had to rest a minute. Then she'd be able to run on to Dilby's.

She sat beside the road listening to the birds. They were awful noisy. They must be getting ready for bed. She stretched her legs out in front of her and tried to quiet her breathing down. A couple of yards away a bird lighted and then swooped right away. Probably scared of her. She saw a flash of bright orange. A daddy robin, she thought.

She closed her eyes, resting, remembering a robin's nest she found once on her way to school. She smiled, thinking of the screechy little birds with their wide-open mouths. The big robin watched over them, all black-eyed and proud, just like those babies were beautiful and bright-feathered instead of all naked and ugly like they really was.

A dog somewhere off in the fields barked loudly and Emmy's eyes flew open. She sucked in her breath and jumped up. She flew down the road. How long was she sitting there? Oh, Lordy!

She ran faster, her long hair streaming out behind her. No more bird sounds now. Over the trees she saw the first pale showing of the moon. Just a tiny bit of darkness. Not dark yet. Still light. Cal might be dying!

She felt strange running alone in the woods. For a

minute she imagined her face was turning into the face
of one of the little animals she used to watch, the ones
with the smart pointy faces—the ones she used to watch
and wonder what they were thinking. She ran harder,
stretching her legs as much as she could.

Her heart began to pound and it occurred to her
suddenly that a person could only run so fast. She slowed
down. She might drop dead herself if she didn't slow
down. That wouldn't help Cal, would it? But a person
could only run so far, and she was near ready to drop
right now. That was for sure.

If she was to faint over by the side of the road there,
nobody might find her till morning, and then what would
happen to Cal? All that running and the fright of seeing
Cal under the ridge there was likely to make anybody go
faint. Especially somebody puny like she was. Cal was
always telling people how puny she was. He always went
around saying how he never would've married her if he'd
known she was going to turn so puny and worthless for
working. Cal always said that.

Emmy felt the buzzy feeling coming back in her
head. She decided to walk over by the edge of the road
just in case she did happen to go faint. Lordy, she was
tired! She rubbed an arm across her damp forehead. It
was queer how her mind kept running back to the time
when her Pop finally forgot about keeping her out of the
woods. Just like it was yesterday, she could remember
that feeling of getting free. It's like getting wings, she
thought, like all of a sudden having wings.

She shivered. It was turning cool. The days might
be getting hot, but not the nights, not yet. Too early in
the spring for that. Chilly night wouldn't be so good for
Cal—not the way he looked. Probably he didn't stand a
chance if she didn't get some help quick.

In the dim light Emmy could see the turning of the
road near the big crippled pine tree. Once you got to the

big pine it wasn't too far off from Dilby's. But just now, right where she was standing, the roadside sheered off. If a person was to fall down right here, nobody would notice. Even if somebody did happen down the road, they wouldn't notice. Not down in that weedy ditch, not until it was light and they came looking.

She could stay still just like the animals did when something was after them. Animals could all do that—just freeze right up, hardly even breathing. They had to save themselves like that. They had a right to do that if something was after them. And wasn't Cal after her every minute of every blessed day? Wasn't he?

Emmy slipped over the edge into the ditch and sat down. Tomorrow when they found her, they would remember how Cal always said she was given to fainting spells. A hundred times he must have said that. But by tomorrow it would be too late for Cal.

This was the 359th "first story" to be published in Ellery Queen's Mystery Magazine . . . *an impressive first story —disturbing, chilling, compelling.*

The author, Mary Louise Downer, is married to Daniel Bush Downer, a producer of industrial and business films. They have four children, all (at the time of this writing) in school, from junior high to postgraduate. Mrs. Downer, a graduate of Pomona College, Claremont, California, has been a reporter and columnist for the Los Angeles Times, *has recently finished a juvenile historical novel, and is now working on an adult mystery novel set in Spain. She and her family spend much of*

*their time, summer and winter, in their mountain cabin
on Lake Arrowhead, yet manage to travel extensively
throughout the United States, Canada, Mexico, Alaska,
and Europe.*

MARY LOUISE DOWNER

After the lights are out

Henry Holdsworthy felt the sweat break out in the palms of his hands as he began to thread the film into the projector, and he was grateful for the concentration it took to get the film aligned just right. With the sweat, the fear inside him began to grow, swelling like mildewed wheat and as rotten and sour-tasting. There was no way he could get out of showing the film; he had resigned himself to that.

From the long couch in front of him came a scream of laughter. "Oh, Milly! You didn't! Honestly, I wouldn't have dared. Would I have dared, George?"

The answer was fervent. "Not bloody likely."

Henry unsteadily poked the end of the film into its slot. His wife, Milly, must have finally finished telling another of her stories about her adventures abroad. He never listened anymore. However, he could see Milly's best friend, Addie Martin, hanging on every word, although she must have heard it all a dozen times before. Addie's husband, George, seemed to have dozed off.

Over the whispers there was another burst of laughter. Henry wondered if Milly was telling her story about swimming on the Riviera and being spied on by a notorious Arabian monarch, who thereafter coveted her for his harem. Or maybe it was the story about that time in Istanbul when she daringly outwitted the white slavers.

In reality, the Arabian monarch had been a turbaned waiter from their hotel on his way home to wife and kiddies, and the white slavers only two bewildered street peddlers trying to sell her a rug.

Addie was still shrieking like a Greek chorus of one. "Milly! You'd be a riot to travel with. Isn't she a riot to travel with, Henry?"

"A riot," Henry answered.

To postpone the moment when the room would be plunged into darkness and the screen would come to life he said, "How about a drink before we start? Addie? George?"

Addie roguishly wagged a bony finger at him. "Oh, I couldn't possibly. After such a *delicious* and different kind of dinner—your dinner was just delicious, Milly, and so *different*. Wasn't it, George?"

George measured off six inches in the air. "Just a short one, Henry. Thanks."

"Oh, you're just terrible, George," Addie shrilled. "Isn't he just terrible, Henry?"

In the butler's pantry Henry poured four fingers of bourbon into a glass and gulped it down. He refilled the glass, added some ice, and taking another deep swig— from the bottle this time—served George his drink. Milly was in the middle of her tale about the time in the islands when she joined the natives in a Tahitian dance. Henry wished he had brought the bottle back with him.

"Something just seemed to come over me—you know how I am," Milly was saying. "All those magnificent brown bodies and the drums and—well, before Henry realized what I was doing, I had kicked off my shoes and was right up there in the middle of everything."

"Oh, Milly! You're too much. Isn't she too much, Henry?"

"Too much," agreed Henry.

"It isn't hard to do, you know." Milly jumped up to demonstrate. "You just shake everything you have just as fast as you can." She winked at George. "It's why natives always look so happy."

"And they always do, too," Addie came in right on cue. "We've noticed how happy natives always look. Haven't we, George?"

"Just another short one, Henry," said George.

It was, of course, after the lights were out that the terror began. Henry sat very still. Waiting. Beside him the machine whirred softly, and across the room the little rectangle of screen flickered and flashed.

Out of the dark came Milly's well-rehearsed narration. "This was the most exciting trip Henry and I have ever taken. Henry had always wanted to go back to New Guinea—he was there during the war, you know." Complacent giggle. "I think he just wanted to see if I could still compete with those natives girls he was always writing about. Right, Henry? Well, I showed him. Wait till you see me with a bone through my nose."

"Oh, Milly," squealed Addie. "You didn't *actually*. George, you don't think she *actually?*"

"Well—" said George.

"Now that's the port of Lae. If you watch closely you can see me getting off the plane—Henry wanted to record my first step on New Guinea soil. There! Did you see? I was standing right there between those two darling pilots. . . . Now that's our room at the hotel. See me waving? The room overlooked the gardens, and the flowers were just gorgeous. See, aren't the flowers gorgeous?"

It had started again. This time Henry pinpointed the

exact moment. As the scarlet and coral splash of flowers appeared on the screen, the room turned cold and was filled with a heavy scent, moist and overpowering, like stepping into a florist shop, or going to a funeral. No one else seemed to notice.

Milly was chattering on. ". . . There I am with the bone through my nose. You get them at the hotel gift shop, you know—"

"She did it! She actually did it! Did you see, George?"

"I see," said George.

". . . And that's our guide, Pieter Van-something-or-other. Isn't he the handsomest thing? And so virile—what I could tell you! I must say he didn't seem to find me unattractive either. Did he, Henry? *Henry.*"

"No, not unattractive," Henry echoed. He kept his eyes fixed on the screen. Repulsive, was more like it. All that simpering and posturing and those fat white knees. Both he and Pieter had drunk a lot that trip.

He tensed his muscles. Right on schedule the air began to hum and vibrate. The walls of the room seemed to shift slightly—nothing he could see, just a feeling that there had been a subtle reorganization of space.

"George, look at that," Addie twittered. "The guide put his arm around Milly. Henry, did you actually let the guide put his arm around Milly?"

"Sometimes," murmured Henry. He wiped his damp hands along his trousers and felt the cold begin to creep upward. He got up and moved to the back of the room. Very carefully he pressed his spine against the wall.

". . . Pieter just couldn't keep his hands off me, poor dear," Milly was saying. "He couldn't do enough for me. He even took me to see the secret ceremony of the Gourd Men. Didn't he, Henry?"

"Dear God," Henry whispered to himself. "That's what he did, all right."

He closed his eyes, remembering. He had paid virile, handsome Pieter $100 to take them to that secret ceremony. Pieter had looked frightened when Henry first suggested it. Then, when he saw the money, he looked frightened and greedy. "Look," Henry had told him. "Every trip I take—same old pictures everyone else gets. I want something different this time. Come on. I'll make it worth your while."

Pieter's eyes glittered and he licked his lips nervously. "But it's taboo." His voice was hoarse. "If we were discovered, and with a woman—" He shuddered. "It means death for a woman."

"I don't intend to take Milly with us, and besides, with my camera we won't have to get too near. I'll use the telescopic lens." He had riffled the wad of bills and laid them in Pieter's lap. "What do you say?"

Of course Pieter had finally agreed, as Henry knew he would; and, as he had feared, Milly refused to be left behind. "A fertility rite," she cried. "Don't be a fool, Henry. I'm going and that's final."

They made their trek into the highlands, a day's march from a tiny village, along trails that were mere threads lacing the forest. They found the ceremonial ring in a clearing in a small valley that was called, Pieter told them, "The-place-on-the-ground-where-the-eye-in-the-sky-watches-the-people-down-below-so-take-no-risks" —or words to that effect. They settled into a strangely fragrant thicket of giant croton about one hundred yards from the clearing where there was a clear view of the fire ring. Pieter absolutely refused to go any closer.

Milly's voice wrenched Henry back to the present. "Addie, George. Watch closely, everyone. The ceremony is about to start. A fertility rite, Pieter said."

"A fertility rite," Addie whispered. "Did you hear that, George? Milly actually saw a fertility rite."

"I heard," said George.

Henry stared at the screen. The Gourd Men, decked out in paint and cockatoo feathers appeared just as he had seen them that day in the hidden valley. The circle of fire burned orange and red, burnishing the Gourd Men's spears and their glistening brown bodies as they danced. . . .

After they returned to the village Henry had bought one of those spears—bought it from a man with crafty eyes who followed him around until Henry paid the outrageous price just to get rid of him. Henry had never been one for souvenirs, but Milly was delighted—said it was a conversation piece and hung it over the fireplace when they returned home. It gleamed at him now in the light from the flickering screen.

". . . now these are the closeups. Aren't they exciting? Look at that old fellow. It's as if you could reach right out and touch him."

With that Henry was plunged deep in his nightmare. He pressed his back hard against the wall as the room began to revolve. Slowly at first—it was always the same; but he knew the room would spin faster and faster until—until what? So far the film had always ended before the chaos overwhelmed him. But each time the uncanny sensations became stronger. . . .

Amazingly, the first time he had shown the film to Milly's mother and assorted relatives, he had noticed nothing unusual. Utterly engrossed in the color and barbaric costuming, elated that at last he had something truly different—something without Milly hogging the foreground —he had accepted congratulations on his technical skill and daring.

Just as he was falling asleep that night he suddenly remembered that Milly's mother had said, "Isn't our little girl the bravest thing? If you had gotten any closer, they would surely have seen you." And Milly had answered, "Oh, don't be silly, Mother. The telescopic lens makes it look closer than it really was." Lying there in bed, a wave of nameless fear washed over him.

Milly didn't know. There had been no telescopic lens. In his eagerness, that day in the New Guinea highlands, he had forgotten to take the lens and had been ashamed to confess his stupidity. He sat up. So what did they mean about closeups?

Trembling, he had gone back to the living room and begun to run the film once again. This was the time he noted the sudden chill that seemed to start along the floor around his naked ankles, and how the scent of flowers pervaded the room. But, since he was fresh from a warm bed and since Milly's mother, an avid gardener, had set bouquets of homegrown flowers all over the house, it seemed only natural. Then.

He remembered how he had pulled his bathrobe closer when the Gourd Men appeared on the screen. Round and round they shuffled, single file, eyes straight ahead, brandishing their spears in random, jerky movements. They looked little and faraway, just as he had photographed them. He began to relax.

Then, to his horror, he saw the change begin. He felt the walls stir, felt a sensation of vertigo as the room began to turn about him. Slowly, slowly, the figures on the screen began to enlarge. It was as if the space between them and Henry had begun to dissolve. That was the only way to describe it. The foreground simply melted away, and he and the dancers were drawn irresistibly closer and closer together.

Reason deserted him, and he sat frozen until the film reached the end, and the slapping of the celluloid against the reel roused him. Too stunned to move, he set about convincing himself that it had been some trick of lighting, some distortion of the atmosphere like a mirage. That was it, he told himself. A mirage.

The next showing of the film was a few nights later to Milly's bridge club. To a woman they sighed and giggled at her descriptions of Pieter's virility. And once again Henry suddenly became conscious of the cold, of the scent of flowers. Only this time there were no flowers, and the fireplace spewed warmth. Then, as the room began to wheel, he realized something new was happening.

In the first place, the enlargement of the dancers occurred almost immediately. But that was only a part. One of the Gourd Men, an old chief whose sinewy arms were corded with muscle under his dark skin, whose nose and ears were pierced with bone, suddenly swung his heavy head as he passed through the picture. It was as if he had glimpsed something from the corner of his eye and was turning to look.

"Milly," Henry said, after the bridge-club girls had departed, "perhaps we shouldn't be showing this film. After all, it was a secret ceremony and we had no right—"

"Don't be a fool, Henry," she said. "It's the best film we have. You're just jealous of Pieter. That's it, isn't it?"

In spite of Milly, Henry knew he had to do something. He cut those frames of the old chief out of the film, splicing the gap smoothly. But it was no use.

During the next showing to a group of neighbors Henry saw a hooded medicine man, who had followed on the heels of the now eliminated chief, turn to stare right into the camera. The glittering eyes seemed to search out and find Henry as he sat cowering in the dark.

It was then Henry realized the entire film would have to be destroyed. But when he gathered up his equipment after their neighbors had left, he discovered the can containing the New Guinea film was missing. He began a frantic search.

"For heaven's sakes," Milly hissed. "What's your problem? I loaned the film to Bernice to show her brother —you weren't the only one in New Guinea during the war, you know. She's going to give it back to Addie and George to bring with them when they come here for dinner tomorrow night so we can show it to them." She glared at him with narrowed eyes. "You've been drinking again. I've told you over and over how I feel about your drinking."

"I may even get drunk," said Henry.

But he hadn't. He paced the floor all that long sleepless night. And today had seemed endless. All day he had tried desperately to retrieve the film. At the Martins' no one had answered his phone calls; no one had been home when he went by the house.

This evening he had arranged to be at the door when the Martins arrived, but Milly snatched the can of film from his hands. "I'll take charge of that," she said. "Henry has some funny idea that we shouldn't show this film anymore."

Feeling the coldness of their eyes, Henry had sighed. "It's all right. I'll show it. . . ."

Suddenly Henry was jerked from his brooding by the awareness that the screen was being flooded with a pulsing intensity of color. The action was speeding up.

Henry clung to the wall, flattening himself against its hard reality. He felt himself the center of a vortex. The humming in his ears grew louder, and above the humming there emerged a sound of chanting. Faster and faster the circling dancers whirled until they merged in a blurring of light.

Out of the blur Henry saw a figure struggle to take form. As if feeding on the distorted radiance, the figure seemed to gather strength. It loomed larger and larger. It began to detach itself from the screen. Henry saw it take a step out into the room. It raised its arm. A spear glittered.

"Look out!" yelled Henry, and lunged forward.

The jury admitted it was a hard case to decide, and the final verdict—that Milly Holdsworthy and Addie Martin had been stabbed to death by an unknown assailant—may always be in doubt.

The jury did agree that robbery must have been the motive, for the room was ransacked, and it was a miracle that both husbands had survived the vicious attack.

It was only natural that Henry and George were the prime suspects, at first. But they were unshakable in their corroboration of each other's innocence.

Besides, the fingerprints on the bloody spear that killed Milly and Addie belonged to neither Henry nor George.

It is more than ten years since we last offered you a Michael Innes story about Inspector Appleby (more recently the Commissioner of Metropolitan Police, and still more recently, Sir John Appleby). Surely that has been much too long a time, and we are delighted to remedy, however belatedly, this unintended neglect.

In "Comedy of Discomfiture" the now-retired Sir John Appleby finds himself a member of a bachelor-type fishing party. His companions are a choice lot: a successful playwright whose fame is declining, his disloyal publisher, a venomous drama critic, and a tycoon with more than a fondness for the ladies.

Now, Appleby liked fishing, but he liked "odd situations" even more—and this "fishing murder" was an odd situation indeed. As in one of the playwright's own dramas, here are comedy and tragedy, the two faces of the theater—and the two faces of Michael Innes' sophisticated style.

MICHAEL INNES

Comedy of discomfiture

In Scotland, trout fishing, almost as much as deer stalking and grouse shooting, is an amusement for wealthy men. Appleby was not particularly wealthy. From a modest station he had risen to be London's Commissioner of Metropolitan Police—a mouthful which his children, accurately enough, had turned into better and briefer English as Top Cop.

Top Cop's job turning out, predictably, to be more administrative than was at all enlivening, Appleby had retired from it earlier than need be, and now lived as an unassuming country gentleman on a small estate, the property of his wife, in the south of England. This, very happily, had proved not incompatible with getting into odd situations. As a country gentleman he also, of course, liked fishing.

So he had accepted Vivarini's invitation to bring a rod to Dunwinnie, although he didn't really know the celebrated playwright particularly well. Now here he was, cheek by jowl with four other piscatory enthusiasts in what had once been a crofter's cottage. Crofters, and all such humbly independent tillers of the soil, had almost vanished from this part of the Scottish highlands. Whether in small patches or in large, the region had been turned into holiday terrain for rich men.

Appleby didn't brood on this. At least the hunting boxes and shooting lodges were, like everything else, thin on the ground. From the cottage one saw only the river— a brawling flood interspersed with still-seeming pools, brown from the peat and with trout enough—with an abandoned lambing hut on its farther bank, and then the moorland that stretched away to the remote line of the Grampians. Dr. Johnson, Appleby remembered, had once surveyed this scene and disliked it. "A wide extent of hopeless sterility," he had written down. "Quickened only with one sullen power of useless vegetation." That had been the heather.

There was a brushing sound in the heather now. Appleby looked up from his task of cleaning fish for supper and saw that his host was returning. Vivarini had been the last to leave the water. He seemed to be a keen angler. In his stained waders, his Balmoral bonnet festooned with dry flies, and with his respectably battered old creel, he certainly looked the part. But perhaps the playwright had enough of the actor in him for that. Snobbery and expensive rural diversions are inextricably tied up together in Britain, and in pursuit of some elusive social status men will go fox hunting who in their hearts are terrified at the sight of a horse. Perhaps Vivarini with his costly stretch of trout stream was a little like that.

Very rightly, Appleby felt mean at harboring this thought, particularly as Vivarini looked so far from well. Even in the twilight now falling like an elfin gossamer over these haunted lands one could distinguish that about the man. Perhaps it was simply that he was under some sort of nervous strain. Appleby knew nothing about the playwright's London way of life, but there could well be things he wanted to get away from. A setup like this at Dunwinnie—a small all-male society gathered for a secluded holiday on a bachelor basis—might well have been planned as wholesome relief by a man rather too much involved in something altogether different.

"Cloud coming up," Vivarini said, "and that breeze from the west stiffening. Makes casting tricky. I decided to stay with Black Gnat, by the way." He indicated the fly still on the end of his line. "A mistake, probably. Not sultry enough, eh?"

Clifford Childrey, ensconced with a three-day-old copy of the *Scotsman* on a bench beside the cottage door, glanced up—not at Vivarini but at Appleby—and then resumed his reading. He was Vivarini's publisher. A large and ruddy outdoors man, he had no need whatever to look a part.

"You deserve a drink, Vivarini," Appleby said.

"Not so much as you do, sweating away as cook. I'll see to it. Sherry, I suppose? And you, Cliff?"

"Sherry." Childrey momentarily lowered his newspaper. "Don't know about the other two. They've gone downstream to swim."

"Right. I do like this American make." Vivarini had leaned his rod against the cottage's low thatched roof. "No more than five ounces to the six feet. Flog the water all day with it."

"Umph." This response came from behind the *Scotsman*, which had been raised again. But the *Scotsman* was tossed to the ground when Vivarini had entered the cottage.

"No need to be supercilious," Appleby said.

"I've been nothing of the kind."

Appleby was amused. "If 'umph' isn't supercilious, I don't know what is."

"Well, well—Freddie Vivarini and I have been chums for a long time." Childrey chuckled comfortably. "A damned odd lot writers are, Appleby. I've spent my life trying to do business with them. Novelists are the worst, of course, but dramatists run them a close second. Always getting things up and trying out roles. What they call *personas*, I suppose. Thingamies, really. Chimeras."

"You mean chameleons."

"That's right. No reliable personal identity. Shelley said something about it. Right up his own street."

"Keats. You think our host is playing at being a sportsman?"

"Oh, at that and lots of other things. What he's run on all his life has been folding up on him. Unsuccessful literary man."

"Unsuccessful?"

"Of course he's made a fortune. But that's what he's taken to calling himself. You're meant to regard it ironically. Uneasy joke, all the same." Childrey checked himself and got to his feet, perhaps aware of talking too casually about his host. "I'll start that grill for you," he said. "I see you'll need it soon."

As if in one of Vivarini's own neat plays, Childrey's exit line brought the subject of his late remarks promptly onstage again. Vivarini was bearing glasses and a bottle which, even in the gloaming, could be seen as lightly frosted. The cottage was not wholly comfortless. Warmth was laid on for chilly evenings, and there was hot water and a refrigerator and a compendious affair for cooking any way you liked, all served by a few cylinders of butane trundled across the moor on a vehicle like a young tank.

Not that their actual culinary regime wasn't simple enough. Elderly Englishmen of the sort gathered at Dunwinnie rather enjoy pretending to be public schoolboys still, toasting crumpets or bloaters before a study fire. Of

course there are limits, and when it is a matter of a glass
of dry sherry or opening a bottle of hock, they don't expect the stuff to reach their palate other than at the temperature it should.

Nor do they care to couch in straw. Appleby was just
reflecting that the cottage's bunks had certainly come
from an expensive shop when he became aware that his
host, uncorked bottle in hand, was laughing cheerfully.

"I heard the old ruffian," Vivarini said. "Trying out
roles, indeed! Well, what if I am?"

"What, indeed? I myself shall remain grateful to you.
This is a delightful spot."

"My dear Appleby, how nice of you to say so. But I
do enjoy fishing, as a matter of fact. And—do you know?—
as far as renting the cottage and this stretch of river goes,
it was actually one of these chaps who egged me on. Positively ran me into it! But I won't say which." Vivarini was
laughing again—although with the effect, Appleby thought,
of a man not wholly at ease. "No names, no pack drill. Ah,
here come Mervyn and Ralph."

Appleby couldn't afterward remember—not even with
a dead body to prompt him—who at the supper table had
introduced the topic of crime. Perhaps it had been Ralph
Halberd, since Halberd was one of that not inconsiderable
number of millionaires to have suffered the theft of some
enormously valuable pictures. This might have given Halberd an interest at least in burglars, although his line—
besides owning shipping lines and luxury hotels—was a
large if capricious patronage of artists expressing themselves in mediums more harmless than thermal lances and
gelignite.

Perhaps it had been Mervyn Gryde, who wrote theatrical notices for newspapers, thus being dignified with
the title of "drama critic" as a result; and the kind of
plays he seemed chiefly to favor were, to Appleby's mind,

so full of violence and depravity that crime might be supposed his natural element.

Or it might have been Vivarini himself. Certainly it had been he who, exercising a host's authority, had insisted on Appleby's recounting his own part in certain criminal *causes célèbres*. But it had been left to Childrey, toward the end of the evening, to insist with a certain flamboyance on toasting the retired Metropolitan commissioner as the finest detective intelligence in Britain. The hock, Appleby thought, was a great deal too good for the toast; it had in fact been Halberd's contribution to the housekeeping and was quite superb. But he acknowledged the compliment in due form, and not long afterward the company decided to go to bed.

Rather to his surprise, Appleby found himself obscurely relieved that the day was over. Everyone had been amiable enough. But had something been stirring beneath the talk, the relaxed gestures, the small companionable-seeming silences?

As he dropped to sleep, Appleby found himself thinking of the deep still pools into which the Dunwinnie tumbled here and there on its hurrying and sparkling scramble toward the sea. Beneath those calm surfaces, whose only movement seemed to be the lovely concentric ripples from a rising trout, a strong current flowed. . . .

He had a nightmare, a thing unusual for him. Perhaps it was occasioned by one of the yarns he had been inveigled into telling at the supper table of his early and sometimes perilous days in the C.I.D. In his dream he had been pursuing gunmen down dark narrow corridors—and suddenly it had been the gunmen who were pursuing him. They caught him and tied him up. And then the chief gunman had advanced on him with a long whip and cracked it within an inch of his face. This was so unpleasant that Appleby, in his nightmare, told himself that here

was a nightmare from which he had better wake up. So he
woke up—not much perturbed, but taking thought, as one
does, to remain awake until the same disagreeable situation was unlikely to be waiting for him.

The wind had risen and its murmur had joined the
river's murmur, but inside the cottage there wasn't a
sound. The single-story building had been remodeled for
its present purpose, and now consisted, like an ill-propor-
tioned sandwich, of a large living room in the middle,
with a very small bedroom at each end. The bedrooms
contained little more than two bunks set one above the
other. Childrey and Halberd shared one of these cabinlike
places, and Appleby and Vivarini the other. Gryde slept
on a cot in the living room. These dispositions had been
arrived at, whimsically, by drawing lots.

Appleby turned over cautiously, so as not to disturb
Vivarini beneath him. Vivarini didn't stir. And Appleby
suddenly knew he wasn't there. It was a simple matter of
highly developed auditory alertness. Nobody was breathing, however lightly, in the bunk below.

The discovery ought not to have been worth a
thought. A wakeful Vivarini might have elected for a
breath of moorland air. Or he might have been prompted
to go to the modest structure, some twenty yards from
the cottage, known as the jakes. Despite these reflections,
Appleby slipped quietly down from his bunk.

It was dark, then suddenly not dark, then dark again.
But nobody had flashed a light. Outside, the sky must be
a huddle of moving clouds, with a moon near the full
sometimes breaking through. Vivarini's bunk was indeed
unoccupied.

Appleby picked up a flashlight and went into the
living room. Gryde seemed sound asleep—a little dark
man, Appleby passingly told himself, coiled up like a
snake. The door of the farther bedroom was closed, but
the door giving direct on the moor was open. Appleby

stepped outside, switching off the flashlight as he did so. He now knew why he was behaving in this way—like an alarmed nursemaid, he thought. It was because of what had happened in his dream.

He glanced up at the clouds, and in the same moment the moon again came serenely through. The Dunwinnie rose into visibility before him, like a sudden outpouring of hoarded silver on dark cloth. On the other bank the lambing hut with its squat square chimney suggested some small humped creature with head warily erect. And something was moving there.

Momentarily Appleby saw this as a human figure slipping out of the door. Then he saw that it was only the door itself, swinging gently on its primitive wooden pivot. But no sound came from across the softly chattering flood, no sound that could have transformed itself into another sound in Appleby's dream.

There were stepping stones here, practicable enough for an active man. But they faded into darkness as Appleby looked; the moon had disappeared again. He had to switch on the flashlight or risk a ducking. He risked the ducking, although he could scarcely have told himself why he disliked the idea of being seen. When he reached the hut he reconnoitered the ground in front of it with a brief flicker close to the earth.

He felt for the door and pushed it fully open; it had been firmly shut the evening before, he remembered, with an old drill pin through the latch. Now he was looking into deep darkness indeed. The hut was no more than a square stone box with a slate roof; it had a fireplace more for the needs of the ewes and lambs than their shepherd; and in one wall—he couldn't recollect which—there was a window which had been boarded up. Treading softly, he moved through the door and listened.

No sound. No glimmer of light. Nothing to alert a

single sense—unless it was a faint smell of old straw, the ghost of a faint smell of carbolic, of tar. Then suddenly, and straight in front of him at floor level, there was an illusive suggestion of light. All but imperceptibly the small glow grew; it was as if a stage electrician were operating a rheostat with infinite care. It grew to an oblong, with darkness as its frame. And now within the frame there was a picture. It was the portrait of Vivarini—but something had happened to his forehead. It was Vivarini himself.

Appleby was on his knees, his ear to the man's chest, his fingers exploring through a sports jacket, a pajama coat. His face close to the still face, he flashed his flashlight into unclosing eyes, saw uncontracting pupils. He turned his head, gazed upward, and was looking at a square of dimly luminous cloud. Nothing more than the moon's reflected light filtering down the chimney had produced that moment of hideous melodrama. Vivarini himself at his typewriter, or pacing his study while dictating to his secretary, couldn't have done better. It was backward into the rude fireplace that Vivarini had crashed, a bullet in his brain. And hence the crack of that ugly whip in the other dimension of a dream. . . .

Twenty minutes passed before Appleby reentered the cottage. Arrived there, he didn't waste time. He gave Gryde a rough shake and rapped smartly on the closed bedroom door. Within seconds his three fellow-guests were around him, huddled in dressing gowns, dazed and blinking.

"Vivarini is dead," Appleby said quietly. "In the lambing hut. Shot through the head."

"My God—so he meant it!" This exclamation was Ralph Halberd's, and it was followed by a small silence.

"One of us," Appleby went on, apparently unheeding,

"must get down to Balloch and telephone for a doctor and the police. But something a shade awkward comes first."

"Awkward?" It was Mervyn Gryde who repeated the word, and his voice had turned sharp.

"Well, yes. Let me explain. Or, rather, let me take up what Halberd has just said." Appleby turned to the millionaire. " '*My God—so he meant it!*' Just what made you say that?"

"Because he told me. He confided in me. It was a fearful shock." In the cold light of a hissing gas lamp, Halberd, who normally carried around with him an air as of imposing board rooms, looked uncertain and perplexed. "On Tuesday—the day we arrived. It was because I happened to see him unpack this thing and shove it under his shirts in that drawer over there. A pistol. It looked almost like a toy."

"Vivarini said he was going to kill himself with it?"

"Not that, exactly. Only that he had thoughts of it and couldn't bring himself not to carry the weapon around with him."

"Did he give any reason?"

"No. It seemed to be implied that he was feeling discouraged. His plays—all those Comedies of Discomfiture, as he called them—are a bit outmoded, wouldn't you say?"

"Perhaps. But, Halberd, did you take any steps? Even mention this to any of the rest of us?"

"I wish to God I had. But I thought he was putting on an act." The patron's indulgent scorn for the artist sounded for a moment in Halberd's tones. "That sort of fellow is always dramatizing himself. And people don't often kill themselves just because they're feeling discouraged."

"That's certainly true. There are psychologists who maintain that suicide never happens except on top of a clinically recognizable depressive state. An exaggeration, perhaps, but no more than that. But here's my point. Whatever Vivarini said to you, Halberd, he can't have made away with himself. I found no weapon in that hut."

There was a long silence.

"That's just according to one witness—yourself—who was the first man on the scene." Gryde's voice was sharper still. And with a curiously reptilian effect his tongue flicked out over dry lips.

"Exactly. You take my point." Appleby smiled grimly. "Anybody can tell lies. But let's see if there's a revolver under those shirts now."

Watched by the others, Appleby made a brief rummage. No weapon was revealed.

"I may have killed him," Halberd said slowly. "And made up a stupid story about suicide, which the facts disprove."

"Certainly you may have." Appleby might have been discussing a hand at bridge. "But you're not going to be the only suspect."

"Obviously not." Childrey spoke for the first time. The least agitated of Appleby's companions, he might have been a rosy infant doubly flushed from sleep. "Nor are we—the four of us here—characters in a locked-room mystery. Why the lambing hut? Why did Vivarini go over there secretly in the night? To meet somebody unknown to us, one may suppose—and somebody who turned out not to care for him."

"It might still have been one of us he went to meet," Appleby said. "But may I come back to the business of going for help? I'm thinking of the weapon. If one of us killed Vivarini, he may then have had enough time to get quite a distance across the moor and back for the purpose of hiding the gun where no search will ever find it. On the other hand, one of us may have it on his person, or in a suitcase, at this moment. Whichever of us goes for help must certainly be searched first. Or perhaps all of us. Do you agree? . . . Good. I'll search each of you in turn—over there in that bedroom—and one of you can search me."

"I'll come first," Childrey said easily. "But behind that closed door. Less embarrassing, eh?"

Appleby's was a very rapid frisking. "By the way," he asked at the end of it, "have you any notion how this fishing party originated? You didn't by any chance suggest it to Vivarini, or in any way put him up to it?"

"Lord, no! Came as a complete surprise to me. We'd been on bad terms, as a matter of fact."

"I'm sorry to hear it. Send in Halberd."

Five minutes later they were all in the living room again. In another ten minutes the whole place had been searched.

"No gun," Appleby said. "But another lie—or the appearance of it. Vivarini told me one of you had egged him on to organize this little fishing party. But each of you has denied it."

"All according to you," Gryde said.

"Yes, indeed. I'm grateful to you for so steadily reminding me. And now, who goes to telephone? It's at least five miles. I suggest we draw lots."

"No. I'm going." It was Childrey who spoke. "Trekking over the moors in darkness is my sort of thing. I'll just get into trousers and a jacket."

"The cunning criminal makes good his escape," Gryde said. "But it's all the same to me." He turned to Appleby. "While Cliff is louping over the heather—I believe that's the correct Scotch word—I suggest we open a bottle of whiskey and have a nice friendly chat."

It didn't prove at all friendly. Childrey's, it struck Appleby, had been the genuinely genial presence in the fishing party; now, when he had gone off with long strides through a darkness with which the moon had ceased to struggle, the atmosphere in the cottage deteriorated sharply.

"Odd that Vivarini should have made *you* that confidence, Ralph." Gryde said this after the whiskey bottle had clinked for a second time against his glass. "And odd that he asked you here. Wanted to make it up with you, I suppose. Tycoons make ugly enemies."

"What the devil do you mean, Gryde?" Halberd had sat bolt upright.

"And it's going to be awkward for that girl. He'd miscalculated, hadn't he? Thought she was just one of your notorious harem, no doubt, and that you wouldn't give a damn. Actually, you were ludicrously in love with her. Not unusual, once a man has reached the age of senile infatuation. Everybody was talking about it, you know. And I'm surprised you agreed to come here."

"One might be surprised that that cheerful idiot Childrey agreed to come." Halberd had controlled himself with an effort in face of Gryde's sudden and astonishing assault. "He told me that *he* had been on poor terms with Freddie. And, for that matter, what about *you*, Mervyn? I believe—"

"I don't filch other men's trollops."

"You certainly don't. What you'd filch—"

"One moment." Appleby had set down his glass—and he plainly didn't mean to take it up again. "If we're to have this sort of thing—and experience tells me it may be inevitable—it had better be with *some* scrap of decency. No venom, please."

"Venom is Mervyn Gryde's middle name." Halberd reached for the bottle, but glanced at Appleby and thought better of it. "Read the stuff he writes about any play in which the *dramatis personae* aren't a bunch of sewer rats. Read some of the things he's recently said about Freddie. He had his knife in Freddie. You'd suppose some hideous private grudge." Halberd turned directly to the drama critic. "How you can have had the gall to accept an invitation from the poor devil beats me, Snaky Merv. That's what they called him at Cambridge long ago, you know." This had the character of an aside to Appleby. "Snaky Mervyn Gryde."

"I'm afraid," Appleby said dryly, "that I can't contribute much to these amiable exchanges. I don't know a great deal about our late host. But of course—as you, Gryde, will be quick to point out—you have only my word for it. What I do see is that this party is revealing itself as having been organized by way of sinking differences and making friends again. And it hasn't had much luck. One result has been that, in your two selves, it brought here a couple of men with an undefined degree of animus against Vivarini. Perhaps Childrey is a third. Can either of you explain what Childrey meant by telling me he'd been on bad terms with Vivarini?"

"I can, because Freddie told me. Not that you'll believe me." Gryde, having apparently seen danger in too much whiskey, was chain-smoking nervously, so that he was like some small dark devil risen from a nether world amid mephitic vapors. "Childrey had refused to do a collected edition of Freddie's plays. And Freddie had found out it was because he was planning something of the sort for a rival playwright. Freddie was absolutely furious."

"I can certainly believe that. But it's scarcely a reason why Childrey should murder Vivarini. Rather the other way about."

"True enough." Gryde laughed shrilly. "But Freddie believed he was on the verge of exposing Childrey in some disreputable sharp practice about it all. He said he could wreck his good name as a publisher, and that he meant to do it."

"And had meantime invited him to this friendly party? It's an uncommonly odd tale."

"I said you wouldn't believe me."

"On the contrary." Appleby's smile was bleak. "I'm

inclined to believe that the dead man told you just what you say he did."

"Thank you very much." It wasn't without looking disconcerted that Gryde said this. "And where the deuce do we go from here?"

"Exactly!" Halberd had gotten up and was restlessly pacing the room to the sound of a flip-flap of bedroom slippers. "Where the deuce—and all the damned to boot!"

"We wait for the local police," Appleby said quietly. "No doubt they will clear the matter up."

"Stuff and nonsense!" There was sudden violence in Halberd's voice. "And I don't see this as an occasion for superior Scotland Yard irony, Appleby. The rotten business is up to you."

"Well, yes. And I'm sorry about the irony. As a matter of fact, I rather agree with you. And I can't complain. You have both been most communicative—about yourselves, and about each other, and about Childrey. Childrey, too, had made his little spontaneous contribution. I really confront an *embarras de richesses,* so far as significant information goes. You have labored as one man, I might say, to give it to me."

"And just what do you mean by that?" Gryde asked sharply.

"Perhaps very little." Appleby yawned unashamedly. "One tends to talk at random in the small hours, wouldn't you say?" He stood up and walked to the open door of the cottage. "Lights in the lambing hut," he said. "Childrey has made uncommonly good time. And here he is."

"And here you are." Clifford Childrey nearly echoed Appleby's words as he stood in the doorway. "I was beginning to think I'd dreamed up the whole lot of you. Too fantastic—this affair."

"Is that," Halberd asked, "what the doctor and the local copper are saying?"

"I don't know about the copper. He's an experienced

sergeant, settling in to a thorough search, and not saying much meanwhile. As for the sawbones, he's the nice old family-doctor type. Agrees, of course, that the poor devil has been stone-dead for at least a couple of hours. Seems to be wondering whether he was dead first and dragged into the hut second. Suspects something rigged, you might say. Position of the body, and so forth. Appleby, what do you say to that?"

"I certainly felt an element of the theatrical to be present. But other things were present, too."

"Clues, do you mean?"

"Clues? Oh, yes—several. Enough, in fact, to admit only one solution to the mystery."

Sir John Appleby glanced from one to another of three dumfounded faces, as if surprised that his announcement had occasioned any effect at all.

"As it happens," he said, "there is rather a good reason why the local sergeant won't find them—the clues, that's to say. But, as he is going to spend some time in the hunt, I propose to while away a quarter of an hour by telling you about them. Do you agree?"

"You'll have your say, I think, whether we agree or not." Halberd had sat down heavily. "So go on."

"Thank you. But, first, I'd like to ask you something. Does it strike you as at all odd that the three of you—each, apparently, with a rather large dislike of Vivarini—should have accepted his invitation to come here in this particular week?"

"He took a lot of trouble to arrange it," Gryde said. Gryde's voice had gone from high-pitched to husky. "Dates, and so forth."

"And there was this let-bygones-be-bygones slant to it." Perhaps because his night tramp had been exhausting, Childrey might have been described as almost pale.

"Just that," Halberd said. "Wouldn't have been decent to refuse. Rum sort of coincidence, all the same—the particular lot of us."

"Coincidence?" Appleby said. "The word is certainly worth holding onto. Vivarini, incidentally, was holding onto something. Literally so, I mean. I removed that something from his left hand, and I have it in my pocket now. I don't intend to be mysterious about it. It was the cord of the silk dressing gown that Gryde is wearing at this moment."

"That's another of your filthy lies!" Before uttering this, Gryde had clutched grotesquely at his middle. Even as he did so, Appleby had produced the missing object and placed it quietly on the table.

"Making a bit free with the evidence, aren't you?" Childrey asked. He might have spoken out of a benevolent wish to give Gryde a moment in which to recover himself.

"Perhaps I am." Appleby offered this piece of innocence with perfect gravity. "As a matter of fact, I've done rather the same thing with what appears to be property—or the remains of property—of your own, my dear Childrey. If photostatic copies of papers with your firm's letterhead are to be regarded as your property, that's to say. You remember the little place we made to boil a kettle, down by the river, the other afternoon? I discovered that a small file of such papers had been burned there. And no time ago at all, I could still blow a spark out of them. Might they conceivably have been awkward, even compromising, documents that Vivarini had managed to get copies of—fatally for him, as it has turned out?"

"It's true about that collected edition," Childrey said abruptly. "I declined to do it, simply because there wouldn't be anything like an adequate market for it. It is untrue that I behaved improperly. And the notion of my killing Vivarini in order to recover and destroy—"

"But there's something more." Appleby had raised a hand in a civil request for silence. "Just to the side of the door of the lambing hut there happens to be a patch of caked mud. The first thing I found was a footprint in it. Not of a shoe, but of a bedroom slipper—with a soft rubber sole which carries a diamond-shaped maker's device on the instep. Yes, Halberd, you are quite right. You are wearing that slipper now."

"Well," Gryde said maliciously, "that's something the sergeant *will* find."

"Actually, I'm afraid not." Appleby looked properly conscience-stricken. "I was rather clumsy, I'm afraid. I happened to tread all over the thing."

"Can we have some explanation of all this madness— including your own totally irresponsible conduct?" It had been after a moment of stupefaction that Gryde had put this to Appleby.

"Why, certainly. Each of you had a motive for killing Vivarini—or at least you can severally think up motives with which to confront one another. And in the case of each of you we now have a clue—a real damning mystery-story clue. There is a fairly simple explanation, is there not? One of you killed Vivarini, then deliberately planted two clues pointing to the other two of you. If only one of these clues was noticed, there would be one suspect; if both, there would be an indication that two of you had been in collusion. But in addition to planting those two clues *deliberately*, the murderer also dropped one, pointing to himself, *inadvertently*. Would you agree"—and Appleby glanced from one to another of his companions— "that we now have an explanation of the observed facts?"

"A singularly rubbishy one," Childrey said robustly.

"Very well, let me try again." Appleby paused—and when he resumed speaking it was almost as if a current of icy air had begun to blow through the cottage. "There *was* collusion—all three of you. And so incompetent have you been in your evil courses that you have all three made first-class errors. Childrey failed completely to destroy the papers he had managed to recover, and Gryde and Halberd both left physical traces of their presence in the lambing hut. Will that do?"

"My dear Appleby, I fear you have a poor opinion of us." Sweat was pouring down Gryde's face, but he managed to utter this with an air of mild mockery. "Should we be *quite* so inept? And there's something you just haven't accounted for: your own damnably odd conduct."

"Do you know, I'd call that right in the target area? Although I'd say it was not so much a matter of my conduct as of my mere presence." With an air of conscious relaxation Appleby began to fill his pipe. "We were talking about coincidence. Well, the really implausible coincidence was *my* being here. Don't you see? I was *meant* to be here. Vivarini wanted me here—and that even though he and I were no more than casual acquaintances. That was the first thing in my head when I found him dead. And it led me straight to the truth."

"The truth!" There was a dark flush on Halberd's face. "You mean to say you know the *truth*, and you've been entertaining us with all this damned rubbish?"

"I certainly know the truth."

"May we be favored," Gryde almost growled, "with some notion of when you arrived at it?"

"Oh, almost at once. Before I came in to tell you that Vivarini had been shot. First I *thought* for a few minutes, you know. It's always the advisable thing to do. And then I went to have a look at the gas cylinders. And that settled it."

"Vivarini," Appleby said, "didn't like any of you. You'd refused to publish him as a classic, you'd reviewed him waspishly, you'd been in a mess with him about a girl. But what he really resented was being treated as outmoded. His so-called Comedy of Discomfiture—you all regarded it as old hat. Well, he decided to treat you to a whiff of that Comedy of Discomfiture.

"After all," Appleby continued blandly and with apparent inconsequence, "I was his guest, you know. I owed him something. It would have been a shame to knock that Comedy of Discomfiture too rapidly on the head."

"The man was a devil," Gryde said. "And you're a devil, too."

"No, no—Vivarini wasn't really an evil man. He had me here so that there would be a sporting chance of giving you all no more than a bad half hour."

"Three hours." Childrey had glanced at his watch.

"Very well. And I've no doubt that he'd taken other measures. A letter on its way to Australia by surface mail, perhaps, and then due to come back the same way. At the worst you'd have had no more than a few months in jail."

"Go on," Halberd said grimly.

"There's very little to tell, really. He spread a few useful lies: that one of you had egged him on to arrange this fishing party; that he was nurturing something between thoughts and intentions of suicide—although that was *not* a lie; that he had evidence of some discreditable sharp practice on Childrey's part. Then, similarly, he prepared his few useful clues: making that footprint, filching the cord from Gryde's dressing gown, making his little imperfectly burned heap of old business letters. After that, he had just one more thing to prepare."

"You mean to tell us," Halberd said, "that he killed himself just for the fun of playing us a rotten trick?"

"Certainly. It was to be his final masterpiece in the Comedy of Discomfiture."

"But surely—"

"My dear Halberd, didn't you notice he was a sick

man? It's my guess that he was very sick indeed—with no more than months, or perhaps weeks, to live."

"My God—the poor devil! Ending his days with a revolting piece of malice." Halberd frowned. "What was that you said about gas cylinders?"

"There are three stored at the back of the cottage. Two contain butane, all right, but the third contains hydrogen. And all he needed apart from that was a fair-sized child's balloon—just not too big to go up that chimney. Plenty of lift in it to float away a very small gun. With this west wind blowing, it must be over the North Sea by now. So you see why he had to die with his head in the fireplace—and why the doctor is puzzling over the odd position of the body."

"The sergeant of police," Gryde said, "isn't puzzling over that footprint. Because you trampled it out of existence."

There was a long silence while three exhausted fishermen stared at a retired Commissioner of Metropolitan Police.

"It will be thought," Appleby said, "that Vivarini was shot by some professional criminal who had an eye on our wallets and who knew he had major charges to face if he was apprehended. Something like that. The police don't always end up with an arrest, but they never fail to end up with a theory of the crime."

"Is it going to be safe?" Gryde asked.

"Fairly safe, I'd suppose." For the first time since his arrival at Dunwinnie there was a hint of contempt in Appleby's voice. "But safe or not, I judge it decent that this particular Comedy of Discomfiture of Frederick Vivarini's shall never be played before a larger audience than it has enjoyed tonight."

"The bitter years behind, the exciting years ahead . . ."

DANA LYON

The bitter years

The woman finished cleaning up the sink from her solitary meal—the chicken breast cooked in wine, the avocado salad, the beaten biscuits that she had made herself, with enough left over to heat for breakfast—and now the little house was in perfect order. The sun, in this rustic mountain village that she had selected for her permanent home, would sink quickly behind the wooded hills, so that there was never a long protracted period of dusk, and now there would be only a few moments left before everything was shrouded in darkness. So she must take her final look of the day at the ground made ready for her new lawn and garden.

Tomorrow, the man Samuel had said; tomorrow the soil will be ready for the seed and then, God willing, you may have a decent lawn for a change. He was proud of his preparations; no one yet had been able to grow a satisfactory lawn in this rocky section of the hills. Many had tried and had succeeded in growing a few scraggly blades. But she was determined to achieve a beautiful lushness out there in back, and then she would buy some awnings and outdoor furniture and perhaps put in a little fountain; and when she got back from her trip she could sit outdoors all summer long and just bask in the beauty and quiet brought to life through her own efforts. During the winters she would travel: Mexico, South America, the Mediterranean; but in the summers she would enjoy the home and lawn and garden for which she had waited so long.

Still glancing out the window she saw a whisk of white leaping onto the dark loam of the readied earth. She was instantly alert, flying out the back door, screaming "Nemo! Nemo!" to her little cat which paid not the slightest attention because it had sunk to its belly in the soft damp soil. Unthinking, realizing only that the cat might sink all the way in, as in quicksand, she stepped into the dirt and found herself plunged into it almost to her knees, before her feet came to rest on the rocky hardness of the ground underneath.

"Damn!" she said to herself, and laughed. "Old fool that I am."

She pulled herself out of the foot-and-a-half depth of the loam, rescued the yowling cat, and plodded back into the house, there to strip and shower.

Oddly enough, she was pleased at the depth of the new soil. The man Samuel had done his work well—had obviously rototilled the rocky ground as well as he could and had then hauled in great loads of topsoil, weed free and fertilized, now lying ready in the sun for tomorrow's fine grass seed. He hadn't cheated. He hadn't, as some garden workers might have done, merely put in a thin layer of dirt over the solid foundation, but had really prepared the grass for a lifetime of growth. (But he had still shaken his head, had still grumbled in the pessimistic manner of these mountainfolk who were too used to disappointment to tempt fate by hoping. "Grass seed just don't want to grow up here," he had muttered while he raked and smoothed, smoothed and raked. "Soil's empty. Air's too thin. Winter's too fierce." But he had kept on raking and smoothing, promising disaster but hoping in spite of himself.)

The woman smiled to herself, wiped herself dry from the shower, got into her night dress and lounging robe, washed the cat much to its enragement (for who, it seemed to be saying, can wash a cat better than itself?), and went to her easy chair in front of the television set.

She was alone. And safe. Safe at last. Happy and comfortable. Rested. Rested for the first time in her life and with that wonderful world cruise waiting for her, after her years of vacationless labor. Only a few weeks ahead now, but time for her to see the new young grass begin to come up and to know that it would be full-fledged on her return months from now. She had never been as content, excited as a young girl, as she was now. The bitter years behind, the exciting years ahead.

She grew weary and exasperated with the television, for in this mountain fastness there were only two stations available and on one there was a rock group, splitting the air with the modern sounds of yelling and shouting, and on the other an old Western, making loud noises, too, but those of the past, shooting and shouting and galloping hither and yon.

She turned off the set and went to her desk drawer, pushing aside the small revolver she kept there because she was living alone, and took out a pile of brightly colored brochures, to look through again, dreaming and visualizing, living in the future, ignoring the past: the magnificent ship where she would have an outside cabin all to herself and could have days and nights of quiet leisure; England, with its magnificent history; the continent, Paris, Venice, everywhere—even Crete—a cruise to last nearly a whole year. Above all, it was to be the first vacation of any kind in so many years that she couldn't even count them.

She gloated over the pictures, the colorful, impossible

descriptions, and once again, as she had a dozen times before, took out the voluminous ticket, the directions, the receipt, the date of sailing, the pamphlets suggesting what kind of clothes to bring with her—all of it, everything, that had once been her impossible dream. Everything was now arranged for: Samuel to cut and water the new lawn, and care for Nemo; the post office to hold her mail (what mail?); Mr. Prescott, the one-man police department, to check her house periodically.

Everything in order, everything waiting. And finally —pure joy—there would be the trip down the mountain in the rickety old daily bus, the air flight to the city, the overnight stay in one of the big hotels, and then the taxi ride the next morning to the great white ship and all that it promised. . . .

At first she did not hear the knock on the door. The house was quiet, the only sound that of Nemo purring at her feet; but she was lost in another world and the sound of the first knock did not penetrate.

It came again, and this time she heard it. Still lost, not even wondering who would be knocking after dusk had fallen, she went to the door and opened it, and saw a small man standing there.

"Yes?" she said, surprised but not yet apprehensive.

"Miss Kendrick?"

Prepared, yet not prepared, she held herself in the vise of total physical discipline. She did not flinch, nor did any expression appear on her face.

"No," she said quietly. "You must have the wrong place."

"I think not," said the man. He was wholly nondescript: five feet six or seven, thinning sandy hair, suit the same color, pale blue eyes.

"My name is Stella Nordway," she said, "*Mrs.* Stella Nordway."

"Oh?" he said, smiling. "You've been married recently?"

"I have been a widow for ten years," she told him. "So you see, you are mistaken."

"May I come in?"

"No," and she started to close the door.

His face altered slightly. A flicker of fury, then almost instantly a mask of mediocrity that could totally obliterate him in a crowd. "I am an investigator," he said, "for the Halmut Bonding Company. They have employed me to find a woman named Norma Kendrick who embezzled more than $100,000 from her employers over the last seven years. They want you, Miss Kendrick. *And* the money."

She said, "You may come in," and opened the door a little wider. He slipped through, instantly found the most uncomfortable chair in the room, short and straight-backed, and sat on the edge of it—as if taking his ease on the sofa might have lulled him into a lack of alertness.

"You are mistaken," she said again, almost helplessly. "I am not—"

"I am a trained investigator," he said. "For the last twenty-three years. This much I know: You worked for the Sharpe Wholesale Hardware Company, as its head bookkeeper. A large and prosperous establishment. You were competent and reliable. There was only one peculiarity about you: During the last seven years you refused to take the three weeks' vacation you were entitled to every year—"

"But I—" she broke in, then bit the words back. He had deployed her into a near admission. "But," she corrected herself quickly, "I have nothing to do with all this, so you see—"

"You are Norma Kendrick," he said. "I can't help admitting that I am rather curious as to what made you suddenly turn into an embezzler. For years you had been taking care of your invalid father and doing your daily stint at the office, coming home to the same routine every night. Then suddenly you decided to help yourself to the company's money. At the end of the first year you realized you couldn't leave your books—they would have been an open admission to the substitute bookkeeper they'd have to assign in your absence. I was appalled that Mr. Sharpe had not been more curious as to why you wouldn't take your vacation each year, but he said he had trusted you completely, since you were the daughter of an old friend and had shown your competence and reliability; and moreover, you had explained your lack of vacations by saying you couldn't leave your father in order to go anywhere, and that you were desperately in need of extra money for your father's medical bills, so if Mr. Sharpe would just pay you what he would have paid your substitute, in addition to your regular salary, you would appreciate it."

The woman sat frozen, afraid to speak, afraid not to. Instead she listened. There had to be a loophole somewhere. "So?" she prodded him, and he looked surprised, perhaps because he had expected another denial from her.

"So instead of a vacation you would frequently take a long weekend, say from Thursday to Monday, or Friday to Tuesday, and during these periods you managed to set up your second identity as Stella Nordway. You wore a blond wig, tinted glasses, more youthful clothes, and you bought this house. You also bought a single ticket for a world cruise. You did these things rather hurriedly, after seven years of dipping into the till, because not only had your father finally died, but the hardware company was about to be sold because the owner was ready to retire. This sale, of course, would entail a careful scrutiny of the books. Well, Miss Kendrick?"

Her mind fluttered.

"Are the police after me?" she said, in a final relinquishment to the inevitable.

He smiled. "Well, no. Not yet. As I said earlier, I work for the bonding company first, your employer second, and of course, as soon as you are located, then the law will step in. The police are also looking for you, but in a different direction. The bonding company will get their money—what's left of it—and the state will get its revenge. Your little house will go—"

He glanced around the neat attractive room and out the window at the dark sky where the stars shone clearly and cleanly in the mountain air. He sighed with pleasure. It would be a lovely retreat for him after too much of a lifetime spent in the city. "Your trip around the world—and how I envied you that—will have to go—"

She was becoming confused. Why weren't the police here? Why hadn't he notified Mr. Prescott, the one-man police force, that this town was harboring a fugitive? Why was this person here, just telling her these things and doing nothing about it? She knew she had lost her gamble, but she had known it was a gamble from the beginning. The bitterness was gall.

The little man spoke again, half smiling.

"Mrs. Nordway—" he began.

"Mrs. *Nordway?*" she echoed. "But you—you insist that I am Norma Kendrick—"

"You can be either one you please," he told her quietly. "It's up to you."

She sank into the nearest chair, completely confused by now, her confusion greater than her terror. "What do you mean?" she stammered.

"Well, just this. You see, you have more courage than I have. More ingenuity. More gambling spirit. I have been tied to a sickly wife for too many years, just as you were tied to your father, and the more I looked after her, the worse her temper grew. She hated being dependent on me. There was no way I could earn enough money for escape. I am what I am. I have saved my company many thousands of dollars, perhaps millions, but my salary remains unimpressive. . . . So what is your freedom worth, Mrs. Nordway?—or should I say Miss Kendrick? Whatever is left of the money you stole?"

She sat in an icy cocoon.

Not fear this time, but rage. She could understand the need for the law to make her pay—that was the consequence of losing her gamble; but to be robbed of everything she had hoped for and worked for and risked her freedom for by this oily inconsequential little opportunist sitting there so smugly—*that* was beyond acceptance.

She stood up. "There is not much money left," she said, careful to keep her voice noncommittal, "after buying the house and my cruise ticket. I would be left destitute."

"I'll take the house off your hands," he said lightly, now that he was winning, "and you can return your cruise ticket. Or, better still, let *me* have it—"

"I don't believe it's transferable," she said, almost absently. "Wait just a minute, I have it right here—" In moving toward her desk she paused for a moment in front of the window, looking out. "How did you get here?" she asked in the same absent voice. "I don't see your car outside."

"I left it down the street a ways," he said, "in front of the church. Under the circumstances it didn't seem like a good idea to let anyone know you'd had a visitor."

"I see," she said, and moved on to her desk where she rummaged around for a moment, picked up what she wanted, and held it close to the folds of her lounging robe. She remembered, for only an instant, that there were neighbors not too far away, so she moved quietly, unobtrusively, over to the television set.

"Do you like Westerns, Mr.—?"

"Jordan," he said automatically. "Why, I—" His voice sounded bewildered. Television? Now?

She turned on the volume control, high, and the crashing sound of cowboys still whooping it up with gun and horse filled the room. She lifted the small gun she was holding, and as he stared at her in his brief final moment of comprehension, she pointed it at him and shot him between the eyes.

There was no place to hide the body. The problem was as simple as that. No cellar in this tiny house; the ground too hard and rocky for digging; no car, for she had never learned to drive—no place at all to hide this neat little corpse with the small round hole in the center of its forehead.

She sat. She did not regret her action, knowing that even if she had realized ahead of time the complications in concealing her act, she would have shot him just the same. Rage had impelled her—not greed, not fear, not impulse—just an outraged need to kill this person, this thing, who was going to destroy her entire life and future for his own grasping ends.

She left him there on the living-room rug where he had quietly toppled from his chair—there was little blood —and moved into the kitchen, staring out the back window at her cherished little garden, at the prepared soil for the new lawn in which she had such high hopes. She was numb with grief at the thought of all her bright plans for the future now seemingly destroyed. Disintegrated. Dead as the little man in the other room.

She stared out through the window at the black night, motionless.

The lawn. The soil. Eighteen inches of black pulverized dirt above rocky hardness. A foot and a half. Deeper really than it actually needed to be. Deep enough? For a little man stretched out flat? With grass seed planted over him and growing into solid sod?

The dirt was very soft and slightly damp. She waited by the window in the dark, so that the neighbors would think she had gone to bed, watching the few scattered lights go out, one by one. This was a town for early sleep and early rising, and she must wait no longer than she had to. . . .

At last the night was black and still. Still as death. She went into her back yard and dug up a space in the soft prepared soil the right size for the little man—though of course only eighteen inches deep—being very careful that the spade made no sound against the harder earth. Her eyes were accustomed by now to the gloom whose only light was cast by the pale stars, and her movements were as silent as the night.

She brought the little man out to the back yard and laid him in his grave, arms decorously against his sides, and started to cover him with earth. She paused. He must lie flat, as flat as possible, for Samuel might want to rake and roll the dirt once more and there must be no chance of his tools going deep enough to strike something solid. It seemed to her that the little man's shoulders were bunched together, the way she had him placed; he must lie flatter, flatter.

The grave she had dug was wide but not deep, more space on either side of him than just above him. She tried again, stretching his arms out wide, at right angles to his body—ah, this was better, this was as flat as he would go. Now she could cover him and forget him. Soon, soon, the grass would flourish above him, entangle itself in its own roots, cover him forever, his identity, his total being now lost in other places. But not here.

Not here.

She went back into the house and slept. Her future was again safe. . . .

It was not until some time later that she knew her plans were meaningless. Day by day she watched her rear lawn and waited with anticipation for the first green blades to rise, almost forgetting what lay beneath them. And the grass did come up. But not very well. It was as Samuel had said, she thought in despair; no lawn would grow decently in these mountains of rocks and barren soil and bitter winters. But the blades did come up, struggling to reach the sun, a patch here, a patch there, so that perhaps there might be some hope after all.

One morning, after a night of soft summer rain, she looked out at her lawn and saw that there was a change; for in the center of it now was a great stand of lush green grass, beautiful and thick and bright, and it was in the form of a cross, growing and flourishing amid the meager struggles of a few pale blades, growing and flourishing, burgeoning in the soft gentle breezes and the warm healing sun. Growing and flourishing.

So that is why the people of the little town wonder about the crazy old woman who mows her foolish struggling lawn twice a week, every week. Not since the first blades came up did she ever leave her house; not once was she ever away from home, even for a brief vacation; not once in the long years that followed did she ever miss the appointed time, rain or shine, spring or fall, when she must cut her lawn.

The kind of story in which Avram Davidson is at his most gentle and charming best . . . about two old spinster sisters who live in Brooklyn, in a house at the corner of

Upshurr and Huyk Streets, and the sisters and their
house are from a long-dead-and-gone era—except that
it can still happen in Brooklyn.

AVRAM DAVIDSON

Summon the watch!

If you want to see New York as New York used to look,
there is no point in looking around Manhattan, the only
place which practices autocannibalism as a matter of policy. The few—the very few—blocks of old buildings which
survive on Minuit's island have, for the most part, become
slums. Old New York, however, does survive, but in the
sister borough.

Upshurr Street in Brooklyn is not very long, and the
legend that it is easy to get lost in Brooklyn is, unfortunately, all too true. Perhaps that is why so much that is
old and good still survives in Brooklyn—perhaps the
wreckers have merely been unable to find their way, and,
finally baffled, have given up and retreated to destroy yet
more areas across the East River.

The two men who arrived at the house at the corner
of Upshurr and Huyk Streets one winter afternoon surveyed it with interest, despite the cold. It was a well-
kept building in the Georgian style, three stories high, and
surrounded by garden. The smaller trees and bushes were
carefully muffled in burlap. The two men mounted the
steps.

"Where's the bell?" one of them asked, after fumbling with his gloved hand.

The other man shifted a camera he was carrying, bent over, and looked. He straightened up and shrugged. "Ain't none. Try that doojigger there," he said.

The knocker—in the form of a lion's head with a long tongue—was banged a few times. The two men waited, stamped their feet, blew out vapor, rubbed their noses. Then the door was opened by a short heavy old woman with long gray ringlets clustering around her broad pink face. "Come in," she urged. "Come in."

"Miss Vanderhooft?" the first man asked. The old woman nodded vigorously, setting the ringlets to bouncing like springs. "My name is—"

"Your name will still be the same if you come inside," she said crisply. They entered, she shut the door. The house was warm, and well furnished in the style of the early nineteenth century.

"My name—" the man began again.

"*My* name is Sapphira Vanderhooft," the old woman said. "My sister, being elder, ought properly to be addressed only as 'Miss Vanderhooft,' but since this fact seems to have passed out of all common knowledge, you may address her as Miss Isabella—come along, come along," she urged, gesturing them to precede her; "and me, as Miss Sapphira."

They found themseves in the living room, or parlor. A coal fire burned in the high basket grate. A few candles shed a soft light which melted into the ruddy glow from the fireplace. Seated in an upright chair was a second old woman, tall and spare, with her white hair parted in the center and drawn back.

"You will excuse me if I do not rise," she said, nodding to them and making a slight gesture with an ivory-headed cane. Embroidery work, hooped and needled, lay in her lap.

"This is my sister," said Miss Sapphira. "Isabella, these gentlemen are from the newspaper. That is, I *hope* that they are gentlemen," she added.

"And I hope that they are from the press," Miss Isabella said. "Have you seen identification, sister? If you are on another errand—soliciting contributions, for example—you won't get any," she went on, as the younger of the two men fumbled in his pocket. "Mr. Caldwell, at the Trust Company, takes care of all that for us. Hmm. What is this?" She examined the card offered her. "It has last year's date on it; how is that?"

The man said that the card's validity ran from April to April, and—as Miss Isabella nodded, and handed it back to him—he at last managed to get out the information that his name was Dandridge and that his photographer-companion was called Goltz.

"Let me have your greatcoats," Miss Sapphira said. "There's no need for you to stand, we aren't royalty. Have whatever chairs you like, but the settle is mine."

Mr. Dandridge, who was thirtyish and thin, and Mr. Goltz, who was fortyish and squat, looked around the cozy, quaintly furnished room.

Miss Isabella broke the momentary silence. "If you've come to do a sensational article for the penny press, young man, the point cannot be too strongly emphasized that we are *not* recluses," she said.

"Certainly not," agreed Miss Sapphira. "The fact that we receive *you* is—or should be—proof of *that*."

Dandridge said, "Well—"

"After that unfortunate affair of the Collier brothers," Miss Isabella swept on, "there was a reporter here from the Brooklyn *Eagle*, and he at once conceded that there was no similarity at all."

"None whatsoever," said Miss Sapphira. "We knew Homer and Langley when they were very young. The trouble with them was simply that they were spoiled.

Aren't you going to say anything for yourself?" she demanded of Mr. Dandridge.

He smiled. Goltz looked bored. "I might begin by saying that my paper isn't a sensational one—and that it's been many years since any newspaper sold for a penny."

The older Miss Vanderhooft sniffed. "Well, it has been many years since we have cared to purchase one," she said. "So your information is of no particular use."

"Also," Goltz growled, "the *Eagle* is outa business."

For a moment the sisters were startled. Then they regained their aplomb. "Ah, well," said Miss Isabella, "it doesn't signify."

Dandridge looked down from a portrait labeled "General J. Abram Garfield." "Our editor thought it would be of interest to the readers to see how the calm and gracious life of another day is still being kept up amid the hustle and—and—" he stumbled, hesitated.

The sisters smiled. "We are, I suppose, old-fashioned, to be sure," said Miss Isabella, "but we will not be shocked if you say the word 'bustle.' Silly fashion, we always thought. And our dear papa used always to say that the garments Mrs. Amelia Bloomer was condemned for wearing were not so very much sillier than the ones she was condemned for *not* wearing."

Miss Sapphira said that she had put the kettle on. "It will sing, presently, and then we shall have tea. Would you like tea? Capital."

Her sister picked up the hoop and took the needle in her fingers. She looked at the reporter, nodded to him encouragingly. Miss Sapphira, on the settle, slid her hand into her pocket, slipped out a tiny silver box, and—when she thought no one was looking—hurriedly took a pinch of snuff.

"Well, now that we are agreed that you are not recluses," Dandridge said, "may I ask if it is true that you have no radio, telephone, or television?"

The younger sister said that it was true. Such devices, she explained, as she might to a child, exuded a malign magnetical influence. Indeed, if it were not for their dear brother's insistence, they would never have allowed the electrical incandescent lamps to be installed. He was dead, poor Cornelius, and they now lived quite alone.

No servants? Ah, that *was* a problem, wasn't it? Well, Emma came in thrice a week to clean—not today, being Monday, but on Tuesdays, Thursdays, and Saturdays. She did the shopping. The sisters would endorse the bills and send them to Mr. Caldwell at the Trust Company, who mailed checks to the merchants. In clement weather the two sisters often walked to the end of the block and back; no farther.

To church? No, no longer, but of course they always had evening prayers, and on Sundays they took turns reading sermons—one of Dr. Talmage's or, sometimes, one of the Reverend Henry Ward Beecher's. They did not, they assured Dandridge, believe a *word* of that dreadful scandal.

"Was there a scandal about him?" asked Mr. Dandridge. "I didn't know that."

The sisters exchanged gratified glances. "You see, Sapphira," Miss Isabella said. "I *told* you it would die down in time!"

"And have you no fears about living alone like this?"

Certainly not. Why should they have? It was a respectable neighborhood. The police always tried the doors at night—not that it was really necessary.

Dandridge cleared his throat. "Now—I don't mean to ask personal questions—but there seems to be a sort of, ah, legend, to the effect that a large treasure is hidden on the premises. . . ." He tapered off with a chuckle.

"Treasure?" asked Miss Isabella, looking at Miss Sapphira.

"Treasure?" asked Miss Sapphira, looking at Miss Isabella.

"No," they said simultaneously. Then, "Do you suppose, sister, that the young man could be referring to the gold"—the photographer, for the first time, looked interested—"which dear papa brought here following the panic of 'seventy-three?" suggested Miss Isabella.

"Are you?" asked Miss Sapphira. The reporter nodded.

Miss Sapphira said, "Well, well. It isn't here any longer. No. We have *long* since turned it over to the government. Now, when was it? Nineteen twenty-three? Nineteen thirty-three?"

"Usurpation!" cried Miss Isabella, thumping her stick on the floor. A faint pink suffused the pallor of her cheeks. "Usurpation and confiscation—though I suppose we could expect little better, with the Republicans in office."

Miss Sapphira, for her part, brushed aside Dandridge's comment that the Democrats were in office at the time privately owned gold was called in. Dear Grandpapa Vanderhooft, she told him, had said often enough that the nation's fiscal policy had never been sound since the Whigs went out of power. And the two old women nodded soberly at this sage, though melancholy advice.

Miss Isabella poured the tea, Miss Sapphira passed around the cake. Mr. Dandridge brushed his lips with a heavy monogrammed linen napkin. "Why do you call it 'usurpation and confiscation,' ma'am—the government's calling in your gold, I mean? After all, you received—they didn't just take it—you got money for it, didn't you?"

Miss Isabella waved her cane. "Only bank notes!" she said angrily. "Shinplasters! And to think they took our good northern gold to Kentucky—a nest of rebels!"

But Mr. Dandridge was no longer concerned with the gold. "And what did you do with all those shinplasters?"

he asked. Miss Isabella was drinking tea, so her younger sister replied.

"It is somewhere around, I suppose," she said. "It doesn't really signify."

Mr. Dandridge got up. "It signifies to *us*," he said. He pointed to Mr. Goltz, who had put his camera to one side and had something else in his hand. "Now, ladies, you are going to show us to your money and we are going to take it. Everything will be done quickly and quietly, and no one will be hurt. Up, please."

The two old women looked from him to the revolver in Mr. Goltz's fist.

"And you a photographer!" said Miss Sapphira, her pink cheeks very pink indeed. "Why, poor Mr. Brady would turn in his *grave* if he knew."

"Led'm," said Goltz, briefly. "C'mon, where's the money, ladies? Where ya goddit stashed away?"

Miss Isabella sighed and started to rise upon her cane. Dandridge reached to assist her, but she drew back with such an expression of disdain that he let his hand fall. "I suppose the quicker you have it, the quicker you'll leave. And 'tis only greenbacks, after all—no better than the credit of the government, and if the government allows banditi such as you to roam the peaceful streets of Brooklyn it has very little credit indeed. . . . I think they may be in the cedar chest."

The cedar chest proved, after prolonged searching, to contain four bolts of linen and approximately one hundred copies of *Godey's Lady's Book,* all in perfect condition. While Goltz glowered, Miss Sapphira picked up a magazine and let out a little cry of pleasure. "Look, Sister! A story by dear grandpapa's friend whom he so often told us about, poor Mr. Poe. I'm *so* glad I've found it. I shall read it tonight."

For the first time Dandridge's control slipped its

mooring. "Quit this fooling around!" he shouted. "I want that money located in ten minutes—or—"

Miss Sapphira said that she wondered if he fully realized what effect this episode would have on the *young* people of the country if it became known. A most deleterious one, she was afraid.

Her sister stood in a pose of deep thought. "It's been so many years—" she said. "Now, could it be in the mahogany press? That is in the next room. I have the keys on my chain, here, but one of you will have to bring the candles."

The afternoon had grown late and dark and the candles, held by Dandridge, shed a scanty light in the cold room while Miss Isabella fumbled for her keys. Goltz said, "I had enough of this. Them candles are too spooky, and I like ta see what I'm doing." He reached up and tugged the cord of the dusty electrolier overhead. The cord snapped off in his hand, but the lights went on. Miss Isabella and her sister clicked their tongues. Dandridge blew out the candles.

"Open it up," he ordered. Miss Isabella complied. Two large cloth bags tumbled out, and—as the two men exclaimed—quantities of paper money poured from them. Dandridge fell on his knees, grinning. Then, as he examined the money, his grin faded. He waved one of the bills toward the Misses Vanderhooft. "Is *this* what the government gave you for your gold?" he demanded incredulously. "The Planters and Merchants Bank of Boggs County, Missouri?"

The sisters sighed, shook their heads.

"So that is where it was? Dear me."

"An unfortunate speculation in wildcat currency on the part of Great-uncle Isaac—dear grandpapa's brother. We never knew him. He fell at the Battle of Pittsburgh Landing in the year—"

A heavy hand beat loudly on the front-door knocker.

A heavy voice called, "Is anything wrong, ladies? Hello, hello! Is anything—"

Miss Isabella, looking Goltz straight in the eye and without changing by a hair's breadth the expression of calm disdain on her face, opened her mouth and called, "Help!" in a clear, level voice. Goltz went livid, raised the revolver, shook his head threateningly. "Help! Footpads!" Miss Isabella called out.

Miss Sapphira took the candelabra and, with an underhand pitch, threw it through the windowpane.

"Stop, thief!" she sang out. "Summon the watch!"

"I hope you don't mind eating from the same cake as those two scant-soaps fed upon," Miss Isabella said. This time *she* cut and passed, while Miss Sapphira poured the tea. Patrolmen Freitag and Johansson shook their heads, swallowed, accepted more. "This recipe comes down to us from the days of Abraham Vanderhooft's second wife. They say that she was an indentured servant before he married her, but it doesn't really signify, does it? And we ourselves descend from the first wife. . . . Dear me, what an afternoon!"

Patrolman Freitag washed down his second slice of cake with half of his second cup of tea. "This guy Dandridge—the real one, I mean, the reporter—he better be careful what he does with his old press cards from now on, instead of throwing them away. I hope," he said, rather anxiously, "that you ladies won't mind too much having to go to court and all that? Because—I guess—well, we could maybe say you were sick and have them come here to take your testimony—maybe."

Miss Sapphira shook her head, setting the long gray ringlets in motion around her pink face. "It is very kind of you young men to be so considerate—but I trust that my sister and I are sensible of our duty as citizens."

Her sister nodded, then asked, as if the thought had

just struck her, how it was that the attention of the two policemen had been drawn to the house so much earlier than usual. Johansson smiled. Freitag smiled. The former answered.

"It was the electric light," he said. "We were just cruising down Huyk Street and we saw the electric light— I mean, the shade and the curtains were drawn, but we could see it was electric. So I says to Freitag, I says, 'Oh-oh. I been living in this neighborhood for thirty years and I never saw no electric lights burning in the Vander-hooft house, not since Mr. Cornelius passed away.' And he says, 'Neither did I, Nels. Never anything but candles.' So we figured we'd better investigate. I gotta give you both credit—what you did, it took courage."

Miss Isabella said, "Poo." Her sister said, "Pshaw. Hog-snatchers is all they were, trying to get above them-selves."

"It was not our idea at all, to install the incandescent lamps," Miss Isabella explained. "It was our brother's. But we have never used them since he died. Such devices exude a malign magnetical influence."

"Isabella," asked Miss Sapphira, "now that so much attention has been drawn to the matter I confess that I am mildly curious myself as to where those bank notes are."

The older sister's ivory forehead creased in thought. Then she said, "Do you know, Sister—I wonder if we did not ask Mr. Caldwell to take them down to the Trust Company and purchase bonds or something with them during the war."

Miss Sapphira considered. "Did we? Perhaps you are right. Perhaps we did."

"Ah, well," said Miss Isabella. "It doesn't signify. More tea for the watch?" she asked.

Once each year Stanley Ellin writes a story especially for Ellery Queen's Mystery Magazine, *and each year readers and critics look forward eagerly to this new story as a mystery event.*

Gertrude Stein might have said, "War is a war is a war is a war." But war is not a rose, and a war is not a war is not a war is not a war.

STANLEY ELLIN

The payoff

The four men aboard *Belinda II* watched the coast guard helicopter racketing its way southward on patrol along the Miami Beach shoreline.

"Handy little gadget," Broderick said, and Yates, echoing the boss man as usual, said, "Very handy."

"Depends," Del said sourly. He glanced at Chappie, who said nothing.

Broderick and Yates were in their middle forties, both of them big and hefty, with paunches showing under their yachting jackets. Chappie and Del were in their early twenties, flat-bellied in swim trunks.

Broderick, glassy-eyed with bourbon, squinted at his watch. "Thirty-five minutes. Last time was thirty-three. Let's call it an even half hour to be on the safe side." He looked Chappie up and down. "You sure that's enough time for you?"

Chappie said, "It's enough," and went back to whetting the blade of his clasp knife on the stone Broderick had turned up in the galley. The blade was four inches long, bowie-shaped.

Broderick, one hand on the wheel, steadied *Belinda II*, keeping her bow toward the swells riding inshore, her motor almost idling. "You absolutely sure?"

Del said angrily, "You heard him, didn't you? What the hell you want to keep picking on him about it?"

"Because we are cutting down on the excuse quotient," Yates said. He was as stoned as Broderick, his face even more flaming red with windburn and Jim Beam. "Because we do not want to hear afterward how you couldn't do it because that chopper didn't allow enough time. Or any other excuse."

"Well, you won't be hearing no excuses," Del said, and Chappie snapped the knife shut and said to him, "Cool it, man. Just get that baby boat over here."

As Del hauled the dinghy alongside *Belinda II* by its line, Chappie shoved the knife into a plastic sandwich bag, rolled up the bag, and thrust it into the waistband of his trunks. The outboard motor had already been clamped to the sternboard of the dinghy. Del stepped down into the dinghy, took his place at the motor. Chappie dropped down into the bow of the dinghy, untied its line, pushed off from *Belinda II*. Broderick joined Yates at the rail of the cabin cruiser, both of them watching with the same tight little smiles. Broderick cupped his hands to his mouth and yelled over the noise of the outboard, "Twenty-eight minutes left."

They were about two miles away from the towering line of hotels and high-rises along the shore. The sunlight was scorching, but a cool gusting breeze made it bearable. Del centered the bow of the dinghy on the big hotel dead ahead, the Royal Oceanic, tried to keep the boat from yawing and chopping too badly as it moved landward. He eyed Chappie, who squatted there on the bow seat, rocking with the motion, his face empty.

"Suppose the layout's changed over there from the. way Broderick told it," Del said. He pointed his chin at the hotel.

"Changed how?"

"Rooms, halls, you know what I mean. That was a couple of years ago he stayed there. They could have tore down things, built up things, so it's all changed around now."

"You worry too much," Chappie said.

"Because I just don't like this kind of a deal, man. We wouldn't even be in it if that big-mouth Broderick wasn't a mess of bad vibrations. Now ain't that the truth?"

"Nothing but," Chappie said.

"You see." Del solemnly shook his head. "Man, it sure is different from yesterday. I mean like up Palm Beach way when they said come on along and they'd give us a hitch right to Freeport. Fact is, I kind of took to them first look."

"Only way to find out about people is move in with them," Chappie said.

They were getting close to shore now. The swells the dinghy had been riding were taking shape as combers that crested and broke on the narrow, dirty-looking strip of sand fronting the hotel. Some people were standing in the surf. One of them shaded his eyes to look at the dinghy. Del swung it around, bow pointing seaward, and cut the motor. He stood up to gauge the distance to the beach.

"Maybe a hundred yards," he said. "Just remember the low profile, man."

"You, too," Chappie said. He slid overboard, ducked underwater, came up shaking the hair out of his eyes. He rested a hand on the edge of the dinghy. "Don't let it look like you're waiting here. Take a ride for yourself. Then when you're back here, fool around with the motor."

He went deep under the boat, swam hard, and when he bobbed to the surface on the crest of a wave he turned and saw the dinghy wheeling away northward. He let the next wave carry him half the remaining distance to the beach. When he got to his feet he found the water only up to his waist. Off-balance, he was thrown forward on his hands and knees by a following wave. As he pitched forward, he felt the plastic bag with the knife in it slither down his thigh. He clutched at it, missed it, and came up with a handful of slimy, oil-soaked seaweed instead. He flung the seaweed aside. Then he saw the bag, open now, the knife showing through it, come to roost on the tide line up ahead. None of the bathers around him seemed to take any special notice as he got to the bag fast, poured the water out of it, wrapped it tight around the knife again, and shoved it back into his waistband.

He stood for a few seconds looking seaward. *Belinda II,* a small white patch on the horizon, got even smaller as it ran out into the Gulf Stream. Overhead there was no helicopter in sight. Nobody to take in the scene and connect the cabin cruiser with its dinghy or the dinghy with the passenger it had just landed.

He turned, crossed the strip of beach to the walled-in sun deck of the hotel. A broad flight of concrete steps led to the sun deck. A lifeguard type in white ducks and a T-shirt marked *Royal Oceanic* stood at the head of the steps, his arms folded on his chest, his eyes on the beach. As Chappie passed by, the eyes swiveled toward him, flicked over him, then went back to surveying the beach.

Lounges in long neat rows took up most of the sun deck. The rest was taken up by a big swimming pool, its deep end toward the beach, its shallow end not far from the rear entrance to the hotel. A lot of the lounges were occupied; the pool was almost empty. Chappie strolled toward the pool, stepped up on the edge of it.

"Hey, you!"

Chappie froze there. He glanced over his shoulder and saw the lifeguard type walking toward him, aiming a finger at him. "You," the man said. "What goes on?" The finger aimed downward now at Chappie's feet. "Bring all that sand up from the beach, mister, you ought to know enough to take a shower before you get in the pool." He nodded toward what looked like a phone booth with canvas walls. "Shower's right over there."

Chappie slowly released his breath. Thumb in the waistband of his trunks, hand covering the bulge of the knife in the waistband, he went over to the shower booth, stepped inside, braced himself against the shock of cold water jetting down on him.

When he walked out of the booth the lifeguard type gave him a nod and a smile, and he nodded and smiled in return. Then he went into the pool feetfirst, keeping a grip on the knife in his belt until he picked up his swimming stroke. He covered almost the whole length of the pool underwater, hoisted himself out at the shallow end. It was only a few steps from there to the hotel entrance. Inside the entrance he was in an arcade, a coffee shop on one side, a souvenir shop on the other. After the searing glare of sunlight outside, the arcade seemed like a cool, damp, unlit cave, but by the time he had walked past the coffee shop he was used to the lighting. A door beyond the shop was marked *Men's Sauna*, and there was a steady traffic coming and going through it.

Chappie went in and entered a long and wide corridor, narrower corridors branching off from it on both sides. It was hot and close here, the air growing steadily hotter and more humid as he walked along counting, and when he turned into the fourth corridor on the left a smell of sweat became unpleasantly noticeable. The walls in this section were all white tile, and each door along the way had a lettered plate on it: *Steam Room, Dry Heat, Showers, Personnel, Service.* The door to the service room was wide open, kept in place by a rubber doorstop. As he passed it, Chappie took quick notice of the shelves of towels and sheets there. Almost out of sight in a corner of the room, someone was hauling towels from a shelf.

When he reached the end of the corridor, Chappie leaned against the wall, bent down as if to examine an ankle, his eyes sidelong on the open door of the service room. Then a boy in sandals and swim trunks emerged from the room with a bundle of towels under his arm. As soon as he was out of sight around the corner, Chappie went into the service room and helped himself to an armful of towels. He carried them back to the end of the corridor which ran into a short hallway that crossed it like the head of a capital T.

The doors in this hallway were numbered. Chappie carefully pushed open Number One an inch and looked inside. The room was small and windowless, its only furnishings a rubbing table and a shelf on the wall with a row of bottles and jars on it. On the table a big man with the build of a football linebacker was getting a rubdown from a masseur.

Chappie left the door as it was and tried the next room. It was empty. The third room, however, was occupied. A man wearing dark goggles lay stretched out on his back on the rubbing table, a cigar clamped between his teeth and pointing up at the ceiling, a sunlamp brilliantly lighting his naked body. A white-haired man, skinny and wrinkled, his face and body tanned a leathery brown. Clearly visible in the glare of the sunlamp was a tattoo on one scrawny forearm, done in garish colors. A coiled rattlesnake, and circling it in bold print the words *Don't Tread On Me.*

Chappie looked over his shoulder. There was no hotel staff man in sight, only some customers walking around in sandals and bath sheets. He got a good grip on the bundle of towels under his arm and went into the room. It reeked of cigar smoke and was hot enough to make him break into a sweat as he stood there closing the door softly behind him. He could feel the beads of sweat starting to trickle down his forehead and chest.

The click of the door lock roused the man. Without turning his head he said, "Benny?"

"No, sir," Chappie said. He moved toward the table. "But he sent me in to check up."

"Check up?" the man said. "What the hell's he trying to do, fix up everybody in the place with a handout?"

"No, sir. But he said you're not to get too much of that lamp on your front and more on your back."

As Chappie walked over to the table, his toe struck something on the floor beside it. A plastic ashtray with cigar ash in it. More cigar ash was scattered on the floor around it. Chappie stacked his armful of towels on the foot of the rubbing table and picked up the ashtray, the clasp knife digging into his groin as he did so. He said, "If you don't mind, sir," and took the cigar from between the man's teeth and deposited it in the ashtray. He put the ashtray back on the floor, pushing it far under the table.

The lenses in the goggles were so dark that Chappie couldn't see the man's eyes through them as he leaned forward over him. The man's head was resting on a folded towel. Chappie lifted the head barely enough to slide the towel out, and found the towel soaked through with sweat. He dropped it on the floor and gently set the man's head down again. "Want me to help you turn over, sir?"

The goggles fixed on him. "You new around here, boy?"

"Yes, sir."

"I thought so. Well, if you know what's good for you you'll help me turn over so nice and easy I don't feel a twinge. Damn bursitis is killing me. So very nice and easy, you hear?"

"Yes, sir."

The man grunted and groaned as he was arranged on his belly. Then he raised his head a little. "What the hell are you saving those towels for? This thing is like an ironing board."

"Yes, sir," said Chappie.

He took a towel from the pile, folded it, and slid it under the man's head. The man rested his head on it. "All right," he said, "now beat it."

Chappie glanced at the closed door. Then he came up on his toes like a bullfighter preparing to plant his banderillas, both arms raised, left elbow out as if warding off an attack. His right hand flashed down expertly, all his strength behind it, and the edge of the palm drove into the nape of the man's neck like an ax blade. The leathery old body jerked violently, the legs snapping backward from the knees, then falling to the table again, one leg shivering. Chappie came up on his toes again, struck again. The leg stopped shivering. The body settled down into the table like a tub of fresh dough poured on it. One stringy arm slipped off the table and dangled there, its fingers half curled.

Chappie pulled the plastic bag from his waistband, took the knife out of it, opened the blade. He pulled the goggles high up on the man's forehead to give himself room, then slashed off the man's ear with one stroke of the knife. There was no welling of blood, just an ooze of it along the line of the wound. He cleaned the knife blade hastily with a fresh towel from the pile, snapped it shut, and put the knife and ear into the plastic bag.

Coming out of the arcade into glaring daylight he was blinded by the sun and almost bumped into a couple of people as he made his way to the pool. He swam fast to the deep end, giving the diving boards there a wide berth, but as he neared the ladder at the deep end there was a sudden loud splash in his face, a blow on the side of the head that pulled him up short.

It was a girl who had jumped off the side of the pool and was now treading water face to face with him. She was about sixteen or seventeen, her long straight hair in strings down her face. She pulled some of the strings aside and said worriedly, "Honest, I didn't mean that. Are you all right?"

"Sure," Chappie said. He rested his hands on her shoulders and she let them stay there. She seemed to like it.

Chappie saw that some of the people standing on the edge of the pool were looking down at them. He released the girl and went up the ladder. "Hey," the girl called after him, "are you staying here at the hotel?" but he didn't answer or look back.

The lifeguard type was still at the head of the stairway to the beach. Chappie slowed down to a casual walk going past the man and down the steps. He took his time crossing the narrow strip of beach and looked out over the pale green water. The dinghy was rocking up and down beyond the line of breakers, its motor pulled up horizontal, Del pretending to fiddle with it. *Belinda II* was barely in sight on the horizon. She seemed to be stationary now, but it was hard to judge from that distance. Chappie looked up. No helicopter showing anywhere.

He waded into the surf, went under a couple of lines of breakers, and swam to the dinghy. As he hauled himself into the bow, Del dropped the motor back into the water, got it snarling into life with a quick flick of the cord. The dinghy aimed for *Belinda II*, bouncing hard, and Chappie said, "Don't make it look like a getaway, man. Cut it down."

Del eased up on the throttle. He looked at Chappie. "You do it?"

"I did it."

"No sweat?"

"No. He looked about ready to go anyhow. And you can swim right up to that door there. You don't even have to walk in front of people." Chappie spat overboard to get the taste of salt water out of his mouth. "There's some massage artist name of Benny who is in for a big surprise pretty soon. Maybe even got it already." He had to smile at the thought.

Del said, "All the same, man, you ain't getting near enough bread for this kind of a deal. And that Broderick is loaded. I mean loaded."

"All I want is what's coming to me, if I wanted more I would have told him so."

"Sure enough. But you know how much that Yates said that *Belinda* boat cost? Forty thousand. And that Caddie of theirs up in Palm Beach. Man, that heap had everything in it but a Coke machine."

"What about it? All they are is a couple of fat old men with a lot of money. You want to trade around with them, just remember that the fat and the old goes along with the money."

Del shook his head. "Then it's no trade, man. What happens after Freeport? You don't figure to come back with them two, do you?"

"Hell, no. I figure we do some of those islands around there. Then maybe Mexico. Acapulco. How does that grab you?"

"Any place as long as it ain't Danang or like that grabs me just fine." Del looked up over his shoulder. "And talking about that—" The coast guard helicopter was in sight again, loudly making its northward run along the coast. "Man, it makes me sick to even hear the sound of them things now," Del said. "I can feel that pack breaking my back all over again."

"Full field pack," Chappie said. "Stuffed full of those delicious C rations."

When they pulled alongside *Belinda II*, Broderick was at the wheel of the cruiser, Yates was at the rail watching them. Yates took the line Chappie handed up to him and made it fast to *Belinda II.* "Well, well," he said, "look who's home again. And with a tale to tell, I'm sure, about what went wrong and why."

Chappie disregarded him. He went aboard the cruiser, and Del, after tilting the outboard motor out of the water, followed him. Broderick looked them over.

"Not even breathing hard," he said. "A couple of real tough ones."

Chappie went over to the card table where Broderick and Yates played gin when someone else was at the wheel. He pulled the plastic bag from under his waistband, turned it upside down, and let the knife and the ear fall out on the table. The ear was putty-colored now, its severed edge a gummy red and brown where the ooze of blood had clotted.

The little smile on Broderick's face disappeared. He released the wheel and walked over to the table, eyes fixed on it. Del immediately grabbed the wheel and steadied it. He said to Broderick, "What the hell you looking so surprised at, man? He told you he could do it, didn't he? And bring back all the proof you wanted, didn't he?"

Broderick stood staring at the table. Then he stared at Chappie the same intent way, wiping a hand slowly back and forth over his mouth. Finally he said in a thick voice, "You really killed somebody? I mean, killed him?"

Chappie nodded at the table. "You think he just lay there and asked me to cut that off him?"

"But who was he? My God, you couldn't even know who he was!"

"I'm in no rush," Chappie said. "I can wait to find out when we see the papers over in Freeport tomorrow. But I'm not waiting until then for the payoff." He held out his hand and wiggled the fingers invitingly. "Right now's the time."

"Payoff?" said Broderick.

"Man, you said it was your ten dollars to my dime I couldn't do it. So I did it. Now it's payoff time."

Broderick said in anguish, "But I swear to God I never meant you to go through with it. I never expected you to. It was just talk, that's all. You knew it was just talk. You must have known it."

"You told him the layout there," Del said. "You told him where to look for somebody he could waste. You were the one scared about that chopper spotting us coming back here. Man, don't you start crawfishing now."

"Now look," Broderick said, then stopped short, shaking his head at his own thoughts.

Yates walked over to him fast, caught hold of his wrist. "Listen to me, Brod. I'm talking to you as your lawyer. You give him any money now, you are really in this up to your neck. And you're not taking them to the Bahamas or anywhere else out of the country. We can make it to Key Largo before dark and they'll haul out right there."

Chappie shrugged. "Freeport, Key Largo, whatever makes you happy." He picked up the knife from the table, opened its blade, held it up, admiring the way the sunlight ran up and down the blade. Then he leveled the knife at Broderick's belly. "But first I collect everything that's coming to me."

Broderick looked down at the knife, looked up at Chappie's face. Behind him at the wheel, Del said, "There's two of us, man," and Broderick pulled his wrist free of Yates' grip on it, shoved his hand into his hip pocket. He came up with a wad of bills in a big gold clip. He drew a ten-dollar bill from the clip and held it out to Chappie. "For ten lousy dollars," he said unbelievingly.

Chappie took the bill, studied it front and back as if making sure it was honest money. Then he slowly tore it in half, held the two halves high and released them to the breeze. They fluttered over the jackstaff at the stern of

Belinda II and landed in her wake not far behind the trailing dinghy.

"That was the nothing part of the deal," Chappie said. "Now how about the real payoff?"

"The real payoff?" Broderick said.

"Mister, you told me that if I pulled it off you'd come right out and say you didn't know what it was all about. You told me you'd look me straight in the eye and say there's just as good men in Nam right now as that chicken company you were with in Korea. Just as good and maybe a lot better. Now say it."

Broderick said between his teeth, "If your idea of a good man—"

Chappie reached out and lightly prodded Broderick's yachting jacket with the point of the knife. "Say it."

Broderick said it. Then he suddenly wheeled and lurched into the cabin, Yates close on his heels. Through the open door Chappie watched them pour out oversized drinks.

"Key Largo's the place," he said to Del at the wheel, and as *Belinda II* swung southward, picking up speed as she went, Chappie stood there, his lip curled, watching the two men in the cabin gulping down their Jim Beam until Yates took notice of him and slammed the cabin door shut as hard as he could.

Maria Morales was a jewel of a woman—scrupulously honest, a marvelous housekeeper and cook. Lyle Waverly, eligible young bachelor and society doctor, could hardly believe his good luck in getting Maria to run his house, and when the women in his life openly admitted that "Maria is a miracle . . . a perfect servant!"—well, he

couldn't have been more pleased. And when Dr. Waverly
needed more than a devoted servant, when he needed
someone he could trust implicitly, Maria was there.

HELEN NIELSEN

The perfect servant

Lieutenant Brandon was trying to bridge a generation gap when the woman walked into the police station and deposited a wad of currency on the counter. The trio of teen-agers he had charged with collecting hubcaps that belonged to irate citizens seemed unimpressed with the idea that they had committed theft, and then the woman, who was in her middle forties, shabbily dressed and wearing a look of quiet despair in her eyes, relinquished a cheap money clip containing the bills and said, "Please, who is the officer I see about this?"

Brandon nodded for a uniformed officer to take away the teen-agers, grateful for a release from the pointless conversation, and asked the woman to state her problem.

"I was walking down the street—down Broadway," she stated, "and I saw this on the sidewalk. I picked it up. It is money."

Brandon pulled the bills out of the clip. There were three twenty-dollar bills, three tens, and two fives. "One hundred dollars," he said.

"Yes," the woman agreed. "I counted, too. That's a lot of money for someone to lose."

It was a lot of money, and the woman looked as if she had never had her hands on that much at any one time in all her life. Brandon called the desk sergeant to fill out a report and explained to the woman that the money would be held for thirty days, during which time the real owner could report his loss, describe the bills and the clip, and have the money returned, or, failing a claimant, the money would then become the property of the finder.

"Your name?" asked the sergeant.

She hesitated. "Maria," she said. "Maria Morales."

"Occupation?"

"I have no work now. When I work I am a domestic."

"Address?"

She gave the number of a cheap roominghouse in the Spanish-speaking section of town. She told them she was very poor, unemployed, and without any property of her own. When the report was offered for her signature she placed both hands on the desk. A plain gold band adorned the third finger of her left hand.

"Just sign here, Miss Morales," the sergeant said.

"Mrs. Morales," she corrected. "I am a widow."

Brandon caught the desk sergeant's eye and shook his head in wonder.

"You should get those cocky young kids back in here to see this," the sergeant suggested.

"Waste of time," Brandon answered. "They wouldn't appreciate anything this square. Don't forget now, Mrs. Morales, in thirty days you check back with us. Chances are you'll get the money—or at least a reward."

"Thank you," she said in a very soft voice, "but I would rather have a job."

A young reporter from the Tucson daily came into the station just as Maria Morales was leaving, and Brandon, the bitter taste of the cynical teen-agers still in his mouth, related the incident of the honesty of Maria Morales. It was a slow day on the newsfront and when the morning papers came out, the story of the unemployed widow and the $100 was written up in a neat box on the front page.

By noon Lieutenant Brandon was flooded with calls from people who claimed the money, and also with job offers for Maria Morales. Having developed a protective interest in the widow, he took it upon himself to screen the offers and decided that the best prospect was Lyle Waverly, a bachelor and a physician with a lucrative practice among the country-club set.

Waverly needed a housekeeper he could trust. He owned a fine home in one of the better suburbs and entertained a well-heeled social set. He offered Maria a home, a good salary, and free medical care for as long as she remained in his employ.

Brandon approved the credentials and gave Waverly the woman's address, feeling the kind of inner warmth he always got from delivering Christmas parcels to the Neediest Families.

Maria Morales was extremely pleased with young Dr. Waverly. He was easy to work for. The house was large but new, and there was a gardener to help with the heavy work. She was an excellent cook but, aside from breakfast, the doctor seldom dined in. He was a busy man in more ways than one, which was only natural for one so attractive and increasingly affluent.

It soon became apparent that the doctor's love life was divided between two women: Cynthia Reardon, who was twenty-three and the sole heir of Josiah Reardon of Reardon Savings and Loan, and Shelley Clifford, ten years older, who had an additional handicap of being already married to Ramsey Clifford, the owner of Clifford Construction Company. Clifford was a huge burly man of fifty who had too little time to spend with a lovely wife who liked younger men.

Maria observed these things with professional silence, and long before Dr. Lyle Waverly was aware of his destiny, she knew that Cynthia had the inside track and would eventually get her man.

Life was pleasant in the Waverly house and Maria had no desire to return to the kind of employment she had recently known. She began to plot a campaign of self-preservation. When the doctor gave her an advance on her salary, she purchased fitted uniforms with caps and aprons for the frequent cocktail parties he gave for his wealthy friends and patients.

He soon learned that a caterer was no longer necessary. Maria's canapés became the envy of every hostess, and she herself became a topic of conversation not unwelcome in the tension created whenever Cynthia and Shelley were present on the same occasion. Shelley had the prior claim—a fact made obvious by the way she took over as hostess. She was the "in" woman fighting against the inevitable successor, and only Clifford's preoccupation with business could blind him to what anyone else could see. Of the two women, Maria preferred Shelley, who was no threat to her own position as mistress of the house. Shelley wanted only Lyle Waverly; Cynthia wanted his name, his life, and his home.

"Maria is a miracle," Shelley explained at the second party. "Imagine finding someone with her divine talent who is honest as well. Why, she's a perfect servant!"

"An honest woman?" Cynthia echoed. "Impossible! No woman can be honest and survive! Maria must have a few secrets."

Maria smiled blandly and continued to serve the ca napés.

"I refuse to believe it!" Dr. Waverly announced. "All my life I've searched for a pure woman and this is she!"

"Perhaps you'd better marry her, darling," Shelley said. "You could do worse."

That remark was aimed at Cynthia, and Maria didn't wait to hear the reply. She returned to the kitchen and began to clean up the party debris. It was sometime later,

after most of the guests had gone home and even Ramsey
Clifford had taxied off to catch a late plane for a business
appointment, that she heard Shelley berating Dr. Waverly for his interest in Cynthia Reardon. Maria returned to
the living room to collect abandoned glasses and saw them
alone.

"You needn't think I don't know what you're doing,"
Shelley was saying. "You needed me when you were beginning your practice—you needed my contacts and influence. Now you want a younger woman."

"Shelley, please," the doctor begged.

"No, I'm going to have my say! You want a younger
and a richer woman, don't you, darling? What better
catch than Josiah Reardon's sexy daughter? You'll never
hold her, Lyle. She'll wear you like a pendant until she's
bored with you. She's used up half a dozen handsome
young men already."

"I'm not a child!" Waverly protested.

"No. You're a man and vain enough to think you can
use Cynthia Reardon. I'm warning you, you'll be the one
who gets used!"

"You're jealous," Waverly said.

"Of course I'm jealous. I love you, and I need you,
Lyle. Now *I* need *you*—"

Maria retreated quickly to the kitchen before she was
noticed. Sometime later the doctor came in carrying the
glasses. All the guests were gone. He loosened his tie and
drew a deep breath. "The things they don't teach you in
medical school!" he sighed. "Maria, you are the only sane
person on earth. You must never leave me."

"I'll fix you a hot milk," Maria said.

"Oh, no—"

"A bromide?"

"Brilliant idea. Are you sure you never worked the social route before?"

Maria's face darkened. "I worked for women," she said.
"I didn't like it. They talk about you in front of others.

'You just can't trust anyone these days,' she said with savage mockery. 'They'll steal you blind and expect to get paid besides!' "

Waverly laughed. "I think I understand why honesty is so important to you. By the way, the thirty days are up. Did you ever go back to claim that hundred dollars?"

"Tomorrow," Maria said. "Tomorrow I go."

"Good! I hope it's there. If it isn't I'll give you a bonus to make up for losing it."

Maria returned to the police station the next day. Lieutenant Brandon gave her a paper to sign and then handed her the money, which was still held in the money clip made of cheap metal with a silver dollar for decoration. None of the claimants could identify the exact denominations of the bills or describe the clip, so the money was now legally hers.

"How's the job?" Brandon asked.

"The best one I ever had," Maria said.

"Now, that's what I like to hear! There's some justice in the world after all."

"Yes," Maria said, and slipped the money into her handbag.

Her position at the Waverly house continued to improve. She had her own room and, with an adequate household budget, was able to buy food less fattening than the starchy diet of the poor. She soon replaced her uniforms with a smaller size and had her hair done once a month. She was beginning to feel and look more like a woman. Waverly soon took notice.

"Maria," he said, "you never told me about your husband. He was one lucky guy. What was his name?"

"Wa—" she began.

"Juan?"

She smiled softly. "Yes," she said, "his name was Juan."

"Handsome?"

"Of course!"

"And a passionate devil, I'll bet! What do you have going for you now? There must be a boyfriend somewhere."

The doctor had been drinking. He slipped a friendly arm about her shoulder.

"No boyfriend," Maria said.

"No? That's a shame! What's the matter? With legs like yours you could still do a fancy fandango. I'll bet you've done many a fancy fandango in your day."

"In my day—yes," Maria admitted.

"Then get back in circulation. Take a night off once in a while. Take tonight off. I'm going out with Miss Reardon."

"In that case, I think I should make you another bromide."

"No, you don't! I'm just a teensy-weensy bit drunk and I need much more fortification tonight. I'm going to ask Miss Reardon to marry me."

"She will accept," Maria said flatly.

"That's what I'm afraid of. You see, Maria, I've never been married. I'm afraid of marriage. I like women but I like my freedom better."

"Then why—?"

"Why marry? Because it's the thing to do. It's stabilizing. It builds character. It's what every rising young doctor should do, Maria, but I'm still scared. I don't like to be dominated."

"Then don't be dominated," Maria said. "Be the boss."

Waverly picked up his glass. "I'll drink to that," he said.

But it was Maria who feared the marriage more than Waverly. No sooner was the engagement announced than Cynthia began to reorganize the household, and Maria began to worry again about her security. Waverly caught her reading the want ads and demanded an explanation.

"What's the matter? Aren't you happy here?" he asked. "Do you want more money?"

"No," Maria said.

"Then what's wrong?"

"Things will change after you marry."

"What things? Don't you like Miss Reardon?"

"It's not what I like. It's what Miss Reardon likes."

"Stop worrying. Nobody's going to treat you the way you were treated before I found you. I like you and that's all that matters. I'll tell you something I was going to keep secret. I've had my lawyer draw up a new will—a man does that when he gets married. I've made a five-thousand-dollar bequest in your behalf. Now do you feel more secure?"

Maria was reassured, but she had lived long enough to take nothing for granted except money in the bank. Dr. Waverly was impulsive and generous, but Cynthia Reardon was a spoiled, strong-willed girl and Shelley Clifford's description of her character was more accurate than anything a prospective bridegroom was likely to see. What's more, Shelley didn't give up the battle simply because the engagement was announced. The mores of Dr. Waverly's social set, Maria learned, were more liberal than her own.

Shelley immediately developed symptoms requiring the doctor's professional attention at indelicate hours—particularly when her husband was away on business. There were surreptitious calls going both ways. When Waverly finally refused to go to see Shelley again, she came to see him. Traveling over an unpaved, circuitous drive, Shelley's small imported coupe made the trip between the Clifford estate and the doctor's house with increasing frequency.

It was a shameful thing, Maria reflected, for a woman to cling so to a man. As much as she had loved her husband, she would have let him go the minute he no longer wanted her. But no matter how many women Walter might have had before their marriage, he was faithful to his vows. Walter—not Juan. Juan Morales was the name of the father Maria barely remembered. Walter Dwyer was the name of the man she had wed. But when one must work as a domestic for the Anglos, it seemed better not to let it be known that she had once been married to an Anglo, had once lived like a lady.

She had been hardly twenty when Walter married her, but Walter was a gambler and gamblers die broke. After settling with the creditors, there was nothing for the widow Dwyer to do but return to Tucson and again become Maria Morales, domestic.

She had nothing left of the past but what Walter had called her "Irish luck," but her mind was no longer servile. She saw things now with the eyes of Mrs. Walter Dwyer, and what she saw was troubling. When a woman lost at love it was the same as when a man lost at cards. If she cried, she cried alone. What she could never do was cling to anything that was finished.

If Cynthia Reardon knew what was going on, she showed no outward sign. She might even be enjoying Shelley's humiliation. If Ramsey Clifford knew what was going on, he was indifferent. Eventually Dr. Waverly had it out with Shelley in a verbal battle over the telephone. Maria didn't eavesdrop. It was impossible not to hear him shouting in his study.

"No, I won't come over tonight!" he shouted. "There's nothing wrong with you, Shelley, and I won't come over tonight or any other night! I suggest that you get another doctor. I have no time for a chronic neurotic."

It was cruel, but it seemed to work. The telephone calls stopped. Two weeks before the scheduled wedding, Cynthia Reardon moved into the doctor's house and Maria's moral values were again updated. It seemed to be accepted practice in the young doctor's circle and Maria made no comment.

But her worst fears about her future status were soon confirmed. She couldn't please the new mistress, who took Maria to task on the slightest provocation. The good days were finished. Cynthia was vicious. She would get whatever she wanted on her own terms either by using her sex or the lure of Josiah Reardon's wealth and prestige. If there was any doubt of who would rule the Waverly manse, it was decided the night of Josiah Reardon's prenuptial dinner party.

Once a week Dr. Waverly spent a day at the local free clinic, and, because Cynthia didn't care about these things, he sometimes talked about this work with Maria. It was the one thing of which he was genuinely proud, and because of it she was proud of him. A twelve-year-old Mexican boy had been under his care for some time. Minor surgery had been performed and confidence carefully built for the major surgery which, if successful, would restore him to a normal life. Half of the battle, Waverly assured her, was in the rapport he had established with the frightened boy. On the evening before the scheduled major surgery Reardon gave his dinner party. Maria heard the doctor try to get Cynthia to change the date.

"I have nine-o'clock surgery," he said. "It's imperative that I get my rest."

"You're not the only doctor at the clinic!" Cynthia scoffed.

"But this is a special case!"

"And Daddy's dinner isn't, I suppose! Lyle, you must be mad. You know Daddy doesn't change his plans for anyone, and this is a very special occasion. You see, darling, you're the first man I've ever known that Daddy liked. He thinks you're a stabilizing influence for me. I happen to know what his wedding present is going to be. What would you think of fifteen percent of the Reardon Corporation?"

Dr. Waverly thought through a few moments of absolute silence. "You're dreaming."

"Then I must have dreamed the papers I saw Daddy's lawyer drawing up. That's what the dinner is for tonight— the presentation of the gift. Now I know you can get somebody else to take over for you tomorrow. It's not as if you had a paying patient. It's just one of those clinic cases."

Maria held her breath and said a silent prayer, but she lost. Waverly went to the dinner with Cynthia. It was almost two A.M. when he returned and, minutes later, Cynthia was at the door. Maria heard them laughing in the entry hall.

"You shouldn't have come here," Waverly said. "The old boy doesn't know we've jumped the gun, and he might not like it."

"He would loathe it—but who cares? Darling, isn't it wonderful? You see, I didn't lie to you. We've got something to celebrate."

"It's so late—"

"A little nightcap—please."

Maria, listening from the kitchen, sighed and went back to bed. In the morning she arose, made a pot of coffee, and carried it up to Waverly's room. He was asleep. Cynthia opened one eye and then threw a pillow at her.

"Nobody called you!" she whispered angrily.

"The doctor has a hospital call—"

"Cancel it! Tell them he's sick or something. Can't you see that he's asleep? If you don't call the hospital this minute, I will!"

Maria retreated from the room. She went downstairs and phoned the hospital to inform them that Dr. Waverly couldn't perform the nine-o'clock operation. It was noon before the doctor came downstairs and that was just a few minutes after the hospital called to tell him that the boy had died on the operating table. It was a small event in the life of a young doctor who was slated to become the most popular society doctor in the area, but it destroyed Maria's last vision of Camelot.

She remembered that Walter, who was crude and uneducated, had once left a game during a winning streak— and that was the one thing he had taught her a gambler should never do—to donate blood to the black porter who parked his car at the casino each night. The friend who took over Walter's hand had lost everything, but that hadn't mattered because the porter lived and Walter came back as happy as a schoolboy playing hookey. And so Maria was thoroughly disenchanted with her position at the Waverly house even before the night that Shelley Clifford returned.

It was four nights before the wedding. Cynthia, tired from rehearsals of the ceremony, had gone up to bed and taken two sleeping pills. The doctor was preparing a deposit slip for the visit to the bank that he wanted Maria to make for him in the morning. Maria went to the front door when the bell rang and there was no way to keep Shelley out of the house. She had been drinking and was hysterical. One eye was blackened and she had a cut on one cheek. Her husband, she explained when Waverly hurried out of the study, had learned of their relationship and beaten her. Her story might be true or untrue, but the doctor's reaction was firm.

"You can't stay here!" he insisted.

"Just for tonight," she begged. "Ram's been drinking, too. I'm afraid to go home."

"I don't believe you," Waverly said. "Ram Clifford doesn't drink."

"He did tonight. I'm afraid, Lyle. I'm afraid he'll kill me!"

Maria watched the doctor's face. He looked as if he thought that might be a good solution. Firmly he took Shelley by the shoulders and turned her back toward the door.

"Then go to a hotel," he said.

"Why can't I stay here?"

"Because I won't let you."

Waverly was trying to keep his voice down. When Shelley noticed him glance apprehensively toward the stairs, she sensed immediately what he was trying to hide. Her eyes widened. "*She's* here, isn't she? Cynthia's *here!*"

And then she laughed and pushed Waverly away from her. "You couldn't even wait for the marriage! Oh, that's beautiful! Now wouldn't old Josiah Reardon love to know about this! His daughter may be a swinger, but the old boy's a stickler for the proprieties! And there's nothing more conservative than a savings and loan corporation, darling. When they hear about this you may not get that partnership and seat on the board of directors."

"Get out of the house!" Waverly ordered.

"Oh, I will, I will—just as soon as I've run upstairs to check—"

She lunged past him and started to run up the stairs. Waverly was about two steps behind her when the liquor, the shock, and the injuries caught up with Shelley. She was more than halfway up the stairway when she stumbled and fell against the railing. She shrieked and grabbed at the air and then, as both Waverly and Maria watched in horror, she plummeted over the railing and fell to the marble floor of the entry hall. There was a sickening sound as her head struck the marble. She was dead when Dr. Waverly reached her.

For a few moments he was too stunned to speak. Then he turned to Maria. "You've got to help me," he said.

"What do you mean?" Maria asked.

"You saw what happened. It was an accident—she killed herself. But I can't have her found in my house like this. Can you drive a car, Maria?"

"Yes."

"Good. Cynthia's asleep. The pills I gave her will last until morning. I'll get my car out of the garage and you follow me in it. I'll take Mrs. Clifford's body in her car and leave it out on that shortcut she uses."

Maria hesitated.

"Do you understand what I've said?" Waverly asked.

"I understand," Maria said, "but suppose the police come—"

"Out on that unpaved stretch? No chance. Anyway, I'll be the one taking the risk. I'll have the body with me. If you see a police car, just keep going."

"Still, there could be trouble," Maria said.

"Maria, there's no time to argue! I'm not going to hurt Mrs. Clifford—she's already dead. But I can't afford a scandal now. This is a matter of self-preservation!"

"With me, too, it is a matter of self-preservation," Maria said coldly.

It took the doctor a few seconds to understand Maria's words. He had taken her for granted too long a time to make a sudden change without a certain anguish. When he finally did understand, he asked how much self-preservation she had in mind.

"A will is risky," she said. "Wills can be changed. Five thousand dollars in cash is more reliable."

"I don't have that much money in the house," he protested.

"I'll take a check," Maria said.

Minutes later, the doctor's check tucked away in her handbag, Maria drove Waverly's sedan at a safe distance behind Mrs. Clifford's little sports car. There was no traffic at all on the narrow road. When they reached a wide shoulder forming a scenic view over a ravine, Waverly stopped the small car and parked off the roadway. Maria stopped the sedan and watched him carry Shelley Clifford's body to the edge of the shoulder and toss it into the shrubbery.

Waverly then returned to the car and emptied Shelley Clifford's handbag of all cash and credit cards. Leaving the emptied purse on the seat, and pocketing the items that a robber would steal, he then took out his pocketknife and jammed it between the treads of one rear tire, letting out the air. The scene was set: a flat tire on a seldom-used road; a passing car hailed and a grim harvest of murder and robbery.

Waverly folded his pocketknife and walked to the waiting sedan. He drove the car back to the house himself and then he and Maria scrubbed away the bloodstains on the marble entry floor.

When they had finished, Waverly said, "Nothing happened here tonight."

"Nothing," Maria agreed, "except that there's a bloodstain on your coat sleeve, Doctor. Give me the coat and I'll sponge out the stain before I go to bed."

Waverly pulled off his suit coat and gave it to her without hesitation. "Don't call me in the morning," he said. "I'm going to take a couple of sleeping pills myself."

Maria took the coat to her room but she didn't sponge out the blood. She turned off the light and tried to sleep. When that didn't work, she got up and packed her bag. In the morning she got the doctor's bank deposit from his study, the suitcase and the stained coat from her room, and then, because the keys were still in the ignition, drove the doctor's car to the bank. Ordinarily she would have taken the bus. Today was urgent. Because she was so well known at the bank, and particularly after having made the doctor's deposit, she had no difficulty cashing the check for $5,000.

On the return trip she took the unpaved shortcut. No other cars passed and she reached Mrs. Clifford's abandoned coupe unseen. Drawing alongside, she tossed Dr. Waverly's coat into the front seat, and then drove on.

Both Waverly and his fiancée were still asleep when Maria returned the doctor's sedan to the garage. Then, bag in hand, she walked to the bus stop.

Shelley Clifford's body was found early in the afternoon. The story of her death was on the evening television newscasts. An apparent victim of a casual murderer, her death inspired urgent editorial demand for increased police patrols and an end to permissive education. Ramsey Clifford offered a $10,000 reward for the apprehension and conviction of her murderer. It wasn't until the third day after Shelley's body was found that Lieutenant Gannon came to Dr. Waverly's house. He carried a small bundle wrapped in brown paper.

"I've been doing some checking, Doctor," he said. "I understand that you and the late Shelley Clifford were very good friends."

"You've picked up some gossip," Waverly stated.

"I don't think so. We didn't release all the evidence we had in her death when the body was found. We needed a little time to check out something that was found on the seat of her car—" Gannon ripped open the package and held up Waverly's suit coat. "We've traced this to your tailor, Dr. Waverly, and we've matched the bloodstains to Mrs. Clifford's. Now all we want from you is an explanation of what it was doing in her car."

On the fourth day after Shelley Clifford's death a smartly dressed, middle-aged woman checked into a hotel on the Nevada side of Lake Tahoe. She signed the register as Mrs. Walter Dwyer and then took a stroll through the casino because the atmosphere of a gambling town made her feel closer to Walter. Later, upstairs in her room, she studied the Tucson newspaper she had picked up in the lobby and was amused to learn that the police of that area were conducting an intensive search for her body.

Confronted with his blood-stained jacket, Waverly had told the truth—but he wasn't believed. When it developed that his housekeeper had last been seen on the morning of Mrs. Clifford's death cashing a $5,000 check at Waverly's bank, Lieutenant Gannon formed the theory that Waverly had used Maria Morales to get him some ready cash in the event the doctor was linked to Mrs. Clifford and had to leave the country, and had then disposed of the woman so she wouldn't talk.

It was all nonsense, of course, and Maria was sure that Gannon could prove nothing. No crime had been committed. The worst that could happen to Dr. Waverly was that his marriage would be called off. That was a little sad since he deserved Cynthia Reardon as much as she deserved him. The other thing that would happen— and this was the reason she had placed the doctor's coat in Mrs. Clifford's car—was that the community would be made aware of Waverly's true character. This was impera- tive, in Maria's mind, in view of the nature of his profession.

Mrs. Dwyer remained at the hotel for several weeks. By that time the Tucson papers no longer referred to the Shelley Clifford affair, and she could assume that it was in a state of permanent limbo with no need for her reap- pearance to save Waverly from a murder charge.

Before leaving the resort, Mrs. Dwyer put a down payment on a smartly furnished condominium apartment which, the salesman assured her, would bring prime weekly rental in high season. Mrs. Dwyer explained that she traveled in her work and would occupy the apartment only a few months of the year, but that it was nice to have roots somewhere and a woman did need a good invest- ment for her retirement years.

A few days later, a shabbily dressed woman, wearing a look of quiet despair in her eyes entered the Tahoe bus station. She carried a cheap suitcase and a handbag con- taining $100 in a money clip. The bills were old—in fact, they were the same bills, in the same money clip, that Maria Morales, who was then nineteen and the prettiest cocktail waitress on the Strip, saw drop from Walter Dwyer's pocket as he bent over a casino gambling table. Maria had nothing of her own but a $10 advance on her salary, and when she returned the $100 to Dwyer he was so impressed by her honesty, and other attributes, that he took her to dinner. A week later they were married and the marriage was for love—not the cheap bargain that Dr. Lyle Waverly had tried to make with Cynthia Reardon. The money and the clip had been Walter's wedding present.

"Keep it for luck," he said. "Your Irish luck."

In the bus station Maria bought a ticket to Sacramento, the state capital of California. There would be many wealthy people in that area who were so nervous about their own corruption that they would be eager to hire a housekeeper honest enough to go to the police station with $100 found on the street while looking for a job.

Walter had taught her never to walk out on a winning streak.

To give you a provocative idea of what Patricia McGerr's story is about, here are some alternate titles we considered:
> *Bait the Cop*
> *Round Robin*
> *Accessories After the Fact*
> *Somebody's Telling the Truth*

But because the story is so fiendishly clever, we decided on the title below.

PATRICIA McGERR

This one's a beauty

"This one's a beauty," Captain Rogan said cheerfully as he climbed into the car beside Sergeant Pringle.

It was an odd term to apply to a murder, but the sergeant nodded agreement. By Homicide Squad definition it described any investigation that could be wrapped up without overtime. And the case they were headed toward on this crisp January evening was, it appeared, right at the top of that category. The desk man had recorded the call at 7:47.

"This is Horace Sanderson," the authoritative voice at the other end had announced. "I want to report a murder. I've shot a man in my office."

So all they needed to do was visit the scene, hear his confession, and bring him in. As the captain said, "This one's a beauty."

"Sanderson," Pringle ruminated while he eased the car away from the curb. "Don't I know that name from somewhere?"

"You should," Rogan returned. "If he's never made a monkey of you on the witness stand, you're a lucky exception."

"Oh, sure, the big defense lawyer. No, I haven't testified in any of his cases, but I've heard plenty from those who have. They say he gets an extra charge out of making our guys sweat."

"Too right." Rogan's lips twisted wryly in personal recollection. "On cross-examination he can turn you around till you misspell your own name. But now it's our turn. I'm going to like seeing Mr. Horace Sanderson in the dock."

"Weird, isn't it, that after all the raps he's beaten for other people he'd turn himself in without a fight."

"It has to mean the evidence against him is airtight," Rogan said with satisfaction. "Sanderson knows criminal law up and down, backwards and sideways. If he could've seen the smallest loophole he'd never have started off by admitting he did it."

"Maybe he'll claim self-defense," the sergeant suggested.

"On the phone he called it murder. He knows every

meaning of that word and it doesn't include justifiable homicide."

"How about not guilty because of temporary insanity?"

"That's one he might try," Rogan conceded, "but it won't affect our schedule. All we want are the facts. If he decides to take the psycho route it'll be the D.A.'s headache. Unless the lab boys slow us down, we'll be drinking squad-room coffee again before ten o'clock tonight."

It was a short ride to the building that housed the Sanderson law offices. Pringle parked in front and the two men rode the elevator to the fourth floor. The only door that showed a light was lettered "Sanderson, Sanderson & Sanderson, Attorneys-at-Law." At Rogan's sharp rap it was opened by a tall broad-shouldered man of sixty-odd whose physique, grooming, and general air of affluence fitted him to intimidate the most hostile witness.

"You made fast time, gentlemen," he complimented them. "Captain Rogan, I believe." He paused to nudge his recollection. "Ah, yes, you were the arresting officer in the Hutchins murder, weren't you? A pity you got the wrong man. And your colleague—" He looked questioningly at Pringle. "I don't believe our paths have crossed before."

"This is Sergeant Pringle," Rogan snapped. Acquittal of the man he was sure had killed Tom Hutchins was still a rankling memory. "It's my duty to inform you that you are not required to answer—"

"Skip the litany," Sanderson cut him off. "I'm well informed as to my rights and I'm already represented by counsel. If you'll come into the next room I'll show you the corpse and tell you what happened."

A cool, cool customer, Rogan thought with reluctant admiration. *His head's halfway in the noose, but he's the same take-charge guy as he is in the courtroom.*

Sanderson crossed the reception room to open an

inner door. He passed through it, then stepped aside to unblock the view. Sprawled on the dark green rug of what appeared to be a conference room was a man's body.

Rogan dropped to one knee beside it. Lifting the left wrist he felt for a pulse, though he was sure he wouldn't find one. The blood-matted hair at the back of the head indicated that a bullet must have entered the brain to bring instant death.

"D.O.A.," he told Pringle. "We'll want the technical unit and the morgue wagon."

"Use the phone on the desk in the corner, Sergeant," Sanderson said helpfully.

Rogan straightened and looked down at the dead man. He had fallen forward, but the face was turned to rest on one cheek. Rogan felt a glimmer of recognition.

"An old friend, Captain?" Sanderson asked. "His name is—or was—Chet Tankersley."

Gambler, confidence man, jack-of-many-crooked-trades. The computer in Rogan's head punched the appropriate slots. No loss to society. He liked the case even better.

"You shot him?" he asked.

"With this gun." Sanderson stepped around the body to approach the long table that filled two thirds the length of the room and pointed to the weapon that lay on its mirror-bright surface. "I have a license for it, of course. A criminal practice can bring in some rough characters, so I keep it loaded and ready in my desk."

Is he laying a basis for self-defense after all, Rogan wondered, then looked again at the victim and was reassured. The shot had come from behind and the position of the body showed that Tankersley had been on his way out of the office.

Pringle had finished telephoning. "They're on the way, Captain," he reported.

"Fine. Now we'd better hear your story, Mr. Sanderson."

"I'm waiting to tell it," he assured him. "I want my lawyers present, of course."

Three private offices were connected to the conference room. On each was a name. Horace T. Sanderson, Sr., Horace T. Sanderson, Jr., Paul A. Sanderson. The lawyer walked to the center door—his own—and opened it to say, "Come out, boys, I need you."

"My sons and legal counsel," he introduced the two young men who answered the summons. "Horace, Junior, and Paul." Paul, the younger one, was a slim replica of his father, while Horace, Jr., slightly overweight, with narrow eyes and soft lips, showed no sign of the hard courage and sharp intelligence that marked the other two. Junior must favor the maternal line, Rogan decided. If the firm is to go on, it will be Paul who takes the old man's place.

"Sit down, gentlemen." Sanderson took a seat at the end of the table farthest from the body, with one son on each side. Sergeant Pringle stayed at a desk near the door. Rogan turned one of the chairs around and straddled it to retain a sense of mobility.

"I'll get right to the point." Sanderson, Sr.'s tone seemed more suited to chairing a board meeting than to confessing a crime. "This afternoon, Sonny—that is, Horace, Junior—told me he was being blackmailed. Tankersley had a certain document bearing Horace, Junior's signature that could, if made public, lead to his disbarment. Tankersley asked twenty-five thousand dollars and was coming here today after office hours to collect.

"Sonny had managed to raise fifteen thousand on his own and asked me for the balance. I advised him not to give the man one cent and said that I would deal with him myself. My two sons, therefore, left the office at five-thirty, the usual time, and drove home together. I stayed behind and was alone when Tankersley arrived.

"I told him there would be no payoff, now or ever, and threatened him with arrest for blackmail unless he immediately gave me the incriminating document. It was,

I admit, a bluff and it failed. That paper, as Tankersley well knew, would not only end my son's career but cast doubt on the integrity of our law firm. He grew abusive and said I had until noon tomorrow to change my mind. If by that time he did not receive the entire sum, the document would be delivered to the secretary of the Bar Association.

"Well, gentlemen, what could I do? I looked at that miserable creature who held in his hand my family name, my son's future, the professional reputation I'd built with such care." His voice rose to the dramatic height that had swayed so many juries. "Something exploded in my brain."

He paused and Rogan exchanged a quick glance with the sergeant. So it was to be a plea of temporary insanity.

"He walked out of my office. I took the gun from my drawer, followed him into this room, and shot him. Then I phoned my own house. Paul answered. I said I wanted them both here and they drove right back. I explained what had happened and, as my counsel, they advised me to notify the police and make a clean breast of it. Which I have just done."

"And the document that Tankersley was holding?" Rogan asked.

"I took it from the dead man's pocket, tore it into small pieces, burned the pieces, and flushed away the ashes. I apologize for destroying evidence, but I believe my motive is clear enough without making public what I've killed a man to keep secret."

Before Rogan could answer, a rap on the outer door signaled the arrival of the technical unit. Admitted by Pringle and instructed by Rogan, they set about their routines with camera and other equipment. The captain returned to the three Sandersons.

"I appreciate your giving us such a straightforward story," Rogan told the father.

"I like to make your job easy when I can, Captain,"

Sanderson, Sr., returned with sham geniality. "Besides, I really have no choice. The body is in my office. The bullet came from my gun. Tankersley may even have told some-one about his appointment with Sonny. I know better than to try to buck those odds."

"Then the next step is to go to headquarters, get your statement typed and signed, and—"

"I'm familiar with the procedure," Sanderson re-minded him. "And I'm sure you'll follow all the rules. We can't charge police brutality tonight, can we, boys?"

"No, we can't," Paul answered for them both. His glance at Rogan held the same glint of mockery as his father's. "Our client's statement was freely given and is correct in almost every detail."

"Almost?" Rogan felt a stir of apprehension on the edge of his complacency.

"He's made one significant error," Paul continued. "Sonny didn't say anything to Dad about being black-mailed. Sonny told me."

"Oh? Then you passed it on to your father?"

"Certainly not. I agreed with my brother that we'd better keep it to ourselves. So I told Dad I had some work to finish, and he and Sonny left together. After that every-thing happened just as my father reported it—except it was I who waited here for Tankersley. I'm the one who shot him."

"You—" Rogan left the sentence suspended.

"It's his word against mine, Captain," Sanderson, Sr., said. "Which of us do you believe?"

"I'll get that answer from your other son." Rogan's eyes moved to Horace, Jr. "Did you tell your father or your brother about the blackmail? Which one rode home with you?"

Sonny's gaze stayed on the tabletop. His voice was low, with each word forced through stiff lips.

"I didn't tell anybody," he answered. "And I didn't

go home. I said *I* had work to finish and let Dad and Paul leave without me. When Tankersley came I told him I had only fifteen thousand. He said it wasn't enough, he was sure my father would give me the rest sooner than see me disgraced. I said I didn't want Dad to know and he laughed at me. He said I had until twelve o'clock tomorrow noon to raise the whole twenty-five thousand or—as Dad told you—he'd turn the paper over to the Bar Association. I couldn't let that happen. So when he started to go, I—I shot him."

"Where did you get the gun?"

"Out of Dad's drawer. I know where he keeps it."

"Let's see if I have the picture straight. Tankersley left your office, you ran into your father's room, took his gun, and—"

"No," Sonny interrupted. "I was already in Dad's room when I talked to Tankersley. I'd put the money in his safe and wanted to be where I could get it out right away if he agreed to settle for what I had."

"And you?" He turned to the younger brother. "Where did you conduct the interview?"

"I'm the junior junior partner," Paul returned smoothly. "My room is small and my desk cluttered. When Dad's away I take my visitors into his office."

Very carefully arranged, Rogan thought glumly. Tankersley's fingerprints will show up only in the father's office—just as all three stories indicate.

"We're a close-knit family," Sanderson explained. "I told my two sons that I was guilty and that they shouldn't interfere. But you know how it is with young people nowadays. No respect."

"One of you killed Tankersley." Rogan organized his thinking out loud. "Then he called the other two back to the office. The three of you talked it over and cooked up this round robin."

"Exactly." Sanderson beamed at him. "So you have two confessions left over. Untidy, isn't it? If one of us is charged, each of the other two will swear he did it. You haven't a prayer of getting an indictment, much less a conviction."

"Don't bet on it, Mr. Sanderson," Rogan said. "You've wasted your time and mine with your phony confessions."

"Only two are phony," Paul murmured. "One of us is telling the truth."

Rogan ignored the interruption. "Now we'll get on with our work, just as we would if all three of you had denied it. We solve a fair number of cases without anybody coming forward to say he did it." He could not resist the sarcasm. "Sometimes we even convict one of your clients."

"Indeed you do," Sanderson agreed heartily. "The city has a very efficient force and I'll observe your work with great interest." He looked beyond Rogan to watch the morgue men cover the body preparatory to its removal. "I don't usually get to see the start of an investigation. But I'm afraid the evidence you'll collect here won't be very helpful. Fingerprints, for instance. I know how important they can be. But we were a bit nervous while we waited for you and we wandered about opening doors and drawers. As a result you'll find all three sets of prints in random order all over the place."

"In other words," Rogan interpreted, "the one who committed the crime gave the other two a step-by-step account of his actions from the moment of Tankersley's arrival. Then the other two reenacted the crime, taking care to touch all pertinent surfaces. No doubt all three of you handled the weapon."

"Naturally." Sanderson's face burlesqued repentance. "I'm afraid we did something even more reprehensible. I call your attention to the holes in the wall near the ceiling.

The two of us who aren't guilty both took a shot up there. Very bad for the paneling, but tests will show that all three of us recently fired a gun."

The old sod's enjoying this, Rogan thought sourly. He's used to being called in to pick up the pieces after his client has made a mess of it and the police have all the evidence. For the first time he's been on the scene ahead of us, able to set the stage to show exactly what he wants us to see. He's handled more murder cases than most policemen and can anticipate all our moves, plus some we might not think of.

"Worried, Captain?" the senior Sanderson prodded.

"Just trying to work out a timetable." Rogan left his chair and walked to the head of the table to place himself between father and older son. "You said your sons left here at five-thirty." He focused on the father. "How long does it usually take to get home?"

"In normal traffic, twenty-five minutes."

"And what time did you phone them?"

"Six-fifteen. My interview with Tankersley was brief."

"Then I can assume they got back here at six-forty. Right?"

"Give or take five minutes, that's correct."

"That gave you a full hour to discuss the situation, make a plan, and arrange the—er—stage effects. I'm inclined to agree with you, Mr. Sanderson, that we won't find evidence here to point to the one who actually committed the murder." He waited for the other man's lips to curve into a satisfied smile before adding, "It may be easier to discover which two went home."

Rogan whirled to face Horace, Jr., and leaned down till their noses were only inches apart. "Tell me, Sonny," he barked, "who drove the car home?"

"Dad always—" The young man broke off, gulped air. "I mean, I don't know who drove tonight. I didn't go home. I told you, I stayed here. I—" His eyes darted to his father, seeking rescue.

"Don't bully the boy," Sanderson said softly. "He's already told his story."

"But he was about to tell a different one. He started to say that you drove home and he rode beside you. That places Paul in the office at the time of the murder."

"So it does," Paul agreed. "You see, I was telling the truth all the time."

"Don't talk nonsense, Captain," Sanderson ordered. "What Sonny started to say was 'Dad always drives.' And that's true. When the three of us are together, I'm always the driver. But I wasn't in the car this evening, so I presume Paul took the wheel. That's how it usually is, isn't it, Sonny?"

"Yes, I—I don't care much for driving."

And you don't care much for this game of bait-the-cop either, Rogan added mentally. Sanderson, Sr., and Paul are riding every wave, but Sonny looks as if he's about to go under. Judging by the way he acts, he's guilty as hell, but that doesn't move me forward. Unquestionably he's guilty of falling into a blackmail trap—which makes him responsible for what happened tonight, even if someone else did the shooting.

Rogan walked down the table to confer with Sergeant Pringle, then returned to the Sandersons.

"Thought of some more questions, Captain?" the father asked.

"The same one," Rogan answered. "Which of you three killed him? We're going to look for the answer in places where you didn't have time to doctor the evidence. Your house and your car, for instance."

"Good thinking," Sanderson applauded. "Since you can't find the guilty one, maybe you can pin down the two who are innocent. The car's parked in the garage under this building, but I doubt if it will yield any secrets. Will it, Paul?"

"No, Dad," the younger son answered confidently. "You see," Paul told Rogan, "after I asked my father and brother to come back here, it occurred to us that you'd be curious about who drove and who was in the passenger seat. So I went down with a clean cloth and wiped off the wheel, the door handles—did a general cleanup job. Your fingerprint man is going to draw another blank."

"But you didn't go all the way home with your clean cloth, did you?" Rogan asked. "Or did you alert someone there to take care of it?"

"No," Paul conceded. "Mom's out of town and we're batching it this week. You'll get a fine collection of prints at home. But since that's where the three of us live, I don't know what you expect them to prove."

"Don't underestimate the captain's intelligence," his father advised. "He's thinking of spots like doorknobs which might indicate who was the last man to go in or out."

"How disappointing for you," Paul said. "There's an electric gadget in the car that opens the garage door. The stairs go right into the center hall with no need to turn any knobs."

"Don't overlook the telephone," Sanderson suggested. "If it was Paul who answered my call, as I said he did, his prints will be on top. Unless he was in his own room at the time, in which case the prints won't prove anything."

"No more," Paul seconded, "than can be proved if Dad took my call on his bedside phone."

"Just to complete the circle, Sonny," Rogan asked without enthusiasm, "who answered the phone when you called home?"

"Paul did. But I asked him to let me talk to Dad."

"You're not forgetting," Sanderson put in, "the possibility of witnesses?"

"I'm sure you didn't forget it, either," Rogan returned.

"The boys assured me there was no one else in the elevator or in the garage when they left here and, of course, by the time they got back, the building was empty. If we weren't sure of that we wouldn't be taking this line."

"But the streets and sidewalks weren't deserted," Rogan reminded him. "There's no way on earth you can be sure that someone won't come forward who saw you somewhere along the way."

"No doubt many people saw the car," Sanderson agreed. "But it was dark by five-thirty and I challenge anybody to make positive identification in a moving vehicle under those conditions. Especially when there's such a strong family resemblance."

So now, Rogan told himself, we're back to Go. Sanderson has foreseen every possible move. He reads my thoughts even before I think them.

Rogan left them to pace restlessly around the table. Since Sanderson is so knowledgeable about how the official mind works, I'd better stop thinking like a police officer and try to get inside the murderer. There must be some place he's slipped up.

He looked back at his antagonists. Sanderson, Sr., and Paul were talking in low tones. Sonny watched them warily. Who scares Sonny most, Rogan wondered, his father or me? Is he shaking because he may be tagged for murder or because he may not be able to stick to the lie the old man's making him tell? Junior's getting closer and closer to the edge. If I could talk to him alone, he'd break. But the other two won't let that happen.

Rogan went into the office marked with the name of Horace, Jr., and sat down at a desk whose bare top could indicate either extreme efficiency or that he was given very little to do. An inspection of the nearly empty drawers tended to support the second theory. Sergeant Pringle came in to report that the car, as predicted, showed no clue as to its most recent occupants.

"Tough going, Captain," the sergeant commiserated. "You got a favorite?"

"I like Sonny for it," Rogan answered. "His father and brother are the smart ones, the glib ones, the two who can stick to a lie and sidestep any trap that might give them away. If one of them had killed Tankersley, it's not likely they'd set up an escape route that would be shut off if Sonny broke under pressure. But with Sonny as the killer, the three-way confession lets him tell nothing but the truth. That way Sonny knows the answer to every question we ask and only the other two need to be quick-witted."

"He looks like a very nervous boy," Pringle said. "Too bad you can't lean on him a little."

"Maybe I can. I'm thinking about a breath test."

"The kind the traffic squad uses on drunk drivers?"

"That's it. Can you get a machine up here in a hurry?"

"Right away." Pringle looked puzzled, but he didn't ask any more questions. While he telephoned, Rogan moved on to the office of Sanderson, Sr., where the technicians were turning up an abundance of prints that pointed nowhere. Then he looked into Paul's room, which confirmed the younger son's statement about its smallness and clutter. When the sergeant announced the arrival of an officer with a breath machine, Rogan escorted all of them to the table.

"You don't seem to be making much progress, Captain," Sanderson jibed.

"I'm still trying to eliminate the two who are lying," Rogan answered. "We've established that they arrived home about twenty minutes before the phone call that brought them back. The question is, how did they spend that time at home?"

"An intriguing question," Sanderson said. "Unfortunately, since none of us admit having gone home, there's no one to answer it."

"So I'll have to guess. What does a successful lawyer

do at the end of a hard day's work? I think he unwinds over a drink. Am I right?"

"Absolutely," Sanderson agreed. "My personal preference is a very dry martini. But I don't see how that's relevant."

"I'm going to ask you to cooperate in an experiment. We have here a machine that measures blood alcohol content. If three of you blow into it and two register a recent intake of alcohol—well, you follow my reasoning, I'm sure."

"You'll put it down that those two were relaxing at home while the third was committing murder. Very ingenious." Sanderson's tone was indulgent. "I've never seen one of these before. Always been curious about how they work."

The officer placed the box-like machine in front of Sanderson, twisted a dial, and put a narrow tube into his hand.

"Just blow into it," Rogan directed. "The needle will tell us if you've had a drink."

Sanderson followed instructions. The needle stayed at zero. The officer turned the machine to Paul, who provided a breath sample with the same result.

"Another good idea gone wrong," Sanderson said in mock sympathy as the machine was moved in front of Sonny. "There's one flaw in your reasoning, Captain. We're civilized people who treat our before-dinner drinks with ceremony. We don't rush from car to bar." He looked at his older son who was regarding the machine with a suspicious scowl. "Go ahead, Sonny. It won't bite."

"This is stupid," Sonny said.

"Play the game," his father ordered. "Give the captain his full quota of hot air."

The officer lifted the tube to Sonny's mouth. His scowl deepened, but he gave a quick exhalation. The needle moved to the left.

"Alcoholic content point zero eight," the officer read. "At his weight that's about four ounces."

"What?" Sanderson exploded. "That's impossible. Sonny wasn't even—" He broke off, clamped his lips shut.

"Go on," Rogan prodded. "Finish the sentence. 'Sonny wasn't even at home tonight!' Of course he wasn't. You wouldn't have been so willing to take the test if you weren't sure there were no drinks taken at your house. What you didn't allow for was the possibility that Sonny gave you a censored account of his activities after you left the office. He probably has a habit of not telling you things you'd disapprove of."

"I don't know what you're getting at," Sanderson said. "Your machine's obviously broken."

"That can be checked," Rogan said impassively. "You've been a step ahead of me all the way, Mr. Sanderson. Too bad you don't have as thorough an understanding of your older son. He had a twenty-five-minute wait from the time he killed Tankersley until you two got back here. He was alone with a dead body, facing a murder charge and—maybe worst of all—about to have to explain it all to you. It should have occurred to you that he'd need a stiff drink to steady his nerves. Then you'd have found the vodka bottle he has hidden in his desk and fitted it into your triple confession. You see, Sonny, it doesn't pay to lie to your father."

"Why, you—" Sonny made a lunge toward Rogan.

"Shut up, you fool," his father barked. "Sit still and keep your mouth shut."

"*You* told me to blow in his machine." Sonny turned furiously on his father. "I didn't want to do it, but you think you're so damn smart. I shouldn't have phoned you. I should have taken my fifteen thousand and headed for Mexico. I knew your fancy scheme would never work."

"It came close," Rogan said pleasantly. "Do you and

Paul want to withdraw your confessions now?" he asked
Sanderson. "Or will you wait until you're charged as accessories after the fact?"

---

*It was the oddest thing that ever happened to eight-year-
old David or to his mother and father. It was the oddest
thing that ever happened in the Park Avenue apartment
house where David and his parents lived, or for that matter, that ever happened in the whole city of New York.
And it wasn't just oddness. It was something more. . . .
Evan Hunter is the author of* The Blackboard Jungle, *and
as Ed McBain he created the 87th Precinct and has been
giving us some of the best police procedurals written by
an American. "Someone at the Door" is atypical Evan
Hunter, and you'll find it subtler and far more meaningful
than it may at first appear.*

EVAN HUNTER

Someone at the door

David's mother took him with her to Paris the day after
his eighth birthday, which was July the fourth.

Paris was all lights. It was the best time he ever had

in his life. Even if the business with the doorbell hadn't happened when they got back from Paris, he *still* would think of Paris as the best time he ever had. They were staying at a very nice hotel called the Raphäel on Avenue Kléber. Hardly anyone spoke English at the Raphäel because it was a very French hotel, and English was grating on the ears.

David learned a lot there. He learned, for example, that when someone asked *"Quel temps fait-il?"* you did not always answer, *"Il fait beau,"* the way they did in Miss Canaday's class even if it was snowing. He told this to Miss Canaday when they got back from Paris, and she said, "David, I like to think of the weather as being *toujours beau, toujours beau."* He used to speak to the concierge on the phone every morning. He would say, *"Bonjour, monsieur, quel temps fait-il, s'il vous plait?"* And the concierge would usually answer in a very solemn voice, *"Il pleut, mon petit monsieur."*

It rained a lot while they were in Paris.

He and his mother had a suite at the Raphäel, two bedrooms and a sort of living room with windows that opened onto a nice stone balcony. David used to go out on the balcony and stand with the pigeons when it wasn't raining. The reason they had a suite was that his mother was a buyer for a department store on Fifth Avenue, and they sent her over each year, sometimes twice a year, to study all the new fashions. What it amounted to was that the *store* was paying for the suite. David's father was account executive and vice president of an advertising agency that had thirty-nine vice presidents. The reason he did not go to Paris that summer was that he had to stay home in New York to make sure one of his accounts did not cancel. So David went instead, to keep her company. He wrote to his father every day they were in Paris.

Escargots were little snails, but they didn't really look like snails except for the shell, and they didn't taste like them at all. They tasted like garlic. David and his mother ate a lot of *escargots* in Paris. In fact, they ate a lot of everything in Paris. They used to spend most of their time eating. What they would do, his mother would leave a call with the desk for eight o'clock in the morning. The phone would ring and David would jump out of bed and run into his mother's bedroom and ask her if he could talk to the concierge for a moment. *"Bonjour, monsieur,"* he would say, *"quel temps fait-il, s'il vous plait?"* and the concierge would tell him what kind of day it was and then he would hand the phone back to his mother and lie in her arms while she ordered breakfast.

Every morning they had either melon or orange juice, and then croissants and coffee for his mother, and croissants and hot chocolate for David. The chocolate was very good; the room waiter told them it came from Switzerland. They would eat at a little table just inside the big windows that opened onto the stone balcony. His mother used to wear a very puffy white nylon robe over her night-gown. One morning a man in the building opposite waved at her and winked.

The salon showings usually started at ten in the morning. Some days there were no showings at all, and some days they would go to the showing at ten and then have lunch and go to another one at two, and then another one around cocktail time. His mother was a pretty important buyer, so she knew all the designers and the models and they used to go in the back and everybody would make a fuss over David. He didn't mind being kissed by all the models, who all smelled very nice. Once, when he went back before a showing, two of the models were still in their brassieres. One of them said something in French (she said it very fast, not at all like Miss Canaday or the concierge) and the other models started laughing, and his mother laughed, too. He didn't know what was so funny; he'd seen a *hundred* brassieres in his lifetime.

For lunch they used to like the cheese place best; it was called Androuet, and it had about 800 cheeses you could choose from. Every now and then they would go to a place on the Left Bank, but that was only when his mother was trying to impress a designer, and then David was supposed to just keep his mouth shut and not say anything, just eat. They had the most fun when they were alone. One night in the restaurant on top of the Eiffel Tower, his mother ordered red wine for him. She held up her glass in a toast and he clinked his glass against hers and saw that she was crying.

"What is it?" he said.

"Nothing," she answered. "Taste your wine, David. It's really lovely."

"No, what is it?" he insisted.

"I miss Daddy," she said.

The next day he sent his father a card from Notre Dame. On the back he wrote, as a little joke, "Can you find Quasimodo?" He had read *The Hunchback of Notre Dame* in *Classics Illustrated*. His father wrote back and in his letter he sent a thing that he had one of his art directors work up. It was a composite paste-up from the monster magazines, with very big type across the top saying: "Yes, *this* is Quasimodo! But where oh where is DAVID?"

The 14th of July, Bastille Day, fell on a Sunday and that was lucky to begin with because it meant there were no showings to attend. David woke up at eight o'clock and then slept for another two hours in his mother's bed and then they had breakfast and she said, "David, how would you like to go out into the country for a picnic?"

So that's what they did. They hired a car and drove out down by the Loire, where all the French castles were, and they stopped by the river and had sausage and bread and cheese and red wine (his mother said it was O.K. for him to drink all the wine he wanted to while they were in France) and then they drove back to Paris at about seven in the evening, getting caught in the traffic around the Etoile. Later they stood on their little stone balcony and he held his mother's hand and they watched the fireworks exploding over the rooftops. He didn't think he would forget those fireworks as long as he lived.

The next week they were back in New York.

The week after that the doorbell started to ring.

The building they lived in was on Park Avenue and there were two apartments on their floor—their own and Mrs. Shavinsky's, who was an old lady in her seventies and very mean. Mrs. Shavinsky was the type who always said to David as he came off the elevator, "Wipe the mud off your shoes, young man." Mrs. Shavinsky wore hats and gloves all the time because she was originally from San Francisco. She was constantly telling the elevator operator, as if he cared, that in San Francisco all the ladies wore hats and gloves.

Even though there were only two apartments on the floor, there were four doors in the hallway because each apartment had two doors, one for people and the other for service. Their own main-entrance door was on one side of the hall, and Mrs. Shavinsky's was on the other side. The two service doors were in a sort of alcove opposite the elevator. They hardly ever saw Mrs. Shavinsky (except she always managed to be there when David got off the elevator, to tell him about his muddy shoes) until the business with the doorbell started, and then they practically lived in each other's apartment.

The first time the doorbell rang it was two o'clock in the morning on July 29th, which was a Monday.

David's bedroom was right behind his mother's and when the doorbell rang he sat up in bed thinking it was the telephone. In fact, he could hear his mother lifting the phone from the receiver alongside her bed, since she thought it was the phone, too. She said, "Hello," and then the ringing came again, from the front door, and there was a short silence. His mother put the phone back on its cradle and whispered, "Fred, you'd better get up."

"What?" David's father said.

"There's someone at the door."

"What?" he said again.

"There's someone at the door."

His father must have looked at the clock near the bed because David heard him whisper, "Don't be ridiculous, Lo. It's two o'clock in the morning." His mother's name was Lois, but everybody called her Lo except David's grandmother, who called her Lois Ann, which was her full name.

"Someone just rang the doorbell," his mother said.

"I didn't hear anything," his father said.

"Fred, please see who it is, won't you?"

"All right, but I'm telling you I didn't hear anything."

The doorbell rang again at just that moment. From the other end of the apartment, where the housekeeper slept, David heard her yelling, "Mr. Ravitch, there is somebody at the door."

"I hear it, Helga, thank you," David's father called, and then a light snapped on and David heard him swearing as he got out of bed. David went to the doorway of his room just as his father passed by in his pajamas.

"What is it?" David whispered.

"Someone at the door," he said. "Go back to bed."

His father walked through the long corridor leading to the front door, stubbing his toe on something in the dark and mumbling about it, and then turning on the light in the entrance foyer.

"Who's there?" he said to the closed door.

Nobody answered.

"Is someone there?" he called out.

Again there was no answer. From where David was

standing at the end of the long hall he heard his father sigh and then he heard the lock on the door being turned and the door being opened. There was a moment's hesitation, then his father closed the door again and locked it, and began walking back to his bedroom.

"Who was it?" David asked.

"Nobody," his father answered. "Go back to sleep."

That was the first time with the doorbell.

The second time was two nights later, on a Wednesday, and also early in the morning, though not at two o'clock. David must have been sleeping very soundly because he didn't even hear the doorbell ringing. The thing that woke him up was his mother's voice saying something to his father as he ran down the corridor to the front door. Helga had come out of her room and was standing in her pajamas watching his father as he went to the door and unlocked it. David's mother was wearing the same white nylon puffy robe she used to wear when they were in Paris.

"Did they ring the doorbell again?" David asked her.

"Yes," she said, and just then his father opened the door.

"Who is it?" David's mother asked.

"There's no one here, Lo."

"But I heard the bell. Didn't you?"

"Yes, I heard it."

"I heard it, too, Mr. Ravitch," Helga said.

"I wonder," David's father said.

"What do you think?" David's mother asked.

"Maybe someone rang it by mistake."

"Monday night, too?"

"It's possible."

"And left without waiting for the door to open?"

"Maybe he was embarrassed. Maybe he realized his mistake and—"

"I don't know," David's mother said, and shrugged.

"It all seems very peculiar." She turned to David and cupped his chin in her hand. "David, I want you to go back to bed. You look very sleepy."

"I'm not. We used to stay up much later than this in Paris."

"How you gonna keep 'em down on the farm?" his father said, and both his mother and Helga laughed. "Listen, Lo, I'd like to check this with the elevator operator."

"That's a good idea. Come, David, bed."

"Can't I just stay to see who it was?" David asked.

"There's probably some very simple explanation," his mother said.

The elevator operator was a man David had never seen before, about fifty years old, but with a hearing aid. David knew the other elevator man in the building, but he supposed this one always had the shift late at night, which is why he'd never seen him before. The man told his father his name was Oscar and asked him what the trouble was.

"Someone just rang our doorbell."

"Yes?"

"Yes. Did you take anyone up to our floor just now?"

"No, sir. Not since I came on, sir."

"And when was that?"

"I came on at midnight, sir."

"And you didn't take anyone up to the eleventh floor all night?"

"No, sir."

"What is it?" David heard a voice ask, and he looked past his father to the opposite end of the hallway where Mrs. Shavinsky had opened her door and was looking out. "What's all the noise about?" she said. "Do you realize what time it is?" She was wearing a big flannel nightgown with red roses strewn all over it, printed ones. Her hair was in curlers.

"I'm terribly sorry, Mrs. Shavinsky," David's father said. "We didn't mean to awaken you."

"Yes—well, you did," Mrs. Shavinsky said. "What's going on?"

"Someone rang our bell," his mother said.

"Good morning, Mrs. Shavinsky," David said.

"Good morning, young man," Mrs. Shavinsky said. "It is far past your bedtime."

"I know," David said. "We're up to catch the bell ringer."

"Did you say someone rang your bell?" Mrs. Shavinsky asked, ignoring David and looking at his mother.

"Yes. Monday night, and now again."

"Well, who was it?" Mrs. Shavinsky asked.

"That's what we don't know," David said. "That's why we're all here in the hallway."

"It was probably some d-r-u-n-k," Mrs. Shavinsky said.

"No, it wasn't no drunk, ma'am," Oscar said. "I didn't take nobody up here."

"Then why would anyone want to ring your bell at three-thirty in the morning?" Mrs. Shavinsky asked, and no one could answer her.

Later David's mother kissed his cheeks and the tip of his nose and his forehead and hugged him tight and tucked him in.

Mrs. Shavinsky told David about her demitasse cups the next day, and when he hinted that he would like to see them, she asked him to wipe off his feet and come into the apartment. The apartment smelled of emptiness, the way a lot of apartments smell when there is only one person living in them. She had her demitasse collection in a china closet in the dining room. David told her it must be fun to have a big dining-room table like the one she had, and then he looked at her demitasse cups, which were really quite nice. She had about thirty-seven cups, he guessed. Four of them had gold insides. She said they were very valuable.

"How much do they cost?" he asked her.

"You should never ask anyone that," she said.

"Why not?"

"Because it is impolite."

"But you told me they were valuable, Mrs. Shavinsky."

"They are," she said

"Then why is it impolite to ask how much they cost?"

"It's not only impolite," she said, "it's impertinent as as well."

"I'm sorry, Mrs. Shavinsky," he said.

"They cost several thousand dollars," she said. Her voice lowered. "Do you think the bell ringer is after them?" she asked.

"After what?" he said.

"After my demitasse cups?"

"I don't think so," he said.

"Then why would he ring your bell at three-thirty in the morning?"

"I don't know, Mrs. Shavinsky, but it seems to me if he was after *your* cups he would ring *your* bell. Maybe he's after *our* cups."

"Do you have a valuable collection of demitasse cups, too?" Mrs. Shavinsky asked.

David shook his head.

"Then how, would you please tell me, could he be after *your* demitasse cups, if you do not even *own* demitasse cups?"

"I meant our coffeecups. In the kitchen."

Mrs. Shavinsky wasn't sure whether or not he was making fun of her, which he wasn't, so she sent him away.

That night the doorbell rang at one o'clock in the morning.

David was asleep but his father was still awake and watching the news on television. The doorbell rang and David's father leaped out of bed at the first ring and ran down the long hall to the front door and pulled open the door without saying a word.

There was no one there.

"Damn it!" he yelled, and woke up the whole house.

"What is it?" David's mother called.

"Damn it, there's no one here," his father said.

"What is it, Mr. Ravitch?" Helga called from her bedroom.

"Oh, go to sleep, Helga," his father said.

David was awake by this time but he knew better than to ask his father any questions. He just lay in bed watching the ceiling and realizing that the doorbell had rung again, and his father had gone to answer it again, and again no one was there. Through the wall separating his bedroom from his mother's he heard his father going into the room and getting into bed, and then he heard his mother whisper, "Don't be upset."

"I *am* upset," his father whispered back.

"It's probably just someone's idea of a joke."

"Some joke."

"He'll grow tired of it."

"He's got Helga scared out of her wits."

"She'll survive."

"How the hell does he disappear so quickly?" his father whispered.

"I don't know. Try to get some sleep, darling."

"Mmm," his father said.

"There."

"Mmmmm."

While David was investigating the hallway the next day, Mrs. Shavinsky's housekeeper came out with the garbage. Her name was Mary Vincent, but David was not sure whether Vincent was her last name or just part of her first name, the way "Ann" was part of his mother's "Lois Ann." When Mary Vincent came out with the garbage he was pacing off the number of steps from the stairway off the service alcove to the front doorbell.

"What are you doing, David?" Mary Vincent said.

"There are fifteen paces," he said. "How long do you think it would take to run fifteen paces from our door to those steps?"

"I don't know. How long would it take?"

"Well, I don't know, Mary Vincent. But whoever is ringing the doorbell manages to disappear before we can open the door. If he doesn't use the elevator, he *must* use the steps, don't you think?"

"Unless it's an inside job," Mary Vincent said.

"What does that mean? An inside job?"

"Somebody in the apartment."

"You mean somebody in *our* apartment?"

"Could be," Mary Vincent said, and shrugged.

"Well, that would mean just my family." David paused. "Or Helga."

"I didn't say nothing," Mary Vincent said.

"Why would Helga want to ring the doorbell in the middle of the night?"

"I didn't say nothing," Mary Vincent said again. "All I know is she was mighty angry while your mother and you were away in France and she had to stay here and work, anyway, without no kind of a vacation."

"But she is getting a vacation. Mother asked her if she wanted to take her vacation when we went away or in August sometime, and Helga said August."

"That ain't what she told me right here in this hallway, David."

"When was this?"

"When we were putting out the garbage."

"I mean *when*."

"When you and your mother were in France."

"Well, that sounds awfully strange to me," David said.

"It sounds strange to me, too," Mary Vincent said, "that somebody would be ringing your doorbell in the middle of the night."

"I don't even see how Helga could manage it," David said.

"Her bedroom is right close to the service entrance, ain't it?"

"Yes, but—"

"Then what's to stop her getting out of bed, opening the back door, ringing the front doorbell, and then coming in again through the back door and right into her bed? What's to stop her, David?"

"Nothing, I guess. Only—"

"Only what?"

"Only why would she want to?"

"Spite, David. There's people in this world who do things only because it brings trouble and worry to others. Spite," Mary Vincent said, "plain and simple spite. If I was you, David, I would keep my eye on her." Mary Vincent laughed, and then said, "In fact, I would keep *both* my eyes on her."

David started keeping his eyes on her that very night because the doorbell rang at exactly 2:13 A.M. David had a watch that was waterproof and shock resistant—his grandfather had given it to him for his seventh birthday. When he heard the doorbell ring he jumped up in bed and turned on the light and looked at the watch, and it was exactly 2:13 A.M.

"There it goes again," he heard his father say in the next room, but David was listening for sounds coming from the back door. He didn't hear anything. The doorbell rang again.

"Let him ring," his father said. "If he thinks I'm getting out of bed every night he's crazy!"

The doorbell rang again. David still hadn't heard a

sound from Helga's room. He kept looking at the sweep hand of his watch. It was now 2:15.

"Are you just going to let it ring?" his mother whispered.

"Yep," his father said.

"All night?"

"If he *wants* to ring the damn thing all night, then I'll *let* him ring it all night."

"He'll wake up Mrs. Shavinsky."

"So he'll wake up Mrs. Shavinsky."

"He'll wake up the whole building."

"Who cares?" David's father said, and his mother giggled, and the doorbell kept on ringing. David still hadn't heard a peep from Helga.

"Mom?" he said.

"David? Are you awake?"

"Yes. Do you want me to see who's at the door?"

"You stay right in your bed," his father said.

"Someone's ringing the doorbell," David said.

"I hear it."

"Shouldn't we see who it is?"

"We know who it is. It's some nut who's got nothing better to do in the middle of the night."

"Mom?"

"You heard your father."

"Are we just gonna let him ring the damn thing all night?" David asked.

"What?" his father said.

"Are we gonna let him ring the damn thing all—?"

"I heard you the first time," his father said.

"Well, are we?"

"If he wants to. Go to sleep. He'll get tired soon enough."

The bell ringer didn't get tired soon enough. David kept watching the red sweep hand on his wristwatch; the bell ringer didn't get tired until 2:47 A.M., more than half an hour after he had begun. In all that time Helga hadn't said a word. It was almost as if she wasn't even in the house.

For the next two weeks the doorbell rang almost every night at 2:00 in the morning or a little after. David's father let it ring each time, without getting out of bed to answer it. Once, while the doorbell was ringing, David sneaked out of bed and went to the other end of the apartment, near the service entrance, to see if Helga was in her room. But the door to her bedroom was closed and he couldn't tell if she was there or not. The doorbell woke the entire family each time but they simply pretended it wasn't ringing. Each time David's mother would come into his bedroom after the doorbell had been ringing awhile, to see if it had awakened him.

"David?" she would whisper.

"Yes, Mom."

"Are you awake?"

"Yes, Mom."

"You poor darling," she would say, and then she would sit on the edge of his bed and put her hand on his forehead, the way she would sometimes do when she thought he had a fever, though he certainly didn't have any fever. The doorbell would continue ringing and his mother would sit in her nightgown in the dark, her hand cool on his head. In a little while she would kiss his closed eyes and he would drift off to sleep, not knowing when she left him, not knowing when the doorbell stopped ringing.

This went on for two weeks. By the end of that time David was getting used to waking up at two in the morning and getting used to his mother's visits each time the doorbell rang. He was beginning to think, though, that once Helga left on her vacation, the doorbell ringing would stop. He was beginning to think that Mary Vincent was right—that Helga was ringing the bell just out of spite, just to cause trouble and worry for others.

But on August 12th, Helga left and that night at two

o'clock the doorbell rang. It couldn't have been Helga because she had taken a plane that morning at Kennedy Airport, bound for Copenhagen, where her parents lived.

The next day David's father called the police.

It was David's guess that his father had suspected Helga, too, because he told the two detectives right away that it *couldn't* have been the housekeeper since she was now in Denmark. That explained why he hadn't called the police up to now; he *had* thought it was Helga and had expected her to quit ringing the bell after a while.

The two detectives didn't look anything like television policemen at all. One of them looked like Mr. Hartman, who had the candy store on Madison Avenue, and the other one looked like Uncle Martin, David's father's brother. Mr. Hartman did most of the talking.

"When did your housekeeper leave?" he asked David's father.

"Yesterday morning."

"And you say the doorbell rang again last night?"

"Yes, it did."

"Who else lives on this floor?" Mr. Hartman asked.

"Mrs. Shavinsky and her housekeeper."

"Her name is Mary Vincent," David said.

"Thank you, son," Mr. Hartman said. "Would either Mrs. Shavinsky or her housekeeper have any reason to want to annoy you?"

"I don't think so," David's father said.

"He may be after Mrs. Shavinsky's demitasse cups," David said.

"What was that, son?" asked the one who looked like Uncle Martin.

"Mrs. Shavinsky's demitasse cups. They're worth thousands of dollars."

"If the intruder wanted *her* cups," Uncle Martin said, "why would he ring *your* doorbell?"

"That's just what I said to Mrs. Shavinsky."

"Is there anything you can do about this?" David's father asked the detectives. "Can you leave a man here?"

"Well, that would be a little difficult, sir," Mr. Hartman said. "We're always shorthanded but especially in the summertime. I think you can understand—"

"Yes, but—"

"What we *can* do, of course, is to dust the hallway and the doorbell for fingerprints."

"Will that help?"

"If the intruder left any prints it could help a great deal."

"And if he didn't leave any prints? If, for example, he was wearing gloves?"

"Then it wouldn't help at all."

"Well, if you can't leave a man here," his father said, "and if dusting or whatever you call it doesn't come up with any fingerprints, what are we supposed to do? Just let this person keep on ringing our doorbell forever?"

"I suppose you could spend a night sleeping in a chair near the door," Mr. Hartman said. "That might help."

"How?"

"You could open the door as soon as the bell rang."

"We never know when it's going to ring," David's father said, "or even *if* it'll ring at all. There's no pattern to it."

"Well, perhaps you could spend a few nights sleeping by the door."

"I could spend a few *weeks* sleeping by the door," David's father said. "Or maybe even a few *months.*"

"Well," Mr. Hartman said.

"Well," David's father said, and then everybody was quiet.

"Mrs. Shavinsky thinks it's some drunk," David said.

"It might be, son," Uncle Martin said.

"He doesn't use the elevator."

"He probably comes up the service steps," Mr. Hartman said. "We'll talk to the elevator operators and ask them to keep their eyes open. Though, you know, there's the possibility he comes down from the roof. I'll check and see if there's a lock on the roof door."

"Why would anyone be doing this?" David's father asked.

"The world is full of nuts," Mr. Hartman said. "This is something like calling up a stranger on the telephone, only this guy uses your doorbell."

"But how long will he continue bothering us?"

"Who knows?" Mr. Hartman said. "It can go on forever or he can get tired next week. Who knows?"

"Well," David's father said.

"Well," Mr. Hartman said—and that was that.

That night David's father slept on a blanket in the entrance hall and the doorbell didn't ring.

The next night he slept in the bedroom and the doorbell rang at two o'clock.

The night after that he slept in the bedroom again but this time the doorbell didn't ring.

At breakfast the next morning he told David's mother there was no way to figure this damn thing out but that night he slept just inside the entrance door again. David woke up with a nightmare at about one o'clock and went into his mother's bedroom. He climbed into bed with her and she held him in her arms and said, "What is it, darling?"

"I'm afraid," David said.

"Of what?"

"That he'll get Daddy."

"No one's going to get Daddy."

"Suppose Daddy opens the door and he's standing there? Suppose he kills Daddy?"

"No one's going to kill Daddy. Daddy is very strong."

"Suppose. What would we do?"

"Don't worry about it. Nothing's going to happen to Daddy."

"I don't want anything to happen to Daddy."

She put him back in his own bed in a little while and he lay there and looked at his watch and wondered if the doorbell would ring that night. He was just falling asleep again when it went off. It went off with a long loud ring and then a short sharp ring but by that time his father was on his feet, making a lot of noise and unlocking the door as quickly as he could and throwing the door open and running into the hallway.

David lay in bed with his heart beating faster and faster, waiting for his father to come back. At last he heard him close the door and walk through the apartment to the bedroom.

"Did you see him?" David's mother asked.

"No. But I heard a door slamming."

"What do you mean?"

"As I was unlocking *our* door, just after the ringing, I heard a door slamming somewhere."

"Probably the door leading to the service steps."

"Yes," David's father said. He paused. "Where's David? Is he asleep?"

"Yes. He had a bad dream a little while ago."

"Poor kid. What shall I do, honey? Do you think our friend will be back tonight?"

"I doubt it," David's mother said, and paused. Her voice through the bedroom wall sounded very funny when she spoke again. "Come here," she said.

That night was the last time the doorbell rang.

What had happened, David supposed, was that his father had frightened the intruder away. He had jumped to his feet at the first long ring and was already unlocking the door by the time the intruder had pressed the bell the second time, which was probably why the second ring had been so short. The intruder must have realized a trap had been set, so he ran for the service steps just as David's father unlocked the door. That was probably the sound his father had heard—the service-steps door slamming behind the intruder as he ran away. David's father didn't get to see anyone by the time he rushed into the hallway, but he certainly must have scared whoever had been ringing the bell because that was the end of it.

In September school started and Helga came back from Denmark with stories about everything she had done. David began thinking about Paris again only because Helga had just come back from Europe. He would lie in bed each night and think about Paris and one night he suddenly got the idea. He began laughing and then stuck his head under the pillow because he didn't want them to hear him in the bedroom next door. He kept laughing, though, under his pillow. It seemed to him that it would be a great joke. The more he thought about it, the funnier it seemed.

He took his head out from under the pillow and listened. The apartment was quiet. He threw back the covers, got out of bed, tiptoed to the door of his mother's bedroom, and peeked in. She was lying with his father's arms around her, the blanket down over her hip, sort of.

David covered his mouth with his hand because he felt another laugh coming on and then he tiptoed to Helga's bedroom. Her door was closed. He could hear her heavy breathing behind it.

He went to the service door of the apartment.

Carefully he unlocked the door without making a sound, trying his best not to laugh. Then he opened the door and peeked out into the service alcove. No one was there. It seemed to him that he could almost hear the whole building breathing in its sleep.

He picked up an empty milk bottle from where it was standing outside the service door and used it to prop the door open and then went out of the service alcove and into the area just outside the elevators. He listened to make sure the elevator wasn't coming up and then he went to the front door.

He almost laughed again.

He listened.

He couldn't hear anything.

This was going to be a great joke.

He reached out for the doorbell.

He rang the bell once. He heard it ringing inside the apartment. What he was going to do was run right back through the service entrance and then pretend he didn't know what had happened, if he could keep a straight face. He was only going to ring the bell that once, as a joke. But somehow, standing there in the hallway with the building asleep all around him, he rang the bell again. And then, he didn't know why, he rang it again. And again.

As he rang it he could remember the phone ringing each morning at eight o'clock at the Hôtel Raphäel, and his running into his mother's bedroom and climbing into her bed to ask the concierge *Quel temps fait-il?* He kept ringing the bell and ringing it. He didn't even hear the front door when it opened. His father was in pajamas, his mother was standing beside him in her nightgown.

"David!" she said. "What are you doing?"

David started to smile, half expecting his mother to laugh or run her hand over his head. But instead she was looking down at him with a very puzzled look on her face and he decided not to smile because he had the feeling something terrible was going to happen, though he didn't know what. He ducked his head.

"I'm sorry," he said.

They were all quiet for a while and then his father said, "Why did you ring the doorbell, David?"

"I don't know."

"You rang it, didn't you?" his father said.

"Yes."

"Well, why?"

"I thought it would be a good joke."

"A *what?*" his father said.

"A joke."

"A joke? After all we went through last month? You thought it would be a joke to—"

"I didn't do it last month."

"I know that but how could you—"

"This is the first time I ever rang it."

"I know that," his father said, and the hallway became silent.

"Why did you do it, David?" his mother asked.

He looked up at her, wanting to explain, but a hundred crazy things popped into his head instead. He wanted to say, Mom, do you remember the little stone balcony with the big windows where we used to have our breakfast every morning, do you remember the man who waved and winked at you? He wanted to say, Mom, do you remember the models kissing me at the salons and those two with their brassieres that time, the way you laughed, do you remember? Do you remember driving out to have a picnic lunch by the Loire on Bastille Day, and the wild traffic around the Etoile that night when we drove back into the city, and the fireworks later, do you remember holding my hand on the little stone balcony outside our room?

"Why?" she asked again. "Why did you ring the doorbell, David?"

"I don't know," he said.

"You *must* have had a reason," his mother insisted.

"No, Mom," he said. "I didn't have any reason."

She kept looking at him.

His father sighed then and said, "Well, it's very late. Let's all get back to bed."

When our managing editor finished reading the manu-script of "Report on a Broken Bridge," she sent the story to us with the following comment: "This has a Citizen Kane *quality, and yet an individuality all its own." Our interest was immediately aroused.*

Well, you know, our managing editor was right on target—she hit the bull's-eye.

If on finishing this story you are not impressed, or worse, if you do not like it, let the story simmer for a while. We think your mind will keep coming back to it again and again.

DENNIS O'NEIL

Report on a broken bridge

It wasn't love or money that drove Otis Belding to his very thorough suicide: It was something bigger, lots bigger, and knowing about it is pushing me toward a premature demise, too.

You know, boss, we might have guessed the *why* of his death if we'd bothered to think about who he was, where he came from, and especially what he'd accomplished. I'd already completed my investigation by the time I got around to looking at the movies that kid happened to be taking when Belding made his spectacular exit; but as soon as I saw them I knew my guesses were correct. I sniffed an apocalypse.

You're now reading this night letter and you'll never see the prints I've forwarded to the New York office, so I'll give you a preview. Here's what the kid's camera caught:

Background: the Bridge Research complex. Foreground: a lake, placid, dotted with tiny ripples, deep-blue near the shore and powder-blue in the center. In the far distance: the Ozark Mountains. Above: more blue, streaked with wisps of white. And around, everywhere: deep-green—leaves that look heavy enough to use as anchors.

Enter Belding, in a sleek shiny aluminum dinghy, rowing to the mididle of the water—rowing despite a hefty outboard perched on the stern. (At this point the kid changed to a telescopic lens.) Belding carefully cuts off the end of a long brown cigar, places the gold cigar clipper and severed tip in the pocket of his shirt, puts fire to the cigar with a gold lighter. Draws, exhales, slowly gazes up, down. Then he cautiously edges to the bow and sits on top of the wooden keg: The boat lists, and he has a few bad moments getting balanced. He does, though, and after another long look at the scenery he reaches down with his cigar and calmly touches a fuse stuck in the keg's lid.

He sits quietly and I'm pretty sure he's smiling. Sits relaxed as a stone, peacefully smoking. There is a hard red flash and the camera shakes violently, and searches randomly, glimpsing a small army of frogs leaping like dervishes, and then focuses on where Belding had been. He isn't, not any more. There is only a widening circle of dirty gray in the powder-blue, and a cloudlet of bluish haze crowning a roiling column.

It reminds me of the climax of an arty foreign flick—the kind that beats you over the head with Profound Symbolism and in which the director uses the H-bomb mushroom the way a comic strip uses exclamation points.

My favorite headline was on page three of the *Daily News*, amid human-interest drivel about our indian summer heat wave. You remember: BOY WONDER MULTIMILLIONAIRE ENDS WITH A BANG.

Before the ink was dry on that little paradigm of class journalism you had me and my hangover in your office. The air-conditioning was on the blink—again!—and your bald pate was sweat-shiny enough to use as a shaving mirror. You looked like you'd been moldering in a rain forest for a couple of centuries, and coherency was not your strong trait, not that morning. I understood from your sputtering that Otis had done himself in, that the board had panicked, and that unless we could demonstrate that our late president had shuffled off for reasons unconnected with the affairs of Bridge Enterprises, Inc., our stock certificates would soon be worth something less than bus transfers. I concurred and hied away to shoot the trouble.

By noon I was aboard an Eastern jet out of Newark, grimly contemplating the early market report in the first edition of the *Post*: Bridge Enterprises was selling at $31\frac{1}{2}$, down 7 in the first two hours of trading. My wallet ached: I own 300 shares myself.

I picked up a St. Louis paper while waiting for my rent-a-car at Lambert Field: At the day's closing we were selling at 29.

I drove southwest wondering why nobody touts the beauty of that part of the country. There's nothing out here so awesome as the Grand Canyon or as numbingly spectacular as the Rockies, but nonetheless the geography is lovely—soft-edged hills and quiet valleys and lush forests. That land, west of St. Louis, is feminine America, loving and open: Maybe if I'd ever found a human equivalent I wouldn't be typing this with a Beretta in my lap.

Ugliness begins about five miles north of Belding's birthplace, a town called Feeley that used to be small and isn't now because our company built a lead-refining plant close by. Along came Bridge Enterprises and zapped seventy-five acres of trees and bulldozed seventy-five acres of grass and filled a stream with pulped garbage, bringing population and prosperity. Belding's gift to his childhood. Swell gift. The stink is so powerful it must have seeped into the soil; the sky is the color of sooty canvas; the buildings are as shocking as tarantulas on a loveseat. Up there in our air-conditioned, pastel-hued headquarters we just don't realize how gruesome the nitty-gritty is.

Feeley itself can't have changed much. Basically it's one square containing a post office, a bar with liquor store attached, an I.G.A. supermarket, a funeral parlor, and a gas station. Sundry other businesses and a scattering of houses border the square, and more are abuilding. I patronized the liquor store, obtained a fifth of my favorite, and the information that one Hap Elsenmeyer had once been Otis Belding's boyhood buddy. I went to see old buddy Hap, owner of the gas station.

Detective fiction is full of scenes in which the amiable private eye loosens the tonsils of suspicious locals with a dram of the barley. No lie, boss. Elsenmeyer is obviously a man familiar with a bottle. I had to merely hint, to sort of wave the bottle nonchalantly. Old Hap told an adolescent to mind the pumps and we retired to his office.

He produced cracked china mugs with the panache of a carny conjuror producing bunnies, and I poured. The room was pleasantly old-fashioned—even had an overhead fan that sort of sloshed the humidity around—and the pungent smell of petroleum was a relief from the lead fumes outside. We opined on the heat, agreed it sure was fierce for November, and nitter-nattered our way to talking about Otis.

I won't attempt to transcribe Elsenmeyer's dialect in all its drawly splendor. You'll have to be satisfied with the bones of the story he told me.

Otis Belding's real-life Horatio Alger saga began with a hook and a worm. The lad was a pure genius at finding fishing holes. From age six on he had hunches where they'd be biting on any given morning, and the hunches were always dead-center. That was a useful talent for him, giving him a tot of social acceptance and putting food in his belly. Came fishing time his schoolmates forgave him his pa, the town ne'er-do-well, and his ma, the town crazy. During the winter Otis starved and was taunted; summers, he ate fresh fish and was grudgingly respected. Elsenmeyer once asked Otis how he could be so gol-ding *certain,* and Otis said he didn't know, he just had these *feelings.*

He was, in effect, orphaned at the age of ten. His father expired in a ditch one winter night and the authorities carted his mother off to the county mental hospital, where she died some years later. An aunt did a perfectly rotten job of guardianship. Mostly, Otis lived alone in a shack near the site of the future refinery, getting to school now and again, somehow surviving the cold months. Age eleven, he discovered games and took his first hesitant steps toward the Dow Jones index and a cask of high-grade blasting powder.

A bunch of the good old boys used to meet in the back room of the tavern evenings for cards. Friendly poker, two-bit limit. Otis took to hanging around, probably to escape the cold of the shack. I'm guessing now, but I think he must have swiped some money from his aunt's purse one day and wangled himself a seat at the table. Played smart, according to Elsenmeyer—real smart. Uncanny smart. Walked away with enough dollars to stand beers for the bunch, root beer for himself. Kept out a stake, though, and sat in the following session, and every session thereafter, and won more than he could have made in a whole summer's field laboring. The boys were mildly amazed but, I gather, tolerant. Otis became a pet topic of Feeley conversation.

A trucker named Batson J. Frink ended Otis' poker career. Frink pushed a tractor-trailer rig for a Kansas City outfit and often joined the game when he was passing through. Nobody much liked Frink, but nobody told him, because he was big and mean. He was also a sore loser. He lost heavily to Otis on July 4, 1951—Elsenmeyer remembers the date exactly—and didn't enjoy it, not one bit.

He waited for Otis outside the bar while Otis was buying drinks, caught the boy, dragged him behind the building, and beat him mercilessly. Elsenmeyer was a witness; he tells it with a connoisseur's glee—how the trucker punched Otis to blood and bruises, broke a rib, kicked out teeth. Finally Frink was too tired to continue. He paused to catch his breath—and heard his death pronounced.

Sitting against the rear wall, Otis looked up through swollen eyelids and said, "You're going to die tonight." Just those five words, spoken with absolute conviction. Frink must have been shaken by them, because he went to his rig and drove off.

I checked with the highway patrol. The official report confirms Hap Elsenmeyer's story. Between 9:00 and 9:15 on the night of July 4, 1951, a tractor-trailer driven by Batson J. Frink was rounding a steep curve eight miles south of Feeley. The load in the trailer apparently shifted, causing the rig to topple off the road, down into a gulley, and explode. The cargo of magnesium ingots caught fire. Frink's body was never recovered.

Leaving Feeley, I had my first intimations that our late leader had been a hint spooky. Then I thought, no, it was only a coincidence. Sure.

The data you supplied led me next to East St. Louis. The records there showed that Belding had resided in a boardinghouse near the Obear Nestor bottle factory, which is not any urban gem of a neighborhood, believe you me. A Mrs. McNally was, and is, the landlady. Picture the dark side of the moon and see McNally—a walking crater, this senior citizen, and easily 90 percent malice. The remaining 10 percent praises the memory of Otis Belding.

"A *good* boy," she insisted. "Best boy I ever knew."

To prove the assertion she pointed to a plaster Virgin set on a doily on a shelf in the parlor. "Bought me that with his first big winnings, Otis did," Mrs. McNally crowed. "Ain't it lovely?"

You bet, Mrs. McNally, I agreed. Now about those winnings—

Belding's co-boarder had been a man named Lewis Thalier, a wine jockey and doer of odd jobs at a racetrack, Cahokia Downs. Thalier, it seems, had been a big noise in the twenties. The usual weepy history: He'd lost everything in the '29 crash, cocooned himself inside the grape, and never really emerged. Until young Otis appeared, that is.

In the beginning Otis developed his gambling talent —studied the horse forms Thalier brought home and had the wino place bets for him. Thalier noticed that the lad won consistently, and he began making duplicate bets. Thalier prospered, as did his youthful mentor. After a particularly spectacular afternoon with the ponies Thalier fueled himself with champagne—no more California port for *this* ex-tycoon—and reminisced, aloud and at length. Dug forth from his trunk a sheaf of gaudy stock certificates, displayed them to Otis, and discoursed regarding the market.

Otis was interested, and how. He exhausted Thalier's lore and the next morning got an armful of books from the public library. He spent days poring over the books and the financial sections of local papers and, when he learned of its existence, *The Wall Street Journal.* Then he bought Thalier a new suit and embarked on his second and penultimate career.

"The other boarders' eyes plain bugged when they see old Lewis and Otis come out on the porch looking like a bandbox," Mrs. McNally croaked warmly. "They go over the bridge downtown and come back with a big envelope. They spread a bunch of papers on the kitchen floor and look at them like they was gold or something. 'We gonna be rich,' Lewis says. Young Otis, he nods his head yes."

Belding stayed at Mrs. McNally's for nine years. Thalier resurrected dormant expertise in food, drink, music, and in the midst of that slum they lived lavishly. Each Wednesday Thalier obediently guided a spanking limousine across the bridge and returned bearing a fresh envelope and the grandest largess that St. Louis could provide—records, clothes, prime steaks, bonded bourbon.

"Boarders was green with envy," Mrs. McNally solemnly assured me.

Let it be noted that Belding's appetites extended beyond his stomach, as is normal, and as the gossip columnists have frequently observed. With whom is not relevant, and anyway, you'll have a chance to leer further on in this narrative.

Belding terminated the slum idyll on his twenty-first birthday. He and Thalier drove across the Eads Bridge for the last time, saw a lawyer, signed papers, and returned to the boardinghouse. At the curb Belding took the wheel, said good-bye to Thalier, and went away without bothering to collect the belongings from his room. Thalier was official owner of $100,000 worth of blue-chip securi-

ties; Belding held for himself $600,000 worth of wildly
speculative issues.

Thalier's income kept him happily juiced for his remaining half decade: His liver had the privilege of suc-
cumbing to only the finest French and Italian vintages.

Our accounting department will confirm that Mrs.
McNally still receives a check for $400 every month—
more than the old witch deserves.

I won't bore you with my pursuit of the Belding success saga. What you're getting, boss, is pure poetry; if
you want prosaic details send another lackey for them.
Suffice to say, for a week I relearned what we both vividly
know. If you've forgotten any of it read the clippings from
Time, Fortune, Forbes, The Wall Street Journal, et al.

Boy Wonder Belding could do no financial wrong:
He got rich, richer, damn near richest. Two weeks before
the beginning of the great computer boom he bought the
software outfit. Two weeks prior to the McDonnel-Doug-
las merger he bought McDonnel. Two weeks before the
Apollo contracts were awarded he bought Texas Instrument. And two weeks before the start of the TV season
that made camp as obsolete as button hooks he unloaded
that corny television show. The list goes on and on, like a
list of Howard Hughes' fondest dreams.

I'm an investigator, an expert snoop, so I snooped,
thoroughly and relentlessly; through the pads in Malibu,
Newport, and Acapulco; the permanent suite in Las Ve-
gas; the yacht; and I disproved to my complete satisfaction the hoary notion that the wealthy can't be happy.
Listen, he was *happy.* Young, healthy, handsome, and
able to buy spares of anything—a regular bouncing bundle
of sybaritic joy was Otis Belding. Until last September.

In 1966 he formed Bridge Enterprises and unleashed
on the world the hokey motto that graces our letterheads:
Building Bridges to the Future. Otis Belding believed
those words, I think. He was cut from a fairly idealistic

cloth; he was maybe that rare mass entrepreneur who actually saw himself and his affairs as a force for progress. Sure, he engineered dirty deals, but he was unique in *admitting* them, and he had an excuse. You remember the speech he delivered at the convention of the National Association of Manufacturers—the lines quoted in all the press releases: "I regret having harmed a few relatively innocent parties. I harmed them in order to insure a brighter tomorrow for their children."

Horrible speech. Honest sentiment, though. Bear it in mind while I take you to upstate New York.

I won't give you my impressions of our Hudson River plant: You've already been treated to my description of the Feeley refinery, right? Well, the Hudson facility isn't quite as bad, not quite. A lot of money was spent on landscape cosmetics.

The manager, Tyrone Thomas, gave me the grand tour. He's a proud fellow. He speaks of extracting detergent phosphates from raw chemicals like a frat brother boasting a conquest. I understood maybe one tenth of his rap. We finished the tour at the wide grass terrace between the plant and the river. Looking out over the Hudson, with the industrial labyrinth at my back, I could almost forget where I was, except that I felt the vibration of drainage pumps through my shoe soles and saw the churning of the water where the pipes empty into it.

"You can see for yourself this is the finest facility of its kind in the world," Thomas was saying. "Per diem gross is forty tons. We hope to up that the coming fiscal period."

"Very impressive," I said. "Was Mr. Belding pleased?"

"Pleased as Punch. Gave me a bonus, promised another."

"No problems?"

"None worth talking about. We had some trouble with the radicals at the beginning, but Mr. Belding handled it all right."

"Radicals?"

Thomas smiled wearily. "Not the card-carrying sort. The dupes. At least, I think they're dupes."

I asked, "Who exactly are they?"

"The crowd from the university. They did a lot of picketing when we first went into operation. Men with the beards and the hair, girls with the signs and the beads —the whole shebang. It got on the TV news shows."

"They have something against phosphates?"

"They have something against progress," Thomas said righteously. "Darn fools. Claimed we were ruining the environment. That's a pile of you-know-what. Look around, judge for yourself. This land was going to waste before Bridge moved in. Nothing here but chipmunks. We pumped millions into the local economy, put five thousand men to work, going to take another two thousand if we get a go-ahead on the new wing. I ask you, is that *ruining?*"

"Did Mr. Belding do anything about the protests?"

"Oh, sure. He met with 'em on four or five separate occasions. He was a heck of a sight more patient than I'd've been in his position. He volunteered to put in the sod we're standing on and the drainage network underground. Cost a bundle, but they weren't satisfied. They said we're killing fish. Imagine. All that fuss over some fish. Heck-fire, I'd've offered to buy 'em a carload of fish to shut 'em up. Finally Mr. Belding promised to finance a research laboratory and that got rid of the pests."

And it got rid of me, too. I left Thomas to his phosphates and tucked myself into a motel for the night. You're getting nowhere, I told myself sternly, and myself agreed. My notebook and tape recorder were jammed with information, true, but I'd discovered no tidbits absent from *Who's Who.*

The only thing I had learned was that Otis Belding never—*never*—made a financial mistake. I'd always assumed he must have committed a blunder or two along

the way, even as you and I. He hadn't. Not one blunder.
He'd cast his mortal remains to the lake breeze with a
perfect financial record and although his tranquillity had
been infinitesimally marred by the Hudson protests, they
shouldn't have upset him much, considering that they
clued him to the sweetest tax-dodge-cum-public-relations-
coup a multimillionaire could wish for. Compared to the
Bridge Research Center, Carnegie's libraries were so many
sandboxes: The intellectuals applauded, the I.R.S. con-
doned, and the Silent Majority didn't hear about it, as
usual. In short, the Center is another monotonous success.

As I was leaving the motel the next morning you
phoned and told me that the corporate fortunes were im-
proving—we were selling over 30 again—and you said I
should stay with the investigation another twenty-four
hours, prepare a document to exhibit in the annual stock-
holders' booklet—show the Bridge Family that their officers *care*—and bring my expense account home. We'd
gone through the motions and that was sufficient. You
said.

As it happened, I *did* nail the reason for the suicide
within a day, but if I hadn't I would have hung with the
case regardless. Suddenly you didn't seem so almighty impressive, boss; suddenly your wrath held no terrors for
me. Nor the loss of my job, either. Conclusion: Subcon-
sciously, I had the answer. Or I was on the edge of an
inkling—no, in this context, better call it a premonition.

I had two more people to see. Dr. Harold Seabrook,
head of the Research Center, would be in Europe until
Thursday, his secretary told me long distance. So that left
Miss X—Belding's mistress. I'd known about her, of course,
as had you and most of the guys in the executive suite.
Otis Belding's bucolic lady was the worst-kept secret in
the company. As acting chief of security I'd made it my
business to obtain her name and address; more, I'd run a
somewhat-more-detailed-routine check on her—wouldn't
do to have Belding victimized by an adventuress, I ra-

tionalized. I needn't have worried. Sandra Burkholt is nobody's *femme fatale.*

Frankly I was curious. What manner of woman, I
wondered, would cause a man like Belding to abandon his
string of pneumatic starlets, theatrical *grandes dames,* and
society sweethearts? Because abandon them he did—
lopped them off like diseased limbs last summer, about
the time he established the Research Center. My field
personnel said *la Burkholt* was thirty-two, single, living
alone in a small isolated house not far from the Center,
and the mother of an illegitimate son. Belding probably
met her in November 1968, while she was employed as a
typist at the Feeley refinery. It's possible he'd known
her earlier, during his miserable childhood.

I arrived at her house at dusk on Wednesday. There
was a sports car in the driveway, no other signs of prosperity. On the contrary. A bent rusty tricycle lay on the
walk; the grass needed cutting; the house itself needed
shingles and paint. Hardly a magnate's love nest.

She answered my knock and led me into the living
room. The inside was a perfect reflection of the exterior:
shabby furniture, cracked linoleum floor, peeling wallpaper. And Sandra completed the motif. She isn't homely:
There are lingering phantoms of an artful feline girl in her
bold glance, in her quick sensuous smile. But she's worn.
The red hair is stringy and faded, the skin rough, the figure sagging. Had Belding liked his women pitiable? Was
it really love?

Feeling strangely like an archaeologist prowling an
ancient temple, I followed Sandra to the bedroom they
had shared and viewed Belding's artifacts: a medium-
priced portable phonograph, a mixed collection of records,
and the books and magazines he'd read himself to sleep
with. Three sorts of reading matter, divided into separate
piles. Books on extrasensory perception, ranging from
inexpensive paperbacks to footnotey tomes to science-fiction novels. Stuff on ecology of approximately the same

range, including a complete set of Sierra Club publications and a series of pamphlets from Barry Commoner's group at Washington University. And history books, mostly comprehensive texts. I paged through them, to no avail: Belding had not been an underliner.

We went into the kitchen. I unobtrusively turned on my tape recorder while Sandra concocted lemonade. That's right, boss—lemonade. As remarked, Miss Burkholt is not a *femme fatale*.

"I'll have to ask you to hold down your voice," the tape recorder echoes Sandra as I write. "My boy is sick in the next room there. Generally he's healthy as a horse. Must be one of those viruses."

Me: "I hope he feels better."

Sandra: "Thank you."

Me (hesitantly): "Did you know Mr. Belding well?"

Sandra: " 'Course. Not long, but well as can be. We were lovers."

Me (embarrassed): "Forgive me for asking—but did he buy you gifts? Did he have an arrangement with you?"

Sandra (chuckling, bless her): "You mean was I a kept woman? No, sir. Oh, he bought little presents for the house and for my boy. He brought me a Mixmaster once, was I think the biggest thing. He never give me money and I didn't ask for any. Didn't expect any. It was purely a man-woman thing with us. I liked him. I believe he liked me. I'll miss my Otis."

Me: "Did you notice any recent change in his behavior?"

Sandra: "He was always—well, odd. Funny, he could be touching you and somehow not be there at all, like he'd left his body behind. Oh, yes, there was one present Otis brought on his last visit I forgot about. He said something strange—"

She was interrupted by a thump from behind the wall. We rushed into the boy's cubbyhole. The child was lying in a tangle of quilt beside the bed, breathing in harsh rattling gasps. He was drenched with sweat, his skin wax-white. He wasn't suffering from virus; the kid was dying.

"We'd better get him to a hospital," I said.

Sandra wrapped him in the quilt and carried him to my car. I pegged the speedometer needle at seventy most of the distance to the local clinic. The decrepit general practitioner there diagnosed a ruptured appendix and confessed he had no facilities for treating acute peritonitis. I knew a clinic that did—coincidentally, the best medical setup in that area is at the Bridge refinery in Feeley. I got on the phone, chartered a private plane, and alerted one of those bright young specialists the company boasts of recruiting that Sandra and her son were on the way.

At the airfield I gave her my card and asked her to call the office if she or the boy needed anything. She promised she would.

Not being tired yet, I drove into the Ozark foothills, toward the center. I surrendered to bizarre reflections—bizarre for me, anyway. Not since I'd been an altar boy waiting scared in the musty closeness of the confessional had I contemplated eternity. Maybe it was the country. If there are ghosts, they lurk in those hills, flash briefly, mockingly in headlight glare, and rattle forebodingly in leaves. Or maybe it was simple shame, an attempt to excuse my lack of professionalism. I hadn't seen Sandra earlier, during the Feeley phase of the inquiry, and that oversight had been wasteful, costly. But if I *had,* then I wouldn't have been there to bully medicos and pilots, and the boy might not have got the attention he needed. I entertained the notion that I served a benevolent destiny. Fate? Predestination? Whose will was my master? Certainly not Belding's.

Bridge Enterprises can be proud of its Research Center. Architecturally it's the best we have: Instead of the usual eyesore, the building is dignified—predominantly vertical lines harmonizing with the surrounding pines. I parked in the visitors' lot and admired the floodlit scene a bit. A guard demanded to know who I was. Then, miraculously transformed by my credentials, he hefted my bag and escorted me to the VIP quarters. Nice digs. Pastel and Danish plastic modern. Home away from . . .

A shaft of sunlight across my face woke me. I put on my most expensive lightweight suit and a white-on-white shirt-tie combo—to impress the scientific yokel with my Manhattan class.

Huh-*uh*. I doubt that Dr. Harold Seabrook *can* be impressed. He's a large chunk of dour impatience—six-six, big-bellied, features drawn as though his jowls were weighted. He doesn't speak: He spews.

We met in the lounge. As we talked he traced tiny precise geometrics on the Formica table top in a spilling of iced tea.

"I can give you five minutes," he said brusquely.

I was annoyed. I'm a bigger corporate cheese than Seabrook. "You've got somewhere to go?" I asked.

"I've got to see about saving the human race from itself," he replied, managing not to sound corny. "I won't do it prattling with you."

"Funny," I mused sarcastically. "I read your job description. It said 'ecologist,' not 'messiah.'"

"No difference," he snapped.

Having nary a comeback to that I asked, "What exactly are you doing with the company's money? What's the project?"

He raised a brow. "At the moment? We're seeking a way to reduce the so-called 'greenhouse effect.'"

"You're messing with flowers?"

His tone put me back in knee pants and a dunce cap: I was the second grade's biggest dumbo, he the exasperated teacher. He said, "You've noticed the weather? Not enough heat is escaping into space. Pollutants have formed a curtain that traps short-wave radiation near the ground, and the temperature is rising to—"

I interrupted, "I don't need a pee-aitch-dee to tell me it's a hell of a hot November. I'm sure you geniuses will dope out the damnedest refrigerator in twenty years and we'll give you either a gold watch or a Nobel Prize, take your choice."

"Many of my colleagues would agree with you," he said with unexpected gentleness. "I do not, and neither did Otis Belding. He had a theory that a critical point will come in our poisoning of earth, and when it does the planet will simply stop living—*stop*. All the life-support systems will disintegrate at once, and that will be the end. Finish. No more. We may have a few days, or a few hours, to regret our stupidity."

"That doesn't sound like it makes a lot of sense, Doc."

"I didn't think so either, at first. But I was reasoning conventionally. Then I pursued a line of research that Otis suggested and—" His voice changed: The gentleness was gone. "You've wasted enough of my time."

He pulled a folded memo sheet from his yellow-stained lab jacket. "Otis said I was to give you this."

My name was scrawled on it, in Belding's handwriting.

"Hold it, Doc," I said. "I never *met* Otis Belding. He didn't even know I exist. You want me to believe he addressed a note to me personally before he died and left it with you? No way."

"Facts are facts," he said, getting up. "Excuse me."

He was gone, that fast, leaving another protest snagged in my throat and a zero limned in cold tea on the table. Vowing to humble him later, I opened the note. It read:

"There's nothing to be done. It is too late. See model in my office."

Signed: Otis Belding.

I obtained the key to his private office from the receptionist, climbed to the top floor, and entered. The room was barren as a Trappist cell—furnishings consisted solely of an army cot and a metal stand on top of which was a scale model of the Eads Bridge. The model was broken. Someone had hit it and broken it in half. It was a bridge that went nowhere.

There was a question yet to be answered. I used a phone in the lobby to call Sandra.

"How's your son?" I asked.

"He's doing nicely. That nice Dr. Benedict said he caught it in time. I want to thank you."

"My pleasure. Sandra, you remember what you were saying? About a present Otis bought?"

"That was the funniest he ever did. It was a gun—a pistol. I still have it, though Lord knows what I'll ever do with a gun. He gave it to me and said, 'If you love your son you'll do him this favor.' I suppose he was joking."

"Could be. 'Bye, Sandra."

I strolled outside and ambled across the sweep of lawn, down to the lake. No hurry, not anymore, for me, for you, for anyone. Because it's obvious why Otis Belding killed himself. He had a genius for prophecy, remember? I figure he had premonitions about the future—premonitions that slowly grew to convictions until, two weeks before an event, they became certainties. Once he became aware of something, he could predict its course. He became aware of ecology, he saw the "critical point" coming; he saw his future—our future—and sought refuge with a simple woman and her son, and failing to find comfort he chose to die.

Exactly thirteen days ago he chose to die.

I know how he felt. Like a man standing on a broken bridge.

I have my gun, and I've always hated being the last one out.

So—good-bye, boss.

*Is there anyone who even approaches Michael Gilbert in
the writing of legal-detective stories? . . . Here is another strange and fascinating mystery hidden this time in
a deed wallet in the files of Messrs. Preece and Sexton,
lawyers for a certain Colonel Ambrose Spender who had
once distinguished himself for daring Intelligence work.
What deep dark secrets are buried in the archives of an
established law firm like Preece and Sexton?*

MICHAEL GILBERT

Accessories after the fact

Malcolm Preece settled himself in the far corner seat of
the last first-class carriage on the 7:50 train from Woking
to London. The seat was one in which long usage had
given him almost prescriptive rights. After blowing his
nose and wishing his regular traveling companion, Mr.
Satterthwaite, good morning, he turned to the obituary
columns of *The Times.*

A familiar name caught his eye.

"I see that one of our local celebrities has gone," he
said.

"Not Miss Pringle?" said Mr. Satterthwaite. "Dear,
dear, and we all thought she'd make her century."

"No. Not Miss Pringle. Colonel Spender."

"I heard he'd been ill. He was a tough old boy. We
thought he might have got over it."

"Not this time," said Mr. Preece and handed his copy of the paper to Mr. Satterthwaite, across a small woman who had presumed to occupy the seat between them. Mr. Preece suspected that she didn't have a first-class ticket.

"*Spender, Ambrose. After a painful illness gallantly borne. Died in Guilford Infirmary. No flowers. Donations to the Imperial War Graves Commission.*"

"An eccentric character, by all accounts," said Mr. Satterthwaite.

"He was one of my clients," said Mr. Preece, with a note of reproof.

"Then I withdraw the remark. If he was a client of the firm of Preece and Sexton he must have been a man of the highest repute."

"He had had a rather odd career," conceded Mr. Preece. "He called himself Colonel Spender. I had been told, in strict confidence"—and here Mr. Preece glared at the small woman as if daring her to repeat something overheard, in confidence, in a first-class railway carriage—"that he was awarded this rank, and a number of English and foreign decorations, too, for daring Intelligence work behind the enemy lines."

"I only knew him vaguely," said Mr. Satterthwaite. "He had one of those houses in Knaphill Woods, didn't he? Rather nice houses, but a bit isolated."

"Not exactly isolated. A bit remote."

"Wasn't that where they found that woman—what was her name?"

"Mrs. Slaney."

"Mrs. Slaney. That's right. She'd been knocked on the head. But not robbed or—er—assaulted. The police never solved it."

"It was a complete mystery," said Mr. Preece, "and it looks as if it will stay that way. It's nearly two years since it happened. The trail must be very cold by now."

The small woman, who was tired of being ignored, said defiantly, "My aunt's cook, who was walking out with one of the policemen, told her that the case was *not* closed. They had a clue. And he told her what it was—in confidence, of course."

"Oh?" said Mr. Preece.

"Really?" said Mr. Satterthwaite.

Both gentlemen then retired behind their newspapers and did not utter another word until the train reached Waterloo Station.

If a certain disparity in temperament produces the happiest marriages, the same might be said of professional partnerships. Certainly the legal practice of Messrs. Preece and Sexton, though not long established in Bedford Row, managed to get along well enough, although it would have been hard to find two men of more widely different characters than Mr. Preece and Mr. Sexton.

Malcolm Preece was correct in dress and deportment, conservative in outlook, and extremely conscientious in his work. He was normally the first to arrive at the office and often the last to leave. David Sexton was casual, empirical, and occasionally, in Mr. Preece's view, unnecessarily flippant. However, it was a combination of talents which seemed to work. As Mr. Preece sometimes remarked to his clients, "If there's a theoretical solution, I can usually work it out. If I'm stuck, David Sexton can often find a practical answer."

While they were opening and sorting out the mail, a ritual which they carried out together every morning, Mr. Preece told him of the death of Colonel Spender.

"Yes," said Sexton, "I saw it in *The Times*. I thought I'd get his will up so that we could have a look at it. I believe you're his sole executor, aren't you?"

"I think I am," said Mr. Preece.

He was untwisting the string which held down the flap of the deed wallet. The first things which slid out as he opened it were a long legal-looking envelope, then a smaller square one.

"That's the will," said Mr. Preece. "What's the other one? I don't seem to remember it."

Sexton picked it up. On it, neatly typed, were the words: *To be placed with my Will, and opened only at my death*—followed by the initials, also typed, *A.S.*

"It always seems curious to me," said Mr. Preece, "that people will employ a solicitor to make a perfectly sound will for them, and then clutter it round—hand me that paper knife, would you?—with so-called 'letters of instruction,' which are legally ineffective and, in any event, so woollily drawn that they can't be carried out—good heavens!"

"What is it?"

"I can't believe it. It's not possible!"

"*What* isn't possible?"

"Colonel Spender—no—"

Sexton grabbed the single sheet of notepaper from his partner's hand, read it, and whistled.

"Well," he said, "the old devil. I knew he was a queer cuss, but this beats everything."

"Do you think it's true? It can't be, can it? It's some sort of joke."

"If you think it's a joke," said Sexton, "the most sensible thing would be to tear it up and forget about it."

"Good heavens, we can't do that. If the colonel took the trouble to leave it with his will, he must have meant me to act on it. As his executor, I've no choice."

"Then you'll have to show it to the police. They'll have to make their minds up what they're going to do about it. Come to think of it, there's not much they *can* do now, is there?"

"I suppose not," said Mr. Preece thoughtfully. "No."

The typewritten slip was short and to the point. It said: "Theresa Slaney was a poisonous bitch. I knocked her on the head and have few regrets. I'm leaving this note with my Will in case some other poor devil gets suspected of it. She had plenty of enemies, God knows. Incidentally, if the police don't believe me, ask them whether or not they found an artificial pigskin glove near the body."

The note was unsigned. The two lawyers were still looking at it when the telephone rang.

So strong is the association of ideas that, even as Mr. Preece stretched out his hand to lift the receiver, he hesitated. "Suppose it's the police," he said. "What am I to say?"

"Why should it be the police?"

"No reason, really, I suppose. No. I'm being stupid."

Mr. Preece lifted the receiver. The girl on the switchboard said, "Oh, Mr. Preece. It's Colonel Spender for you. I'll put you through."

Mr. Preece had just sufficient presence of mind to hand his partner an extension, and both of them listened to the wheezy voice at the other end.

"Thought I'd ring you up," it said. "Just seen *The Times* myself. Thought I'd better explain, in case you jumped to the wrong conclusion. Ambrose Spender was my cousin. Distant cousin. Same names. Soon as I get out of this damned hospital I'll be round to see you. Got one or two things to discuss. Important things. Good-bye for now."

Mr. Preece looked at Sexton, and Sexton looked at Mr. Preece. There was a long silence. The younger man recovered his voice first.

"I think we'd better put this back in its envelope, don't you?" Sexton said. "After all, the instructions were that it wasn't to be opened *until* death."

"Pretend we haven't seen it?"

"That's right."

"We can't do that."

"Why not?"

"As an Officer of the Court—" said Mr. Preece.

When he used these words, Mr. Preece, unlike many solicitors, really meant something by them. He saw himself dressed in some undefined but imposing legal uniform, defending the ancient rules and practices of the law against all attackers.

When he heard the fatal words, Sexton realized that it was no occasion for flippancy. He said, speaking slowly, "If you feel that we can't ignore this information, even though it has come into our hands in an irregular manner —for we had of course no right to open the envelope until we were *sure* that Colonel Spender was dead—then where do you visualize our duty lies?"

This was the right approach. "Irregular" and "duty" were words which Mr. Preece understood.

He said, "We shall have to consider our next move very carefully. In my submission, we have a double duty in the matter: a duty to our client not to involve him prematurely—and an equally important duty to the public not to suppress vital information about a crime. Indeed, to suppress it entirely would make us guilty of compounding a felony."

"Accessories after the fact?"

"Something of that sort." Like most solicitors whose practices were confined to conveyancing and probate, Mr. Preece really knew very little about criminal law. "And have you considered that the police are certainly still working on the case? The files on a murder are never closed. Someone was mentioning, only this morning, that the police had a clue. Why, they could even be on the point of arresting some innocent person! If we produced this information *after* that happened it would certainly be suspect. We might have manufactured it ourselves. The note is only typed—"

"And on a Remington standard machine," said Sexton. "We've got half a dozen of them in the office."

"Now that you mention it," said Mr. Preece, "it is even possible it *was* typed in this office. I recollect that when Colonel Spender came to discuss his will he arrived early for his appointment and was put in one of the smaller office rooms which happened to be empty—the waiting room was being redecorated at the time, you remember."

Sexton examined the note more closely. "I think you're right," he said. "And what's more, he used a sheet of *our* paper. It's that cream-laid quarto that we had a stock of. The girls used to complain that it was so thick they couldn't take proper carbon copies."

"I've been thinking," said Mr. Preece. "I know the superintendent of police at Woking quite well. In fact, we've played golf together more than once. Suppose that I give him this information, without revealing where it comes from."

"He's certain to want to know. What will you say when he asks you?"

"It's perfectly simple. I shall say that the source of the information is connected with one of my clients, and is therefore privileged."

"I see," said Sexton doubtfully. "I hope he remembers he's a friend and not just a policeman."

However, when Mr. Preece presented himself at Woking Police Station that evening, he was told that the friendly golf-playing superintendent was on leave and would be absent for a fortnight. This was disconcerting. He hardly felt that he could withhold vital information that long. He found himself talking to a much younger and less friendly inspector. As soon as Mr. Preece mentioned the name of Theresa Slaney, the inspector said, "I think, sir, you had better wait for a few minutes. The case was handled by Central. It won't take long to get hold of Superintendent Marker. I happen to know that he's over at Weybridge."

It took forty minutes to bring Superintendent Marker to the station and by that time Mr. Preece, who had already completed a full day's work, was both hungry and tired.

The superintendent was a huge man with a red face, who looked as if he had been poured into his enormous blue suit and left to set. He had also missed his dinner and this may have made him even brusquer than usual. He said, "I understand you've something to tell us about the Knaphill case. I was in charge of that case—in fact, I still am, so you can tell me about it." As he said this he signaled to a uniformed sergeant who had come in behind and was now seated unobtrusively in the corner with notebook open and pencil poised.

This was so different from the friendly chat which Mr. Preece had anticipated that he hardly knew how to begin. It occurred to him that he ought to establish his own *bona fides* first. He said, "My name is Malcolm Preece. I work—"

"That's all right," said Superintendent Marker. "I've looked you up in the Law List. And got your local particulars from the sergeant here. It's just the information I want."

"It has come to my knowledge," said Mr. Preece, picking his words carefully, "that a document exists in which a local resident confesses that he was responsible for the Slaney murder."

"Let's see it."

"I am afraid I'm not allowed to let you have it."

"Who wrote it?"

"I can't tell you that."

"How did you get it?"

"That is also confidential."

"You'll have to tell someone sometime. Why not tell me now?"

"There will be no compulsion on me, at any time, to reveal the source of my information," said Mr. Preece with all the dignity he could muster. "It is privileged, as between solicitor and client."

The superintendent made a noise deep down in his throat. It sounded like the noise of a hungry lion. He said, "This isn't a matter of who-owes-who-tuppence-halfpenny. This is a case of murder. If you've really got any information, cough it up quick. If you haven't, let's all go home."

"As to whether this information is privileged, I'd be happy to refer the matter to the Law Society. And may I add that I don't care for your manner."

"I don't give a brass monkey if you like my manner or not," said the superintendent, getting up. "You've dragged me out when I was just sitting down to my first hot meal in two days. If you nuts are going to come along with phony confessions, you might at least have the kindness to do it in office hours."

He signaled to the sergeant, who was grinning broadly. "Come on, son," he said, "let's get home."

Mr. Preece was very angry, too. But it occurred to him that he had not fully delivered the message he intended. He said, "Before you go, I might also add that I wonder if you ever found the glove?"

There was a moment of total stillness. Then, without seeming to have moved, Superintendent Marker was back at the table, staring at Mr. Preece, and the sergeant was sitting down again in the corner, notebook open and pencil poised.

It was as though a film director had said, "Cut. We'll take that scene again." Only this time it wasn't the same scene. The superintendent had lost all trace of fatigue and boredom. He had settled his massive form into his chair, with the air of one who was prepared to stay in it all night.

"Well, Mr. Preece," he said, "*what* was that about a glove?"

The next two hours were easily the most unpleasant that Mr. Preece had ever spent. He had never imagined that the same question could be asked so many times and in so many different ways. At the end of it he was quite surprised to find that it was only nine o'clock. He would not have been greatly surprised if it had been midnight. His housekeeper, Mrs. Biddlecomb, was waiting for him, looking worried.

"I couldn't imagine what had happened to you," she

said. "I rang the stationmaster. He said your train was on time, and he'd seen you on it. I put your dinner in the oven, but it'll be all dried up."

"I'm sorry," said Mr. Preece. "Serve it up in five minutes." Then he pushed past the astonished Mrs. Biddlecomb, went into the library, and poured himself out a large whiskey. It was the first time that he had ever drunk spirits before dinner.

"It's quite clear," said Sexton, "that you can't stop now. You've got to let them have the whole story."

"That's quite impossible," said Mr. Preece. He had not slept well, but the coming of morning had restored some of his self-possession, and the familiar surroundings of his office had gone a long way to complete the cure.

"Why is it impossible?"

"Because they'll go straight down to the hospital and start questioning Colonel Spender. He's a sick man. If that superintendent starts on *him*, it'll probably kill him."

"It's his own fault. He's brought the whole thing on himself by writing that damn silly note."

"And how are we going to explain to the colonel about opening it?"

Sexton said, with a touch of impatience, "Tell him the truth. It was a mistake. And a perfectly natural one—"

"I know—but—"

"Have you considered what may happen if you don't come clean?"

"What do you mean? What could happen? They can pester me with a lot of silly questions, but they can't arrest me."

"Can't they?"

"What for?"

"For the murder of Theresa Slaney."

Mr. Preece stared at him as though his partner had gone mad.

Sexton said, "Do you know what you were doing on the evening of March twenty-fifth, two years ago?"

"Of course I don't. But I can soon find out."

Mr. Preece was a methodical man. His working diaries for the last six years were stacked in a shelf behind his desk. "March twenty-fifth? That was a Friday. I'm usually at home on a Friday. On Thursday I see I went to the local Law Society dinner. And on Saturday I played bridge. I assume that on Friday I was at home."

"Alone?"

"Naturally. As soon as Mrs. Biddlecomb has cleared and washed the dinner things and laid my breakfast, she goes home."

"Which would be about what time?"

"She's usually away by nine. Why?"

"I've been reading up the case. The medical evidence was that Mrs. Slaney died shortly before or shortly after midnight. Her house is about fifteen minutes' walk from yours, through Knaphill Woods."

"But—you're joking, aren't you? This is a piece of your nonsense, David. What possible motive could I have for killing the woman? I knew her by sight, it's true, but I don't think I'd ever spoken to her."

"It was strongly hinted at the inquest that Mrs. Slaney was a high-class prostitute. Appointments by telephone. It was also hinted that a lot of her customers were respectable citizens in the neighborhood, and that she was making quite a bit of money on the side by gentle blackmail. The police were pretty certain that she was killed by one of her customers she'd squeezed too hard, or too often."

"But good heavens, you're not suggesting—"

"*I'm* not suggesting anything. But the police don't know you as well as I do."

"But," said Mr. Preece, "even if—I mean—even if there was the slightest simulacrum of truth in this fantastic suggestion, why should I have gone out of my way to call the attention of the police to myself?"

"Their minds work in a peculiar way," said Sexton. "I'm afraid that the sequence of ideas which may occur to them is this: You read in *The Times* of the death of your neighbor and client, Colonel Spender. He was an obvious candidate for Mrs. Slaney's favors. He was a great womanizer and he lived in the neighborhood, alone since his wife died. He probably has no alibi for the night in question. So you—the real murderer—decide to foist it on to him and close the case forever.

"You arrive ahead of me at the office—which you did, incidentally—type out this confession on office paper with an office machine—they'll be able to prove all that easily enough—then go down to the strongroom and put the 'confession' with the will. Knowing, of course, that we'll have it up at once since you're the executor of the colonel's estate. I mean—it's plausible."

Mr. Preece, whose face had been growing redder and redder, said in a stifled voice, "I think you're right. I'll go round this evening."

"I see," said Superintendent Marker. He said it in a voice so neutral that the words were devoid of meaning. "Was it you or your partner who opened this—what did you call it—deed wallet?"

"I think I opened it myself."

"Could you describe it?"

"It's a stout manila folder." Mr. Preece demonstrated the size with his hands. "We have one for each client. It would have deeds and documents in it. And any will or codicil. Important documents which we keep under lock and key."

"And when do you suppose this—this other envelope—was put in it?"

"The will was dated almost exactly a year ago. I assume the envelope was put away with it. Clients often put a letter of wishes with their wills."

"You assume? You don't remember?"

"I can't say that I definitely remember it. I put documents away every day. The person who certainly *will* remember it is Colonel Spender."

"Yes," said the superintendent. "I expect he might have. You see, he died this morning."

While Mr. Preece was still gaping at him, the superintendent added, "I'll have to take instructions on this. I'd like to ask you not to go away in the meantime."

"What do you mean, go away?"

"Go abroad."

"I've no intention of going abroad," said Mr. Preece, with dignity. "I shall be going to my office at precisely the usual hour tomorrow."

"That'll be very convenient, sir. For I shall probably be calling on you."

The superintendent was as good as his word. He called the next morning at ten o'clock, bringing the sergeant with him. They faced Mr. Preece and Mr. Sexton across the table on which lay the Spender deed wallet.

"So this is the one, is it? Name on the outside. I see. And a number. You keep things in good order in your office, Mr. Preece."

"We have a considerable number of papers to look after."

"But it's only the important ones, like this, that you keep locked up?"

"That is so."

"Where do you keep them?"

"In the strongroom, in the basement."

"And who has the keys?"

"My partner, Mr. Sexton, and myself."

"I see," said the superintendent. He had been fiddling with the string, and now the wallet fell open; the will in its long legal envelope and the smaller white envelope both slid out onto the table. The superintendent, who was holding the wallet, gave it a shake. "There's more inside," he said. "What would they be?"

"The deeds of his house at Woking, I imagine," said Sexton. "And there are a couple of deeds of covenant in favor of the local hospital, I fancy. Why don't we have a look?"

The superintendent gave the wallet a shake. The first thing which came out, with some difficulty, was a packet of deeds. Then came two separate deeds. Finally, three white envelopes.

"Hullo," said Mr. Preece. "What are those?"

Each one had, typed on it, the words: *To be placed with my will and opened only at my death.*

"Good heavens!" said Mr. Preece. "What on earth—"

"They must have got stuck behind the deeds," said Sexton. "Shall I—?"

He looked at Mr. Preece, who looked at the superintendent, who was watching impassively.

"We might as well," he said. "Maybe they say he changed his mind and *didn't* do it, after all."

The first note was short. It said: "I should like my executors to inform the American ambassador that I shot President Kennedy."

The second was shorter still. It said: "I am Jack the Ripper."

"Well," said the superintendent. "That's two more mysteries solved, isn't it?" The atmosphere seemed suddenly to have got lighter. "I've been making a few inquiries about Colonel Spender. I understand he was a rare old leg-puller. As a matter of fact, we shouldn't have taken a lot of notice of the first note if it hadn't been for his mentioning the glove. That was odd. Because we did find a glove, a single one, under the body. We kept it up our sleeves, as you might say."

"But," said Mr. Sexton, "if you didn't tell anyone, how did Colonel Spender find out?"

"We had to institute a lot of inquiries. It was a foreign glove—artificial pigskin, made in Belgium. What happened, I've no doubt, was that someone told someone else —in confidence, of course—and they passed it on. These things get about. You know how it is."

Mr. Preece nodded.

"I'm sorry it's all come to nothing," said the superintendent. "But that's the way with these inquiries. We have to follow up each line until it runs out. Come on, son."

"I'll show you out," said Sexton.

When they had gone, Mr. Preece sat staring at the little pile of documents on the table in front of him, a frown on his face. He wasn't thinking about the glove. As the superintendent said, these things got out. Women in railway carriages who had aunts who had cooks who were walking out with policemen—that sort of thing. What was bothering him were the other envelopes. He himself had emptied the deed wallet and was certain there had been nothing else in it.

However, as he had sometimes remarked to his clients, "If there's a theoretical solution, I can usually work it out. If I'm stuck, David Sexton can often find a practical answer."

We usually think of Edgar Allan Poe's C. Auguste Dupin (1841) as the world's first fictional detective. And that statement is true, in a modern sense. But, of course, there were forerunners—among others, Daniel (in the Bible), Voltaire's Zadig (1747), William Leggett's Jim Buckhorn (1827), François Eugène Vidocq (1828), and Charles Dickens' "officers from Bow Street," Blathers and Duff (1838).

Similarly, we usually think of Edgar Allan Poe's
The Murders in the Rue Morgue *as the world's first
locked-room detective story (1841). And that statement
is also true, in a modern sense—the forerunners were primitive attempts at the theme of the "hermetically sealed
chamber." And after Poe, of course, came the remarkably
ingenious development of the locked-room gambit—by
Joseph Sheridan Le Fanu (1851), Thomas Bailey Aldrich
(1862), Israel Zangwill (1892), Gaston Leroux (1907), and
the king of them all, John Dickson Carr–Carter Dickson.*

*Now, one would think, since the limits even of
mental and creative ingenuity are not infinite, that in 131
years the multitudinous mysterymongers would have exhausted the plot possibilities of the locked-room murder.
Perish the thought! Infinity is a long way off. Here, for
example, is a brand-new wrinkle on the locked room—
and it will, we guarantee, positively baffle you.*

EDWARD D. HOCH

The Leopold locked room

Captain Leopold had never spoken to anyone about his
divorce, and it was a distinct surprise to Lieutenant
Fletcher when he suddenly said, "Did I ever tell you
about my wife, Fletcher?"

They were just coming up from the police pistol
range in the basement of headquarters after their monthly
target practice, and it hardly seemed a likely time to be

discussing past marital troubles. Fletcher glanced at him sideways and answered, "No, I guess you never did, Captain."

They had reached the top of the stairs and Leopold turned in to the little room where the coffee, sandwich, and soft-drink machines were kept. They called it the lunchroom, but only by the boldest stretch of the imagination could the little collection of tables and chairs qualify as such. Rather it was a place where off-duty cops could sit and chat, which was what Leopold and Fletcher were doing now.

Fletcher bought the coffee and put the steaming paper cups on the table between them. He had never seen Leopold quite this open and personal before, anxious to talk about a life that had existed far beyond the limits of Fletcher's friendship. "She's coming back," Leopold said simply, and it took Fletcher an instant to grasp the meaning of his words.

"Your wife is coming back?"

"My ex-wife."

"Here? What for?"

Leopold sighed and played with the little bag of sugar that Fletcher had given him with his coffee. "Her niece is getting married. Our niece."

"I never knew you had one."

"She's been away at college. Her name is Vicki Nelson, and she's marrying a young lawyer named Moore. And Monica is coming back east for the wedding."

"I never even knew her name," Fletcher observed, taking a sip of his coffee. "Haven't you seen her since the divorce?"

Leopold shook his head. "Not for fifteen years. It was a funny thing. She wanted to be a movie star, and I guess fifteen years ago lots of girls still thought about being movie stars. Monica was intelligent and very pretty —but probably no prettier than hundreds of other girls who used to turn up in Hollywood every year back in those days. I was just starting on the police force then, and the future looked pretty bright for me here. It would have been foolish of me to toss up everything just to chase her wild dream out to California. Well, pretty soon it got to be an obsession with her, really bad. She'd spend her afternoons in movie theaters and her evenings watching old films on television. Finally, when I still refused to go west with her, she just left me."

"Just walked out?"

Leopold nodded. "It was a blessing, really, that we didn't have children. I heard she got a few minor jobs out there—as an extra, and some technical stuff behind the scenes. Then apparently she had a nervous breakdown. About a year later I received the official word that she'd divorced me. I heard that she recovered and was back working, and I think she had another marriage that didn't work out."

"Why would she come back for the wedding?"

"Vicki is her niece and also her godchild. We were just married when Vicki was born, and I suppose Monica might consider her the child we never had. In any event, I know she still hates me and blames me for everything that's gone wrong with her life. She told a friend once a few years ago she wished I were dead."

"Do you have to go to this wedding, too, Captain?"

"Of course. If I stayed away it would be only because of her. At least I have to drop by the reception for a few minutes." Leopold smiled ruefully. "I guess that's why I'm telling you all this, Fletcher. I want a favor from you."

"Anything, Captain. You know that."

"I know it seems like a childish thing to do, but I'd like you to come out there with me. I'll tell them I'm working and that I can only stay for a few minutes. You can wait outside in the car if you want. At least they'll see you there and believe my excuse."

Fletcher could see the importance of it to Leopold,

and the effort that had gone into the asking. "Sure," he said. "Be glad to. When is it?"

"This Saturday. The reception's in the afternoon, at Sunset Farms."

Leopold had been to Sunset Farms only once before, at the wedding of a patrolman whom he'd especially liked. It was a low rambling place at the end of a paved driveway, overlooking a wooded valley and a gently flowing creek. If it had ever been a farm, that day was long past; but for wedding receptions and retirement parties it was the ideal place. The interior of the main building was, in reality, one huge square room, divided by accordion doors to make up to four smaller square rooms.

For the wedding of Vicki Nelson and Ted Moore three quarters of the large room was in use, with only the last set of accordion doors pulled shut its entire width and locked. The wedding party occupied a head table along one wall, with smaller tables scattered around the room for the families and friends. When Leopold entered the place at five minutes of two on Saturday afternoon, the hired combo was just beginning to play music for dancing.

He watched for a moment while Vicki stood, radiant, and allowed her new husband to escort her to the center of the floor. Ted Moore was a bit older than Leopold had expected, but as the pair glided slowly across the floor, he could find no visible fault with the match. He helped himself to a glass of champagne punch and stood ready to intercept them as they left the dance floor.

"It's Captain Leopold, isn't it?" someone asked. A face from his past loomed up, a tired man with a gold tooth in the front of his smile. "I'm Immy Fontaine, Monica's stepbrother."

"Sure," Leopold said, as if he'd remembered the man all along. Monica had rarely mentioned Immy, and Leopold recalled meeting him once or twice at family gatherings. But the sight of him now, gold tooth and all, reminded Leopold that Monica was somewhere nearby, that he might confront her at any moment.

"We're so glad you could come," someone else said, and he turned to greet the bride and groom as they came off the dance floor. Up close, Vicki was a truly beautiful girl, clinging to her new husband's arm like a proper bride.

"I wouldn't have missed it for anything," he said.

"This is Ted," she said, making the introductions. Leopold shook his hand, silently approving the firm grip and friendly eyes.

"I understand you're a lawyer," Leopold said, making conversation.

"That's right, sir. Mostly civil cases, though. I don't tangle much with criminals."

They chatted for a few more seconds before the pressure of guests broke them apart. The luncheon was about to be served, and the more hungry ones were already lining up at the buffet tables. Vicki and Ted went over to start the line, and Leopold took another glass of champagne punch.

"I see the car waiting outside," Immy Fontaine said, moving in again. "You got to go on duty?"

Leopold nodded. "Just this glass and I have to leave."

"Monica's in from the West Coast."

"So I heard."

A slim man with a mustache jostled against him in the crush of the crowd and hastily apologized. Fontaine seized the man by the arm and introduced him to Leopold. "This here's Dr. Felix Thursby. He came east with Monica. Doc, I want you to meet Captain Leopold, her ex-husband."

Leopold shook hands awkwardly, embarrassed for the man and for himself. "A fine wedding," he mumbled. "Your first trip east?"

Thursby shook his head. "I'm from New York. Long ago."

"I was on the police force there once," Leopold remarked.

They chatted for a few more minutes before Leopold managed to edge away through the crowd.

"Leaving so soon?" a harsh unforgettable voice asked.

"Hello, Monica. It's been a long time."

He stared down at the handsome, middle-aged woman who now blocked his path to the door. She had gained a little weight, especially in the bosom, and her hair was graying. Only the eyes startled him, and frightened him just a bit. They had the intense wild look he'd seen before on the faces of deranged criminals.

"I didn't think you'd come. I thought you'd be afraid of me," she said.

"That's foolish. Why should I be afraid of you?"

The music had started again, and the line from the buffet tables was beginning to snake lazily about the room. But for Leopold and Monica they might have been alone in the middle of a desert.

"Come in here," she said, "where we can talk." She motioned toward the end of the room that had been cut off by the accordion doors. Leopold followed her, helpless to do anything else. She unlocked the doors and pulled them apart, just wide enough for them to enter the unused quarter of the large room. Then she closed and locked the doors behind them, and stood facing him. They were two people, alone in a bare unfurnished room.

They were in an area about thirty feet square, with the windows at the far end and the locked accordion doors at Leopold's back. He could see the afternoon sun cutting through the trees outside, and the gentle hum of the air-conditioner came through above the subdued murmur of the wedding guests.

"Remember the day we got married?" she asked.

"Yes. Of course."

She walked to the middle window, running her fingers along the frame, perhaps looking for the latch to open it. But it stayed closed as she faced him again. "Our marriage was as drab and barren as this room. Lifeless, unused!"

"Heaven knows I always wanted children, Monica."

"You wanted nothing but your damned police work!" she shot back, eyes flashing as her anger built.

"Look, I have to go. I have a man waiting in the car."

"Go! That's what you did before, wasn't it? *Go, go!* Go out to your damned job and leave me to struggle for myself. Leave me to—"

"You walked out on me, Monica. Remember?" he reminded her softly. She was so defenseless, without even a purse to swing at him.

"Sure I did! Because I had a career waiting for me! I had all the world waiting for me! And you know what happened because you wouldn't come along? You know what happened to me out there? They took my money and my self-respect and what virtue I had left. They made me into a tramp, and when they were done they locked me up in a mental hospital for three years. Three years!"

"I'm sorry."

"Every day while I was there I thought about you. I thought about how it would be when I got out. Oh, I thought. And planned. And schemed. You're a big detective now. Sometimes your cases even get reported in the California papers." She was pacing back and forth, caged, dangerous. "Big detective. But I can still destroy you just as you destroyed me!"

He glanced over his shoulder at the locked accordion doors, seeking a way out. It was a thousand times worse than he'd imagined it would be. She was mad—mad and vengeful and terribly dangerous. "You should see a doctor, Monica."

Her eyes closed to mere slits. "I've seen doctors." Now she paused before the middle window, facing him.

"I came all the way east for this day, because I thought you'd be here. It's so much better than your apartment, or your office, or a city street. There are one hundred and fifty witnesses on the other side of those doors."

"What in hell are you talking about?"

Her mouth twisted in a horrible grin. "You're going to know what I knew. Bars and cells and disgrace. You're going to know the despair I felt all those years."

"Monica—"

At that instant perhaps twenty feet separated them. She lifted one arm, as if to shield herself, then screamed in terror. "No! Oh, God, no!"

Leopold stood frozen, unable to move, as a sudden gunshot echoed through the room. He saw the bullet strike her in the chest, toppling her backward like the blow from a giant fist. Then somehow he had his own gun out of its belt holster and he swung around toward the doors.

They were still closed and locked. He was alone in the room with Monica.

He looked back to see her crumple on the floor, blood spreading in a widening circle around the torn black hole in her dress. His eyes went to the windows, but all three were still closed and unbroken. He shook his head, trying to focus his mind on what had happened.

There was noise from outside, and a pounding on the accordion doors. Someone opened the lock from the other side, and the gap between the doors widened as they were pulled open. "What happened?" someone asked. A woman guest screamed as she saw the body. Another toppled in a faint.

Leopold stepped back, aware of the gun still in his hand, and saw Lieutenant Fletcher fighting his way through the mob of guests. "Captain, what is it?"

"She— Someone shot her."

Fletcher reached out and took the gun from Leopold's hand—carefully, as one might take a broken toy from a child. He put it to his nose and sniffed, then opened the cylinder to inspect the bullets. "It's been fired recently, Captain. One shot." Then his eyes seemed to cloud over, almost to the point of tears. "Why the hell did you do it?" he asked. "Why?"

Leopold saw nothing of what happened then. He only had vague and splintered memories of someone examining her and saying she was still alive, of an ambulance and much confusion. Fletcher drove him down to headquarters, to the commissioner's office, and he sat there and waited, running his moist palms up and down his trousers. He was not surprised when they told him she had died on the way to Southside Hospital. Monica had never been one to do things by halves.

The men—the detectives who worked under him—came to and left the commissioner's office, speaking in low tones with their heads together, occasionally offering him some embarrassed gesture of condolence. There was an aura of sadness over the place, and Leopold knew it was for him.

"You have nothing more to tell us, Captain?" the commissioner asked. "I'm making it as easy for you as I can."

"I didn't kill her," Leopold insisted again. "It was someone else."

"Who? How?"

He could only shake his head. "I wish I knew. I think in some mad way she killed herself, to get revenge on me."

"She shot herself with *your* gun, while it was in *your* holster, and while *you* were standing twenty feet away?"

Leopold ran a hand over his forehead. "It couldn't have been my gun. Ballistics will prove that."

"But your gun had been fired recently, and there was an empty cartridge in the chamber."

"I can't explain that. I haven't fired it since the other day at target practice, and I reloaded it afterwards."

"Could she have hated you that much, Captain?" Fletcher asked. "To frame you for her murder?"

"She could have. I think she was a very sick woman. If I did that to her—if I was the one who made her sick— I suppose I deserve what's happening to me now."

"The hell you do," Fletcher growled. "If you say you're innocent, Captain, I'm sticking by you." He began pacing again and finally turned to the commissioner. "How about giving him a paraffin test, to see if he's fired a gun recently?"

The commissioner shook his head. "We haven't used that in years. You know how unreliable it is, Fletcher. Many people have nitrates or nitrites on their hands. They can pick them up from dirt, or fertilizers, or fireworks, or urine, or even from simply handling peas or beans. Anyone who smokes tobacco can have deposits on his hands. There are some newer tests for the presence of barium or lead, but we don't have the necessary chemicals for those."

Leopold nodded. The commissioner had risen through the ranks. He wasn't simply a political appointee, and the men had always respected him. Leopold respected him. "Wait for the ballistics report," he said. "That'll clear me."

So they waited. It was another forty-five minutes before the phone rang and the commissioner spoke to the ballistics man. He listened, and grunted, and asked one or two questions. Then he hung up and faced Leopold across the desk.

"The bullet was fired from your gun," he said simply. "There's no possibility of error. I'm afraid we'll have to charge you with homicide."

The routines he knew so well went on into Saturday evening, and when they were finished Leopold was escorted from the courtroom to find young Ted Moore waiting for him. "You should be on your honeymoon," Leopold told him.

"Vicki couldn't leave till I'd seen you and tried to help. I don't know much about criminal law, but perhaps I could arrange bail."

"That's already been taken care of," Leopold said. "The grand jury will get the case next week."

"I—I don't know what to say. Vicki and I are both terribly sorry."

"So am I." He started to walk away, then turned back. "Enjoy your honeymoon."

"We'll be in town overnight, at the Towers, if there's anything I can do."

Leopold nodded and kept on walking. He could see the reflection of his guilt in young Moore's eyes. As he got to his car, one of the patrolmen he knew glanced his way and then quickly in the other direction. On a Saturday night no one talked to wife murderers. Even Fletcher had disappeared.

Leopold decided he couldn't face the drab walls of his office, not with people avoiding him. Besides, the commissioner had been forced to suspend him from active duty pending grand-jury action and the possible trial. The office didn't even belong to him anymore. He cursed silently and drove home to his little apartment, weaving through the dark streets with one eye out for a patrol car. He wondered if they'd be watching him, to prevent his jumping bail. He wondered what he'd have done in the commissioner's shoes.

The eleven-o'clock news on television had it as the lead item, illustrated with a black-and-white photo of him taken during a case last year. He shut off the television without listening to their comments and went back outside, walking down to the corner for an early edition of the Sunday paper. The front-page headline was as bad as he'd expected: DETECTIVE CAPTAIN HELD IN SLAYING OF EX-WIFE.

On the way back to his apartment, walking slowly, he tried to remember what she'd been like—not that afternoon, but before the divorce. He tried to remember her face on their wedding day, her soft laughter on their honeymoon. But all he could remember were those mad vengeful eyes. And the bullet ripping into her chest.

Perhaps he had killed her after all. Perhaps the gun had come into his hand so easily he never realized it was there.

"Hello, Captain."

"I—Fletcher! What are you doing here?"

"Waiting for you. Can I come in?"

"Well . . ."

"I've got a six-pack of beer. I thought you might want to talk about it."

Leopold unlocked his apartment door. "What's there to talk about?"

"If you say you didn't kill her, Captain, I'm willing to listen to you."

Fletcher followed him into the tiny kitchen and popped open two of the beer cans. Leopold accepted one of them and dropped into the nearest chair. He felt utterly exhausted, drained of even the strength to fight back.

"She framed me, Fletcher," he said quietly. "She framed me as neatly as anything I've ever seen. The thing's impossible, but she did it."

"Let's go over it step by step, Captain. Look, the way I see it there are only three possibilities: Either you shot her, she shot herself, or someone else shot her. I think we can rule out the last one. The three windows were locked on the outside and unbroken, the room was bare of any hiding place, and the only entrance was through the accordion doors. These were closed and locked, and although they could have been opened from the other side, you certainly would have seen or heard it happen. Besides, there were one hundred and fifty wedding guests on the other side of those doors. No one could have unlocked and opened them and then fired the shot, all without being seen."

Leopold shook his head. "But it's just as impossible that she could have shot herself. I was watching her every minute. I never looked away once. There was nothing in her hands, not even a purse. And the gun that shot her was in my holster, on my belt. I never drew it till *after* the shot was fired."

Fletcher finished his beer and reached for another can. "I didn't look at her close, Captain, but the size of the hole in her dress and the powder burns point to a contact wound. The medical examiner agrees, too. She was shot from no more than an inch or two away. There were grains of powder in the wound itself, though the bleeding had washed most of them away."

"But she had nothing in her hand," Leopold repeated. "And there was nobody standing in front of her with a gun. Even I was twenty feet away."

"The thing's impossible, Captain."

Leopold grunted. "Impossible—unless I killed her."

Fletcher stared at his beer. "How much time do we have?"

"If the grand jury indicts me for first-degree murder, I'll be in a cell by next week."

Fletcher frowned at him. "What's with you, Captain? You almost act resigned to it! Hell, I've seen more fight in you on a routine holdup!"

"I guess that's it, Fletcher. The fight is gone out of me. She's drained every drop out of me. She's had her revenge."

Fletcher sighed and stood up. "Then I guess there's really nothing I can do for you, Captain. Good night."

Leopold didn't see him to the door. He simply sat there, hunched over the table. For the first time in his life he felt like an old man.

Leopold slept late Sunday morning and awakened with the odd sensation that it had all been a dream. He remembered feeling the same way when he'd broken his

wrist chasing a burglar. In the morning, on just awaken-
ing, the memory of the heavy cast had always been a
dream, until he moved his arm. Now, rolling over in his
narrow bed, he saw the Sunday paper where he'd tossed it
the night before. The headline was still the same. The
dream was a reality.

He got up and showered and dressed, reaching for
his holster out of habit before he remembered he no longer
had a gun. Then he sat at the kitchen table staring at the
empty beer cans, wondering what he would do with his
day. With his life.

The doorbell rang and it was Fletcher. "I didn't
think I'd be seeing you again," Leopold mumbled, letting
him in.

Fletcher was excited, and the words tumbled out of
him almost before he was through the door. "I think I've
got something, Captain! It's not much, but it's a start. I
was down at headquarters first thing this morning, and I
got hold of the dress Monica was wearing when she was
shot."

Leopold looked blank. "The dress?"

Fletcher was busy unwrapping the package he'd
brought. "The commissioner would have my neck if he
knew I brought this to you, but look at this hole!"

Leopold studied the jagged, blood-caked rent in the
fabric. "It's large," he observed, "but with a near-contact
wound the powder burns would cause that."

"Captain, I've seen plenty of entrance wounds made
by a thirty-eight slug. I've even caused a few of them. But
I never saw one that looked like this. Hell, it's not even
round!"

"What are you trying to tell me, Fletcher?" Suddenly
something stirred inside him. The juices were beginning
to flow again.

"The hole in her dress is much larger and more
jagged than the corresponding wound in her chest, Captain. That's what I'm telling you. The bullet that killed

her couldn't have made this hole. No way! And that means maybe she wasn't killed when we thought she was."

Leopold grabbed the phone and dialed the familiar number of the Towers Hotel. "I hope they slept late this morning."

"Who?"

"The honeymooners." He spoke sharply into the phone, giving the switchboard operator the name he wanted, and then waited. It was a full minute before he heard Ted Moore's sleepy voice answering on the other end. "Ted, this is Leopold. Sorry to bother you."

The voice came alert at once. "That's all right, Captain. I told you to call if there was anything—"

"I think there is. You and Vicki between you must have a pretty good idea of who was invited to the wedding. Check with her and tell me how many doctors were on the invitation list."

Ted Moore was gone for a few moments and then he returned. "Vicki says you're the second person who asked her that?"

"Oh? Who was the first?"

"Monica. The night before the wedding, when she arrived in town with Dr. Thursby. She casually asked if he'd get to meet any other doctors at the reception. But Vicki told her he was the only one. Of course we hadn't invited him, but as a courtesy to Monica we urged him to come."

"Then after the shooting, it was Thursby who examined her? No one else?"

"He was the only doctor. He told us to call an ambulance and rode to the hospital with her."

"Thank you, Ted. You've been a big help."

"I hope so, Captain."

Leopold hung up and faced Fletcher. "That's it. She worked it with this guy Thursby. Can you put out an alarm for him?"

"Sure can," Fletcher said. He took the telephone and dialed the unlisted squad-room number. "Dr. Felix Thursby? Is that his name?"

"That's it. The only doctor there, the only one who could help Monica with her crazy plan of revenge."

Fletcher completed issuing orders and hung up the phone. "They'll check his hotel and call me back."

"Get the commissioner on the phone, too. Tell him what we've got."

Fletcher started to dial and then stopped, his finger in mid-air. "What *have* we got, Captain?"

The commissioner sat behind his desk, openly unhappy at being called to headquarters on a Sunday afternoon, and listened bleakly to what Leopold and Fletcher had to tell him. Finally he spread his fingers on the desktop and said, "The mere fact that this Dr. Thursby seems to have left town is hardly proof of his guilt, Captain. What you're saying is that the woman wasn't killed until later—that Thursby killed her in the ambulance. But how could he have done that with a pistol that was already in Lieutenant Fletcher's possession, tagged as evidence? And how could he have fired the fatal shot without the ambulance attendants hearing it?"

"I don't know," Leopold admitted.

"Heaven knows, Captain, I'm willing to give you every reasonable chance to prove your innocence. But you have to bring me more than a dress with a hole in it."

"All right," Leopold said. "I'll bring you more."

"The grand jury gets the case this week, Captain."

"I know," Leopold said. He turned and left the office, with Fletcher tailing behind.

"What now?" Fletcher asked.

"We go talk to Immy Fontaine, my ex-wife's stepbrother."

Though he'd never been friendly with Fontaine, Leopold knew where to find him. The tired man with the gold tooth lived in a big old house overlooking the Sound, where on this summer Sunday they found him in the back yard, cooking hot dogs over a charcoal fire.

He squinted into the sun and said, "I thought you'd be in jail, after what happened."

"I didn't kill her," Leopold said quietly.

"Sure you didn't."

"For a stepbrother you seem to be taking her death right in stride," Leopold observed, motioning toward the fire.

"I stopped worrying about Monica fifteen years ago."

"What about this man she was with? Dr. Thursby?"

Immy Fontaine chuckled. "If he's a doctor I'm a plumber! He has the fingers of a surgeon, I'll admit, but when I asked him about my son's radius that he broke skiing, Thursby thought it was a leg bone. What the hell, though, I was never one to judge Monica's love life. Remember, I didn't even object when she married you."

"Nice of you. Where's Thursby staying while he's in town?"

"He was at the Towers with Monica."

"He's not there anymore."

"Then I don't know where he's at. Maybe he's not even staying for her funeral."

"What if I told you Thursby killed Monica?"

He shrugged. "I wouldn't believe you, but then I wouldn't particularly care. If you were smart you'd have killed her fifteen years ago when she walked out on you. That's what I'd have done."

Leopold drove slowly back downtown, with Fletcher grumbling beside him. "Where are we, Captain? It seems we're just going in circles."

"Perhaps we are, Fletcher, but right now there are still too many questions to be answered. If we can't find

Thursby I'll have to tackle it from another direction. The bullet, for instance."

"What about the bullet?"

"We're agreed it could not have been fired by my gun, either while it was in my holster or later, while Thursby was in the ambulance with Monica. Therefore, it must have been fired earlier. The last time I fired it was at target practice. Is there any possibility—any chance at all—that Thursby or Monica could have gotten one of the slugs I fired into that target?"

Fletcher put a damper on it. "Captain, we were both firing at the same target. No one could sort out those bullets and say which came from your pistol and which from mine. Besides, how would either of them gain access to the basement target range at police headquarters?"

"I could have an enemy in the department," Leopold said.

"Nuts! We've all got enemies, but the thing is still impossible. If you believe people in the department are plotting against you, you might as well believe that the entire ballistics evidence was faked."

"It was, somehow. Do you have the comparison photos?"

"They're back at the office. But with the narrow depth of field you can probably tell more from looking through the microscope yourself."

Fletcher drove him to the lab, where they persuaded the Sunday-duty officer to let them have a look at the bullets. While Fletcher and the officer stood by in the interests of propriety, Leopold squinted through the microscope at the twin chunks of lead.

"The death bullet is pretty battered," he observed, but he had to admit that the rifling marks were the same. He glanced at the identification tag attached to the test bullet: *Test slug fired from Smith & Wesson .38 Revolver, serial number 2420547.*

Leopold turned away with a sigh, then turned back. *2420547.*

He fished into his wallet and found his pistol permit. *Smith & Wesson 2421622.*

"I remembered those two's on the end," he told Fletcher. "That's not my gun."

"It's the one I took from you, Captain. I'll swear to it!"

"And I believe you, Fletcher. But it's the one fact I needed. It tells me how Dr. Thursby managed to kill Monica in a locked room before my very eyes, with a gun that was in my holster at the time. And it just might tell us where to find the elusive Dr. Thursby."

By Monday morning Leopold had made six long-distance calls to California, working from his desk telephone while Fletcher used the squad-room phone. Then, a little before noon, Leopold, Fletcher, the commissioner, and a man from the district attorney's office took a car and drove up to Boston.

"You're sure you've got it figured?" the commissioner asked Leopold for the third time. "You know we shouldn't allow you to cross the state line while awaiting grand-jury action."

"Look, either you trust me or you don't," Leopold snapped. Behind the wheel Fletcher allowed himself a slight smile, but the man from the D.A.'s office was deadly serious.

"The whole thing is so damned complicated," the commissioner grumbled.

"My ex-wife was a complicated woman. And remember, she had fifteen years to plan it."

"Run over it for us again," the D.A.'s man said.

Leopold sighed and started talking. "The murder gun wasn't mine. The gun I pulled after the shot was fired, the one Fletcher took from me, had been planted on me sometime before."

"How?"

"I'll get to that. Monica was the key to it all, of course. She hated me so much that her twisted brain planned her own murder in order to get revenge on me. She planned it in such a way that it would have been impossible for anyone but me to have killed her."

"Only a crazy woman would do such a thing."

"I'm afraid she was crazy—crazy for vengeance. She set up the entire plan for the afternoon of the wedding reception, but I'm sure they had an alternate in case I hadn't gone to it. She wanted some place where there'd be lots of witnesses."

"Tell them how she worked the bullet hitting her," Fletcher urged.

"Well, that was the toughest part for me. I actually saw her shot before my eyes. I saw the bullet hit her and I saw the blood. Yet I was alone in a locked room with her. There was no hiding place, no opening from which a person or even a mechanical device could have fired the bullet at her. To you people it seemed I must be guilty, especially when the bullet came from the gun I was carrying.

"But I looked at it from a different angle—once Fletcher forced me to look at it at all! I *knew* I hadn't shot her, and since no one else physically could have, I knew no one did! If Monica was killed by a thirty-eight slug, it must have been fired *after* she was taken from that locked room. Since she was dead on arrival at the hospital, the most likely time for her murder—to me, at least—became the time of the ambulance ride, when Dr. Thursby must have hunched over her with careful solicitousness."

"But you *saw* her shot!"

"That's one of the two reasons Fletcher and I were on the phones to Hollywood this morning. My ex-wife worked in pictures, at times in the technical end of movie-making. On the screen there are a number of ways to simulate a person being shot. An early method was a sort of compressed-air gun fired at the actor from just off-camera.

These days, especially in the bloodiest of the Western and war films, they use a tiny explosive charge fitted under the actor's clothes. Of course the body is protected from burns, and the force of it is directed outward. A pouch of fake blood is released by the explosion, adding to the realism of it."

"And this is what Monica did?"

Leopold nodded. "A call to her Hollywood studio confirmed the fact that she worked on a film using this device. I noticed when I met her that she'd gained weight around the bosom, but I never thought to attribute it to the padding and the explosive device. She triggered it when she raised her arm as she screamed at me."

"Any proof?"

"The hole in her dress was just too big to be an entrance hole from a thirty-eight, even fired at close range—too big and too ragged. I can thank Fletcher for spotting that. This morning the lab technicians ran a test on the bloodstains. Some of it was her blood, the rest was chicken blood."

"She was a good actress to fool all those people."

"She knew Dr. Thursby would be the first to examine her. All she had to do was fall over when the explosive charge ripped out the front of her dress."

"What if there had been another doctor at the wedding?"

Leopold shrugged. "Then they would have postponed it. They couldn't take that chance."

"And the gun?"

"I remembered Thursby bumping against me when I first met him. He took my gun and substituted an identical weapon—identical, that is, except for the serial number. He'd fired it just a short time earlier, to complete the illusion. When I drew it I simply played into their hands. There I was, the only person in the room with an apparently dying woman, and a gun that had just been fired."

"But what about the bullet that killed her?"

"Rifling marks on slugs are made by the lands in the rifled barrel of a gun causing grooves in the lead of a bullet. A bullet fired through a smooth tube has no rifling marks."

"What in hell kind of gun has a smooth tube for a barrel?" the commissioner asked.

"A homemade one, like a zip gun. Highly inaccurate, but quite effective when the gun is almost touching the skin of the victim. Thursby fired a shot from the pistol he was to plant on me, probably into a pillow or some other place where he could retrieve the undamaged slug. Then he reused the rifled slug on another cartridge and fired it with his homemade zip gun, right into Monica's heart. The original rifling marks were still visible and no new ones were added."

"The ambulance driver and attendant didn't hear the shot?"

"They would have stayed up front, since he was a doctor riding with a patient. It gave him a chance to get the padded explosive mechanism off her chest, too. Once that was away, I imagine he leaned over her, muffling the zip gun as best he could, and fired the single shot that killed her. Remember, an ambulance on its way to a hospital is a pretty noisy place—it has a siren going all the time."

They were entering downtown Boston now, and Leopold directed Fletcher to a hotel near the Common. "I still don't believe the part about switching the guns," the D.A.'s man objected. "You mean to tell me he undid the strap over your gun, got out the gun, and substituted another one—all without your knowing it?"

Leopold smiled. "I mean to tell you only one type of person could have managed it—an expert, professional pickpocket. The type you see occasionally doing an act in nightclubs and on television. That's how I knew where to find him. We called all over southern California till we came up with someone who knew Monica and knew she'd dated a man named Thompson who had a pickpocket act. We called Thompson's agent and discovered he's playing a split week at a Boston lounge, and is staying at this hotel."

"What if he couldn't have managed it without your catching on? Or what if you hadn't been wearing your gun?"

"Most detectives wear their guns off-duty. If I hadn't been, or if he couldn't get it, they'd simply have changed their plan. He must have signaled her when he'd safely made the switch."

"Here we are," Fletcher said. "Let's go up."

The Boston police had two men waiting to meet them, and they went up in the elevator to the room registered in the name of Max Thompson. Fletcher knocked on the door, and when it opened, the familiar face of Felix Thursby appeared. He no longer wore the mustache, but he had the same slim surgeonlike fingers that Immy Fontaine had noticed. Not a doctor's fingers, but a pickpocket's.

"We're taking you in for questioning," Fletcher said and the Boston detectives issued the standard warnings of his legal rights.

Thursby blinked his tired eyes at them and grinned a bit when he recognized Leopold. "She said you were smart. She said you were a smart cop."

"Did you have to kill her?" Leopold asked.

"I didn't. I just held the gun there and she pulled the trigger herself. She did it all herself, except for switching the guns. She hated you that much."

"I know," Leopold said quietly, staring at something far away. "But I guess she must have hated herself just as much."